A Soul to Steal

By Rob Blackwell

This work is entirely fictional. Any similarity between characters
and persons, living or dead, is purely coincidental and pretty much
all in your head. While Leesburg and Loudoun County, Va., are real
places, I have taken liberties with the geography.

For Maia, of course

"The dominant spirit, however, that haunts this enchanted region, and seems to be commander-in-chief of all the powers of the air, is the apparition of a figure on horseback, without a head. It is said by some to be the ghost of a Hessian trooper, whose head had been carried away by a cannon-ball, in some nameless battle during the Revolutionary War, and who is ever and anon seen by the country folk hurrying along in the gloom of night, as if on the wings of the wind.

Such is the general purport of this legendary superstition, which has furnished materials for many a wild story in that region of shadows; and the spectre is known at all the country firesides, by the name of the Headless Horseman of Sleepy Hollow."

—Washington Irving, "The Legend of Sleepy Hollow"

"The situation is a good deal worse than we expected. Robert has barricaded himself within the castle walls and refuses to see me or Doctor Frank.

I have grave concerns for his well being. Based on discrete inquiries into his activities, it appears your son has been publicly proclaiming himself some kind of Celtic prince with mystical powers. My contacts tell me he has some kind of 'event' planned for the feast of Sanheim—All Hallow's Eve.

I know you have always tolerated your son's youthful artistic endeavors, but I worry he has gone too far. Word of his indiscretions could undermine your position if they reach London. I beg you to travel here as soon as you are well. There are some things that should best be discussed in private."

—Letter from David Burns to Sir Crowley, Oct. 16, 1873
Horace Camden, "The Prince of Sanheim."

Chapter 1

Wed., Oct. 4, 2006

Quinn stood in the living room, a large kitchen knife clutched in his hand. It had been the first thing he thought of when he woke up, bolting from bed and heading straight for the only weapon he had in the apartment.

Just what good a knife, or any weapon, would do him was not clear. It did not even make him feel better. He just stood at the door, waiting for something to come through it.

It was a dream, of course. Just another in a long string of nightmares. But it didn't matter. He could not shake the feeling—no, the certainty—that something was coming for him. It could arrive at any minute. Worse, it may already be here.

Quinn's hands were sweating. The sound of his breath was so loud he held it briefly just to ensure there was no one else there. How many nights had he stood here, waiting for a demon that wouldn't show? How much sleep had he even had?

He glanced at the clock on his wall, saw the hands creep past 5:42 a.m. He mentally calculated that he had four hours sleep even while he anxiously watched the door.

It would pass, he knew. He could not even remember how long he had been standing here. Fifteen minutes? Twenty? His heart was still racing. If he was lucky, he hadn't screamed this time. If he had, he was certain to hear about it from Gertrude upstairs, who seemed to believe he was shouting in the middle of the night as a result of Satanism or some bizarre sexual practice. Somehow the real reason—a bad nightmare—just didn't cut it with her.

He wondered if he could at least bring himself to sit down. That was usually the first step toward calming down. Never taking his eyes off the door, he retreated to his armchair on the back wall.

Janus had often joked that Quinn was the only guy he knew whose recliner was angled away from the television. Quinn never told him the reason why.

After another fifteen minutes, the feeling of something watching him, waiting for him, began to subside. By the time 6:15 a.m. rolled around, he could at least look away from the door for 30 seconds at a time.

By 6:40 a.m., he felt good enough to get himself a drink, pulling a Coke from the fridge, popping its top and gulping it down in giant sips.

He lay down on the sofa and thought briefly of picking up the remote. But he worried. What if he turned on the TV and his dream was on it? It had happened before.

He should be used to this, he thought. His nightmares began when he was a kid—but back then there was at least some feeling of relief when he woke up.

Lately, Quinn had not felt that way. Instead, his dreams had taken on a tangible feel. The sound of a horse chasing him, the smell of the pine forest as he ran through it, even the feel of his feet slipping in the clay as he ran down a hill. In contrast, waking life felt vague and indistinct, as if it were the dream and not the other way around.

Quinn heard a thump at the door.

He was out of his chair in an instant, the knife back in his hand. The Coke in his lap had spilled to the ground, now seeping out its remaining brownish liquid onto the white carpet. He waited for the thing to come through the door. After what felt like an eternity he realized the noise had not been caused by any monster.

It had just been the delivery kid dropping off newspapers near his front door. Quinn's body sagged in relief. He sighed and went back to the kitchen, putting the knife on the counter and picking up some paper towels to soak up the spilled soda.

He waited another ten minutes before going to the front door, opening it quickly and pulling the two papers inside. The first was the *Washington Post,* a must for anybody living in the suburbs of the District of Columbia. He dropped it on the ground as he sat back down.

Instead, he turned his attention to the *Loudoun Chronicle.* The lead story had a headline, "Loudoun Board rejects new subdivision." Another talked about a push to protect the site of a Civil War skirmish off Route 15. There was a giant photo of a football player catching a ball underneath a headline that read "Potomac Falls claims victory over Broad Run."

At the bottom of the page was a smaller headline that said "Phillips Farm Debate Started."

"Jesus, that will get their attention," Quinn said sarcastically to the wall. The wall had never answered him, but Quinn had begun to worry in his present state it might. Then he knew he'd be in real trouble.

He sighed. The tiny by-line—By Quinn O'Brion—would undoubtedly go unnoticed by most who bothered to read the story. But it hurt just a little to know he had worked two days on a story only to see the headline turn into a bright neon sign warning people not to read any further.

"Phillips Farm Debate Started," he said. "Why don't they just say: 'Boring White People Fight More,' or 'Trouble Sleeping? Read Further for Cure.'"

Quinn didn't read any further.

It was hard not to be frustrated working for a paper that seemed to publish the same stuff every week, poring over the most minute details of life in Loudoun County, Virginia. Year to year, you talked to the same people, wrote many of the same stories. And even when you had a good story—and the Phillips Farm debate mattered, he believed—it probably wouldn't register.

He dropped the *Chronicle* on the ground and picked up the *Post.* He leafed through it to find the "Loudoun Extra"—a 15-page insert that attempted to replicate a local paper. The *Post* had been on a kick lately. Seeing increasing numbers of readers turn to the Internet for news—which was free—the paper had begun local inserts in several regions.

The end result was that fewer residents felt the need to subscribe to papers like the *Chronicle*. It did not matter that the *Chronicle*'s staff had worked here longer or knew people better. People didn't want to subscribe to two papers anymore.

He glanced at the Extra's headlines and groaned. "Gibson set to unveil new Phillips plan."

"Shit," Quinn said.

He read the story quickly. Sure enough, Paul Gibson, the chairman of Loudoun's board of directors, had begun circulating a plan that would give a developer two-thirds of the old farmstead, but protect the rest under a conservation easement.

All his work, Quinn thought, and his story was already outdated. There was seldom anything worse than waking up and discovering you had been scooped. How had it happened? He had talked to everybody, including Gibson. And no one had breathed a word about any new plan. Damn.

He did not even need to look at the by-line. He knew Summer had beaten him and she would find some way to bring it up the next time they met.

Quinn dropped the paper in disgust and got up. He stumbled down the hall to the bathroom. He stopped when he passed the mirror above the sink. In the reflection was a 30-year-old of average height and regular build—he was thin enough, but not in great shape. He put his hand through his brown hair. Were those gray hairs? Maybe it was the nightmares. Was he good looking? He didn't know. There seemed little exceptional about him.

Except...his eyes. He stared back at himself with electric blue eyes. An old girlfriend had once told him his eyes were the only reason she had agreed to go out with him. She had been on the verge of saying no when she looked him in the eyes. And then she changed her mind.

Quinn smiled, but the expression held little humor in it. If his eyes had ever been arresting, he doubted anyone would notice now. His skin looked gray and pallid, as if he hid himself from the sun. And his eyes were surrounded by dark circles, the sign of a man who does not sleep well.

Jesus, he thought, I look...*haunted*.

He turned on the water and washed his face, as if to brush the look away. But the only change that occurred was his reflection now looked wet.

Screw it, he thought. It didn't matter. But just as he turned and reached for the shower faucets, he paused and listened intently. Quinn grabbed the side of the shower door to steady himself. That couldn't be right, could it? He walked into the hallway slowly and then to his window to look outside. His apartment faced the back, looking over a brief sparse of woods before another cluster of apartment buildings.

He opened his window. Over the sounds of traffic winding its way through Leesburg and beyond the call of birds, it was the sound of a horse running. The sound caused his stomach to seize up and he struggled not to be sick. It sounded close.

Quinn tried to dismiss it out of hand. Horses in Loudoun were hardly unusual, he thought. It meant nothing. But how could he hear these things? Most people wouldn't hear the sounds of a horse if one were twenty feet away, much less through a bathroom wall—not to mention an apartment.

Quinn shut the window. He didn't want to think about it. Didn't want to remember it. It was nothing but a horse lover out for a ride and there was no sense in making it into some kind of demon. He had enough real demons to worry him, didn't he?

He sighed as he stripped and turned on the shower. Mentally, he ticked off the things that had already gone wrong with his day: He got four hours sleep, began his morning threatening a door with a kitchen knife and was scooped by Summer Mandaville, *Post* reporter and pain-in-the-butt.

The only benefit to starting the day in such a lousy manner was that at least things weren't likely to get any worse.

But he was wrong about that, too.

LH File: Letter #1
Date Oct. 1, 1994
Investigation Status: Closed
Contents: Classified

Dear Mr. Anderson,

Some of what I tell you will be lies. I don't mean to get us off on the wrong foot, but I thought I should make that clear from the outset. There is, at least, a good reason for this caveat. Within the day, this letter will be in the hands of the police and they will pore over every detail, real and imagined. If I only offered truth, it might provide them with a roadmap to me and I'm not quite prepared for that. Yet.

I am a longtime reader of the Chronicle—that part is no lie, I assure you. In particular, your work has captivated me. It's something in how you write about crime. It seems pedestrian in others hands. But you offer me enough details that I can almost hear the squeal of tires at a roadside accident and smell the smoke from the fire. You are very talented and I have no doubt you will go far.

So allow me to hand you the biggest story of your career.

Approximately 6.7 miles from here to the northwest, just past Waterford on Clover Hill Road, lying in a shallow stream bed, you will find a body. While it's possible some local urchin will spot it first, it's sufficiently fresh that I think it likely you could be the first on the scene. Whether you want to see it yourself, or call the police, I leave up to you.

The name of the victim is Henrietta Verclamp. I had nothing against her. She was an attractive 37-year-old artist given to painting nature scenes and we chatted quite amiably shortly before her death. Even when she saw the knife, she didn't really understand. And why should she? Monsters lurk in the dark, not the daylight, and most don't stop to chat.

To help you with color for your story, I will tell you this: She attended George Mason University and studied history.

Art was something she took up to pass the time when she returned home to Leesburg, Va., while she decided what she wanted to do with her life. On a lark, she entered one of her paintings into a competition and the rest, as they say, is history. She won. In the 15 years since, she has never achieved widespread fame. But I think you will find her reputation was good and growing.

She had wonderfully red hair, an easy laugh and a certain twinkle in her eye when she smiled. Oh, in case it's relevant, she screamed delightfully when I sliced into her. Unfortunately, I cut a little too close to the left lung and she began choking on her own blood, which rather diminished the effect.

No one heard her. She died at 11:33 a.m. this morning. Her parents, whom she mentioned still live in Leesburg, undoubtedly think she is out painting. Can you call them and tell them yourself, or is that too tacky? I really wish I understood more about the niceties of reporting. I mean, that way you would get a great scoop, right? Be able to tell all about their reactions right as they hear their only daughter has been murdered? That would make for great color, I would think. God, I wish I could see it, but I'll have to rely on you to convey what you can. I leave it to you to best judge the situation. I can't know everything and your work has left me sufficiently impressed that I'm confident you will know the best way to handle it.

Now for your questions. I suppose the biggest one is: Why? As you know, it's the hardest question for anyone to answer. Why does a man feel like watching football on a Saturday afternoon, a cold beer in his hand as he kicks his feet up on the couch? No, that's a bad analogy.

Why does a woman enjoy a good game of tennis with her best friend on a Sunday morning? That's better—more active. Believe me, murder is an aerobic workout.

My point is: You do these things because on some level, they are a lot of fun. A way to relax. A way to blow off steam after a hard day's work. And I figured it was a good way to start the month off right.

There are other reasons. I wouldn't want you to think I murdered her just for fun. I did it because I wish to prove a point: the world is changing. It's something indefinable in the air and water. History is a cycle of the rise and fall of civilizations and individuals. There comes a certain point where the apex has been reached and everything begins slipping into darkness.

That point has now come. When it turned, I can't exactly say, but I feel it under my skin. Underneath the perfume of the roses, you can begin to scent the rot and decay setting in.

I don't mean this just at a national level. You can feel it here too. Maybe you already do. You are a perceptive man.

Loudoun County has stayed much the same as it has for 200 years. But that is beginning to slide. Fairfax County is growing and expanding. Pretty soon, the future will be at the door. There will be immigrants, developers and yuppies flooding through our gates. And that will bring with it the enemy of all humankind: change.

Change is inevitable, but there are times in life when we must make a stand. I intend to do so. My medium is the one best understood by every being on this planet, from the lowly maggot to us—fear.

Don't worry, I won't single out immigrants or minorities. I'm not prejudiced and—in all honesty—that would be trite and predictable. For terror to be most effective, it has to be indiscriminate. You can't ever believe you are safe. You have to always be looking behind you, wondering who is there in the shadow beyond the streetlight. So, starting today, everyone is up for grabs.

I will be the thing people fear. And for all time, my name will send a shiver down everyone's spine. It will become synonymous with the creeping darkness.

Today is the first day of October. By the end of it, five women, five men and five children will be rotting in the ground. You cannot stop me, just as you cannot stop change. I am night. I am cold. I am flesh rendered and torn. I am steel. I am the harbinger of fall: I am death.

You can call me Lord Halloween.

Chapter 2

Wed., Oct. 4, 2006

Kate woke up thinking about a corpse.

The image should have been faded like an old photograph wearing around the edges. But instead it felt fresh, more real than yesterday, as vivid as a minute ago.

There was a buzzing sound. She had to clear her head with some effort (she could still clearly see the hand lying awkwardly off the bed—the flesh was pink but it was cold to the touch) and realize it was just the alarm clock.

Her hand reached out and fumbled over buttons until the noise stopped.

She took a dim account of her surroundings and tried to let the dream go. Of course, it wasn't really a dream at all. It was a memory, a related but fundamentally different beast.

It felt stuffy in the room. Kate got up and walked to the sliding glass door. She opened it and felt a breeze blow past. She walked out onto the balcony of the Hotel Leesburg and was treated to a partial view of the town. Zoning laws did not permit any tall buildings within the city limits, so the view was a poor one.

Still, she breathed in the crisp fall air and took in the orange color of the leaves. It might have been beautiful, but she barely noticed. Why is it always the same? The image of walking across the ground floor of her childhood home, so real she could feel the carpet beneath her toes.

In the dream, she knows what is happening above her but cannot stop. She's stuck on repeat, a character in an old home movie doomed to do the same thing again and again. But the dream (or the memory, it didn't matter anymore) could not explain why she was here—why she had come back. Kate stared down the street and felt her hands grip the cold rusty railing. What was she doing here?

She could hear the chirping of birds, with one long mournful call breaking through the morning air. It was the only answer she received.

Would you know it if you went crazy? There was supposed to be a catch—you can't be crazy if you wonder if you are insane. But it didn't feel like a blanket exemption. What happens if you can look at your own behavior, evaluate it coldly in the light of day, recognize it for utter lunacy, but can't stop it?

There was no reason for her to have left Ohio, a suitcase thrown in her trunk, and return here. Not a good one anyway. Did she expect an answer, or healing, or...

She let the thought drift off. Compulsion. What she felt was a compulsion, an obsession, and she hadn't been able to stand it anymore.

Kate turned and walked back inside. She sat on the bed and put her head in her hands. Before she could even begin to be depressed, the familiar anger took over, the feeling growing quickly inside her. Why? It was a question that echoed in her head every second of every day. Why had this happened to her?

She stood back up again and walked to the bathroom to take a shower. As she turned on the water, she tried to block out her own thoughts. There were no answers inside her head. She had to trust the instinct—the compulsion—that brought her back here. She hoped some answers were out there somewhere.

It was not until after she toweled off that she saw it. She had just begun to brush her teeth and absentmindedly looked in the mirror. When she looked up, she saw a word written in the mirror. It had been drawn in careful strokes as if the writer had taken their time. Kate was so surprised, she stumbled back through the bathroom door.

"Sanheim," it said.

For a moment, Kate almost screamed. But when she opened her mouth, no sound came out. Instead, when she blinked, the message was gone. All she saw was fog on the mirror.

She shook her head. She was going crazy. It was as simple as that.

One way or another, this had to stop.

*****

Quinn sat in his usual place at the Leesburg Starbucks and stared out the window. It had become a ritual, this stop, and he knew it was a bad idea. Starbucks was a giant pit that he threw money into. He could have purchased a coffee maker—it might have even produced better coffee—but somehow coming here made him feel better. Maybe it made him feel less alone.

He picked through the main section of *The Washington Post*, waiting for something to catch his eye. But aside from the usual political scandals, the various fights in Congress and the inevitable crime stories, there was little to be found. Certainly nothing distracting.

And then she walked in. Quinn felt the cool draft sweep by him as the door swung open and then shut. Out of the corner of his eye, he saw her blonde hair flip off her shoulder—the result of a casual toss of her head. Her hair just brushed her shoulders and curled a little in various directions. It was simple, yet elegant, like her khaki slacks and white blouse.

By now, Quinn was staring shamelessly. No doubt, she was beautiful. Petite and graceful, roughly his age, with delicate hands as she counted out her money for the cashier. But she was compelling in a way Quinn could not begin to explain.

When she turned to find a seat, Quinn almost caught his breath as he saw her bright blue eyes. With great effort, he stopped staring, but continued to steal glances as she stretched out in an armchair to read the paper.

He had never been so drawn to a stranger before, nor so observant of her every detail. Her silver earrings, the way her fingers rested on her eyebrow as she read.

He shook his head. This was stupid. It was nothing more than a reaction to two dateless years and too much time spent around women who were too old to court. It was a new face, that was all, he told himself. A new face with a great looking body.

Suddenly she caught him watching her. But like a child caught staring, he couldn't even pretend that he wasn't. They held each other's gaze for a moment and then she looked back down at her paper—his paper, his employer in fact. After a while she got up and barely looked his way as she left the Starbucks.

When she was gone, he let out a large sigh, like he had been holding his breath the whole time. What was his problem?

She would be gone now, he thought. If there was destiny involved, surely it had just slapped him in the face and passed him by.

He tossed the paper in a recycling bin and left the shop.

*****

Quinn stared at his desk and for the 15th time this week wondered how he got anything done. The desk was beyond a disaster—it was a crater filled with papers, pads, pens, highlighters and paperclips. Underneath all of it could be the Dead Sea scrolls, but Quinn seriously doubted he would ever know.

It was a pile of rubble that shifted from place to place, exposing bare brown areas of desk. He didn't think the entire desk would ever be seen again, at least not while he worked there.

Scattered around were various pieces of Tupperware, which he hoped would find their way back to his apartment one day. But considering that every day he forgot they were there, he thought they would have to get up and walk home themselves.

Quinn slung his bag onto an extra chair and flicked on the computer. The computer had no sooner booted up then a little sign appeared in the window.

"How could you perform an illegal function yet, you dumb machine?" Quinn asked it.

Quinn turned off the computer and started again.

He hated computers. Clearly the feeling was mutual. A day that went by without a major computer fault eating one of his stories or just generally going haywire was an event to celebrate. Quinn thought maybe it would help if Ethan actually shelled out some real money for this place, but that was like asking for a miracle.

His thoughts were rudely interrupted by Kyle, who practically burst through the door from the stairwell, walked quickly to his desk and threw his bag on a chair.

"Fantastic," Kyle declared, to nobody in particular. "Absolutely fantastic."

Quinn didn't reply. You didn't bother replying to Kyle. In a way, his manner of conversation was like a bad computer program. No matter what input you gave, the output would be the same.

"I mean fantastic," Kyle said again, for the first time really turning to Quinn.

"What is fantastic?" Quinn asked, not exactly expecting it to make any difference.

"The fire last night. Whooh, boy," and Kyle shook his head as if he could not *believe* someone had not seen this "fantastic" thing. "Makes me wish I were still a fireman."

"Thought you were a policeman," Quinn shot back.

"Of course, of course," Kyle said, as if this were a minor detail. "But we handled fires all the time. But last night. Last night was…"

He stopped as if searching for the right word.

"Fantastic?" Quinn offered, smiling slightly to himself.

"Yes," Kyle said, and pointed to Quinn, gesturing with his finger to his nose. "Yes. Absolutely fantastic. This stupid kid was playing with matches in the garage and managed to light some dry wood lying around."

"Doesn't sound too bad," Quinn said.

"Yeah, well, you should have seen what happened next," Kyle said, savoring the moment, his hands twitching slightly while his eyes shifted away from Quinn and stared into space.

"The kid ran out, got his parents. And they ran in. And the father saw it, right? He knew what was going to happen."

"What happened?" Quinn asked, still vaguely looking more at his computer, which looked like it was crashing again, than Kyle.

"The gasoline, man," and Kyle came up right next to Quinn, as if to whisper conspiratorially. "Two cans of it—just sitting there. You wouldn't believe it. When it went off, it was like a bomb. A large explosion."

"Jesus, was anybody hurt?" Quinn asked, for the first time really looking at Kyle. But Kyle still had that far away look, as if he were replaying the whole thing in his mind.

"Was anybody hurt?" Quinn repeated, with more emphasis.

"What? Oh, no," Kyle said. "No, the guy knew there was no way. He just got his family out and ran. Ran and ran. But the garage really went up. I saw that fire burning, and whew! What a doozy. Fireguys said they hadn't seen one like that since the gas explosion over in Ashburn."

Quinn didn't respond. He didn't want to talk about the gas explosion in Ashburn.

Janus and he had been the first on that scene—before even the police arrived. It wasn't a pleasant memory.

"Amazing," Kyle said again, shaking his head.

"But nobody got hurt," Quinn repeated.

"No, no," Kyle said and his voice appeared to echo with disappointment.

Quinn wasn't sure though and quickly dismissed it. Injured people might make a better story, but he doubted even Kyle was that cold-blooded.

The guy was a softie, despite a muscular build and an almost fu-Manchu mustache—not to mention an obsession with WWF wrestling that bordered on serious psychosis. He wanted the story, but he wasn't the type to really want someone dead.

"Amazing," he said again and wandered back to his desk.

Quinn rolled his eyes.

Within two hours, much of the rest of the staff started to arrive.

Janus showed up first, predictably announcing himself by chucking a mini-basketball at Quinn's head.

"Head's up," he yelled a second before he cut it loose.

Quinn nabbed it out of the air with terrific speed.

"Jesus, how the bloody hell did you pull that?" Janus asked.

"Quick reflexes," Quinn replied.

"Like you knew it was coming," Janus muttered.

"I've told you before—you Welsh boys can't throw too damn well. Too busy playing soccer," Quinn said and grinned.

"Like you throw better?" Janus asked, but he was chuckling. "I'm sorry about the story."

"The what?" Quinn replied.

"Come off it, mate. I saw the Summer story," Janus said.

Quinn grimaced and lied, "It sucked."

"It didn't and you know it," Janus replied.

His voice was not entirely unsympathetic, however. He had his own issues with Summer, to be sure, but even photographers knew what it was like to see a better picture in somebody else's paper.

"What do you want me to say? She beat me," Quinn said.

"Well at least you beat her the week before," Janus replied.

"What, the stalker stuff?" Quinn said. "I guess, but no one will remember, and she didn't exactly give me credit when she did the same story two days later."

"You expected her to? That's optimistic of you."

"No," Quinn said. "I suppose actually following the basic tenets of journalistic civility is too much to ask."

Janus laughed, turned and walked back to the darkroom in the corner of the newsroom—the place where the photographers worked, lived and breathed. Quinn briefly wondered why they still called it a darkroom. With everything having gone digital several years ago, there was no need to keep it dark anymore.

He had little time to think about it, however, before Rebecca came out of her office and took a sharp look around.

"Why isn't anybody in the conference room?" she asked the staff loudly, glaring at them all. "Don't we have a meeting anymore or did I miss a memo?"

Nobody pointed out that it was only two minutes after ten o'clock and that that was hardly late. Instead, they all looked at each other and scrambled to get in the room after her.

Chapter 3

"Fifty men went up a hill,
None of them came down.
Fifty men went to him,
None of them were found."
—Traditional Scottish Rhyme, circa 1880s

Less than 20 minutes after accepting the job at the *Loudoun Chronicle*, Kate was already beginning to have doubts. Before she had made the rather impulsive decision to come back here, she had carefully considered the pros and cons.

The paper had been around for nearly two hundred years, was well entrenched in the community and was one of the few paid subscription papers left in the area after recent expansions by *The Washington Post*. Since the *Post* was unlikely to hire her, and journalism was the only career she ever considered, the *Chronicle* felt like the right place to be.

But her sense of balance had forced her to acknowledge some unpleasant truths. The *Chronicle*'s subscription was dwindling; its stories often lacked polish; and she feared it would be more provincial than she was used to.

Within those first few minutes, she knew she had been right on all counts. They were nice, of course. Lawrence, the editor, introduced her around to smiles and nods from all sides. But the meeting then became a series of inside jokes, unsubtle digs between reporters and general confusion.

To add to her doubts, the guy she had seen in the coffee shop this morning—the one who could not stop staring at her—was here making a repeat of his morning's performance.

She had the feeling that he was trying to be subtle, but if so, it wasn't working. Every time she looked away, she could feel him watching her.

The sensation wasn't threatening—she had no malicious vibe off him—just unnerving. Momentarily, the thought flitted through her mind that she had something on her face, or was somehow dressed inappropriately. But if that were true, only one guy noticed, and she thought that was unlikely.

Rebecca tried to keep the meeting going by listing various sections of the paper: Schools, Crime, Politics, Business and Sports. It was life divided into easy-to-understand categories that had little bearing on the world outside—life as a series of boxes. Not that Kate saw any other way to run a paper; it just felt forced.

But the meeting was bogged down from the get-go. The schools reporter was feuding with the crime reporter. The guy who was staring at her—Quinn—was bickering with the political reporter. The sports reporter wouldn't say two words together, earning him the anger of Rebecca, and the business reporter was nowhere to be found.

About the only good thing was that it was over quickly. Rebecca, though clearly annoyed, waded through the options and quickly chose those she thought would be on the front page. But the overall feeling was provincial—no doubt about that.

Within minutes of leaving the meeting, it only became worse. Kyle, the crime reporter, was waiting for her outside, anxious to talk.

"Do you know what the key to being a good reporter is?" Kyle began.

On the face of it, this was an offensive question. Did she know what being a good reporter was? Well, she had been doing it for three years; she certainly hoped so.

"Oh here we go," said another voice, one of the photographers.

Kate glanced at Bill. He was a huge guy, fat from every angle, but cheerful and friendly.

"What?" Kyle said, looking annoyed.

"Don't let him bother you," Bill said.

"Kyle, are you bothering the new girl already?" a new voice piped in from behind Kate.

It was Janus—she remembered the name because it sounded like a girl's, but was spelled differently.

Behind Janus, Kate noticed the guy from the coffee shop—Quinn.

"Not a problem," Kate replied to Janus.

"Anyway," Kyle said, clearly irritated at the interruptions and the crowd around him.

"Oh, is Kyle going to give his watch speech again?" Janus asked, and thrust out his hand to Kate. "The name's Janus."

"He's Welsh," Quinn said behind him. Quinn thought it was possible this was the worst opening line he had ever used on anyone, but it had just popped out there.

Janus turned and looked at him with mock offense.

"How dare you bring my ethnicity into it?" he said, far too loudly. "I tell you, Kate, the racial stereotyping around here is just ridiculous."

"It's best if you ignore him," Quinn said, sticking out his own hand for Kate to shake. "He won't go away, but you will gradually tune him out."

"Gentlemen, I believe I was talking to the lady," Kyle said.

"Right, right," Janus said. "Mustn't get in the way of the watch speech."

"The watch speech?" Kate asked, a little bewildered at the motley collection of guys around her.

"As I was saying, the most important part of being a reporter is..."

Janus shot up his hand and Bill quickly followed. Quinn laughed and Kyle ignored them all.

"The most important part is to set your watch ahead by three minutes," Kyle said, looking very serious.

The others started chuckling.

"Set it three minutes ahead?" Kate repeated, feeling like she was being put on.

The others started laughing again.

"Don't listen to them," Kyle said again, waving his hand dismissively. "It's very important."

"Why?" Kate stammered, completely at a loss.

"So that you will never be late," Kyle said, still looking very intense.

"How would that help?"

Kyle stared at her a moment, giving her a blank look at why she couldn't see the wisdom in what he was saying. Then he smiled.

"It's very simple," he said, while Janus and Bill started talking amongst themselves. "All reporters like to procrastinate, yes?"

Kate nodded.

"And all reporters are always about two minutes late to everything, right?"

"I guess," she said.

"A-ha," he said, looking pleased with himself. "Well, if you set your watch just three minutes ahead, it gets you moving. You look at it and instead of being late by two minutes, you are just in time."

"Oh," Kate said.

"It's very simple, but I can't tell you how many times it has saved my butt," Kyle said, still smiling intently.

"I see," she replied. She paused, waiting awkwardly for something to save her. "Well, that seems very helpful."

"Of course, you could just leave earlier," Quinn said.

Kyle grunted in disgust.

"Yeah, sure," he said. "You could, yeah. You make fun of me, but how many times are you late to something, Quinn? Huh?"

"All the time, Kyle," he replied.

"You see?" Kyle said, looking at Kate in triumph. "You see? I'm never late. I'm always one minute early. It makes all the difference in the world, Kate."

Kyle jabbed his finger in Quinn's direction.
"All the difference," he said again.

"That's super, Kyle," Janus said, and put his arm around Kyle to start moving him away. "You're scaring the poor girl. Worse, you're scaring me."

"Did you forget your medication again, Kyle?" Bill asked.

Kyle shook off Janus, gave him a dirty look and stomped away.

"Thanks, Kyle," Kate called after him, but he glanced balefully at Bill and Janus.

"I'd stay out of his way today," Quinn told them.

"Nah," Bill replied. "He'll get over it."

"Don't worry about Kyle," Janus said. "Something will explode or some robbery will happen and he'll be happy again."

Laurence popped his head out of his door.

"Janus, Quinn, good," he said. "I want you to give Kate the tour, will you? Take her around, show her the place."

"That's the first five minutes," Janus said.

"Yes, well..." Laurence said.

"It's okay, we'll do it," Quinn replied. Laurence retreated back into his office.

"Janus is right, though," he said afterward. "This won't exactly eat up your whole day."

"It's all right," she said. She smiled at Quinn.

"Well," he said. "Uh, I guess you can see the newsroom. If you walk straight ahead, you'll find the graphics department."

They walked just a few feet down the hall. As they did, Kate sized up her three companions. Quinn was handsome, though he looked tired. Janus struck her mostly because of his size. He looked no taller than her, at about 5 feet 4 inches, with straight black hair and brown eyes. Given how talkative he had been in the staff meeting, she wondered if he was the kind of guy to have a Napoleon complex. Stepping next to him, she also distinctly smelled the aroma of cigarettes on his clothes.

Bill was a big guy, not quite obese but well beyond chubby, Kate observed. She felt almost mean thinking that because he was so nice. About medium height with brown eyes and black hair, he looked pleasantly cheery, as if someone had recently complimented him. Maybe it was just a good day, but she had the impression he usually looked that way.

"About the only thing worth seeing here is the printing press," said Janus.

"It's cool you actually see it," Kate said. "At the *Gazette*, we never did. It was all sent off-site."

"It's cool," Quinn said, and he opened the double doors that led downstairs.

They walked down there and saw the paper run just beginning. The rumble of the press would soon be so loud they would have to start yelling to make themselves heard. They watched it for a moment.

In the corner a sign said, "Safety is our number one priority. We have not had an accident in..." and in magic marker it finished, "54 days."

"Not a very encouraging record," Quinn said when he saw Kate looking at it. "Come on, you can see back here where it all comes out."

They walked around the gigantic machine to get to the back.

"The *Loudoun Chronicle* is a broad sheet," Quinn said, pointing up. "If you look up there, you can see where the screens come in. Everything is sent electronically from upstairs, then photographed and placed on the screens. It gets sent through in sections, then comes out over there."

He pointed to a few places.

It took Quinn a minute more before he realized Kate wasn't watching him. He looked to see her staring at the far corner of the room. There was nothing there that he could see.

"Kate?" he asked. Janus and Bill followed her gaze, looked back at Quinn, and shrugged.

"Kate?" Quinn asked again. She didn't respond for a minute.

"What happened there?" she said finally.

"Happened where?" Quinn asked, and looked back at the spot.

"There," she said, and pointed to a spot on the floor. Quinn saw nothing but a very dusty piece of cement.

The three men exchanged quizzical looks.

"There's nothing there," Quinn said, feeling a little concerned.

Kate walked up and looked down.

"It's right..." she trailed off.

Quinn followed her. He looked down and saw nothing.

"Are you okay?" he asked her.

She turned and looked at him, then back at the floor.

"Trick of the light," she said. "I just thought I saw something—that's all."

She did not sound convincing, but Quinn let it go.

"Sure," he said.

"Hey, guys," Bill said. "Are we done with the tour yet? Anyone up for lunch?"

Kate nodded, said she was hungry, and they headed out the back door. On his way out, Quinn noticed her look back at the corner of the room.

"Are you okay?" he asked again.

She met his gaze.

"Yeah," she said. "What could be wrong?"

Outside, he noticed her hands shaking, but he knew enough not to say anything.

*****

They went to a small Italian deli for lunch and Kate tried to forget about what she had seen, though the thought of it kept coming back. She was surprised at how easy it was to hang out with these people. She had this idea that reporters were supposed to be constantly moving, as they had back in Ohio. No one had time for lunch there.

But she supposed a weekly paper was bound to be different and if there was a more relaxed atmosphere, she wondered why she felt herself missing the all-consuming pressure of a daily deadline.

"It's different, isn't it?" Quinn asked.

"What?" Kate said, startled out of reverie.

"Working here," he replied, and smiled at her.

"You read my mind," she said, and really looked at Quinn.

In jeans and a red button-down shirt, he appeared casual and comfortable, but she felt some vibe coming off him. He seemed...nervous. Like a guy on his first date or something. It never occurred to her that she might have had something to do with that.

"No, I just know how it goes," he said. "When I came back here after working on the Hill..."

"You worked on Capitol Hill?" she asked.

"Yeah, for *Congressional Quarterly*," he said.

"Nice," Kate replied.

"I suppose," Quinn said. "But when I got back here, it was kind of crazy. I had gone from a constant deadline to a paper that just seemed to take its time."

"Hey, some of us enjoy our relaxation time," Bill chimed in.

"Too much from the look of it," Janus said, and patted Bill's belly. Bill brushed Janus' hand away with a look of bemused irritation.

Quinn barely acknowledged them.

"Anyway, it was a switch," he said.

"I'll bet," Kate said, and tried again to size Quinn up. She had this nagging feeling that she knew him from somewhere and the more he talked, the more difficult it was to shake it. But she couldn't place him to save her life.

"So Laurence said something about you coming from a daily paper and I thought I could relate," Quinn said.

"Yeah," she said. "I guess I'll get used to it."

"If you worked for a daily, why did you come down here?" Quinn asked.

That, my friend, is the million-dollar question, Kate thought. She was damned if she knew. Instead of saying that, however, she just smiled.

"I needed a change of scenery," she said.

"So you came to Loudoun?" Janus asked. "Boy, did you take the wrong train to Clarksville."

"You don't like it here?" she asked him.

"Well, I do, yeah," Janus said. "But I'm a loon, so I don't think that tells you much. I guess I got my mates here and they pay me to take lovely photos. But I don't know what anyone else sees in it."

"You should be in tourism, Janus," Bill said.

"I just mean it's a pretty boring place," he said.

"That wasn't the impression I had," Kate said.

"Oh, you just wait," Janus said, picking up his turkey sandwich and biting into it. "Wait till you have lived here for six years. Then tell me how exciting it is."

"It isn't that bad," Quinn said quickly.

"Then why did you move away, bucko?" Janus asked through a full mouth.

"I moved back, didn't I?" Quinn replied.

"Why was that, anyway, Quinn?" Bill asked. "I always meant to ask."

Quinn shot a dark look in Janus' direction, who held up his hands in a 'What did I do?' gesture.

"Just didn't like it there, I guess," Quinn replied.

"I would have thought it would be exciting," Kate said.

For a moment, she saw an odd look cross his face and then it was gone.

"Maybe it was too exciting," he said, and appeared to want to leave it at that.

"Speaking of excitement," Janus said, finishing off his sandwich even as Bill got up to get another. "I think you and I need to get going, right?"

Quinn looked at him blankly.

"Where?" he asked.

"I thought Buzz told you—we have to go see that coin-sorting place for the profile, right? Remember? I take the pretty photos and you write your boring article?"

"Oh damn," Quinn said. "I forgot."

He looked at his watch.

"We are supposed to be there in 10 minutes," he said. "We'll never make it."

"You know, if you had just set your watch 3 minutes ahead, Quinn," Janus started.

"Get stuffed," Quinn said. "Let's go."

He looked apologetically at Kate.

"I'm sorry to run out on you, but duty calls," he said. "We'll see you back at base, right?"

"Sure," she said.

"And sorry to leave you alone with Bill," Janus said, watching as the portly photographer wandered back to the table with another sandwich. "Don't let him get too fresh."

"I won't," she smiled, and watched Quinn wave before they walked out the door.

As Bill sat down and began to munch on his sub, Kate let out a small sigh.

She wondered again just what she had she gotten herself into.

Dear Mr. Anderson,

I confess that I'm disappointed. I wouldn't say angry—not yet anyway—but disappointed. When I chose you, it was with the expectation that you would make me famous. Instead, you appear to be cooperating with the police in covering me up. Since Ms. Verclamp's death, I've seen two articles on her murder, not one of which has even hinted of my existence.

There is no good reason for this. It can't be that you don't believe I'm the killer. I gave you the precise location of her body and I'm told you made the call yourself to police after reading my first missive. So what's the hold up? Did the police tell you that you would be interfering in an investigation? Did they say my letters would only panic the public? Nothing like a serial killer on the loose to get the blood circulating, right?

So you wrote two very drab pieces, the first on the death and the second a profile of the victim. Though the profile was touching—I note with pride you used my suggested color—the whole thing feels pedestrian. I wanted to make a big splash with my first kill and now everyone is probably assuming Ms. Verclamp had an angry boyfriend. They don't even know I'm out here.

This makes me unhappy, Mr. Anderson, and I wish to warn you upfront that a second mistake of this nature will not be tolerated lightly. Consider this my second gift to you—I'm letting you off easy this time. I'm not threatening you, Mr. Anderson—I have no wish to see you harmed—but you must understand my position. I aim to make a name for myself, and see you as my partner. And right now, my partner isn't pulling his weight.

Let's hope things improve this time around. The next body is lying on the outskirts of Ida Lee Park, in the woods behind the tennis court. The police will identify him as Michael Weissman, a promising 16-year-old who attended Loudoun High School. So that police can be sure I'm the killer, I'll offer the following tidbits. He wasn't killed where his body is now located—and he tried to fight his attacker. He failed, of course, but I give him credit for trying. I stabbed him in the lower abdomen and watched as he tried to crawl away. He bled to death eventually, but I have to admit it took longer than I expected.

I'll leave you to find out more about his background. We didn't have much time to talk. Did he have a girlfriend? What did he want to be when he grew up? How hard do you think his parents will take it? I'm tempted to give them a call myself—that would really give you something to write about: "Killer Taunts Dead Boy's Family."

But perhaps that can wait. Fear is a contagious thing, but sometimes it's best to let it spread slowly. I trust that in this next article, you will mention me properly. Feel free to quote from my letters to you—they are on the record, as always.

Oh, and you might want to get a move on. It's only Oct 5th, and I have a lot more killing to do before the month is up. I'd prefer it if my victims knew who was gutting them, so I'm trying to keep things slow until the word gets out. Please don't disappoint me again. I promise you that you will regret it.

Yours Sincerely,

Lord Halloween

Chapter 4

"As far as serial killers go, Lord Halloween was more flashy than scary. True, he terrified the area he haunted, but it seems impossible, when compared with some of the more famous killers of the 20th century, that this person should stand out. Yes, LH murdered with impunity. Yes, LH tortured several victims. But his fetish with Halloween is so trite that I give him lower marks than many of his contemporaries. About the only thing that gives me pause is that he got away with the murders. Most killers secretly want to be caught. It's clear LH didn't."
—Arnold Cosgrove, "Stop Me Before I Kill Again: Serial Killers in History."

Lord Halloween could wait forever. It was hard to say how long he had been standing alongside the road. He didn't move or speak or show any other signs of life. He just stood there, looking in front of him. Patience was one of his virtues, he knew. Probably the only one.

He had waited 12 years. He thought that was long enough. There was some consideration, even as late as this morning, that he should wait one more year. After all, 13 had great significance among the superstitious. But everything was prepared and he didn't have the heart to put away the tools of his trade for one more year. The truth, he knew, was that he didn't want to wait another year—didn't want to dream about this for another 12 months.

On the road, nothing stirred. Somewhere there was a faint rustling of leaves as the wind blew them around in the darkness, but everything else was still. He certainly did not move. He would wait for the right moment. He had waited this long, he could afford the time now. If today wasn't the day, well...

He stopped himself. Today would be the day. His hands twitched with the thought of it and he smiled faintly. He stared out at the road. Today had to be the day. He felt it in his bones.

He waited in the darkness.

*****

Mary Kilgore felt the car sliding to the left and fought with the steering wheel to bring it under control. She felt a flurry of panic, fearing it would career into the woods beyond the road. But just as that seemed inevitable and the trees loomed above her, the car suddenly came back to the right.

She pumped the brakes furiously and successfully brought the car to a stop. She sighed in relief at first, happy to be safe. But it occurred to her soon after that something serious had happened to her car and that she might not be able to get it moving again.

She unbuckled her seatbelt and got out of the car. Certainly she hadn't hit anything—there hadn't even been a bump in the road. She wondered if it was the transmission, or engine failure and cursed herself that she didn't know more about cars. That had always been Donald's arena and now he was gone.

She sighed again and walked to the front of the car. Mary took one look at the battered front right tire, and even to her untrained eye, she could see what the problem was. The tire looked like it had come apart. She thanked her stars at least she had been able to bring her car under control before she crashed. But when was the last time she had changed a tire?

It took no time for her to think about Donald again. If he were here...

But he isn't here, Mary told herself. He is not going to come to the rescue this time, or any other time. She felt a wave of self-pity coming on and struggled to throw it off.

She looked back at the road. It was deserted, of course. It was the very reason she had come this way—a short-cut to get to the Middleburg town meeting on time, for once. But now she wished she had stuck with her normal route. If she had, she could have flagged a dozen cars down. Right now, the prospect of any showing up seemed farfetched.

She went back into the car and pulled out her cell phone. She flicked it on and waited to see if she would get a signal. She didn't. Instead, the phone simply displayed a message, "No service."

"Damn," she said. She tossed the phone back in the car and flipped the switch that opened the trunk. She would just have to hope that there was a jack and a spare tire in there. If not, she faced a long, lonely walk in the dark. In Loudoun, there was little to be frightened of, but she still shivered at the thought.

It seemed like just the other day she had read in the *Chronicle* about someone in Loudoun spotting a mountain lion near the area. What if she ran into it in the dark? What if some bear wandered down this way? Already, she had a disturbing sense of being watched, but dismissed it as paranoia.

The sooner she changed the tire, the better. To her surprise and immense relief, she found both a jack and a spare in the trunk.

"Damn you, Donald," she said out loud again. "I can do this without you."

The bastard was probably off with his 25-year-old tart right now.

She stopped herself. That was no help. She needed to stay focused. She returned to the front wheel with a sense of purpose. But as she walked, her foot scraped against something. Bending down, she saw that she had stepped on a nail.

"Crap." The nail had caused the flat.

Then she saw two more nails on the road. Looking back, she could see a few more faintly glinting in the moonlight.

"Damn it," she said. Someone had put nails out here. Probably some kid, she thought, and silently she cursed them. They could have gotten her killed. She wondered what kind of little punk had done this.

Mary was still bent over when she heard a sound on the pavement behind her.

Wheeling around, she stared off into the darkness and saw nothing.

"Is somebody there?" she asked.

Maybe the kid was here to see what kind of results his prank brought.

"Show yourself, if you're there?" she called again.

At first there was nothing. Just the sound of a faint echo of her own words. And then she jumped at a voice coming from behind her.

"Sorry," the voice said. "I didn't mean to sneak up on you like that."

She turned around to see a figure standing on the other side of her car.

"It's okay," she said, and smiled in relief. "I just..."

And her smile faded. He said he hadn't meant to sneak up on her, but how was that possibly true? Hadn't she heard him behind her a second before? Why hadn't he called out? She looked around and saw nothing near them. Where was his car?

"It's alright," he said again, and took a small step forward. "Looks like you got a flat."

"Yeah," she said, although she looked at him warily. "Some kid put these nails here and I must have run over them..."

But the words dried out on her lips. Her tongue briefly flickered to the roof of her mouth as her heart seemed to spring directly into her throat. This was no kid.

"Yeah, you have to watch out for stuff like that," he replied. She could see that he was smiling, but it failed to reassure her. To Mary, the smile appeared distinctly predatory, like some kind of cat (*a mountain lion*) that had found its prey. Instinctively, she took a step back.

"Yeah," she muttered, and wondered if her fear was obvious.

He took another step forward and rested one hand on the hood of her car.

"Well, what do you say, let me see if I can help you with that," he said, but he made no more forward moves.

She could see now in the faint moonlight that he had the other hand behind his back. It made her more nervous. She had no idea what to do. Should she run? Her brain was running through options but coming up blank. Panic was setting in.

"No, I'm okay," she said, straining to keep her voice calm. "I just called my husband, Donald. He should be on his way."

"Really? That's great," the man replied. "I'm surprised that you would get any reception out here. You know they've been debating putting up a cellular tower out here, but the damn environmentalists won't let them. They say it would 'mar' the landscape, I think. I don't know that much about it, of course. I don't much care for that kind of news."

Mary took another step back. She had hoped her ruse would cause him to back off. But it was obvious it hadn't. The terrible truth finally clicked in: this was a trap. The nails, the dead-zone, the lack of any nearby help. She had a brief flicker of a memory of watching a mouse struggle on a glue trap near her stove. She had hated watching the thing slowly die, thrashing and screaming and begging for help. But she was that mouse now, she knew. And she was beginning to think her fate would be even worse.

"Well, it did," she said, and sounded lame even to herself. "I was surprised."

"Well, yeah, you would be," he said. "I mean, you must have a great carrier around here."

He took his hand off the car and took another step forward.

"Look," Mary said. "I don't know what you are doing out here, but..."

"Waiting for you," he replied calmly, and the smile slipped from his face.

Now that the smile was gone, she found she wanted it back. In the light, he now looked blank and impassive and his eyes appeared dead.

"You put the nails here," she said. It wasn't a question. There was no need to ask.

He nodded and took another step forward. Mary took another back. She wished desperately she had taken her purse out with her. There was an old can of mace in it. As she was, she felt helpless.

"Well, I can't leave *everything* to chance, can I?" he said.

"No," she said, though she had no idea what he was talking about. "I suppose not."

She looked briefly at her shoes. They were pumps, not exactly running sneakers.

"I mean, I was just lucky someone came this way, you know? Not many people bother anymore. Do you know why that is?"

She couldn't bring herself to say anything. Instead, she backed away again. Her face felt taut and she could feel pain all through her chest. Every muscle in her body had tensed now and she fought the urge to just run blindly into the surrounding woods.

"It used to be a great make-out area, you know?" he continued, taking another step forward even as she walked back. "The kids all came this way and pulled off the side of the road. Sure, it was a shortcut, but it was so dark out here. You could get away with anything and there would be nobody around to hear."

"I didn't know that," she said, still trying to think of what to do.

"No, if you had, you probably wouldn't have come," he said.

"Because you would have known what happened to them. You must be new to the area, Ms..."

"I'm not going to tell you my name," she said.

"Pity," he replied. "I'll just have to read about it in the paper, then."

"What?" she asked.

"When they find your body," he said. "They won't find it for a while, of course. But when they eventually identify you from your dental records, then I'll see the name."

"Oh, dear God," she said, and was startled to find water running down her face. She was crying. She didn't know a person could cry from terror.

"He won't help you, my dear," he said. "Anyway, I put a stop to kids coming out here. Do you have any kids, Ms. Soon-to-be-very-dead? They could have told you how. Twelve years ago—on this very night—I gutted two of them. I mean, I really went to work. Not the way I will on you. No, I was younger then, and didn't have enough artistry."

Mary was sobbing now, unable to help herself.

"Anyway, just one couple. That was all it took. And in 12 years, they never came back. I know because I waited to see. But they were smart enough to stay away. Too bad for you though."

"Please," she said. "Please don't do this."

She took another step backward.

"If you don't put up a fight, I'll make it quick," he said. "I promise."

"No, no, no, no," she stammered out, and she felt another emotion now. She felt a kind of raw anger coming out of her. These men, she thought. For how many years had she put up with Donald? And now she was finally free of him and this guy comes along? It was unfair. It wasn't right. She wasn't supposed to die like this. She was supposed to go quietly in her bed, surrounded by grandchildren.

She felt the anger wash over her and was surprised by how good it felt. Anything that broke through the fear.

"If you do fight, well…" he said. "I'm out of practice, but I remember well enough how to inflict pain."

She heard his words and felt a click in the back of her head. She wasn't going to give in to the urge to run away. If she did, he would be on her in seconds.

Mary stopped moving back. The fear that had so flooded her had given way. Dim memories of her best friend, Gladys, teaching her a move from a self-defense class, flickered to life. And as she watched this man advance, a plan formed in her mind.

She had stopped crying. She was through crying. Instead, she quickly bent down on the ground and felt along the side of the road.

"Just what the hell do you think you are doing?" he asked, and he was moving, faster than she anticipated.

But not quite fast enough. Grabbing hold of gravel she had felt along the road, she threw it at his face as he approached. He cried out and stumbled back, putting his right hand to his head.

It was a good start, but not enough. Still feeling the anger bubbling inside her, she moved toward him. Remembering what Gladys had told her, she put her hands across him on his shoulder and drove her knee deep into his groin.

He doubled over and fell to the floor, dropping something in his left hand as he did so. She looked to see a long, curved knife—a machete.

"You bitch," he said.

She stood back, surprised at what she had done. As suddenly as it had come, the anger she felt left her and the fear came running back. She had to get away—get away before he recovered.

Turning on her heels, she ran into the forest, hoping to put distance between them. Sooner than she had anticipated, she heard him cry out.

"I'll find you, you know that?" he screamed, his words echoing through the forest all around her. "There isn't anything for miles. I'll find you. Do you know what I will do then?"

She ran faster, cursing herself for her pumps.

"You won't get far," he shouted after her.

She ran for her life. She ran faster than she ever had.

But ultimately, the man was right.

Mary Kilgore did not get far.

Chapter 5

Friday, Oct. 6

The only thing that Quinn could remember was that he had been running for his life. Somewhere the Horseman had been behind him, laughing at him and swinging his almighty sword. Quinn knew it was only a matter of time before he caught up.

He woke drenched in sweat and immediately jumped out of bed. The urgency in his dream was still with him and he fought down the urge to run. Where would he run to?

He paced through his apartment and then got in the shower. As the water poured over him, he attempted to sort through what he felt but it was impossible. He kept hearing noises outside his door and despite telling himself it was nothing, he could not bring himself to believe it.

He's here. The Horseman is here. And he's waiting for you.

He felt the bile in his throat rise up and Quinn closed his eyes and leaned into the water stream. The Horseman is not out there. The Horseman is not real. He is not even a myth or a legend. He is a fictional creation of Washington Irving. That is all he ever was or is.

No, a voice in his head said. He's real and he's waiting for you.

Quinn looked down at his hands, which were shaking. He clenched his eyes closed as he washed his hair, willing himself not to see the nightmares in his head. Wasn't there the sound of someone pacing outside his door? Was that the sound of the door opening? He was sure he could hear it. But when he opened his eyes and pushed aside the shower curtain, there was nothing.

There is nothing here, Quinn told himself. But why didn't he believe it?

He sat down on the porcelain edge of the tub and let the water continue to hit him. What is wrong with me? How long am I going to feel the effects of this childish nightmare?

He had to think of something else, but found it hard to do. Every time his mind latched on to something, he could hear the hoof beats again in his ears. He could feel the blade approaching his neck, the branches tearing through his flesh.

"Enough," he cried, and said it out loud for good measure.

It was then that he thought of her, and from the moment he did, the sound of the chasing horse seemed to recede. Kate. He thought of how she looked the first time he saw her. He remembered the sound of her voice. The memories calmed him, and for the first time since he woke up, the feelings of his dream receded.

He should call her, ask her out. But as soon as that thought appeared in his head, the ridiculousness of it came right after. He didn't know her number or where she lived. And how dumb would he look asking her out after knowing her for exactly two days?

He stood up and finished soaping himself. As he did, he processed the past two days. He had barely seen Kate on Thursday, since Laurence had her out tracking a story in the far northern part of the county.

Quinn knew he had been single too long. He stepped out of the bathtub and dried himself. Maybe that was all it meant. That she was the first potential girlfriend he had met in a long time. He could just be lonely.

All he knew was that she seemed like the only good, tangible thing in his life. And he didn't even know if she was aware of his existence. Did it matter? Sometimes the hope for something was better than the real thing. It was something to focus on, something to distract you.

He sighed as he threw on clothes. Nightmares and dreams. Those were the only things that felt real.

*****

Across town at the Leesburg Inn, Kate was awake, lost in thought. She felt unsettled. She had felt that way from the moment she crossed the border from Maryland.

But her dreams the night before had been worse than normal. She was back at her childhood home, of course—it was too much to hope for some variety there. But it had seemed different, more intense.

She went onto her balcony as she had two days before. There was a reason she was here, she felt sure of it. She placed her hands on the railing and stared at the treetops.

But she couldn't just wait around. Today she had to start taking some kind of action. Starting with Mom, she thought. It was time to go see her mother.

*****

Quinn practically jumped out of his chair when Buzz said hello behind him. He didn't think anyone else was in the office yet.

"Sorry to startle you," Buzz said, although he didn't look very apologetic. Quinn thought he looked smug. The old man enjoyed sneaking up on people. He felt it gave him an "edge."

"Yeah, Buzz," Quinn said, dismissively.

Quinn leaned back in his chair to look at Buzz again. The guy looked haggard and unshaven. Quinn thought it odd that he somehow always looked this way. He never had a full beard, but constantly seemed like someone who had stayed at a party too long, perhaps having a little too much to drink. Buzz's clothes were loose fitting over his wiry frame. You could almost say he looked homeless, except Quinn thought he looked more like the proto-typical reporter—the kind of guy that shows up with a fedora hat and a pencil over his ear. Those guys never looked neat. They always looked rumpled.

Buzz had first become a reporter in Vietnam. Maybe in those days it didn't matter what you looked like because you were just as likely to end up dead.

"You need to listen more carefully, Quinn," Buzz said. "It could save your life."

Jesus, I'm surrounded by psychos, Quinn thought.

"I'll remember that," he said.

"I'm serious, my boy," Buzz said again. "In the jungle, you had to listen at all times."

"We're not in the jungle, Buzz," he replied.

"We're always in the jungle, Quinn. Don't forget that."

"Yeah, I get it," Quinn said, and felt frustrated. He had come here for peace and quiet, not one of Buzz's exceedingly bizarre lectures.

"No, you don't," Buzz said, and looked at him strangely. "But you might, real soon."

"I don't follow you," Quinn said.

"The Lord is back in his manor," Buzz said, looking around him carefully. He said it in a whisper even though there was no one to be seen in the office.

"The who is back where?" Quinn asked, hardly believing he was having this conversation.

"The Lord is back," Buzz said.

"What are you talking about? And why are we whispering?" Quinn asked.

"Lord Halloween has returned," Buzz said.

"Oh," he replied, relieved. He had thought it was something serious. Instead, he fought off a chuckle. "Gotcha. Back in the manor. Right-o."

"You don't believe me?" Buzz asked, notching his eyebrows together in an expression of repressed anger.

"Buzz, it isn't like this is the first time you've warned me," Quinn said, only to receive a blank look. "Last year? You warned me not to cover the 'Harvest Celebration' protest down in Sterling. You told me he would be there."

"Oh, I'm sure he was, my boy," Buzz said, looking intently at Quinn. "Just like I'm sure he is around now."

"Then why hasn't he done anything?" Quinn asked. "I mean, I know he was a big deal back in the day, but if he was here, why not make his presence known? They caught him, Buzz. Remember?"

"Pah," Buzz replied, and waved his hand in disgust. "Holober was a patsy."

"Just like Oswald, right?"

"Don't get me started on Oswald," Buzz said.

Quinn tried to contain his laugh, but let it out anyway.

"I know, I know," Quinn said. "It was the CIA in it with the Mob..."

"You listen to me," Buzz said, and jabbed his finger in Quinn's chest. "You should pay attention when I say Lord Halloween has returned. He's here. I can feel it."

"Then where are the dead bodies, Buzz?" Quinn replied, and pushed Buzz's hand out of his way. "We should have seen at least one by now, right?"

"You wait," Buzz said. "You wait."

Quinn knew there was no use arguing with Buzz. There was no point in even trying to reason with a man so buried in his own conspiracy theories.

"Okay," Quinn said.

It appeared to suffice.

"He's out there," Buzz said again, almost to himself. "In the jungle, you have a sense for these things."

Quinn felt an urge to ask if that was where Buzz left his sanity—back in the jungle. He put his hand to his head.

"Sorry to doubt you, Buzz," he said. "But it's been a long morning."

Buzz leaned back and eyed him for a minute.

"I only tell you because the rest of these guys would think I'm crazy," he said.

Now why would they think that? Quinn thought.

"Laurence only wants an excuse to fire me," Buzz said. "He'd say I was trying to panic the staff."

"Laurence does not want to fire you," Quinn said.

Buzz snorted in patent disbelief.

"You wait," he said. "He's just biding his time."

"He just wants you to come to staff meetings again."

"Right," Buzz said. "So they can mock me to my face? So they can tell me how to do my job better? So Rebecca can start complaining again?"

"It isn't like that," Quinn said.

"Maybe not to you," Buzz said, pointing again, this time thankfully away from Quinn's personal space. "But you don't remember. No, I won't go to them. He can fire me for not attending staff meetings if he wants. But I won't go."

Quinn looked at Buzz and it was hard not to be taken in with his earnestness. There was no doubt he believed it all. Why he trusted Quinn was beyond his understanding.

"That girl is here to replace me, did you know that?" Buzz asked.

"Why do you say that?" Quinn asked, glad at least to be thinking of Kate again.

"She told me yesterday she wrote some business stories," he said.

"She's written a lot of things, Buzz," Quinn replied. "Including business. I think that was her way of volunteering, that's all."

Buzz paused to consider this.

"Well, she doesn't have my experience, that's true," he said, obviously carrying on some type of internal conversation as well.

"Relax," Quinn said, as calmly as he could. "They are not trying to take your job."

"You wait," Buzz said again, but he didn't continue. Instead, there was a significant pause. "Can you do another business profile for me?" he finally asked.

"But I'm already doing the coin-sorting place," Quinn said. "I was just working on that."

"I know, I know," Buzz said. "I wouldn't ask, my boy, but I..."

He turned up his hands in a shrug.

"I won't ask you for one next week. I promise."

"I've heard that before," Quinn said.

"This time I mean it."

"I've heard that too," he said.

"I know, I know," Buzz said.

"Why not ask Kate?" Quinn asked, and when Buzz gave him a blank stare added, "The new girl?"

"Laurence told me he had her working on other things," Buzz said.

"How about Alexis?" he asked. "Or Helen?"

"They both refused," he said. "I need it for my pages. I swear this is the last time I'll have you do double duty.

"Please. They'll fire me if I don't get in enough stories. They are just waiting..."

"Okay, okay, okay," Quinn said. "What's the story?"

And that was how Quinn found himself two hours later driving out to Middleburg.

*****

Kate stood before her mother's grave, reading the inscription for the hundredth time.

"Sarah Blakely," it said simply. "Beloved wife and mother."

That was it. Somehow she thought there should be more. Something that made this grave stand out from the hundreds of others.

Carefully, she leaned down and put the pot of flowers by the memorial. This at least gave the impression that someone cared about her mom. When she arrived, it had looked deserted. She looked at the grave and felt guilty.

"I'm sorry I haven't come in a while, Mom," she offered. "It's just..."

Her dad made the trip at least once a year. Even after he remarried, he still came down. He invited Kate, of course. But she never wanted to come and he wasn't the type to force an issue.

"Dad's doing well," she said. "He likes Anne well enough but I don't think he ever got over you. I guess you're just that great."

She smiled. She thought that she should feel more, but instead she just felt numb. She tried to picture her mom and couldn't call up an image.

"I'm sorry," she offered. "I don't know what else to say."

She stood there staring at the inscription. She felt like there was something more she was supposed to do, but she couldn't think of what. She had spent so long feeling the anger from the day her mother died, she was unsure she wanted to think too much about it anymore.

But unfortunately, that had meant not thinking much about her mother anymore either. Not a day went by when she didn't think about it at some time or another. It had hung over her life like a dark cloud and she didn't think it would ever go away.

Since she had arrived in town, she had been forced to think about it. The memories and the dreams made it feel like it had occurred just a few days ago, not more than a decade before.

"Wherever I go, some part of me will always be here, Mom," she said. "I can never leave it."

She hadn't visited the grave in years, but it was easy to remember where it was. It was always there in the dreams. She shouldn't have come back. She had thought it might make it better, but now that seemed laughable. Instead, she was either waking up screaming or seeing things near the printing press. That vision had seemed so real...

She fought it off. Some part of her felt like pulling her hair out. She could never talk about this. Her mother's death was an untreated wound she kept hidden from the world. It kept her weak and bleeding, but she would never let anyone see it. Sometimes she wished she had died too. She flexed her hand and stared at her mother's grave. This was it. This was the way it would be. She would move on, but... this will always be here.

She jumped as she heard the gate swing open behind her. Reacting on instinct, she moved herself behind a tree for cover.

She saw a man walking down the path. It took a minute as he came closer to realize she knew him—it was Quinn from the paper. She watched him walk around the bend and made a move to follow. She wondered just what the hell he was doing here.

Kate watched as he walked down the hill and through the inner gate at the back. He paused, looking out at the pond below the cemetery. Then he walked forward and sat on a bench on the hillside.

Kate moved slowly and with great uncertainty. She felt like she was intruding somehow and forgot that it was he who had disturbed her moment at her mom's grave. But he appeared to be merely sitting on the bench and made no move to do anything else.

Part of her thought she should leave. She should turn around and leave him in peace. But another side wanted desperately to know what he was doing. She also felt some kind of pull towards him, as if she couldn't quite walk away even if she had wanted to.

Instead, she moved carefully. As she came closer, she could tell the bench was made out of marble. It appeared to be a memorial to someone, but obviously placed there so people could sit on it. She paused and wondered how to approach him.

Lacking a better idea, she moved so that she was in his peripheral vision and called out, "Hello Quinn."

He jumped up, whirling around. For a moment, he looked ready to run away.

"It's Kate," she said. "I didn't mean to startle you."

"I know," he said, shaking his head slightly. "It's just, well, I didn't expect to see you here."

"What were you expecting?" she asked, and smiled at him.

"Well, I wasn't expecting anyone to jump out at me," Quinn said. "And certainly not someone who isn't in a hockey mask or something."

"Sorry about that," she said, as she walked towards him. "Do you mind if I join you?"

"Not at all," he said and gestured for her to sit down. "What are you doing here?"

"I was working out this way," she lied. "I saw you walk in and I was curious."

"Wow," he said, and smiled at her. "You must be a good reporter."

"I tend to follow my instincts," she said.

"I can see that," he said.

"I just wanted to see what you were doing," she admitted.

"Honestly," he said, "I'm just here to think. I feel very calm here."

"So you come here often?" she asked.

"Only when I have had a rough day," he said and laughed.

"Well, now we are talking," she said and smiled. "What caused your rough day?"

She swung her legs around so she straddled the bench, then lifted one leg up and wrapped her arms around it.

"I don't want to bore you to death," he said.

"No, no," she said. "Look, I haven't had much conversation lately that isn't about watches, or Bill's treatise on the bologna sandwich. I could use a decent one."

"All right," he said, and grinned. "I'm game."

"So what's the problem?" she asked.

"Where do I start?" he laughed. "Buzz has got me running around God's green acre working on business stories. Helen keeps bringing up a story about dog shit, and Laurence's idea of a raise is about 500 bucks a year."

Kate laughed. She couldn't help it.

"Dog shit?"

Quinn laughed back.

"Apparently, it's quite the health issue. Nobody is cleaning up after their dog, people step in it, kids get sick and basically it's the end of Western civilization."

"Wow, that sounds like a great story," Kate said, and smiled so he would know she was kidding.

"That's Helen. She's very generous. Not to mention pushy." Quinn stared back at the wall.

"I'm also getting my butt kicked by Summer and I haven't slept more than four hours a night in roughly a gazillion years."

"Summer?" Kate asked.

"Local *Post* reporter. Thinks she's God's gift to journalism. You'll meet her soon enough."

"Well, the sleeping part I can relate to. I have bouts of insomnia myself," Kate said.

"Oh, I can fall asleep easily enough, but..."

"Dreams?"

"Dreams are nice fluffy things where you get the girl and save the day. What I have is definitely not that. And it feels so real. I mean, I can hear sounds, feel the gravel beneath my feet... it all seems so intense. Then when I wake up, I don't want to go back to sleep."

Kate nodded in agreement. She didn't want to say anything—she really didn't know Quinn—but she could relate more than she wanted to admit.

"You have the dream a lot?" she asked instead.

"Every October," he said, looking out at the pond.

"That's strange. Only one month a year?"

"It started a little earlier this year, but yeah, always around now. And every year, it's worse. If I had my way, I would prefer not to dream at all. Ever again."

"Would you?" she asked as he turned back toward her.

"Yeah," he said with more conviction. "I would. I'd kill to get rid of that dream. It infects everything else around it. I think about it way too often. Does that make any sense?"

"A lot, actually," she replied. "But I don't know if I could give up on dreams. I think maybe they are the closest thing to magic we have. They show us worlds that never existed, places we've been that are long gone and give us the ability to talk to the dead."

Kate did not say what she was really thinking. That her dreams were the only place she could still talk to her mother.

"Mine don't show me any of that," Quinn replied. "At least not that I can remember."

"Maybe it's there, you just choose not to remember it," she offered. "Besides, nightmares aren't all bad. Sometimes they can be a warning."

"Oh, believe me, that's what I fear the most," he said, looking back at her. "That's the worst part."

Quinn wanted to tell her the whole truth. He wasn't sure why he didn't. The truth would sound better than he had made it out to be. But he thought he might sound crazy. He worried he might have already gone too far.

It is one of the ironies of life that two people can have virtually the same thought at the same time and never really know it. Kate, too, was close to telling him the truth.

She desperately wanted to talk to someone. About her mother, about her return to Leesburg, about everything. When was the last time she had talked about any of that?

But for Kate, it had been too long since she talked about it. Her experiences had taught her long ago not to let down the wall that kept others out. It might make you feel better for a time, but ultimately, it would only make matters worse.

For his part, Quinn would have been more than willing to tear down his own walls. Since the moment he had laid eyes on her, he had wanted to get to know her, to be her confidant. But it was precisely his desire that kept him from talking. Though he wanted to be close, he was afraid of what she might find out. Afraid that she would see him for what he really was. It seemed better—safer—to stay distant. Best not to let her see how weird his life had become. And so they sat there in silence, staring across the gravestones toward the ducks on the pond.

"This is a nice place," Kate said after a time. "I can see why you come here."

"It's very peaceful," he said. "You are going to think I'm crazy, but sometimes Leesburg feels a little crowded. My mind gets cluttered with stuff. I come here to get uncluttered."

"That makes sense," she said. She looked suddenly at her watch. "I need to get back to the *Chronicle*."

"Well, it was good chatting with you," Quinn said.

"You too," she replied, and stood up. "You want to come with me?"

"I've got a little time to kill," he said.

"You sure? Don't we have that planning meeting to go to in a couple hours?"

Quinn stared at her blankly.

"Phillips Farm?" she asked.

"Oh, yeah," Quinn said finally. During the conversation, it had totally slipped his mind. Laurence had asked if he could give the Phillips Farm beat to Kate so she would have something to focus on. Considering Quinn was having trouble keeping up with his own responsibilities, he had been happy to let it go.

"I think Laurence was hoping you could show me around and introduce me to a few people at Friday's meeting, but if you have some other plans..." she said.

Quinn laughed out loud, then stopped abruptly.

"Oh, you were serious," he said. "No, I'm afraid many of my Fridays involve working. I'd be happy to come, I just forgot about it."

He jumped up. He was suddenly cheerier at the thought of spending much of the rest of the day with Kate. She smiled at him.

"Great," she replied.

They started off down the path side-by-side.

Chapter 6

"The debate over the future of Phillips Farm continued to rage last week, with conservationists threatening to file a lawsuit to block any development of the land. Martha Paletta, director of Protect Loudoun's Heritage, said on Tuesday the group had received a large anonymous donation to continue its quest to stop development by Heller Brothers of the 100-acre property. 'It just proves that people everywhere do not want to see this property destroyed,' she said. Martin Heller, the co-founder of the development firm, said the group's opposition would not deter the company from moving forward. A public meeting with county officials is scheduled Friday."
—Quinn O'Brion, "Phillips Farm Debate Started," *Loudoun Chronicle*

Friday, Oct. 6

Quinn moved through the crush of people to the front of the room. He did not see Kate anywhere. He just hoped she knew where to come. He had gone into Laurence's office for a quick discussion, but when he came out he found a note on his desk that said she had run out for a bite to eat and would see him at the meeting.

Quinn had been disappointed, hoping that maybe they could have dinner together. And when he arrived at the meeting, he didn't see her anywhere. He moved to the front of the room to see a row of chairs reserved for reporters. They didn't often get front row seats. Reporters as a rule tended to prefer the back where they could slip out if events were boring.

"So are you going to give me credit this time?" a voice asked behind him.

Quinn rolled his eyes. He did not turn around.

"Summer, what a pleasure to talk to you again," he said.

A petite brunette with curly hair walked in front of him.

"I'm serious, Quinn," she said.

"Give you credit for what?"

Summer snorted. "For this," she said, and spread her hand out at the room.

"You called all these people here?" Quinn asked. "That's funny, I thought the county did that."

"You know what I mean," she replied.

She put her hands on her hips and glared at him dramatically. On the surface, Summer could be considered pretty. She had a graceful figure, dark brown eyes and an attractive face. But there was an intangible quality below that—everything about her, the way she talked and moved, felt calculated. And beyond the pretty eyes there was something in her stare that reminded Quinn of the dull sheen of a boulder.

"What do you want me to say? It was a great story. You found out about the plan and I didn't. Super job. Way to go, Tiger."

"Thanks, but are you going to give me credit?" she said.

"Maybe," he said and shrugged.

The move appeared to infuriate her, as Quinn knew perfectly well it would.

"Oh, come on. You have to. We reported it first and I'm so tired of everybody..."

"I don't *have* to do anything," Quinn said. "Remember a month ago? Who had the story about the Leesburg First State Bank getting slapped with a fine by the federal government for losing all those files? Last I checked, I exclusively reported that with a document leaked to me from a source. But when the *Post's* Extra ran the story, with your by-line as I recall, I don't remember getting any credit."

"That was different," Summer said. "I told you that I already had that document. If I had relied on your reporting in any way ..."

"Oh, you had the document, did you?" Quinn said. "Is that the rule now? I thought reporters generally gave credit when they got beat to a story, not just when they didn't already know about it."

"Listen, this is totally different..."

"Am I interrupting something?"

Quinn had been so focused on his debate with Summer he hadn't noticed Kate standing right by him.

Summer's attention instantly shifted away from Quinn.

"Hi, I'm Summer Mandaville," she said with a bright smile. "I'm with *The Washington Post.*"

"The Loudoun Extra to be exact," Quinn said.

Summer shot a dirty look in his direction and extended her hand. Kate shook it.

"I'm Kate Tassel," she said. "I'm new with the *Loudoun Chronicle.*"

Quinn could almost see Summer stop the handshake. The smile stayed on the rival reporters' face, but it appeared suspiciously plastic in nature.

"Oh," she said. "Well, that's great. The *Chronicle* could use a fresh face. It's a good little paper. A great place to start."

While Quinn silently fumed at the condescending words "good little paper," Kate jumped to the rescue.

"Actually, I have several years experience already," she said. "I chose the *Chronicle.* I wanted to join a paper that would really dive deeper into local issues. A lot of the larger papers don't have the time or energy to do that."

Summer's smile slipped a little.

"Well, at the Extra..."

"Oh, I think it's a great idea," Kate said. "A free supplement buried in a big paper like that. It's a great little handout."

Quinn watched with glee as Summer struggled to find something to say.

"It was nice meeting you," Summer finally said, in a tone that indicated it was anything but.

"Nice meeting you too," Kate said cheerfully, as if nothing was amiss. "I'm really looking forward to getting to know you better. I'll be covering the Phillips Farm case, so I'm sure we will see each other around."

Summer nodded and walked to the end of the row before sitting down.

Quinn turned to Kate.

"That was fucking awesome," Quinn said. "I have never seen anyone leave her speechless before."

Kate grinned and she seemed to positively glow. She leaned in closer to Quinn and talked softly.

"Her article wasn't that good," she said. "I've just been handed the plan for the farm, and she got a couple facts wrong and missed the most important part. So we already have a good way to come back on this story. Also, your article did a better job than hers of really laying out the situation."

Quinn looked at her to see if he could find a trace of flattery there. But Kate's gaze held no dishonesty in it. She really thinks my story is better, he thought.

"Believe me, I will give her a run for her money on this story," Kate said with a smile that on a competitor would have frozen Quinn in his tracks. "I so look forward to kicking her ass."

Quinn thought he had never heard someone say anything so sexy in his life.

*****

From there the meeting was a blur. While Kate took notes as citizen after citizen spoke about protecting their local heritage, Quinn found it hard to concentrate. He was nominally there as back up, but one look in her direction and he knew he wasn't needed. She knew what she was doing.

After the meeting was over, it was no different. Quinn watched as Kate made the rounds easily with everyone important in the room. Martha Paletta appeared to be practically eating out of her hand as Quinn stood nearby.

"We've got great plans for the place," Martha was telling her. "We have a Christmas tree farm all set up for winter. In the meantime, we've just been planting a large vegetable garden. I know the folks around here aren't much for pumpkins—for obvious reasons—but there's still no reason not to grow some and sell a bundle in Fairfax County. Course I don't think we have the manpower to pick everything out there, but it's a start at paying some of the bills and the Phillips were incredibly kind to..."

Quinn lost interest. No wonder Summer had beat him on this story. A reporter was no good unless his story interested him. You do what you must to fill a paper, but you are never going to really own a story unless it owns you a little too.

Maybe I can take up an interest in dog shit, he thought. I can be the go-to guy for pooper scooper stories. He sighed. Quinn thought he should just be happy with what he had.

Quinn saw that he was not the only one to notice Kate's easy access to the powers-that-be. While Kate sat down briefly with Martin Heller, local developer bogeyman, Quinn saw Summer staring in disgust.

Just because he could, Quinn decided to needle her a little.

"Looks like Kate is fitting in just fine," he said as casually as he could.

"Martin chases anything in a skirt," Summer replied.

Quinn leered at Summer for dramatic effect.

"Last I checked, you were wearing one too," he said.

Summer waved him away.

"The guy won't talk to me since I ran that profile of him," she said.

Quinn thought back to the story three months ago. It hadn't been his beat then—but he was forced internally to acknowledge it had been a good profile. Very tough, but not unfair. Just because Summer was a pain didn't make her a bad reporter.

Of course, he was not about to tell her that. Instead he just grunted and Summer wandered away, casting dirty looks in Kate's direction.

When most of the room had cleared, and Martin had walked away looking pleased with himself, Kate finally turned in Quinn's direction.

"You didn't have to wait for me," she said.

"Well, it was so clear you needed my help."

She laughed. "Yeah, I'm quite shy, I'm sure you noticed," she replied.

"Also, I thought I could give you a lift. I didn't think you had a car."

"I do, although I walk a lot," she said. "But it's getting late. That would be nice."

They walked outside and Quinn took a deep breath. There was a smell in the air. He could never place it, but it reminded him of leaves blowing in the wind, night coming quicker—fall, in other words.

"It smells nice, doesn't it?" Kate asked.

"Nothing like it," he said. "Leesburg's small enough so there isn't much pollution. The air is nice and clean."

He walked her to the car and opened the door for her before getting back in the driver's side.

"So where's home?"

"Leesburg Inn," she said.

"I hope the company is paying for some of that until you find a place."

"What do you think?"

"My guess would be no because they are cheap bastards."

"Good guess," she said.

It was not a far drive. Quinn was more than a little disappointed about that.

"So what's up with you and Summer?" Kate asked.

Quinn practically choked and had to will himself not to stray from the road.

"I deeply hope I misunderstood that question," Quinn replied.

"You don't have to answer if you don't want to. If I hit a nerve or something."

"Well... I... No... I... just."

Quinn looked over at her to see her smiling slyly back at him.

"You're taking the piss, aren't you?" he asked.

"If you mean making fun of you, yes," she replied.

"Sorry—I've been around Janus too long. For the record, there is nothing between Summer and I, nor has there ever been, nor will there ever be."

"Don't worry, it seemed pretty obvious she wasn't your favorite person."

"Kate, I've met many people in my life," he said melodramatically. "A lot of politicians, lobbyists, heads of trade groups. Some are great, but others are the most self-important people you could ever meet. And Summer beats them all with room to spare. She is the most effortlessly self-involved person I've ever met."

"Sounds charming."

"Also, she has a persecution complex a mile wide. She thinks everybody is out to get her."

"Is she right?"

"Well, some of the time. In terms of her reporting though, Summer's intense and definitely no slouch. She's desperate to make it to *The Washington Post*—absolutely consumed by the idea."

"She already works there," Kate said.

"Yes and no. The Loudoun Extra is very segregated from the main paper. So around here she can say she works for the *Post*, but it isn't like she can escape Loudoun exactly. They view her as belonging to a satellite—and slightly inferior—office. So she works her butt off to try and get stories into the main paper. Something that will help her prove to them she's ready for the big time."

"Hard to do, I'll bet."

"Sure. My point is she's tough. If you want to beat her, believe me when I tell you I would like nothing better. But she'll give you a run for your money. You might be able to charm people to tell you the truth, but she will beat them over the head with a stick until they give her what she wants."

"Don't worry, I can be plenty aggressive when I need to be," Kate said.

Quinn looked at her. For a moment, she looked so serious that he was worried he had offended her. But she smiled back at him.

"Here we are," she said.

They pulled into the Leesburg Inn. Quinn pulled up to the door hoping she might stay in the car a while longer, but she thanked him for the ride and was almost out of earshot before he thought to stop her.

"Hey wait," he called.

She turned around.

"I meant to tell you this earlier. Some of us go to this bar on Saturday nights. It would be cool if you could join us."

Kate paused and appeared to consider the offer. Quinn hurried on as if he wasn't nervous, but casual.

"It's the Leesburg Tavern—right off Market Street."

"All right," she replied. "What time?"

"Around seven. We have dinner and there is usually a good band there for an hour or two."

Kate nodded. "Sounds good," she said. And she was through the lobby doors before he could say another word.

Quinn saw her stride through the lobby and lost sight of her.

He felt strangely pleased with himself. He hadn't asked her out, but it was a beginning. Things are looking up, he thought.

He enjoyed the moment, not knowing just how short it would be.

*****

Saturday, Oct. 7

Kate walked over to the Leesburg Tavern with some measure of dread. A part of her wanted to stay inside. Since she had been back, she had fought the urge many times to just pack her bags and head home. In her anonymous hotel room, she could convince herself she was safe. But out in the night air like this, a terrible thought kept popping up.

I'm going to die in this town.

She shook her head. It was nonsense. Understandable, given her history, but stupid. Besides, faced with another night watching terrible cable in a hotel room, what choice did she have? If she was going to live in this town, she would have to put aside her fears and at least try to be social. Otherwise, she worried she would go crazy.

When she pushed open the door and stepped inside, she was immediately hit by a gigantic waft of smoke and the smell of stale beer. Despite the dim lights, she could see the place was outfitted like a kind of hillbilly version of T.G.I. Friday's—there were signs, photos and knick-knacks covering the wall. Most of them, Kate noted, were off-color in taste. "Big Butts welcome, so sit your ass down," said one near the door.

She sighed. Maybe this was not such a good idea.

It took her only a moment to see Quinn, Bill and Janus sitting at a table near the front. Bill waved frantically at her and she moved toward them through the haze of smoke.

"Hey Kate," Janus and Quinn both said when she sat down.

"How are you?" Quinn asked right after.

"Good," she said, and smiled at him.

She didn't know quite what to make of Quinn. The first time she had seen him she had wondered if he was some type of stalker—staring at her from across the Starbucks like that. But by now, he seemed like one of the few people she really knew in the town. She had thought about their conversation in the graveyard and at the Phillips Farm meeting a lot during the day. She didn't know quite what to make of him yet, but she liked him. That much she knew.

"You got here just in time," Quinn said. "The band is just about to show up. As soon as they do, they'll be a line out front."

She nodded. "What band is it?"

"A group called Eddie from Ohio," he answered. "They're local—well, sort of local, at any rate."

"They're brilliant," Janus said, and looked around the table as if daring anyone to disagree. "Kind of a folk-rock thing, like a mix of Janis Joplin and Pearl Jam."

"Pearl Jam?" Bill asked, and snorted. "Did you pull that out of a hat? More like a cross between Janis Joplin and Sheryl Crow."

"Yes, guys, let's do have this debate again," Quinn said, and glared at them.

"Anyway," Janus said, pulling a cigarette from his shirt pocket and lighting it with a silver lighter he fished out of his jacket. "They are one of the best bands that plays here. Second only to the Urban Hillbilly Quartet. Now that's an incredible band. Like a mixture of Bob Dylan and Pink Floyd."

"Okay, now you are just trying to piss me off," Bill said. "Neither one of those is right. They're more free form than that, like a mix of..."

"Please drop this," Quinn said. "Kate has been here for five minutes and you guys are already degenerating into the same argument you have all the time. They're like a bitter married couple."

"Fuck off," the two said in unison.

Kate laughed.

"It's okay," she said. "It's been awhile since I've had a debate about music."

Janus shot Quinn an "I told you so" look.

"Believe me, this is less of a debate and becomes more of a soapbox tourney," Quinn said.

"It's a pissing match," Janus replied, and took a drag on his cigarette, holding it a moment before blowing a puff of smoke in Bill's direction. "One I always win."

"Get bent," Bill said, using one of Janus' favorite expressions.

"It's easy to win a pissing match when you are as large as I am."

Bill rolled his eyes.

"Rebecca is right—you really are a sexual harassment suit waiting to happen," Quinn said.

"Americans are so uptight," Janus said.

"How long have you lived here?" Kate asked him.

"Don't let him fool you," Quinn said. "He's been here long enough that he drinks coffee, not tea, and he makes fun of British people too."

"I make fun of *English* people," Janus said. "There is a difference, you know. The English are prats."

"My Dad is English," Kate said. The conversation stopped, as everyone stared at Janus.

"Well, I guess... maybe not your..." Janus sputtered.

"It's okay," she said. "I was only kidding."

It took a minute for that to sink in. Quinn and Bill started to laugh. Janus waited a second before joining in.

"Well, look at you," he said. "Here only a few days and already making fun of me."

Kate smiled at them. "When in Rome..." she said, and spread her hands.

"You're all right," Janus said. "Now Bill, why don't you get off your rather large exterior and get us a drink?"

"Charming, just charming," Quinn mumbled.

"Why do I have to get the drinks?" Bill asked. "I got them last time."

"Do Quinn and I look daft to you, ya wanker?" Janus asked. "We remember perfectly well last week. We bought rounds and you didn't."

"Now, wait a minute," Bill retorted. "I did so."

"You're embarrassing the lady," Janus said.

"Actually, I..." Kate began, but Janus cut her off.

"See?" Janus said. "Look. She's beet red. Now be a good photographer and get us some drinks."

Bill sighed deeply.

"Okay," he said gloomily. He took the drink orders and went off to the bar.

"You know, he really did buy the round last time," Janus told Kate.

He absentmindedly crushed his finished cigarette in the ashtray at the table. Quinn rolled his eyes again, but chuckled.

"Don't feel too bad for Bill, Kate," he said. "Janus may have tricked him this time, but he does have a habit of sneaking out on paying for drinks."

By the time Bill returned, the band had taken the stage and begun.

To her surprise, Kate found herself enjoying the whole evening. It was true that neither Bill nor Janus were exactly gentlemen, but they were fun guys. A half dozen times during the evening they started arguing, with topics ranging from which country had the best soccer team to the best restaurants in Leesburg.

Quinn, meanwhile, took turns occasionally joining in and then mocking them to Kate right afterward.

For a moment, she felt like she had always been there, sitting at the table, watching the three of them make jokes. It was a remarkably warm feeling, like she belonged here. Like she had never left. She smiled to herself. Maybe this had been why she came back—to escape the ghosts of the past.

But the feeling receded like a wave and she shivered in the hot, smoky room. What had happened she wasn't sure, but suddenly, Kate didn't want to be there anymore.

"Want another round?" Janus asked when the band had finished its set. "Numb-nuts here will buy."

"I swear to almighty God if you call me that again, you short little..." Bill said.

"You'll what? Come on, you'll what?"

Quinn sighed and looked at Kate.

"Seriously, do you want anything?" he asked.

She shook her head and looked at her watch.

"Actually, I should get going," she said.

"See what you did," Janus said, and looked accusingly at Bill.

"Well, if you hadn't been acting like a jerk, I'm sure she would have stayed," Bill replied.

"It's been a great night, guys, it really has," Kate said, and stood up. She lifted her jacket off the chair back.

"Well, I was thinking of leaving, too, you mind if I walk with you?" Quinn asked.

Janus nudged Bill in the stomach and both men chuckled. In a not-so-subtle move, Quinn extended his middle finger and scratched his eye with it. They took the hint, but chose to ignore it.

"Sure," she said, and glanced only briefly at Quinn.

"See you guys later," she said. Quinn waved and the two walked out the door.

Kate pulled her jacket closer to her and shivered in the night air.

"God, it got cold," she said.

"Yeah," he responded.

"You don't need to walk me home," Kate said, though in truth she felt like some company.

"It's all right," he said. "I could use the exercise."

He paused a minute.

"So I hope you had a good time tonight," he said.

"I did," she replied. "I really did."

She opened her mouth to say something more, then shut it. She liked Quinn, but what did she really know of him? It was unwise to say too much. It would raise questions she did not want to answer.

"Good. It's tough when you join up with a new paper. New editors, new beats. But we're a nice bunch. At least some of us are, at any rate."

Kate laughed. "Who isn't very nice?" she asked.

"You don't want to hear me gossip, do you?" he asked.

"Sure," she said. "I'm dying for some good gossip."

"Well, Helen you know about," he said.

"Rebecca seems kind of controlling too," Kate said.

"She is that, but she is also good at her job," he said. "Helen... well... Helen is good at coming up with ideas for other people. And Ethan thinks she just walks on water."

"Who's Ethan?" she asked.

"Ethan Holden—the owner of Holden Inc.," Quinn said and laughed. "You'll meet him soon enough. He is a piece of work. He pays us shit, then demands at every meeting that we need to work harder—with substandard equipment and crappy benefits."

"Seems like a great guy," Kate said.

"He also doesn't have a backbone," Quinn continued as they walked. "Last year, I had a great story about Paul Gibson, who is now the chairman of the board of supervisors. I had sources who told me he had taken money from developers on the side, all the while promising that he would stop development in the county. But Ethan wouldn't let Laurence run it. Or at least that is what Laurence claims..."

"Why not?" she asked.

"Paul and Ethan are friends, of course. Ethan is friends with all the local politicians. Hell, he knows Senators Mark Warner and George Allen personally. He is one of the wealthiest guys in the state and gave pretty decently to their campaigns."

"And Laurence didn't stand up to him?"

"One thing I should warn you—in this job, don't expect much support from Laurence," he said. "Rebecca will fight for you, but Laurence would lose a boxing match against a one-legged man in a wheelchair. I've only seen him angry a few times, and even then, he didn't do anything about it."

"My editor at the *Gazette* was a great guy," Kate said. "I saw him yell at just about everybody—from advertising guys he felt had crossed the line by approaching reporters, to the publisher for interfering."

"Well, Laurence isn't that," Quinn said.

"Why did you come out here?" she said. "People would kill for a job at the *Congressional Quarterly*. You didn't say why you left the other day."

He paused before launching into the whole sordid story.

"My parents died," he said. "They had moved down here from Pennsylvania and just loved it. But some drunk guy from Hillsboro hit them one night and they were gone."

"God, I'm sorry," Kate said.

"I moved into their house for awhile while I sorted everything out and I suddenly felt I couldn't go back. I didn't want to be in D.C. It was too self-involved and politics suddenly lost its appeal. It just didn't seem to mean that much anymore."

"I can understand that," she said.

"So I sold their place and bought an apartment," he said. "I couldn't think of where to go and this just seemed right. So I stayed."

They were approaching the Leesburg Inn.

"That must have been hard," she said, "to lose both your parents."

"It's one of those things that every time I think I've moved on, I get pulled back. I'm not sure I'll ever really move on."

Kate nodded.

They stopped in front of the hotel.

"Well," Quinn said self-consciously, and looked down at his shoes. "Here we are."

Kate stopped and looked at him. "Thanks for walking me home."

She wanted to say something more—about her own mother maybe—but she couldn't. She felt overwhelmed by fatigue and didn't want to think about it anymore.

"Sure," he said. "I hope you'll join us again."

"Anytime," she said.

And then she did something unexpected for both of them. Without thinking about it, she leaned in and kissed Quinn on the cheek. Startled by her own action, she pulled back a little, so that their faces were only inches apart. It felt like something electrical crackled in the air and she pulled away as suddenly as she had started.

"Thanks again," she said.

And then she was through the door and out of sight.

Quinn stood outside looking up. He touched his cheek reflexively. Despite the cool October air, he felt warm inside, like he had drunk a gallon of hot coffee.

He walked home in a kind of daze, not really sure what had happened. There had been something, he thought. And whatever it was, it was powerful. Something had seemed to move between them and only time would tell what.

*****

Across the county, Dee glanced at the waving branches around him and pulled his jacket closer to him. This place gave him the creeps. It had been Jacob's idea, of course, and you couldn't argue with him about something like this.

He twitched reflexively and rocked back and forth on his heels. It was cold, it was dark and he was tired. He wished again for a cigarette and reached in his jacket pocket out of habit.

But there was nothing there, and if Denise had her way, there would never be cigarettes for Dee again.

"Fuck," he swore, and nervously watched as the wind blew through the trees again.

He didn't like it, mostly because the way the branches blew out, it was as if some invisible giant was pushing them aside. It gave him the impression that things were happening all around him and he had no idea what.

"Fuckin-A, Jacob. Where the hell are you?"

As if on cue, he saw headlights appear around the curve on the side of the road. Why they had to come all the way out to Purcellville only God knew. Why they had to come out to the darkest, most isolated place in the goddamn county he was even less sure.

The cops here don't care, Dee thought. They never have and they never will. Maybe they were dumb to it, or maybe they just didn't give a damn. What did he care? Either way, there was no damn reason to come out here.

Dee watched as the car slowed down and pulled up next to his. He continued rocking back and forth on his heels.

Jacob practically threw open the door to his old Volkswagen Jetta and stepped out.

That was Jacob, Dee thought. Never does anything half way.

"What's up, gee?"

It bugged Dee that some skinny white kid would throw around lingo like he was a brother or something, but he was used to it. His friends called Jacob a live wire and though Dee was confident he could kick Jacob's ass, he also knew any victory would be short-lived. Jacob had friends and given who his father was, the temporary satisfaction of putting him down wouldn't be worth it.

"Not much," Dee replied.

Jacob came around the car and pulled a pack of cigarettes out. He held one out.

"Want a smoke?" he asked.

"Shit, man, you know I can't," Dee replied.

"Right, right," Jacob replied. "That bitch Denise got you wound around her little finger, doesn't she?"

"Don't call her that, J," Dee replied.

J is what Jacob liked to be called. Dee thought it sounded stupid, although he recognized the irony in that.

"Whoa, my brother," Jacob said, and raised his hands in mock surrender. "No need to get angry."

"I'm not your brother," Dee said under his breath.

"What did you say?" Jacob asked, his tone shifting slightly to one more menacing.

But Dee was not afraid. Careful, but not scared.

"Nothing," he said. "You got it, or not?"

"Well, well, why don't we cut right to the chase?" Jacob said. "I might have it, but just one question. If she won't let you smoke, how does she allow you to do this stuff?"

"That's not your concern, man," Dee said, and left it at that. He would meet Jacob on his terms, but he would be damned if he would let the little shit into his business.

"You aren't sounding too friendly, Dee," Jacob replied. "I can always take my wares someplace else."

"We don't need to go through this every time, J," he said.

"Don't treat me like your bitch, then," Jacob said evenly. "If you keep on doing it, you could find yourself in trouble."

"I meant nothing," Dee said, but the words caught in his throat on the way out.

Jacob stared at him for a moment, apparently weighing whether or not to do anything.

"All right," he said finally, and reached into his pocket.

It was then that Dee first heard the rumbling. It was low at first, a kind of rhythmic beating that he couldn't place.

Jacob glanced nervously about.

"You invite somebody?" he asked, glaring at Dee.

"Hell no," he replied.

They both looked down the road near them. As far as either of them knew, there was never any reason to come out here. It wasn't even a spot people picked as a make out place. It was too damned creepy.

The rumbling turned into a pounding and grew steadily louder, enough so that Dee could recognize it for what it was.

"Who the hell would be riding a horse at this hour?" he asked out loud.

Jacob shook his head.

It was then that Dee noticed the air had become completely still. A few minutes ago, it had been active, and now—everything was silent. He didn't like it.

"The cops?" Dee asked.

"No fucking way, man," Jacob said. "They don't ride horses around here. Probably some rich dude out for a ride."

Dee glanced at his watch.

"How many fucking rich dudes you know that go riding at 11:00?"

Jacob didn't answer. The sound was now getting steadily louder—almost too loud, Dee thought. Should it echo like this?

"Let's get out of here," he said.

"Don't be such a pussy," Jacob said. "We'll just let them pass by. If he stops, we'll deal."

But Dee, already nervous here, didn't care about the jibe.

"You stay if you want to," he said. "No weed is worth this."

Dee turned to go to his car.

And then he saw it, tearing down the road in front of them. The sound seemed to come from all around them and Dee found it hard to take his eyes off him.

The horseman was riding incredibly fast, his black cape swinging out behind him.

"Holy shit," Jacob said, but Dee didn't look at him. He couldn't look anywhere else.

The galloping grew louder and the wind that had vanished came back with a vengeance. Dee felt blown backward, as if it was moving ahead of the rider in a wave. The branches on the trees above him bent backward and he had trouble breathing.

"Shit, shit," Jacob said.

For a second, Dee tore his eyes away to look at Jacob standing on the road. It appeared he could not move either. He just stood there, almost directly in the horseman's path.

Dee looked back at the rider. He had crossed the distance in remarkable time. Dee clenched his hands and felt sweat gathering on his forehead. He felt the urge to run but was rooted to the ground.

"Holy shit," Jacob said.

Dee looked at Jacob to see what was the matter, but could see nothing.

Looking back at the rider, he knew.

The horseman coming at them—his cape billowing—had unsheathed a sword. And there was a second, much more urgent problem—the rider had no head.

Both boys started screaming then.

The Headless Horseman came full tilt at Jacob, never slowing or pausing. As Dee watched, the Horseman moved to his left side, letting his blade down on a perfect level for Jacob's neck.

Dee wanted to scream or run, but could do nothing.

Instead, time seemed to slow down and he watched as the Horseman blew by them both, his sword clearly going through Jacob's neck.

And then he was gone, riding off into the distance. Dee watched him go, still yelling at the top of his lungs.

When he looked at his friend, he wasn't sure what he expected. But whatever it was, he was in for a shock.

Jacob stood there, in the center of the road—his head still firmly attached to his body—screaming.

Dee moved over to him and was immediately hit with a foul smell. Looking down, he could see that the other boy had wet himself, or maybe something worse.

"What was that?" Dee asked.

But Jacob didn't respond, his lungs gasping for air and then screaming again. Dee looked for a sign of the blade, some cut or scratch.

But instead there was nothing.

All around them, everything had returned to its former shape.

It seemed like the horseman had never been there at all.

Dee ran to his car and got moving. He didn't care about Jacob. He just wanted to get very far away.

LH File: Letter #3
Date: Oct. 8, 1994
Investigation Status: Closed
Contents: Classified

Mr. Anderson,

The article on Weissman was a vast improvement. Even I wanted to cry after reading it. Such promise! Such talent! Such a tragedy!

Your article made his death sing, it really did. 'Bob Weissman stares at a photo of his son, who will now be 16 forever.' Have you been saving that one up? 'All they want to know is why.' Well, you could have told them that, couldn't you? Their son died because he is a sign of the rot that is eating this county from the inside.

Bob Weissman should never have moved here. He's not a farmer, he's not even working class, like most of the Sterling residents. No, he's just another suburbanite.

They will take over Loudoun County, I promise you that. They will overrun us like a plague of locusts, tearing down everything in their path so they can put up rows and rows of shiny, metal boxes with no artistry and less personality than a concrete block. I know them, Mr. Anderson. They did it to Fairfax County already. Falls Church was once a small little town. Now, what is it? Just rows of street lights with tacky stores and sub-par restaurants.

Can you imagine what Leesburg will look like in 10 years, or 20? It will be just another suburb of Washington, D.C., a lifeless carbon copy of Fairfax or Reston. Think of all the history that will be destroyed. Union troops marched through this town, did you know that? They fought with their Confederate enemies at Ball's Bluff. Over in Waterford, there was actually a Union regiment from Virginia. Many of them died, holed up in Waterford Baptist Church yelling for their mothers as their Virginia brothers shot lead into the building.

Weissman and his ilk will destroy this. They won't mean to and that just makes it worse. They'll come because they want a bigger house, and they won't care about the added commute, or the acres of farm land that are plowed over to make their new dwelling space. Did Bob Weissman see his son much? Of course he didn't. He had a 35-minute commute to RBS Industries in Rosslyn.

That's the tragedy here. He grieves for a son he barely knew. He worked so hard to "provide" for his family, he never truly had one at all. Did his son think of that, as he bled to death, slowly dragging himself away from me? He didn't say much, I can tell you that. He just stared at me, whimpering.

Will I stop the Bob Weissmans of the world? I can't. I'm one person and the battle to save this land has not been joined. By the time others figure out what is happening, it will be far, far too late. But I will exact a price to pay. There are real ghosts here, specters that lurk just beyond the streetlight. I am their voice.

Here I am ranting again, I'm afraid. I'm giving your police handlers lots to think about. Maybe I've joined a preservationist organization? I could even be a Civil War reenactor! What do you think? I'm glad you finally thought to use my name this time. I would have been so very displeased if you hadn't. Of course, no mention of the letters—are you planning to save them? Maybe write a book when this is all over? And your description of me is so dry, so impersonal. "Police attribute the murders to a serial killer who calls himself 'Lord Halloween.'" That's it?

But I shouldn't complain. It's a start and we have some time left. I promise this will be a month that no one around here ever forgets.

Yours Sincerely,

Lord Halloween

Chapter 7

"Robert Crowley is hard to quantify. As a poet in his own right, he was mediocre at best. His poems tended to be overly-symbolic with a poor sense of pacing. And yet it would be unfair to leave him out of a discussion of British poetry during the 19th century. Other poets at the time considered him bold and innovative, and later, better masters of the art were influenced by him. But it seems his real claim to fame unfortunately comes from the rather bizarre circumstances surrounding his disappearance. That—if nothing else—assured he was unlikely to be forgotten."
—Ross MacFarlane, "Scottish Poetry Through the Ages"

Monday, Oct. 9

Quinn sat in the early morning darkness staring at his living room wall. He was not really conscious of being there—his thoughts had drifted somewhere else—and it was only with a sudden start he realized he had been staring at the same spot for over an hour.

He supposed it must have been some manner of dreaming, though he knew he was awake.

Maybe this will be enough sleep today, he thought grimly. He couldn't be surprised, or even too disappointed. After Saturday evening had gone so well, it was only natural that the night would go badly. The nightmares, always intense, always realistic, had been worse than ever.

So bad, in fact, that sleeping on Sunday night did not appear to be much of an option. Instead, he had stayed up—at first by watching the TV—and then by reading. He had not nodded off—though he felt incredibly tired—but his mind had wandered.

Quinn stood up abruptly and crossed over to the window. Sometimes he thought he could still hear the sound of hoof beats out there.

But he heard nothing this morning. He tapped his fingernail against the glass and then turned around to get in the shower.

*****

He was at work by 7:00 in the morning, far ahead of everyone else. He had three goals for the day: the first, and most important, was to talk to Kate again. He wondered if her brief kiss on his cheek had felt the same to her—the electric impulse that had spread through his body. He doubted it. Then he smiled at himself. This is what it was like when he was depressed and running on no sleep. He doubted everything.

The second goal was to attend Sheriff Brown's press conference on the stalker. Quinn leaned back in his chair. Well, maybe "stalker" was a little strong. Peeping-Tom, perhaps? It didn't matter. The story had provided him with fodder for two months. A man, always hiding in shadow, spying on houses in Leesburg's outskirts. More than a dozen people thought they had caught a glimpse of him, and on at least two occasions, police had been called out to find evidence of an attempted break-in.

It was, sad to say, Quinn's favorite story at the moment. He had slim pickings in the town itself and crime was usually crowded out by Kyle. But Kyle had dismissed the stalker story as unimportant—a phantom no less—and so it had become Quinn's. And if now it was a story "with legs," it remained in Quinn's purview.

He hated the idea that he could be territorial—he despised Helen's insistence that any article on the board of supervisors go through her first—but good stories were hard to come by.

Though he was not expecting much, he assumed the sheriff would face the normal angry parents and concerned citizens during the conference. Enough for a story. Enough so that Quinn actually had something other than business to write for the week.

He sighed. It was not supposed to be like this.

The phone startled him out of his reverie and for a minute he glared at it like it was some strange alien being. It was so early in the morning, who the hell would be calling him?

"Quinn O'Brion," he said, picking up the line.

There was silence on the other end.

"Hello?" he asked again.

"Quinn," the voice said. "I didn't expect you to be there."

It took a second for Quinn to place the voice.

"Then why were you calling now, Gary?" he asked.

They both knew why. Gary was notoriously hard to catch on the phone, mostly because he hated talking to the press. Quinn was an exception. But Gary still felt that every conversation with Quinn endangered his job with the Leesburg police.

He was probably right.

"Uh..." Gary drifted off.

"It doesn't matter," Quinn said quickly, worried Gary would hang up.

"What's going on?"

There was a long silence on the other end.

"Gary?" Quinn asked. "You still with me?"

"Yeah," Gary said finally. "I'm here."

"Cat got your tongue?"

"The press conference is off."

"What? Why? Did they catch him?" Quinn asked hopefully. His pulse quickened as he smelled a good story.

"If they caught him, don't you think there would be a bigger press conference?" Gary said. "They certainly wouldn't cancel it."

"So what's going on?"

"I'm not sure."

Quinn waited. This was the best policy with squirrelly sources. Secretly they want to talk. It is just a question of pausing long enough for them to spill it all out.

"There is a lot of commotion," Gary said after some time had passed.

"What kind of commotion?"

"It's very hush-hush," he said. "They won't tell anybody anything."

"What do you mean by commotion?"

"Yesterday, they called in a bunch of guys," Gary said. "But they never told us what it was for. A lot of us were just standing around with nothing to do."

"So they called in a lot of guys on a Sunday and then didn't do anything with them?"

"About right," Gary replied, keeping his voice low. "And then..."

Quinn paused again. It was all he could do not to ask more questions, but he paced himself. It wouldn't do to rush this.

"Then Stu came out. You know Stu, don't you?"

"Brown's deputy? The one always hovering around him that looks scared of his own shadow?"

"Er... yeah," Gary said. "Anyway, Stu came out and told the boys to go home. Said it was a mistake made by a dispatcher or something."

"That's weird, but I guess it's possible..."

"Well, we all thought so too, but... then he said something weird," Gary said.

The conversation drifted to silence.

Finally Quinn couldn't take it anymore.

"What did he say?"

"He said that we shouldn't mention this to anybody," Gary replied. "He said it would be embarrassing if everybody knew about it."

Quinn laughed.

"Who gives a shit if the dispatcher called in a few guys for no reason?"

"That's what we thought," Gary said.

"And then Stu called a couple guys back. Johnny Redacker and the Kaulbach kid. They looked confused and went into his office. We caught up with them later and Kaulbach looked sick."

"What do you mean?"

"We were at the bar..."

"On a Sunday?"

"Hey, we already had to come into work, why not?"

"Fine, fine," Quinn said. "What do you mean sick?"

"I was telling you," Gary said.

"Okay," Quinn said.

"No sense in me talking to you if you are just going to interrupt," Gary said again.

"Okay," Quinn said. "I'm sorry."

Gary waited.

"I'm really sorry," he said again.

Gary cleared his throat and continued.

"Kaulbach and Redacker came in and the two of them were all sullen and quiet. That isn't like Johnny at all, of course, and we were all curious to know what the hell was going on, so we started asking them questions. But they wouldn't say nothing. Johnny started giving us the procedural bullshit, you know, 'It's against policy,' all that jazz. I swear he is to big for his britches ever since Stu promoted him. Last week, he actually told me..."

"Gary?" Quinn interrupted. It was best to keep the guy on track.

"Right, right," he said. "So Johnny is clamming up and the whole time Kaulbach looks like he is going to faint or something. Finally, he excuses himself. I went after him, because the kid is new, you know?"

"Also you thought he might spill his guts?" Quinn asked.

"Well, that is what he was doing," Gary replied. "He was puking his lungs out. I mean really just pouring it out."

"Okay," Quinn said. "You don't need to paint a picture."

"I asked him if he was okay, you know, after he finished, and he said he was. I asked him what had happened and he said, 'Stu said we could lose our jobs if we said anything.'"

"That it?"

"Well, then this morning I get in early and I find this voicemail from Stu. It said the press conference today is canceled, and if anybody asked why, I was to tell them that Brown is sick or something."

"Pretty lame," Quinn said. "And since when do you handle press? You won't talk to Kyle so..."

"That cocksucker," was all Gary said.

"I know what you think of him," he replied.

"What I think of him? That asshole nearly cost me my job," Gary said.

"I know, I know...."

There was a significant pause.

"I don't know why I was in charge of press today," Gary finally said. "Maybe Fred really is out."

Or maybe not, Quinn mused. Fred Tipper had a reputation as a leaker on the police force. This was mostly undeserved, since his job was to talk to the press. Or more specifically, Kyle. Gary, on the other hand, had handled press only a few times and his dislike of Kyle Thompson was well known.

Gary didn't really like any reporters. The only reason he tolerated Quinn was because of a single favor more than a year ago.

"You know something more," Quinn said. It was not a question.

"Christ," Gary replied, but said nothing.

"Look, I really appreciate what you've said so far," Quinn began.

"Bullshit," Gary said. "Bullshit. Reporters are all alike. You butter us up or you dress us down, but you don't really give a damn. You just want information. You just want a story."

"Yes, I want a story," Quinn said. "But I've given you no reason not to trust me. In fact, quite the opposite."

"You can't always bring that shit up," he said. "You can't keep using it on me."

"Come on, Gary, I'm not using anything," he said. "I'm just trying to get the story."

There was a pause. Silence reigned and Quinn watched the clock on the wall move agonizingly forward a full minute before he talked again.

"What are they hiding?" he asked, when he could take it no longer.

"I don't know," Gary replied.

"But you know something," Quinn said.

"The Kaulbach kid..."

Quinn let the pause come. He steeled himself to wait. If he hurried, Gary would realize he could just hang up the phone. Sometimes there was a magical effect on sources. If you ask a question, they feel compelled to answer it. But push it too far and you lose them. Quinn waited.

"He kept saying something," Gary began again.

"What?"

"He kept saying, 'I found her head. I found her head.'"

"Found who's head?"

"Well, I finally asked him," Gary said. "Look, I can't be telling you this. This is my ass on the line."

"Think about it Gary, why did they put you in charge today?"

"I don't know."

"Sure you do," Quinn said. "You hate reporters. You tell them nothing. You've made no secret about it. Stu doesn't trust Tipper—he never did. He'll leak. But you won't."

"Because they trust me," Gary said. "And I'm betraying that..."

"No, because you got burned by Kyle and Summer," Quinn said. "You said something off the record and they put it in their stories. But they don't know about us. Why? Because I didn't burn you. I went out of my way to protect your son and I didn't have to. A cop's kid dealing marijuana is a big story..."

"Shut up, okay?" Gary said. "You don't have to remind me."

"Kyle doesn't know I talk to you—my own editor doesn't know," Quinn said.

This last part was a bold lie—Rebecca knew damn well who his source was. But she would never give it up.

"No one will know if you leak to me," Quinn said. "You know you can trust me. They won't know."

"All right," Gary said finally. "All right."

"Tell me what you know," Quinn said.

"They found a body, in the woods, on the gravel road between here and Waterford," he said.

"Hearse Road?"

"Yeah," Gary said.

"They found a body. Murdered?"

"She was decapitated, Quinn," Gary said. "That kind of thing doesn't tend to happen accidentally. The Kaulbach kid spilled the story along with his guts. The woman was missing a head—clean cut from her shoulders."

Quinn felt a momentary stab of panic. In his head, an image played from his nightmare. The Horseman was bearing down on him, a sword in his hand, preparing to remove his head. He could feel the blade about to cut into his flesh.

Quinn pushed it away.

"And Kaulbach found the head," he said.

"They were called out there to search," Gary said. "Originally they wanted to have a whole pack do it, but they stopped."

"Why?" Quinn asked.

"Because they're scared," Gary said. "Scared this isn't a murderous lover or something..."

"Scared it's the Horseman," Quinn said.

"Yeah," Gary said, and then added, "Wait. What? The Horseman? Who the hell is the Horseman?"

"No one," Quinn said quickly. "I sometimes get my serial killers mixed up."

"I'm not going to say who I was thinking of," Gary said.

"Lord Halloween," Quinn said. "That's who they are worried about."

"Look, I was truthful at the beginning here," Gary said. "I don't know much. We don't know that it is that guy at all. Hell, some people still even think it really was Holober. But even if it wasn't... He has been gone 12 years, for Christ's sake. It's just..."

"Just what?" Quinn asked.

"The brutality of it is unusual for this town, you know that. And with this time of year..."

"It isn't hard to jump to conclusions," Quinn said. "So are they going to talk about it?"

"Are you nuts?" Gary asked. "If I so much as mention that you are inquiring about a headless woman in the woods, what the hell do you think they will say? They'll clam up."

"So how do I get the story, Gary?"

"That's not my problem," Gary said. "I shouldn't have told you this much. They'll find out who leaked it."

"No they won't," Quinn said.

"They will..."

"They will if you run around acting guilty," Quinn said. "Don't do that. Just act like everything is normal. Just be cool."

"Easy for you to say," Gary said grumpily.

"Look, I appreciate what you've told me..."

"Just don't screw me over," Gary said. "All right? Just don't screw me over."

And with that, he hung up, and Quinn was left in silence.

He looked at the clock. It was still early in the morning and no one else was here. And he had the story of a lifetime.

Almost.

There were two concerns. The first was the vision of his nightmare intruding on reality. The idea that this was the work of a Washington Irving character was absurd and yet Quinn couldn't help but wonder about it. A headless corpse, days after he had been dreaming about a headless rider who enjoys taking trophies. It unnerved him. But he pushed it to the back of his mind. Dream phantoms don't kill people.

The second problem was more banal. He needed confirmation. Regardless of how it works in the movies, a one-source story wasn't going to fly at the *Chronicle*. In theory, Gary could be making stuff up or have his facts confused. Quinn trusted him, but he wasn't enough. Considering the return of Lord Halloween would panic just about everyone, he had to make sure the story was 100% solid.

But Quinn also knew he could not call the known world. Doing so could alert Summer or someone even more important to what's going on. This was a major scoop—likely the biggest one of his career—and he would be damned if he was going to let it get away. How he acted would be critical. The police were trying to keep this quiet. That was fine by him. The *Chronicle* wouldn't publish for two days—a lifetime for a story like this.

If whatever was going to happen broke today, it would be old news by the time the *Chronicle* came out. But if the police wanted to keep a lid on this... that changed things.

He had to be careful, building the case so it wouldn't break until precisely the right time. This had to work but he was going to need help. He dialed Janus' number.

*****

He was so busy the next few hours, he didn't even see when Kate walked in. Only when his stomach started rumbling at 12:30 did he look up and notice her there. She seemed absorbed in whatever she was doing.

He got up and crossed over to her desk.

"Hey," he said, in what he hoped was a casual way.

She looked up at him.

"Hey stranger," she replied. "I saw you over there working the phones. What has you so busy?"

Quinn thought for a moment. It was a risk to bring her in on a story like this. He really knew very little about her. On the other hand, she had been a reporter at a good city paper and Laurence had mentioned something about police beat experience. She might be an asset. Quinn glanced around nervously.

"How about we discuss it during lunch?" he asked.

She chuckled.

"Now I really am curious," she said. She picked up her purse and grabbed her jacket.

"Where to?" she asked.

Chapter 8

Janus was standing in the entrance to La Villa Roma when they walked in.

"I figured I would find you here," Janus said.

Quinn nodded and they walked over to a booth. The table still had the remnants of its previous occupant's lunch on it, but Quinn barely noticed. Janus picked it up and set it on a nearby table before settling into the booth across from Quinn and Kate.

"What did you find?" he asked Janus.

"There's a lot of activity," Janus said. "They chased me away in a goddamned hurry."

"Figures," Quinn said.

"Wait a second," Kate began. "What's going on?"

"Can we trust her?" Janus asked, and Quinn could tell he wasn't kidding. For all of Janus' swearing and sometimes obnoxious behavior, there was no one else you wanted on your team. On stories like this, he was the most professional photographer you could ever want.

Quinn caught his breath and opened his mouth to speak.

"What do you think?" Kate asked, and looked at both of them slowly. Her gaze seemed to pierce right through Quinn. "On Saturday, you guys were all joking and now Janus is looking as serious as I've ever seen him. You can trust me. Now please tell me what the hell is going on."

"I think we can," Quinn said and looked back at Janus. He nodded.

"All right," he said.

Quinn kept his voice low as he related to Kate his conversation with Gary that morning, although he did not tell them his source.

"So who were you on the phone with the rest of the morning?" Kate asked Quinn.

"Right now just making the rounds on the stalker," he said. "I'm trying to find out why they canceled the press conference."

"But you know that..."

"Yeah, but they don't know that I know," he said. "I wanted to find out what the cops have told some of the heads of the citizen patrols."

"I doubt very much they told them there was a dead body in the woods," she said.

"Nope," Quinn replied. "But they were stupid enough to tell them different stories. Bill Browson, who heads up the Leesburg Family Council, was told that Sheriff Brown had to testify in court unexpectedly. But Rev. Athearn was told that there was simply no new information. They both might be true, but I doubt it."

"Sloppy," Kate said.

"Yeah, because they had to do it fast," Janus said.

"Why are you wasting time on this?" she asked. "Why not just confront the police?"

"I could," he said. "But what would that do? The story needs time to simmer. The cops think they can keep a lid on this, but there is no way this doesn't start to leak out. Sooner or later, something always does. The more people that know, the easier getting confirmation will be. If I ask too many questions too soon, the right people are going to get scared and clam up. I want to see how many times I get the same story."

"But if you just asked..."

"This isn't Ohio, Kate," Janus said. "These cops don't like or trust us very much. They're secretive down to their core. A lot happens in this town they don't like to talk about. The first time Lord Halloween struck, a lot of people lost faith in the police and they never got it back. It's created a siege mentality at the police force."

"But you could force them to talk, just by asking a lot of questions," she said.

"If I do that today, they could find my source," he said. "And that won't help me. Let them see me asking everyone in town—they will hear about it. They'll get nervous and when I call them tomorrow they won't ask who gave me the story. They'll figure I pieced it together."

"But what more do you know?" Kate asked.

Quinn gestured at Janus.

"He's been my eyes in the sky," he replied. "I'm waiting for his report."

"Quinn called me this morning and had me head out to the site," he explained to Kate.

"Where the body supposedly is?" she asked.

"We didn't know exactly where, but..." Quinn said.

"We know where now," Janus said.

"What did you find?" she asked.

"The cops are swarming around the woods along a side road between Leesburg and Waterford. They've roped off a whole chunk of it. It isn't very well traveled, but..."

"Not exactly subtle," she said.

"They never are," Quinn replied. "Secretive, but not subtle."

"I got there and parked far enough away," Janus said. "I started taking photos pretty far back. I have a good telescope lens, so I could see quite a few uniforms combing the woods."

"Did they see you?"

"Not at first," he said. "I got pretty close before anyone came over to me. When they did, though, you would have thought I killed the lady."

"What happened?"

"A whole bunch of cops—like five or six—started coming toward me and shouting and shit," he said. "I switched the film because I figured they might try and hurt the camera, but they weren't that dumb. Instead they just started trying to intimidate me."

"What did you do?" Kate asked.

"I told them they could go fuck themselves," Janus said and grinned.

"This is his usual response to most inquiries," Quinn said.

"Really?" she asked.

"Oh yeah," Quinn said, holding up his hands. "Honest to God."

"So I imagine they took that well," she said.

"Well, I also showed them my press badge," Janus added. "That made them calm down, but one of them went running back and brought out Stu."

"Who's Stu?"

"Brown's deputy," Quinn said.

"What did he say?" Kate asked.

"He didn't say jack," Janus replied. "I asked him what the hell was going on. I said I got calls from some locals about the police out here, so I came to take some pictures and I get the fucking Nazis coming down on me."

"Good, good," Quinn said.

"No locals called, I assume," she said.

"Not a bloody one," Janus replied. "So Stu just glares at me and you can see the hamster wheel running in his head. Then he said something about how it was dangerous and there was a chemical spill in the woods and how I needed to keep away from the area."

"If it was a chemical spill, where were the masks and suits?" Quinn asked.

"Bingo, man," Janus said. "Exactly the question I asked him. He just told me to leave."

"Is that about it?" Quinn asked.

"Well, I got enough art for you," Janus said. "But I will tell you this. Those kids—the other cops—they were scared. You could just feel it coming off them. I don't know if they were told the chemical bullshit or not, but I doubt it. Whatever body is back there, I think it's pretty messed up."

"Or they didn't just find a body," Kate said.

"Meaning?" Quinn asked.

"They found something else," she said. "Something that is worrying them."

"Like?"

"A note," she said. "Lord Halloween's calling card."

"Wait a minute," Quinn said. "We don't know that yet. I agree it's a possibility—maybe even a good one, but..."

"How many murders happen in October, for God's sake?" Kate asked.

"I know," he replied evenly. "But it is far too early to tell yet. We have to find out more."

There was a silence between the three of them.

"I might be able to help," she said finally.

The two men looked at her.

"How?" Quinn asked her.

"Do you trust me?" she asked him and the two of them stared at each other.

"I said I did," Quinn replied.

"Then let me worry about it," she said. "I have some experience with police procedure. And I may have a source."

"Whoa, hang on, we can't let this get out," Quinn replied.

"You have to trust me, Quinn," she said.

"I'm not going to burn you. But if this story is what we think it is, this source will know. And he won't lie to me about it."

"How is that possible? You just came to this town," Janus said.

Kate didn't answer him.

"You've been here before," Quinn said. "Haven't you?"

Kate looked at both of them, but said nothing. She looked at her watch.

"I have to run guys," she said. "But I promise I'll keep this quiet for you. If he comes through, I'll let you know."

She stood up and started to walk away. Suddenly, she came back to the table.

"Quinn?" she said.

"Yeah?" he asked uncertainly.

"Thanks for trusting me. You won't regret it."

And she left them both watching her leave.

"Wonderful girl," Janus said. "Either I'm going to kill her or I'm beginning to like her."

"*Empire Strikes Back*?" Quinn asked.

"Nah, man," he said. "Original *Star Wars*. You are off your game today. And if she screws us, you will have blown the biggest story of your life. Return of a brutal serial killer?"

"I know what I'm doing," Quinn replied.

"I hope you're right," Janus said. "We don't know an awful lot about her, you know. And notice how she didn't answer if she had been here before? I'm not the reporter, but when someone doesn't answer a question, it usually means there is a story."

"I know," Quinn said.

"You dig her?" Janus asked.

Quinn just looked away.

"We've got a lot of work to do."

"So you aren't going to answer my questions now?"

"I don't know how to answer it," Quinn said. "Yeah, I 'dig' her."

"Good," Janus said. "God knows you've needed a girlfriend in the worst way."

"Leave my personal life alone," Quinn said.

"Why start now?" Janus asked. "Just be careful about trusting her too far. She's holding back. That much is obvious."

"I'll be careful," he said.

Janus grunted and they finished the rest of their lunch in near silence.

*****

Kate stood outside on the curb, uncertain exactly what to do. The barrier between her and the door was little more than 10 feet of grass, but it felt like something infinitely more dangerous. As if the grass would swallow her whole if she stepped on it.

Finally, with what felt like a momentous effort, she stepped forward and crossed quickly to the door.

Maybe no one will be home, she thought, ignoring the fact that she would have to come back at some point. Or did she? She could just tell Quinn it hadn't worked out. Her source was no good.

You aren't doing this for him, she told herself. You know damn well why you're doing this.

Kate rang the doorbell and waited an eternity before it finally opened.

An attractive-looking woman in her late 50s stood there.

"Can I help you?" she began, and then stopped abruptly. "Oh my God. Katrina? Is that really you?"

Kate nodded and the woman hugged her violently before escorting her through the front door.

"I can't believe it," the woman said, though Kate could hardly hear her.

She was too busy looking around. She had thought some of this might seem familiar to her, but either the house had changed or her memory was refusing to kick in.

"I can't believe it," she said again.

"Hi, Mrs. Redacker," Kate said finally, still looking around the room. She felt no tingle of familiarity. Her brain's insistence that there must be something here, anything that she should remember only made the place feel more alien and this meeting more strange.

"Call me Sue," the woman gently said. "Calling me that makes me feel so old."

And then Kate spotted it. A large photo was on the back wall in the family room they had just walked into. It was an old picture of four adults and two little girls. She didn't need to look hard to see one of them was herself.

"Well, my goodness," Sue Redacker continued. "When did you get into town? Your father didn't say anything about coming down here and Johnny just spoke to him..."

"My dad isn't here," she said, more abruptly then she meant it. "I came down here on my own."

"Oh," Sue said. "Of course. It's so hard for me to think of you as all grown up, you know. Are you in town on business, or just touring Virginia? You should have told me. We would have been happy to have you stay here."

"It's okay, Mrs. Redacker," Kate said. "I'm all right. I was offered a job here, at the *Chronicle*."

"And you took it?" Sue said.

"Yeah," Kate said, and smiled grimly. "I took it."

There was silence in the room as Kate continued to look around. There were a few other photos—mostly of the Redacker's daughter Julia—that looked familiar. But nothing else.

"I'm sorry, dear," Sue continued. "It's just your father never wanted to hear the word 'Leesburg' mentioned, so I'm surprised..."

"It's all right," Kate said and smiled. "Really. I know it's weird."

"Then why, if you don't mind me asking?" Sue asked, and looked at Kate intently.

"I don't know, to be honest," Kate replied. "Maybe it was to see the place again. I'm not sure."

"Well," Sue said, and let out a breath. "I'm certainly glad you're here. Will you stay for dinner? I don't think Johnny will be much longer."

"I can't," Kate said. "It's my first week and I have a lot of stuff to do."

"Well, come by later this week then," Sue said. "I'm just so happy to see you. I talked to Julia last night and I know she would love to see you."

"That would be great," Kate said. "I hate to cut right to the chase, though, but I need your help."

Kate hated herself a little. The Redackers were good people, but being here—standing with this woman—felt intensely painful. Now that she was through the door, she just wanted to leave.

Sue looked startled, but nodded her head.

"Anything, dear," she said. "You know that."

"My dad doesn't know I'm here," she said. "I would appreciate it if you didn't tell him."

"But..."

"Please."

There was a long pause.

"I was your mother's friend for most of her life and I respect your father a great deal," Sue replied. "I don't think it's a good idea to lie to him."

"I'm not asking for that," she said. "Just don't bring me up."

Slowly, Sue nodded.

"Okay," she said. "For now. But that's not what you came for, is it?"

"It's not, no," Kate replied. "I need Mr. Redacker's help."

Sue waited, but turned slightly away.

"With what?" she asked, and Kate could see she was looking at the photo of Kate's mom on the far wall. "Did you know he was promoted just a few months ago?"

"There was a dead body found today," Kate said suddenly. "Out past Leesburg."

"Oh my God," Sue said, inhaling.

"Or it might have been found earlier. I'm not sure."

"How could Johnny help you with something like that?" Sue asked.

"We are working on a story about it," Kate said.

"Well, he isn't allowed to talk to the press, dear," Sue said.

"This isn't a normal murder, Mrs. Redacker."

"Then what is it?"

"We don't know, exactly," Kate said. "But we hear rumors. That there may be more than a single corpse."

There was a long pause. Sue looked uncomfortable and Kate fought the urge to just leave the room. She hated doing this, having this conversation. It felt like she was watching herself from a million miles away. She was handling this poorly.

But she had to know.

"Well, I don't know how he can help you with that."

"Is it him?" Kate asked her.

"Who?" Sue replied, but she was walking into the kitchen. Kate followed her.

"You know who I mean," Kate said.

Sue stopped and slowly turned around.

"Trina," she said, and Kate winced at the use of her mother's nickname for her. "They caught that man. You can't just...."

"Does Mr. Redacker really think Holober was the guy?" Kate asked. "He's told my father that, but does he really believe it?"

Sue didn't answer.

"I didn't think so," Kate said. "And I don't either. Which means he could still be out there."

"He's not," Sue said.

"Maybe," Kate said. "But I need to make sure. I need to know what else was found by that body. Notes, clues, anything. Do the police think it's him?"

Sue walked back into the kitchen.

"I don't know anything about this," she said.

"But you can ask Mr. Redacker," Kate said. "He would know."

"It's not that simple," Sue said. "This is crazy. I'm sure it isn't that man... they caught him."

"They didn't, Mrs. Redacker," Kate said, and moved closer to her. "They didn't. You know it, I know it, my father knows it. And I feel like I've just been waiting for him to show up again."

"Trina, he's not coming back. And you can't expect Johnny to..."

"I know I don't have a right," Kate said. "But I think my mom does. Don't you understand? He murdered her and he's still free."

"No," Sue said adamantly. "They caught him."

"What if they didn't?" Kate asked.

"It's not him," Sue said.

"If it's not him, I need details," Kate said. "There are rumors a note was found by the body. I need to know if that is true."

There was no rumor of any such thing, but Kate had to go out on a limb. If it was Lord Halloween, there would be a note. There was always a note.

"Tell him it's me who wants to know," Kate said.

"So you can put it in the paper?" Sue asked. "That the murderer is still out there?"

"To warn people," Kate said. "Don't you think my mom would want that? Wouldn't you? If this guy really is back and we don't tell people, someone could die who doesn't have to."

"But if you run a story like that, people will panic," Sue said. "It will be like before."

"Maybe not," Kate said. "Maybe this time we'll catch him."

"I'll ask him, but I can't guarantee he can say anything," Sue said. "I can't guarantee anything, Trina."

"I know," Kate replied. "Just ask. Please."

Sue nodded. Ten minutes later, Kate was outside again, gulping down the fresh air. Why had she come back? She swore under her breath. Why didn't she leave now?

But she knew she had to know more. Mrs. Redacker had agreed Kate could call later, when her husband was home. He would tell her what she wanted to know—she hoped.

*****

Quinn was startled by the knock at his door. He closed his *Newsweek* and looked out the peephole expecting to see Bill or Janus there. They dropped by unannounced semi-frequently. But Kate stood there instead. He opened the door.

"How do you even know where I live?" he asked, and gestured for her to come in.

"I'm a reporter," she said simply. "It's my job to know stuff."

She looked around. It was definitely a bachelor's pad. Clothes hung over a light brown armchair that looked like it could have been 20 years old. Magazines were strewn about on the coffee table in front of the TV. She noted with some approval that they were mostly good quality magazines, like the *Newsweek* he had in his hand.

"Sit down," Quinn said, at a loss for what to do. Of course, this is the kind of thing he might have dreamed about. But somehow he doubted she was there to confess undying affection for him. "Can I get you something?"

"No, thanks. You have a nice place," she said, looking around. She had been in guys' apartments a lot worse than this.

"I'm sorry it's so messy," he said. "I don't normally have a lot of visitors."

"No girlfriend?" she asked, and it came out more flirtatious than she meant it.

"Not for a while, anyway," he replied, and shrugged. "Are you sure I can't get you anything?"

"No, it's all right," she replied. "Thanks."

She moved the clothes to a broken down looking sofa and sat down on the armchair.

"What can I do for you?" he asked. "When you didn't show up at the office later, I got a little worried. I asked Laurence about you, but he said you were following up a business profile."

"That's mostly true," she said. "As well as checking out a lead for you."

"Find anything?" he asked.

"Maybe," she said, and pulled a piece of paper from her back pocket. Quinn crossed over to her and picked it up.

The paper had scribbled notes on it, with one name near the top: "Mary Kilgore."

"Who's Mary Kilgore?" he asked.

"Your dead lady," Kate replied.

"Jesus," he said. "How the hell did you get this?"

"Never mind that. Keep reading."

Quinn looked it over.

"This is for real?" he asked in disbelief. "How the hell did you get this? It would have to be someone high in the police department to have these details."

"It's for real," she said. "But there is a catch."

"You aren't going to tell me who it is?" Quinn asked.

Kate nodded. "Actually, it's worse than that."

"How?"

"You can't print just on this. You have to get the police to confirm. Or someone on their staff..."

"You have to be kidding," Quinn said.

"Look, it's the best I can do," she said. "If the guy reads just this, he'll never talk to me again. I promised I wouldn't burn him."

"But they'll never confirm all of this..."

"It's a start," Kate said. "Once they know you have details, they might confirm enough."

"Yes, yes," he said. "Look, it's a great help. Don't get me wrong. I called just about everybody I know today."

"I figured," she said. "But keep me out of it."

"What?" he asked. "Hey, look, this is good stuff. You should get credit."

"No, I don't want my name near this story," Kate said, and looked at him so intently Quinn flinched.

"Why?"

Kate spread her hands. "I just don't."

Quinn looked at her. In one sense, he felt insanely glad to have her there. She had just delivered more details than he could have dug up in three days. But on the other hand, he felt like she wasn't really there at all. She seemed angry about something, but if it was Quinn, he couldn't think why.

"Okay," he said.

"Look, I have to go," she said and stood up.

"Wait," Quinn replied.

"Look, Quinn, I'm wiped out. I don't want to be rude, but..."

"It isn't that I don't appreciate what you've done," Quinn said. "But I need to talk this through. Just for five minutes."

She nodded and waited.

"So this isn't Lord Halloween," Quinn said.

"Disappointed?" she asked.

"No," Quinn shook his head. "It's just, I'm not sure how your source knows that for sure."

"Donald Kilgore has a history of spousal abuse," she replied evenly. "Hell, he had a citation just a year ago for it. My source says the court records will back that up. The word is she had moved out recently and Donald wasn't happy about it. The police think he set a trap for her."

"And made it look like a serial killer?" he asked.

"Sure," she said. "It would distract people. He left a note, but the police said it wasn't consistent with the ones Holober supposedly wrote. He wanted the police to think it was a serial killer."

"Do they have him in custody?" Quinn asked.

"They picked him up an hour ago," she replied.

"I can't believe this," he said finally, still staring at the sheet of paper.

"Just protect me," Kate said. "Tell Janus that I had nothing."

"Look, I don't want to lie to him. We've been through a lot."

"Then swear him to secrecy," she said. "I mean it. I don't even want a hint I was involved."

"Why?" he asked. "Why act like you have something to hide?"

Kate just looked at her watch again.

"I've got to go," she said. "It's late."

"Hey," Quinn said. "You can trust me."

Kate shook her head and crossed the room to leave. But she turned at the door.

"The problem isn't you," she said.

"Oh, if I had a nickel for every time I've heard that before," he replied.

"It isn't," she insisted. "You have to believe that. I just... I can't, that's all. I know you are trusting me with a lot, but I can't. I just need..." She held up her hands.

"I don't know what I need," she said, and pulled open the door.

"Kate," he said and walked to the door. "If you do need something—you can trust me."

"Thanks," she said, and was out the door. Quinn was left looking at the yellow, folded sheet of paper.

Chapter 9

"The hour is at hand. How long have we waited, brothers and sisters, for the feast of Sanheim to arrive? But it is coming, and we will receive our long-awaited reward. Come to St. Bede's chapel by the morning of Oct. 31. You will not be disappointed."
—Letter from Robert Crowley, Oct. 5, 1873.

Wednesday, Oct. 11

By the morning staff meeting, Quinn had already basked in the glow of a thousand congratulations. Everyone but Kyle had told him how great the story turned out, even advertising employees he barely knew.

But it all felt hollow.

It wasn't the play the story got or even how it turned out that bothered him. First, Kate had not looked him in the eye since Monday, and it was apparent to him that something was bothering her.

But something else gnawed at Quinn. The story had gone off without a hitch yesterday. By mid-morning, he had confirmed the victim's name with three others connected with the police department. By the afternoon, the department itself confirmed the victim, her address and that her husband had been taken into custody.

One police officer whom Quinn had never spoken to had called to confirm details of past arrests with Don Kilgore and explained that he had a longstanding abusive relationship with his wife.

In short, by Tuesday evening, he had a perfect story—good sources, a great lead and hardly any revisions from the editor.

But it was his very success that bothered him. It felt too easy.

Everything had simply fallen into place—confirmations from a police department that on a normal day would barely confirm that the sky was blue, an official arrest in the evening and even an unsolicited call from a brand new source.

It fit too well. Quinn's unease increased every time he thought about it. The reporting instinct he had counted on for years—what he jokingly called his "Spidey sense"—was tingling.

He thought he had been on the story of a lifetime. But now he had the distinct feeling he had been used. The story was so right it felt wrong.

It was unnerving and the more congratulations he received, the worse he felt.

What was it Buzz said? Just because you're paranoid doesn't mean they are not out to get you. Quinn thought Buzz was more than a little crazy, but maybe he was right on that one.

He leaned forward and stared at his keyboard. From a distance it looked fine, but when he examined it closely, it had crumbs and small hairs between the keys. It looked nasty. It seemed an apt metaphor.

Almost everyone else appeared happy. Rebecca actually seemed in a good mood, an unusual state for her. And Laurence had already told him twice what an excellent story it was. He acted like some kind of proud father, probably because he knew the paper would sell well today. Murders were more common than they once were—and God knows this town had its own brand of serial killer a dozen years back—but they were rare enough to attract attention.

But Kate appeared more withdrawn than ever. She complimented him briefly in the morning, but hadn't said much of anything else. And she had reason to be happy apart from his story. Quinn noticed Kate's first by-line had ended up on the front page, an exclusive from Martin Heller offering a compromise with the conservationists at Phillips Farm. On any other week, it would have been the lead story. But he could not imagine that Kate would hold that against him.

Rebecca interrupted Quinn's reverie when she started rounding everyone up for the staff meeting. Quinn left his keyboard and followed her into the conference room.

*****

The meeting was already out of Laurence's control by the time Ethan Holden walked in. Kyle had spent 15 minutes discussing the poor quality of the photos with his story, which had touched off a fight with Josh, the head photographer, while Alexis complained bitterly about last minute changes made to her story on the new science lab at Park View High School.

At least two people audibly groaned when they saw Holden open the door and stroll in. He looked at the motley group around the table, smiled briefly, and then walked to the far side of the room.

"Please continue," he said in a deep gravelly voice. "I don't want to interrupt."

Janus snorted and when Holden looked at him, acted like he had a coughing fit.

Laurence placed his palms on the table and began for a third time.

"I think we had a good paper," he said. "Quinn, I want to make sure we keep a close eye on your story. They may have arrested the husband, but if we have new details by next week, we should make sure to stay on top of that."

This was the part of the staff meeting Quinn despised. Laurence did not have a clue what to say now that Holden—his boss—had shown up. He kept glancing in his direction waiting for the inevitable interruption.

Quinn also hated being told to follow the story. Did Laurence really think he wouldn't? That he would just walk away? No, he doubted Laurence did. But he had to say something.

He glanced at Kate, who was the only one not darting glances in Holden's direction. Instead, she seemed to be staring at the wall.

Quinn realized with alarm that Laurence had asked him something.

"Yeah," he said, hoping it was a yes or no question he had been asked.

Laurence nodded.

"I also want to stay on the kindergarten fire," Laurence said.

Kyle groaned quietly.

"What more do you want me to say?" he asked Laurence.

"Interview the parents," Laurence said. "Talk to other kindergartens."

"I don't think there will be a rash of kindergarten fires, Laurence," he said.

"Laurence is right," boomed Holden, and Helen and Alexis both jumped in their chairs.

Laurence looked surprised to have Holden supporting him.

"Kids," Holden said. "It is always about kids. Remember that."

Kyle nodded. The comment had made little sense to anybody but it was safer to nod around Holden.

"Kids," he said again, gravely. "And animals. People love animals."

Here it went. The semi-monthly everybody-loves-animals story.

"We need to put more on the front page," Holden continued. "People connect with animals. Just the other week, Paul Gibson and I went hunting. He told me how important it was that the local paper emphasize this county's wildlife. That way people can appreciate it more."

"By killing it?" Janus asked.

Laurence glared at him, but Holden didn't appear to notice.

"It's important we tell people what is unique about this county, particularly the wildlife," Holden said. "I was hoping we would have a few shots of animals in our special Halloween section, Laurence. Maybe a horse-drawn carriage ride in a pumpkin patch. Don't you think that would be a good idea?"

Heads swiveled sharply in Holden's direction and there was an audible gasp from Alexis. People had been beginning to nod off, but that comment got their attention.

"What Halloween section?" Rebecca asked, looking at Laurence.

"Uh yes, Mr. Holden, I was going to talk with you about that," Laurence replied, and looked away from everyone.

"Yes?" Holden said and looked at Laurence expectantly.

"Well, I thought, maybe in private we could discuss it."

"No time like the present," Holden replied gruffly. "Let's all talk about it. This is going to be a big deal."

"Well, sir, I just wasn't sure that the county is quite ready for this," Laurence said.

"Ready? I would say it's overdue," Holden replied. "We've been doing it in the Fairfax papers for five years. It sells well every time. We need to expand it to Loudoun. None of the other papers even mention..."

"That's precisely my point, Mr. Holden," Laurence replied. "Halloween here is a little different."

"I know, I know, the killer," Holden said. "But that was more than a decade ago."

"Loudoun isn't like other places, Mr. Holden," Rebecca said. "Since 1994, Leesburg has banned any public celebration of Halloween. Shopkeepers are generally discouraged from painting even a pumpkin in the window, much less a ghost. This is not something we want to celebrate here."

"Well, I think it is time people got over it," Holden said.

"With all due respect, I don't think you can just..." Laurence started.

"The paper needs to take a stand," Holden said. "I'll write an editorial. It is time to move on, and..."

"Why, so you can sell a few more papers?" someone said bitterly.

Helen gasped and the entire staff looked toward the origin of the voice. Kate sat there, glaring straight ahead at Holden.

Holden coughed abruptly. He was not used to outright defiance.

"No, of course not," Holden said.

"Then why? Why do they need to get over it?" she asked.

"Kate, I think maybe you should let Rebecca and I handle it," Laurence said gently.

Quinn was too surprised to jump in to help her.

"We can't live in the past, young woman," Holden said. "Banning a public celebration of Halloween is poppycock. It's nonsense. There is no sense tying together the murders with the damn holiday..."

"Why not?" she asked. "He did. I'd say he connected them together pretty well."

"Well, it's time to let that madman go," Holden said. "They caught him. He's dead. People should just move on. What's done is done."

"What about the families of the victims?" Kate asked. "Should they just move on? Forget about it?"

"Look, I'm just saying..."

"I know what you're saying," she said. Holden seemed afraid to look her in the face. "It's over, let's just all forget about it. Well not everyone can do that. Do you want to be the one to remind them? To force it down their throats?"

"Kate..." Laurence said.

"Young lady, I don't know who you are or why you care so much about this, but I'm the publisher of this paper and I don't appreciate your tone," he said.

"She's just trying to say that people haven't forgotten, Mr. Holden," Quinn said, and Laurence and Rebecca both glared at him. "She doesn't mean any disrespect."

But Kate had a look of pure disgust on her face. Disrespect appeared to be exactly what she intended.

"Well," Holden said. "I'm just saying, I think it is about time to put together a section like this."

"I don't know if that is a good idea," Rebecca said.

"Well, I do," Holden said, and banged his hand on the table. "I do think it is about time. We need to move on from this. I want a special Halloween section on my desk by next week. That's it. No more debate."

"Mr. Holden..." Laurence began.

But Holden stood up.

"I bid you all good day," he said stiffly, and walked out.

Laurence put his head in his hands, and Rebecca glared at Kate.

"Kate, you're new here, so maybe you didn't know," Rebecca said. "That was Ethan Holden, our publisher. Don't talk to him that way. Ever."

"Why not? His idea is going to bring up a lot of pain for everybody," Kate said.

"It's just a Halloween section, with ghost stories and a couple pumpkin carving tips, where is the harm?" Laurence asked.

"I happen to agree that it isn't a good idea," Rebecca said, still looking at Kate. "But he is the publisher of this paper. If the man wants a special section, he'll get one."

"Fine," Kate said.

Everyone else sat in stunned silence.

"In fact, I can tell you right now who is going to write it up," Rebecca said. "I think we will start with Kate and Quinn. Mostly because they interrupted what should have been a private conversation between Mr. Holden, Laurence and me."

"I don't think you're being fair," Quinn said.

"Newsflash, Mr. O'Brion: Life is not fair," Rebecca said. "I'll cut Kate some slack because she is new, but I don't want to hear another word from you. Laurence and I will brainstorm assignments and hand them out today. You will both get your stories done. That's all there is to it."

"But..."

"Don't test me," Rebecca said and Quinn shivered involuntarily.

And that was that. The rest of the meeting occurred in near silence. When Rebecca dismissed them, everyone rushed to leave the room.

*****

By the time Quinn got out, he could already see Kate exiting by the side door. He hurried to catch up with her and got to her outside in the parking lot.

"Kate?" he asked her.

She wheeled on him.

"Don't follow me," she said.

"Whoa," Quinn put up his hands. "What did I do?"

"I don't need your help," she said. "That man was an idiot. A goddamned idiot."

"Are you mad at me or at him?" Quinn asked.

Kate glared at him and then paused. She sighed.

"I should leave," she said.

"Well, I'd stay out of Rebecca's way," he said. "She is not exactly peaches and cream when she is pissed off."

"That's not what I mean," she said, shaking her head. "I should leave for good. I should have never come back."

"Hang on," Quinn said, and grabbed her by the shoulders. "Look, it's just a little fight. It will blow over. Come on."

"That's not why. I don't know why I'm here, Quinn. I was just begging for that kind of outburst. Everything is so…"

She clenched her fists into balls. She wanted to scream or hit something. But instead she let her fingers slowly curl back out again.

"Let's go somewhere," Quinn said. "Let's go talk this out."

"I don't think…"

"Come on," he said. "Please. You're upset. I'd like to help."

"You can't," she said. "You can't."

"How do you know?" he responded. "I don't think I can make it any worse."

She paused before finally sighing. "Okay, let's talk. God knows I need to talk to somebody."

"Where are we going?" she asked him when they were in the car. They had been driving in silence for 10 minutes.

"You haven't guessed?" he asked.

And it was then she knew. They were heading back to the cemetery.

"Okay," she said. "Perfect, actually."

They rode the rest of the way quietly. He parked by the front gate and they both got out.

"This is as peaceful a place as there is," he said. "And private to boot."

"It is," she said. "I should come here more often."

"Yeah…"

"Not for the reasons you think," she said and started to walk briskly. "Follow me. Remember how you said I had been here before?"

Quinn nodded, as he and Kate walked down the cemetery's main road.

"How did you know?" she asked.

"Just a vibe," he said.

"Like you had seen me before?"

"No, although I've felt like I do know you from somewhere," he said. "But I knew I had never seen you before. I would have remembered."

"Well your guess was right," she said.

"I gathered that from your reaction," Quinn replied.

She stopped in front of a grave. It took a moment for Quinn to realize this had been done on purpose.

He looked at it. It was a simple marble slab with the inscription, "Here lies Sarah Blakely." There were some dates below.

He looked at Kate quizzically.

"The name doesn't mean anything to you?" she asked quietly.

"Should it?" he asked.

"I'm surprised you haven't come across it in your research," she replied as she stared at the headpiece. "Sarah Blakely was killed 12 years ago. She was the Loudoun serial killer's fifth victim."

There was a pause before Kate said anything more. But Quinn had begun to feel a sense of dread.

"She was also my mother," Kate said simply and turned away from the headstone.

She started to walk down the path. Quinn hurried to keep up with her.

"Jesus," he said and wondered what more he could say. "I'm so sorry..."

"I was born here, Quinn," Kate said. "I even attended Leesburg Middle School."

"Why didn't you tell Laurence that?" he asked.

She stopped.

"Would you?" she asked. "If I had mentioned that I had lived here, there would have been more questions. There are always more questions when you're a reporter. Where did you live? Why did you leave? Do you know Joe Smith, or Judy Doe, or whoever? Sooner or later, it would have been clear who my mother was. And I didn't want that out there."

"Kate, I have no idea what to say," Quinn said. "I lost my parents, so I know what it feels like."

"No offense," she replied and looked back in the direction of her mother's grave. "But it's not exactly the same. Your parents died and it's a tragedy. They were young, you grieve, but you can tell people about it. They can help you. But who helps you when your mother is murdered and the killer is still out there? You can lie, certainly, but that feels like a betrayal. You can tell the truth, but then you can't just leave it at 'murdered' really. It is something that begs for more background.

"So you push it away, because it isn't something you want to talk about. And pretty soon your mother isn't dead anymore, she has been systemically erased. I saw photos of you with your Mom and Dad at your apartment. I have almost none. She died when I was 12 years old—late enough that I can still remember her, but it's fading. If you don't talk about someone, they fade away like an old photograph."

"I'm sorry," Quinn said again.

"So you can see why I was a little upset with the Holden plan," Kate said and laughed. It was not a pleasant sound.

"I can," he said.

"I'm not the only one who will be," she said. "There are more people than me who would just as soon the entire affair stay buried. And that's the real thing. Because Loudoun associates that stupid holiday with the sick bastard who killed people, they can't help but think of him when you start trying to get them to celebrate it."

Quinn was not so sure. Maybe she was right, or maybe it was time for people to move on. For them to see that Halloween didn't equal a literal bogeyman. But he did not think now was the right time to debate this.

They had walked to the edge of the graveyard, where they had sat nearly a week before. It felt like longer ago, Quinn thought. A breeze came across the pond and made him shiver.

"My dad and I left not long after," she said, looking at the pond as well. "And I really never thought I would be back. My life felt like it began at age thirteen and that was that. Some people asked about my Mom, of course. But nobody knew. It was easier to let them think that maybe she had abandoned us. Of course, it never occurred to me I would head back here."

"Then why are you here?" Quinn asked.

She laughed again and turned to look Quinn in the eye.

"That's the thing, Quinn," she said. "I really don't know."

She walked forward and found the bench to sit down.

"I was there, you know," she said.

"Where?" he asked and sat down next to her.

"I was in the house when he murdered my mother," she said calmly.

"My God," Quinn said.

"I didn't know it, of course," she said. "But he did. He knew I was there."

"How?" Quinn started.

"I remember the whole day," she said and her eyes had a distant look. "It was a Thursday and Mom was supposed to be home. The front door was wide open. I yelled upstairs for her, but she didn't respond. In fact, I thought maybe she was out, that the door had just been accidentally left open."

"But it wasn't," Quinn said.

"No," she said. "Her keys were on the table. And the mail was scattered there. I remember I glanced at it to see if there was anything for me. But did I know something was wrong? No. I just shut the door and yelled for Mom again."

"I heard nothing. But I was a little worried. I started to climb the steps. I thought maybe she was in the bathroom or something and couldn't hear me. I got to the top and called again and still didn't hear anything. It was then I thought something was wrong. I can remember the hairs standing up at the back of my neck. But I was twelve and I didn't listen to my instincts. I called her again."

"I walked down the hallway to my parents' bedroom. Then there was a large crash and I turned and ran right to it. It sounded like something had smashed in my room. I was so startled I actually went to look in there and saw that the lamp next to my window had fallen. The window was open and the curtains were swaying in the breeze. The next part I remember in slow motion. I looked out to see a figure run around the side of the house. I think I screamed. I don't remember.

"But what I saw clearly in my mind was that the front door was still unlocked. I had shut it, but I hadn't locked it. In my head, I could see it swinging open again and maybe him coming back up the stairs."

"Jesus," Quinn said, but Kate did not seem to hear him.

"But he had already done what he came to do," she said. "I didn't know that. I actually ran into my parents' room as comfort. I thought I would be safe in there. It didn't occur to me..."

She stopped and looked at Quinn.

"At that age, you feel immortal," she said. "But more than that, your parents seem immortal too. They will always be there to help you, to rescue you. They will know what to do."

"I know," he said.

"And I just thought—I'll be safe in there," Kate said and looked away again. "I remember I could not move fast enough. In my head, he was coming through the door, on his way up the steps, and my feet were made of concrete. I walked into their room and I saw her...I thought she was alive, Quinn. I didn't know. She just seemed to be staring at the ceiling. But then I saw the blood and I..."

"It's okay," he said. "You don't have to finish."

"I think I do," she said. "I've never talked about it. Not with boyfriends, friends, therapists—even my father. I wouldn't. But the truth is that I don't remember much else. There was blood everywhere. I don't know why I hadn't seen it when I walked in. I know I screamed. I screamed for days, it felt like. He's coming back, I kept thinking. He's coming back for you. I went to the phone and somehow there was blood on my hand. I thought it was mine, I didn't know..."

She stopped and took a long breath.

"I made the call, but didn't see it," she said.

"See what?" he asked gently, when she stopped again.

"The note," she said calmly.

"Lord Halloween's calling card," he said, mostly to himself.

"Yes," she replied. "But I didn't know that. How could I? My parents had kept any news of the murders as far away from me as they could. I didn't know what I was looking at. I can still see it in my mind. I'm scared out of my mind, dialing 911 and there's this post-it note stuck right by the phone. I didn't even think about it. I was screaming into the phone to the operator and then I read it."

She stopped again and Quinn felt compelled to ask.

"What did it say?"

She looked at him.

"It said, 'Happy Halloween. Your father can't protect you and you are now on my list. Like mother, like daughter. See you soon, Trina.'"

"My God," he said again.

"He even knew her name for me," Kate said. "I still don't know how he knew that. She was the only one who called me that. Everyone else called me Kate, but my full name is Katrina, and she said Trina."

"What did you do?" he asked.

"I screamed some more," she said. "The operator had no idea what was going on, but they sent the police. I didn't wait for them though. I was certain he had come back in, that he had been waiting for me to find the note. Even then, with my mom's body a few feet away, I started thinking in terms of my own survival. The police found my mother with little difficulty. But it wasn't until one of them checked the attic later that they found me. When the cop came up, I felt certain it was him. I started screaming as soon as he saw me and it took my father picking me up before I stopped."

"Jesus," Quinn said.

"My whole world shattered," she said. "I sometimes wonder who I would have been if that day had never happened. I see her sometimes—in my mind—this different woman who thinks about a career and a life. But you never know, do you? It wasn't just my mom's murder, of course. That would have been enough. 'See you soon, Trina.' That was what did it.

"We left town days later. My dad was a cop. He knew the force would be out there trying to avenge his wife. But he had a daughter to protect and I was beyond hysterical. He did not do a large funeral. He was too scared.

"His wife had been murdered and his daughter threatened— he slept by the side of my bed with his gun every night. By then we were at the Leesburg Hotel, checked in anonymously, of course."

"You were worried the killer would find you?" Quinn felt like an idiot asking.

"I was not worried, Quinn," she said. He noticed her clench her fists together and put them on her thighs. "No, I was certain. Certain he would find me. That it was just a matter of time. My father couldn't convince me I was safe. The police could not convince me I was safe. Nothing could. I just saw the words 'See you soon, Trina' in my head. I have ever since."

"Even when you moved away?"

"It helped," she said. "It took time, but I felt like it worked. I had dreams of course—the most common of them was him standing behind me as I read the note. I feel his hands around me and then I wake up. But those dreams became fewer and fewer. I thought maybe some day I would be over it."

"Then why....?"

"Why come back here?" she asked. She shook her head.

"In October of last year, the dreams started up again. But they were more intense than ever. And they grew stranger."

"Stranger?"

"I could hear my Mom calling me," Kate said. "In the dreams, I would be walking around—at work at the paper even— and I would pick up the phone and she would be at the other end of it. 'Trina, it's time to come home,' she would say. And I would argue with her, tell her I couldn't go back. But I'd be afraid to tell her why.

'Why can't you come back, Trina?' she would ask, over and over again. But I don't want to tell her.

'Is it because of me, Trina? Are you afraid, Trina?' she'd say.

I tell her, 'Please, Mom. 'I've got work to do, he'll find me. He's waiting for me.'

'He's coming for you there, Trina,' she says. And by then in the dream I'm already home, in her bedroom, and her voice is there, but the body is lying on the bed motionless.

'He's coming for you, Trina' she says again. 'He's in the house.'

In the dream, I can see it, Quinn. The door is opening, he is coming through and walking up the steps. And I'm on the phone again, screaming for help. But it's just my mom on the other end.

'See you soon, Trina,' she says.

And then her voice is gone. Another male one, much deeper, takes her place and I hear it and it makes me want to vomit.

'Your father can't protect you and I will find you,' he says. 'See you soon, Trina,' And then he's laughing. And I can see him coming down the hallway at the same time.

And then I wake up."

Quinn shivered.

"I'm so sorry," he said. "I've had nightmares in my time, but that's…"

"Horrible?" she asked. "I fought it off last year. The dreams kept coming, growing worse and more real every single day until Halloween came. I thought I was going crazy."

"And then?"

"It stopped," she said. "Just like that. November 1 came and it all ended. And I felt so relieved, like it was gone for good."

"But it wasn't…."

"No, it wasn't," she said. "It started sooner this time. It was August when it began. And I could feel it building in my brain. I just could not take it."

"So you came here?" Quinn asked in disbelief.

"I had to, Quinn," she said. "Something in my brain is telling me I needed to come back here. I don't think it's my Mom, but..."

"Then what?"

"I don't know," she said. "I don't think it's him either. Because in my dream, she tells me he is coming anyway and I think she is right."

"That he is coming for you?"

"It doesn't matter, Quinn," she said and stood to face him. "I see him everywhere, in everything. Do you know what that is like? To live your whole life waiting for the bogeyman to show up? I have dreams where the post-it note is on my door. Whether he is coming or not, I have let this man shadow me for so long it doesn't matter. I see him around every corner, in everything. He lives in my mind rent-free. I had to come back."

"But what if he's still here?" Quinn asked. "The murder the other day..."

"It wasn't him," she said. "Do you know I was actually sorry when he told me it wasn't Lord Halloween?"

"Why?"

"Because it would mean it is time to face my fears," she said. "I don't want to be afraid of him anymore. I want to find him and be done with it."

"But..."

"I know it's not sane, but would you do anything different? I can't keep living like this, or if I do, he's killed me already. So I actually wanted it to be that bastard's return. Then I could get busy and find out who he is."

"And you're sure it wasn't?" he asked.

"Aren't you? You wrote the story."

"I don't know, Kate," Quinn said. "The police confirmed it all, very easily. But..."

She waited for him.

"I felt good about it yesterday," he said. "But today, it felt wrong. Like they wanted me to write that story. I actually had a voicemail from Brown's assistant telling me it was a good story. It feels wrong."

"I don't think my source would have lied to me," Kate said, but she looked troubled.

"Are you positive?" he asked. "Because if he..."

"My father was a cop. They were on the force together. He and my parents were friends. I played with Julia, their daughter. Why would he lie to me about this? Of all things..."

"I don't know," Quinn said. "Maybe he didn't."

She sighed and pulled her jacket closer to her.

"I have to find him," Kate said.

"If it's true, and he's still here, how do you know he won't find you first?" Quinn asked.

She looked at him.

"Maybe he will," she said. "But I've been looking over my shoulder for so long, I think I have a leg up. I'll be ready."

"If you wanted it to be him, and you've come back for that, why talk about leaving?" Quinn asked. "You said outside the office you were going to go. Why?"

"Things are so weird, Quinn," she said.

"They weren't already?" he responded.

"It's different now," she said. "I have dreams, but they aren't like before. Sometimes my mom is in them, but then there are these symbols and a word that I don't understand."

"Maybe your dreams are just catching up with your location."

"I don't think so," she said. "And there has been other stuff."

She paused.

"Like?" he asked.

"I'll tell you, but only because you can already tell I'm crazy."

"You aren't crazy," he said, and put his hand on hers without thinking about it. "I don't think that."

She looked at him.

"Thank you," she said.

"So what is the other stuff?"

"One of the very first days I was here, when you gave me a tour of the *Chronicle*, do you remember that?" she asked.

"Yeah," he said.

"When we were downstairs, near the printing press, I saw something," she said. "I asked you and Janus about it."

"I remember you pointing at the floor," he said.

"But you saw nothing?"

"No, I didn't see anything," he replied.

"I saw something, Quinn," she said. "Something that makes me worry I'm cracking up."

"What?"

"There was blood," she said. "There was a pool of blood all over that floor. I looked at my feet and it felt like I was walking in it. I could see it, shiny and deep red, so clearly. And you guys acted like it wasn't there."

"I didn't see anything," he replied.

"You see? That's why I wanted to leave. Everything was so screwed up before and now that I'm here, it seems to be getting worse."

"Did you see it again?"

"I haven't been down there since," she said. "I saw it as clear as day and then while I was talking to you, it disappeared. It's stuff like that. The dreams, the blood, everything... The rational part of my brain keeps telling me to leave before I lose what is left of it."

"Then why stay?"

"Because I think this guy is close, Quinn," she said. "I feel it somehow. I know he will return. Maybe now or maybe next year. But he is still here and I have to find him."

She stopped talking and looked back out across the pond. The wind drifted across it again, blowing her hair back. Her hands clenched the marble bench.

"You have to promise to keep this secret," she said.

"Of course," Quinn replied.

"I shouldn't have even told you."

"I think it's about time you told someone," he said. "You've been bottling this up for too long."

"I know," she said. "And I'm not going to leave. Whatever is going to happen, it finishes now, here. I'm through waiting for him to jump out of the shadows."

"Look, I want you to stay, but..." Quinn said. "What if you're right? If this guy is back, this is the last place you should be. Particularly if he figures out who you are. Every bit of research on him shows he is one for the follow-through."

"That's why you have to help me, Quinn," she said and gripped his hand. "You have to help me find him first."

*****

The stranger watched the two figures talking near the bench. He couldn't tell if they were arguing or not, but they were certainly animated.

He wished he could hear what they were saying. The stranger sighed. Still, he was glad he had followed them out, if only to know for sure there was something going on between the two. He wondered what it meant.

Quinn and Kate, sitting in a tree, not quite K-I-S-S-I-N-G, he thought. He idly wondered which one he should kill first.

Patience, his brain said. Not too soon. You have to take your time, hone your skills.

But it would be so easy, he thought. He could even take one right now.

Patience, that voice in his head said again. Not too quick or they'll connect you. The police are dumb, but they aren't that dumb. Don't be sloppy. You've waited so long.

Kate seemed familiar to him, the stranger thought. She claimed to have never been here before, but there was this strange odor of familiarity to her. It seemed like something on the tip of his tongue—but he couldn't think of it.

Had he known someone named Kate Tassel? He thought about it a moment. He did not think he did.

Breaking his line of sight with them, he moved back through the cemetery toward the grave where they had been standing. They had not been there long, but the stranger wanted to see. It might help him.

He found it and recognized the name immediately.

"Sarah Blakely," he said out loud, just to hear it.

He clapped his hands to his mouth to keep a laugh from coming. No, he didn't know a Kate. But he did know a Trina, didn't he? Yes, yes he did.

Everything made sense now. Her familiarity – even as a child, she had been stunning to look at. And her outburst. He should have known it then. But the last name had thrown him.

It will take more than a last name to hide from me, the stranger thought.

She was little Trina—dear Trina—whose Mom thought about her even while she was being gutted. She called out her name so many times.

He moved back into the line of trees at the back and carefully worked his way to see the couple now standing near the bench.

I have old business with you, Trina, he thought.

He watched as the two walked out of the cemetery together. He noticed they were holding hands. Yes, he was very glad he had followed them.

And this so easily solved the question of whom he would kill first.

"See you soon, Trina," he said out loud as they disappeared around the bend. "See you real soon."

Chapter 10

Thursday, Oct. 12

About the only thing that made Madame Zora's waiting room any different from a doctor's was the faintest smell of lavender in the air, Kate thought.

It was painted off-white with magazines like People stacked neatly on tables next to moderately uncomfortable couches. And there was no sign of what Kate had expected—scented candles, beads or voodoo dolls—not even new age music.

Instead the place had more of a sterile quality.

She was surprised a little by the number of people there—she counted eight. Apparently a lot of people need a psychic healer, or an "alternative medicine guru" as she styled herself now.

Maybe the crowd should not have been surprising. Madame Zora was one of Loudoun's oldest business owners and if her establishment did not have much respect (jokes about it were common), it had at least endured long enough to command a loyal clientele.

Kate shook her head. It wasn't that she disbelieved in something beyond the material world, but this? A semi-doctor's office dedicated to the occult? She found it hard to accept. But she dutifully scribbled something in her notebook. An article on

Madame Zora—Loudoun's most famous (and presumably only) psychic—was to be her contribution to the Halloween section. And though she hated the section, she would at least write a good article. It was a matter of professional pride.

"Kate Tassel?" a sprightly teenage girl with a ponytail asked as she came out of the door on the far wall.

She too had the air of a nurse, clothed in a white coat.

Kate gathered her notebook and stood up.

"Madame Zora will see you now," the girl said and gestured for Kate to follow.

Kate followed her in and they proceeded down a long hallway with several closed doors on either side.

"Have you ever been with us before?" the girl inquired.

Kate shook her head.

"Well, you are in for a treat," the girl said and smiled broadly. "Madame Zora is the best in the business."

Kate wryly wondered what "business" they were talking about.

She was escorted to a red door near what Kate assumed must be the back of the building. The girl knocked, smiled again, opened the door and walked quickly away.

Watching her go, Kate stepped through the doorway and was astounded at the change.

She took a deep breath. This is more like what she had expected.

Rows of creepy dolls lined two bookshelves in the back, all positioned in different ways. A dark maroon drapery hung across one wall and a door in the back was semi-hidden by columns of beads. In the center of the room sat a small round table covered in a gold tablecloth with a single lit candle on it. Two empty chairs sat on either side of the table.

Kate smelled the air—the candle was definitely lavender-scented. She waited for close to a minute before she heard a small hissing sound. The room started to fill with smoke. Kate stood up and started to back away.

"Reporter!" a voice called from above her head. "Stay where you are!"

With some reluctance, Kate sat back down and quietly turned on her tape recorder.

"You are about to meet Madame Zora—the most powerful psychic in the world!" the voice said, and Kate noticed it had a vaguely British accent to it. "Be not afraid to look directly at her, for your heart will be filled with peace and you shall know contentment."

With that, a plume of smoke shot up in the center of the room and when it cleared there was a woman standing there, dressed in a brightly colored robe. She faced away from Kate.

"Why have you come?" Zora asked.

Kate coughed, waved away smoke from her face and tried to speak...

"I shall tell you why you have come," the woman continued before Kate could say anything.

"You have come to test the great Zora. You have come to see if she is a fraud."

"Actually, I ..." Kate started.

"Silence!" Zora shouted. "I know your heart. I know your fears. I know all."

With that, she started to slowly turn until she faced Kate, but Zora kept her eyes closed and her arms crossed in front of her chest.

"I will give you what you seek," Zora intoned. "I will tell you, Kate Tassel, that...."

At that moment, Zora opened her eyes...and stopped.

"Well, Jesus," Zora said and her body language changed dramatically. Her voice now had a slightly southern lilt to it.

"Hell, I'm sorry," she said and Kate felt her jaw beginning to drop. "I got all dressed up because I thought it was some reporter... and... well, crap."

She laughed and shrugged in a you-know-how-it-is way. Kate didn't get it.

Zora turned and pushed a button underneath her table.

"Lou Ann," Zora yelled at the table. "Lou Ann, get your butt in here!"

Zora gave Kate an apologetic look. Kate stayed silent, not sure what was going on.

A moment later, the teenage girl reappeared.

"Yes, Madame Zora," she said when she poked her head through the door.

"Why the heck did you tell me it was the reporter coming?" Zora demanded. "I got all dressed up, used my best show smoke and all. That stuff isn't cheap, Lou Ann. I've told you before you need to pay attention to who you are sending back to me."

Lou Ann looked guiltily around and then turned to Kate.

"But I thought you said..." Lou Ann said and looked plaintively at Kate.

"I am the reporter," Kate said, looking at Zora.

Zora looked stunned.

"But you're..." she said and her voice faltered. "You're the *Loudoun Chronicle* reporter?"

Kate nodded. Lou Ann looked briefly vindicated and shut the door.

Zora appeared flustered and sat down in her chair.

"I don't understand," she said, but Kate had the impression she was talking to herself.

"You were expecting me to come," Kate said, feeling a little defensive as if she was the one at fault.

"Yes, yes," Zora said and looked back at her. "It's totally my fault. Hell, that was impressive, though, wasn't it? My performance? I mean, I felt pretty 'on.' Did I feel 'on' to you?"

"It was..." Kate started. "Impressive?"

"Yeah, it felt pretty good. And now I blew it. And I think that was a really good one, too. Oh well."

"If you want I can go back out and you can start over," Kate said.

"No, no," Zora said and waved her hand. "It's done. No use crying over spilled honey."

"Don't you mean milk?"

"Well, aren't you Little Miss Literal?" Zora said. Then she sighed and leaned back in her chair. "I'm sorry to snap. It's been a tough day and I had really been hoping to wow you. I don't get that many new customers anymore. It's mostly the same people, with the same problems. You always want to jazz it up for the new people."

"Why did you think I wasn't the reporter?" Kate asked.

"Well..." Zora started. "I thought you were in the trade."

"The trade?"

"I thought you were another, oh hell, what's the latest term, 'alternative healer.' I just assumed really. It isn't often..."

Kate waited.

"No sense me prattling on," Zora said. "You can ask your questions. I'm not in the mood to give much in the way of answers, but we'll see what we see, I guess."

"Why would you assume I was in the 'trade'?" Kate asked.

"Honey, you got vibes coming off you like a freight train," she said.

The inner-editor in Kate noted that vibes do not come off freight trains, but she held her tongue.

"I still don't follow..."

"Your aura?" Zora said. "You got a psychic vibe coming off you. I'm surprised I didn't notice it until I saw you."

"What did you see?" Kate asked.

"You're psychic," Zora said.

"I'm not psychic," she replied.

"Well, I don't really care if you think you are or not. You are."

"Wouldn't I know?"

"Not necessarily, honey," Zora said and tapped her brightly-painted fingernails on the table. "Your aura—well, you got a lot of juice. That's all I'm saying."

"Okay," Kate said and scribbled in her notebook.

"Believe me or not, sweetheart," Zora said. "It's your call."

"Well, let's get started with the interview then," Kate said.

"You already turned on the tape recorder," Zora said. "I thought we had started."

Kate felt a little taken aback.

"I didn't think you noticed that," she said.

"I know all," Zora said and smiled. Her far left visible tooth was gold-capped. "Well, I suppose this would go better if I was in character, wouldn't it?"

"In character?"

"Okay," Zora said. "You see all this bulldiddly around me, right? The beads, the kewpie dolls, the scented candles? That's all a joke to you, right?"

"Well..." Kate said.

"It's okay," she replied and spread her hands. "It's a joke to me too. Even the smoke machine, though I really do think it's impressive. Had to order it special and everything."

"Then why..."

"Why do it?" Zora laughed. "Because that is what people expect. Believe me, when I started out in this business, I didn't want to be anywhere near this stuff. I thought I could remake how people saw psychics. But I was young and stupid."

"Why?"

"Because I didn't get any customers," she replied. "I went under my real name—Carol Cuthberson—and put out a helpful sign. This was the 1970s. I thought my power alone would keep me going."

"It didn't?"

"Heck, no," she replied. "You wouldn't believe it now, but in those days I was a looker. And all they saw was a pretty girl who told them some things they wanted to hear, but mostly stuff they didn't. I was right, and I knew it, but they didn't. They felt ripped off without the theatrics of the psychic scene. They had seen so many movies, even by then, that it didn't feel real to them without all the fake crap surrounding it."

"So you played along?"

"Eventually," Zora said. "I worked as a secretary right out of high school. I did the whole 9 to 5 work thing. And it wasn't for me. For starters, I got tired of knowing things I shouldn't, like who was real sick and probably going to get cancer and whose wife was cheating on them."

"You saw that psychically?"

"Saw is probably the wrong word," Zora replied. "But, yeah, I knew it. It was like a gut feeling. I have had it since I was a kid. Sometimes I just knew stuff. I found that the more I listened to that voice, the more I knew. Sometimes all it took was talking to the person, other times I would shake their hand. I used to amuse my girlfriends at Lincoln High by telling them all sorts of gossip. Nobody knew how I got it—and sometimes even I wondered if I was making it up. But this one time, I knew this girl called Colleen had slept with my best friend Jeanne's boyfriend. I told Jeanne and she cried a fit, denied it, and said I was a liar."

"What did you do?" she asked.

"I proved her wrong," Zora said. "I told her to wait by the girl's locker room on Thursday night and see for herself. And sure enough, she saw that little hussy getting it on with her 'loving boyfriend.' If I had a nickel for every time I knew about some adultery, I would be a rich woman."

"So you decided to take up being a psychic as a job?" Kate asked.

"I hated being a secretary," she replied. "Just hated it. I wanted to be my own boss. But I hadn't gone to college and this was the only talent I had."

"You opened your own shop," Kate said.

"I did, right on the outskirts of my hometown," she replied. "And I stayed away from the theater at first. I really did. But while being psychic is a talent, I figured out pretty soon it isn't enough. People want the theater. They need it. It's the same type of person that keeps going to Catholic mass when they don't believe a word of it. People like being mystified. They aren't going to take psychic advice from Carol from Keystone, West Virginia. But they will take the advice of Madame Zora—Psychic of the East."

With that, both Zora's countenance and voice changed. Instead of seeming tired and resigned, she now appeared regal and in command of the room.

"Let me tell you your future, Kate," she said, and Kate was blown away by the change. She seemed like a wholly different person. "Let me gaze through the sands of time and tell you what the goddess Fortuna has in store."

And as quickly as before, Zora slumped back into her chair and returned to her regular voice.

"Be honest—who would you believe? Me or Madame Zora?"

Kate smiled.

"Exactly," she said. "So I left Keystone, moved to Leesburg, and opened up this office here. The worst part about it is that so many people think you're a fake. They see all this bulldiddly and think, 'No way.' I get that. But you know what? Most of those people wouldn't believe me anyway. I've convinced plenty of people I was for real, but I'm not sure if it is the talent or the theatrics that does it."

"You seem somewhat irritated by that," Kate said.

"Do I?" Zora asked and sat up. "I'm not, you know. In a way, I've grown to like it a bit. It's like an actor must feel giving a real fine performance. When you see some people walk out of here, you can just tell their whole world has expanded. They believe, Kate. And I know I delivered it to them."

"But you know some of the stuff is fake?"

"Does it matter?" she asked. "They get the real stuff too."

Kate paused.

"How much of this are you going to want me to print?" she asked. "Surely, it won't help business."

"Sweetheart," Zora said and cocked her eyebrow at her. "You can print what you like. People see what they want to, anyway. And, not to break your heart, but I'm not too worried that the readers of the *Loudoun Chronicle* will have much effect on my business. There aren't that many."

Kate chuckled a bit.

"Maybe not," she said, smiling.

"I like you, Trina," Zora said and the color drained from Kate's face.

"What did you call me?"

"Are you okay?" Zora asked and a look of genuine concern was on her face.

"What did you call me?"

"Trina. That's your nickname, isn't it? I didn't really think about it..."

"It's not my nickname," Kate said evenly. She was flustered but let it go.

"Oh," Zora said. "That's odd. Well, maybe it's just an off day. First, my botched entrance and then..."

"Have the police ever used you?" Kate asked suddenly.

Zora leaned back in her chair.

"Oh," she said and put her hand to her lips. She then pulled idly at her ear.

"What do you mean, 'Oh?'" Kate asked.

"This is about him, isn't it?" Zora asked. "I'm sorry I didn't see it earlier."

"About who?" Kate asked.

"Honey, I know you think I'm a nutball, but you have to believe I really do have some talents. So, yeah, I see stuff others can't. For real. And the minute I called you that nickname, I could see it in my head."

"See what?"

"A press clipping. Of those murders 12 years ago. You are practically throwing it off in waves. I don't know why you care so much about it. I can't see that far, but I can see that."

Kate pushed back her chair.

"I ought to get going."

Zora reached across and grabbed her hand.

"Honey, you don't need to worry," Zora said. "If you don't want to talk about it..."

"I don't."

"Then we won't. There is no need to run away. I have the feeling there has been a lot of that already."

"Look," Kate said. "I like you, but don't think you know me, okay? I'm not some customer you can just snow over."

Zora leaned back again.

"I never thought you were," Zora said. "Well, not since I saw you at any rate."

The two sat in silence for a minute. Kate was unnerved and she felt like she had enough for a story anyway.

Zora took a large breath.

"You want to see the Tarot card bit?" she asked.

Kate nodded. As long as they weren't going to talk about her mother, she would be okay.

"Tarot cards are great little devices," Zora said. "I used to think they were crap. But I made the mistake everybody makes when they see these used. They think the cards somehow have power. And that is, of course, absurd."

"What then?"

"The cards are inanimate objects," she replied. "They have no power at all. But the people—the two of us, for example—have the power. My abilities and my read of the person affect how I shuffle the cards and subconsciously affect what I pull out. It's really quite simple."

"And the cards then tell the future?"

"Well, that's the other part," Zora said and smiled. "The cards don't tell you anything. It's all in the interpretation. And that is done by me. Someone with no talent will just randomly interpret. Maybe they will get lucky. Someone with a little talent even can start discovering fascinating things. If they trust their instincts, the cards can tell them many things."

"The future?" Kate asked and started writing again.

"Maybe," Zora said. "Do you want to see?"

Kate nodded with a slight hesitation

She watched Zora as she shuffled her way through the deck and laid them out on the table. She laid three in the center face down.

"This is just a test run, honey," Zora said. "You can do this with all different kinds of cards in all sorts of ways. I'm just going to do three from the Major Aracana."

With that, her voice changed.

"Now we shall see your destiny," Zora said in her British accent.

She flipped the first card.

Kate was a little surprised to see it was the Hanged Man. A man was suspended upside down from a tree, his feet tied up with rope. Kate had seen this card before—she remembered seeing a friend get her fortune told at the beach some years ago—but then the man had looked peaceful, as if in suspended animation. On this card, the Hanged Man looked in pain, as if he was struggling to get free but failing. His arms were tied behind his back and Kate could see a figure in the distance coming towards him. Whoever it was, the Hanged Man looked panicked about it.

"Strange," Zora said. She flipped the cards over and stared at it. "I use these cards a lot, but I don't remember seeing this version before."

"What does it mean?"

"Probably Lou Ann bought me the wrong pack," Zora said, but her voice sounded unsteady, as if she wasn't sure that was the case.

"All right, though, what does the card mean?"

Zora kept staring at it.

"Well, it can mean many things. Sacrifice, giving up, surrender, even passivity," she said. "But I don't think that's what this one means."

"I don't follow," Kate said.

"Everything is instinct. My gut says you're not the surrendering type and this card—this version of it—is about anything but surrender. I've never seen one like it. But the Hanging Man is also a doorway of sorts. He sees what others do not, from an angle they do not. In this case, he could be an opening to the Truth. To the mystical."

Kate wanted to look away and couldn't. The image bothered her more than she wanted to admit, particularly the look on the Hanged Man's face.

"Isn't he supposed to be peaceful?" she said.

"In every other card I've seen, he is," Zora said, looking up at Kate. She couldn't be sure, but Kate thought Zora looked a little bit frightened. "This card isn't like the others. It's about a journey, one that may be quite painful for you. But it clearly denotes the start of something, something that will look like one thing but be another."

"Like a friend who isn't a friend?" Kate asked.

Zora nodded. "Or something that seems good, but isn't. Or the reverse. The Hanged Man sees things in a different way—he sees what's real."

"He looks like whatever he sees is terrifying him."

"Let's just move on to the next card."

Zora drew carefully from the deck this time, as if she wasn't quite sure she wanted to. With some hesitation, she put the card on the table.

Kate didn't need an interpretation. At a glance, she knew the card: The Devil. A horned, giant beast stood in the middle of the card, holding a trident in one hand and extending his arm to two human figures below him. There were a man and a woman on the card, both naked with horns of their own.

Kate looked up. "If this is a joke, it isn't funny," she said.

But Zora seemed more unnerved than she did.

"The Devil can also mean many things: ignorance, stupidity, prejudice and pessimism," Zora said. "But I think this one is about something else too. It's about sex."

Kate took a look at the card. The human figures weren't looking at the Devil—not even a little bit. Instead, they seemed to be staring at each other with a look of raw desire. Kate wasn't sure how the artist could show it in such detail, but now that she looked at it, it was obvious the two wanted to have sex. And not the kind you see in the movies, or at least not the films she watched. These two people wanted to get it on right there and then and if the Devil was watching them, she doubted they cared.

"Again, this version of the card is unique," Zora said, her voice still unsteady. "The Devil often indicates sexuality, but this is more obvious than on some. There is another thread here as well: obsession and temptation. One thing I know: sex will change everything."

"I'm not exactly a virgin," Kate replied.

"Doesn't matter," Zora responded. "This—whatever this is—is different. Is there anyone you're attracted to? A boyfriend?"

Quinn came unbidden into her thoughts. She had been about to say no, when an image of him popped into her mind. But she hadn't looked at him that way, had she? No, he was just a friend. Then why had she kissed him? Why was she thinking of him now?

"No," she said.

Zora was staring at her.

"I don't need to be a psychic to tell that you're lying," she said.

"It doesn't matter," Kate said.

"Not to me, it doesn't, but it matters to you," Zora said. "This is not your average relationship, that's for sure. If you move forward with this person—if you have sex with him—the world will never be the same."

Kate tried to smile, tried to laugh it off, but none of it felt funny. The more she thought about Quinn, the more she realized she was attracted to him. She was breathing faster, her pulse rate up. She licked her lips. It dawned on her that she was *very* attracted to him and that scared the hell out of her.

"Next card," she said.

Zora hesitated.

"I don't know that it's a good idea."

"Look, we've come this far," Kate responded.

Zora reached into the deck and pulled out the card. Kate noticed her hands were shaking. She already knew what the next card would be. She had known it all along.

The card showed a knight on a dirty, matted horse. The knight held a sword aloft and below him were the trampled bodies of kings, merchants and peasants. Women and children lay sprawled at his feet. The knight himself was a grinning skeleton.

"Death," Kate said. "Well, at least I know what this one means. Is it my death?"

Zora looked back at her. She suddenly seemed worn and very, very tired. Kate knew she wanted to lie, was almost sure she was going to.

"Maybe," she said. "Usually, the answer would be a straight no. I would tell you this is a symbol and nothing more."

"But not this time?"

"Honey, I've never seen these three cards together. The Hanged Man, The Devil and Death? That's a bad combination."

"I'm really missing why you get any return business."

"Do you think I would fake something like this?" Zora said, and her voice was back to having a southern accent. "How stupid do I look?"

"You could just be trying to frighten me," Kate said.

"There are two frightened people in this room at the moment," she said. "Believe me when I tell you that whatever you are into, it's some serious mojo. Truth, Sex and Death."

"Great, I realize the truth, have sex and die," Kate said. "Sounds like a slasher film to me."

"The death card may not mean *your* death," Zora said. "Typically it stands for the end of one cycle and the beginning of another. It's about transformation. Taken together, these cards show a major event in your future, one that could have massive ramifications."

"Including my death."

"Yes, that's a possibility," Zora said. "But there are others."

Kate sat in stunned silence. She looked at the three cards. The man hanging upside down, the couple staring at each other, and the skeleton on top of the horse.

Something gnawed at her about the death card, so she picked it up off the table. The message in the card was clear enough: death takes everyone—men, women and children, from nobility to serfs. The skeleton knight held a sword out in front of him and it was unclear if he had trampled his victims to death, or used his weapon.

There's something familiar in this, Kate thought. But she couldn't quite place it. An image that was similar, but not quite right. It was on the tip of her tongue when she noticed a word written on the sword. The letters were hard to see and Kate had trouble making it out.

"What's this?" she said and pointed to the sword.

Zora took the card from her and stared at it. She reached behind her desk and pulled out a pair of glasses. If you ignored the outfit, she looked like a librarian. Zora examined the word carefully.

"Sanheim," she said finally.

Kate nearly grabbed the card out of Zora's hands.

"I know that word," she said, and felt like the room was starting to spin. She had seen it written in the bathroom mirror just the other day. Then it had disappeared. And hadn't she seen it before that? A memory flashed in her mind. Her mother was dead on the bed beside her and she was holding the phone. Lord Halloween's note was below her. But instead of saying, "Happy Halloween," or anything else, it just had one word: "Sanheim." She must have seen it in her dreams.

"What does it mean?" she asked. "What's Sanheim?"

Zora stared at her.

"Sanheim was the Celtic God of the Dead. It's also a festival celebrated by thousands every year."

"I've never heard of it," Kate responded.

"Not under that name. But believe me, you know it. It's the festival the early Christians renamed when they came to convert the Irish. They started calling it All Hallow's Eve."

"Halloween," Kate said under her breath. "Sanheim means Halloween."

Zora disappeared into the back for a moment and left Kate staring at the card.

"This is about him, isn't it?"

Zora shook her head.

"I don't think so," she said.

"Come on. I get a death card with the word 'Halloween' on it and it isn't about Lord Halloween? What are the odds of that?"

Why does everything come back to him? Kate fought down an urge to run. She didn't believe in divination—not really—but this was her worst nightmare in card form. She had always feared she would die at his hand and this appeared to bear that out.

"Only in Loudoun do they connect Halloween automatically with that guy," Zora said. "It's a celebration that goes back centuries, far beyond the written history we have of it."

"You can't deny it's a strong coincidence."

"But it may just be that, Trina," Zora said, and Kate winced again at the nickname. "I told you before, everything about being a psychic is instinct. When I first called you Trina, I knew from your reaction that there was something about Lord Halloween in your reaction. I still don't know what, but I just felt it. It's the same here—this card isn't about him. His fate may be tied up with yours—I have a hunch it has to be—but nothing here says he's going to kill you."

Kate pushed back from the desk.

"I think I've seen enough in any case," she said.

She flipped off the recorder and stood up.

"Don't leave like this," Zora said. "I'm sorry."

Kate didn't say anything. She was shaken, and badly. Suddenly, nothing seemed too far-fetched. Could Zora be working with Lord Halloween? Is this all a trick to make her more panicked, more afraid?

"I'm not working with him," Zora said, as if she had read her mind. Maybe she had, but Kate didn't care.

"You had better not be," Kate said, and there was venom in her voice. "If I find out you are, God help you."

Zora held up her hands. "I'm not your enemy," she said. "I have a feeling that would be a very bad position to be in."

Kate nodded and turned to walk out.

"There's one more thing you should know," Zora said.

"I'm done listening to this," Kate said.

"The spelling—it's wrong."

Kate paused as she began to head for the door. She almost turned around.

"What spelling?"

"The name on the sword here is Sanheim," Zora said. "The Celtic God of the Dead is spelled Samhaim, similar sounding, but different."

"What does that mean? Maybe somebody forgot to spell check."

"I don't know what it means, Kate. But everything here means something."

With that, Kate walked out the door.

Zora sat at her desk after Kate had left. She had seen more than wanted to admit. A dead woman, lying on a bed. While the cards weren't about Lord Halloween, she had seen something else, too.

"He's coming for you, Trina," she said.

But only her kewpie dolls heard her.

LH File: Letter #5
Date Oct. 15, 1994
Investigation Status: Closed
Contents: Classified

Mr. Anderson,

Half of the month is gone and from my point of view, much of it was a waste. Where is the mass panic? Where is the fear? Where is the publicity? I've killed seven people. You've written about four. You didn't even mention the cop's wife! Do you not know about it? You're supposed to be a reporter, Anderson. I can't hand you everything on a fucking plate.

I can't do everything, Mr. Anderson, and I'm growing so tired of waiting. I've encouraged you, warned you, even threatened you, and I get no respect. Are some of the articles good? Yes, they are all I could ask for. But it's not enough. It's not close to enough.

I want speculation about me. Who am I? Why do I do it? Can the police catch me? All you have are straight-laced stories with no hint of speculation.

How are they supposed to fear me if they never really know who I am? I chose you, Mr. Anderson, because I thought you would give flight to this fantasy of mine. We would be partners. But you are no partner at all. You're just another parasite, another sign of the problem.

So I'm through treating you gently. Write about me the way I deserve, or victim #8 will be familiar to you. Very familiar.

Signed,

Lord Halloween

Chapter 11

This isn't a date, Kate thought. She sat having dinner with Quinn and trying to convince herself over and over. She could see he thought it was. After all, he had asked, and she had immediately said yes. She should have thought more about it, with Zora's predictions still hanging in the air, but she hadn't.

She didn't want to be left alone to think of those Tarot cards and the false psychic. So here she sat, eating bites of her pasta primavera and wondering if she had slipped from the frying pan to the fire. Hadn't those predictions been about Quinn? Shouldn't she be trying to stay away from him?

"So evidently I'm psychic," Kate said for lack of something better to say. Quinn had almost appeared content just to sit in silence. Ordinarily, she would have loved that trait. She hated people who had to have conversation every minute of every day. But not today. Today she was worried the silence would strangle her.

"Huh?" Quinn asked, not sure he had heard her right.

"That's what the great Madame Zora tells me, at any rate," she said and tried not to say it with any bitterness in her voice.

"Someone has to tell you that you're psychic?" Quinn asked. "I thought the point was that you just knew stuff."

"Yes, I thought so too," Kate said. "It's silly. The woman was... a fraud."

"Can't say I'm surprised. There are about a million stories about her in this town."

"She read my fortune," she said, and was horrified she was talking about this. She hadn't meant to bring it up, but it had just popped out.

"Riches, romance and fame?" Quinn asked.

"Truth, sex and death," Kate said.

"Your death?" Quinn asked, because he didn't want to ask about sex. Or, rather, he desperately did want to do so, but was worried that was the wrong approach to take on a first date. "And this woman gets repeat business?"

Kate laughed and it sounded forced to both of them.

"It's nothing," she said. "Like I said, a fraud."

"You don't sound too confident of that," Quinn said.

"Well, it was unnerving," she acknowledged. "It isn't every day someone tells me I'm going to die."

"I hope not," Quinn said. "That would get awful repetitive."

Kate laughed at that and this one came out sounding genuine. She liked him. Her mind flashed back to the pack of Tarot cards.

"How about you? What was your assignment?"

"Terry Jacobsen, the local ghost hunter."

"That sounds decent, right?"

"It was all right, if you believe in that kind of stuff. To be honest, it got a little technical for me. There's a whole theory behind ghosts, involving electromagnetic fields and living people as batteries. It felt a little like science class."

Kate was smiling now. The feeling that she had at Zora's was starting to fade. Now it felt like a bad dream. Cards don't tell the future and psychics aren't real. It's all just smoke and mirrors. There was no reason to let it get her worked up.

"Are there a lot of haunted houses in Leesburg?" she asked.

"He called it 'the most haunted town in America,'" Quinn replied. "He and his team have been to nearly every house or business in the main center of town. He even claims the *Chronicle* building is haunted."

The smile dropped from Kate's face. She had just been starting to enjoy herself. But now she could think of nothing but the vision she had seen in the printing press room.

"Did he say what part?" she asked.

Quinn looked concerned.

"I wouldn't take it too seriously. We probably have..."

"Did he say which part?"

"He just said the basement."

"Where the printing press is."

"Well, yeah, but..."

Quinn stared at her.

"Your vision," he said. "I didn't even think about it when he mentioned it."

"Well, it feels connected to me."

"Then there's one thing else you should hear."

"What?" she asked, and she hated herself a little for asking. She didn't want to know anymore. She wanted all of this to go away.

"When I said I had trouble believing that, the guy just smiled at me. He said there have been complaints from some people. People who work there late at night."

"Complaints about what?"

"I thought maybe people were just hearing the printing press. It can be quite loud and honestly late at night, it's very creepy."

"Complaints about what?" she repeated.

"I don't want to freak you out," he said.

"Quinn, today a woman in a gaudy Middle Eastern dress turned up the three worst Tarot cards you can get during a divination, using a pack of cards she didn't even know she had. I'm having constant nightmares reliving the murder of my mother,

"I have returned to the town of her death against all sane impulses and am constantly looking over my shoulder for a psychotic killer. Add to that a vision of a pool of blood in the workplace and I'd say I'm pretty freaked out already."

"Someone screaming," Quinn said, and looked down. "They hear the sound of someone screaming."

"Jesus," she said. "Then what I saw..."

"I don't know," Quinn said and shook his head.

"It's too weird to be a coincidence," she said. "I see a pool of blood near where a lot of people hear screaming. Something happened down there."

"Maybe," he said.

"Does the building have a history?"

He shrugged.

"I don't know," he said. "I've never looked into it. I hesitate to ask this, but..."

"What?" she said.

"Lord Halloween never killed anyone in that building, did he?"

"No," Kate replied. "I've read every case, believe me. There were three other victims around that area, but no body was ever found there."

"Then maybe it's not connected," he said. "The guy could just be making it up."

"I don't think so," she said. "Maybe it's unconnected, but I want to look into this a little more. I could use some help. You game?"

"What do you need?" he asked.

"Well, I've read the public file on Lord Halloween, but I've been thinking there has to be more."

"Technically, the case is shut."

"No one seriously believes Holober did it," Kate responded.

"My point is the case file should be all public," he said.

"Just my gut: I have a feeling some information was held back," she said. "Maybe there was another victim, someone who could have died in the *Chronicle* building. Or maybe there's something else, but we need help."

"Buzz," Quinn said. "He's obsessed with Lord Halloween: always has been. He might be able to help—at least point us in the right direction."

"Sounds like a plan," Kate said.

"I'll talk to him tomorrow," Quinn said.

*****

Philip Jackman stubbed his toe on a tree root and let out a brief cry. If the woman he was watching through her bedroom window noticed, she didn't show it.

Jackman quietly cursed himself and shook his foot to get rid of the pain. But all the while he kept his eyes on the woman in the window. She was just starting to undress. It was not quite a strip tease, but he felt like she was showing off for him just the same.

Jackman would wait until her light was off and then he might be able to get a closer look. Maybe get up real close to her bedroom window. If he was lucky, he could even find a way in.

He had done that a few times before. He had never gone far—usually something happened like a dog barked or a light came on. But it was just a matter of time before he made it all the way. If at first you don't succeed...

He wanted to watch her sleeping up close. And when she woke up, maybe she would want to do more than sleep. God knows he wanted more. And if she didn't...

Jackman caught his breath as the woman stood up and dropped her robe to the floor. From this angle—15 feet from the window—he could almost make out her....

And then he heard a voice behind him.

"So you're the infamous stalker," it said.

Philip jumped and whirled around. He grabbed beneath his jacket for his knife. Since he first started these little escapades more than six months ago, he had kept the sharp-edged Kelso knife with him. But he had never needed it before.

"Careful what you pull out there, compadre," the figure standing before him said.

But Philip didn't listen. He pulled the knife out and held it in front of him in what he hoped was an intimidating stance.

"Don't come any closer," he said. To himself, the voice sounded too high and weak, unsure of itself.

The figure in front of him laughed.

"You sure have a lot of experience with this, don't you?" he said.

"I've killed before," Philip said, and did his best not to sound nervous.

"Have you? Some little girl you've been watching undress through the window, perhaps? No, I doubt you went even that far."

The figure took a step closer.

"Stay back," Philip said and he fought down the urge to run. How was this going to end? Was he really going to kill this man? He supposed he had to. The police hadn't caught Philip yet and he had been out spying on people so many times he had lost track. He supposed if he was a murderer he could still escape their clutches.

The figure laughed again.

"You know, it's funny," he said. "I'll bet a lot of people think you are a monster. Someone who watches women in their boudoirs and then grabs himself some. And if they saw you here, waving that knife, they might actually be scared."

"That's right, they'd be scared," Philip said.

"Maybe," the figure said and his tone sounded almost thoughtful. "Just like most animals are scared of the wolf prowling in the darkness, waiting to prey on the weak. But what if the wolf met a bear? Do you think the bear would be scared?"

"Shut up," Philip said. "I'll cut you."

Philip was working up a plan. He thought just rushing the figure would be too obvious. It seemed better to feint in that direction and then come at him from the side. Or maybe he could still avoid a fight altogether. The guy couldn't have gotten that good a look at his face.

"I'm the bear, Mr. Stalker-Man," the figure said. "You might scare some people, but to me you are just more meat."

Should he move now, Philip wondered? Maybe get him while he was still talking? But he had the uneasy feeling the figure was just waiting for him to do something, like maybe he was goading him.

"And you are a distraction," the figure said. "I mean, I thought my little trick last week would put me back on the front page, but I have to give the police credit, they actually had a plan and carried it off. Good for them. It just makes things a little more challenging. But I like a challenge. Because killing people is just too damn easy."

"What the hell are you talking about?" Philip asked, feeling even more anxious. This guy wasn't right. Why wasn't he calling the police on a cell phone? Or shouting to the houses around him? Was he trying to act crazy? What was he waiting for?

"Just making talk," the figure said and laughed again.

It made Philip shiver.

"You've been in the papers too long," the figure said. "So I'm going to do you a favor. I'm going to put you in the papers one last time. The obituary column, to be sure, but maybe the police are smarter now. I didn't think so, but..."

Philip made his move. He tried to feint forward, but halfway through the move, his body seemed to go all the way forward. He just rushed the figure, slicing through the air in front of him and hoping to connect with something.

But then everything went wrong. He felt a fist connect with his face and then his knife was out of his hand. His arm was in blinding pain and Philip went down on the ground still firmly in the man's grip.

"God, you are pathetic," the figure said. "The weak preying on the weak. And now it's time to take you out of business altogether. But I'm a nice guy and since you have been so good in providing copy, I'm going to give you one final treat. That woman you've been watching in the window? How about if I introduce you?"

"You're hurting me," Philip said. He felt like his arm was broken. His eyes searched the ground for the knife. He had to do something.

"And you were what? Going to just pop me on the head with that little toy of yours?"

"I'm sorry... I'm sorry," Philip said.

"You really are an insult to any person who was ever branded the Stalker. I actually had high hopes for you, you know. I looked for you for two days and I thought you would be a little more worthy of the attention people paid to you. But you are not even a wolf. You're just a sheep. A pathetic perverted little sheep."

*****

Mary Louise Fanton wrapped her robe around her tightly and wondered if she should answer the door.

Who rings your doorbell at quarter to 11 at night? But whoever it was seemed quite insistent. She wished she had an intercom.

She quickly picked up the phone and dialed Sally, one of her best friends.

"Hello?" Sally said at the other end.

"Hi, it's me," Mary Louise said.

The doorbell rang again.

"Why are you calling so late, Mary, it's nearly..."

"I know," Mary Louise said. "But the doorbell is ringing."

"Who is it?"

"How should I know?" she asked. "I'm afraid to answer it. I thought I should call somebody..."

"Why?"

"In case, you know, it's that stalker or somebody," Mary Louise said.

"I don't think someone like that rings your front doorbell," Sally said.

Mary Louise was annoyed. She was feeling heightened anxiety and Sally sounded nothing more than bored.

"Go to the door and look outside," Sally said.

Mary Louise did, as the doorbell rang again, then sighed in relief.

"It's the police," Mary Louise said.

She opened the door.

"Ma'am, I need to use your phone," the policeman said.

"Sure," she said, and nearly dropped the phone when she saw that he was practically dragging a man in with him. "Oh my God."

"What is it, what happened?" Sally asked.

"I'm sorry, Ma'am," the policeman said. "I found this gentleman outside your premises spying on you. Unfortunately, he broke my radio when I detained him. I'll need that phone."

"I've got to go, Sally," Mary Louise said.

"Is everything okay?" she asked.

"Is that a friend of yours?" the policeman asked.

"Yeah," Mary Louise asked, and the policeman reached for the phone.

She handed it to him.

"Hello," he said into it. "Yes, ma'am, she's fine. This is Officer Kaulbach of the Leesburg Police Force. Your friend will be fine, I just need to use her phone. Then we are going to pay to put her into a motel until we make sure the area is safe. Our suspect might have been working with a partner."

He nodded and listened for a minute.

"Thank you, ma'am," he said and hung up the phone.

He practically threw the detained man into the house and then shut the door behind him. And locked it.

"Is this the stalker the paper has been talking about?" Mary Louise asked. The man on the floor appeared to be whimpering and cradling his arm.

"Yes, Ma'am, I think so," the policeman replied.

"And he was looking at me?"

"I found him right near your bedroom window," the cop said.

Mary Louise pulled her robe even tighter around her.

"Do you have a knife I can borrow?" the cop asked. "The suspect here dropped his."

"Sure," Mary Louise said, and then her voice faltered. "But why would you need a knife? Don't you just want to call for back-up?"

The cop started to laugh. All at once Mary Louise became uncomfortable. She looked carefully at his clothes and was disturbed that what she had taken for a uniform just appeared to be regular blue pants. And he was wearing gloves. She didn't think that was normal. But she had seen a badge...

"What's so funny?" Mary Louise asked.

"You," the cop said and pulled out the badge again. "Take a good look."

He tossed it to her.

Mounted on a nice looking leather case was a simple star. Above, in large letters, it said "To Protect and Serve." But the star itself looked plastic. And when she looked closely, she could see that letters had been scraped off. She read them closely.

"Does this say 'Deadwood Deputy'?" she asked.

"You can still see that, can you?" the cop asked.

"But why would you have a deadwood deputy badge if you were a real..."

Her voice dropped off.

"God, lady, how long did that take you?" the cop asked. He started to laugh again.

Mary Louise looked for the phone and saw it still in his hand.

She backed up.

"Don't run," the cop said.

Mary Louise turned and fled, intending to head for the kitchen and through to the back door. But she tripped over the other guy's body as she ran and fell to the floor.

She was grabbed from behind by a rough hand, who dragged her to her feet.

"What do you say, Ma'am?" the fake cop said. "Want to make the papers?"

137

*****

Quinn felt nervous as he walked Kate back to the hotel. It wasn't thoughts of serial killers or phantom horsemen that bothered him, however.

The last time he had walked her home, it had ended in a kiss. A brief one, yes, but that didn't matter. It had still been fantastic.

He felt more than a little stupid actually. In the midst of all this weird shit going on, what was foremost on his mind was still getting the girl.

Maybe it is always like this, he wondered. Life never really stops and waits for you. Or maybe he needed something to look forward to other than the grim prospect of angry bosses and psychotic murderers. Maybe.

"A penny for your thoughts," Kate said to him.

"I thought you were the psychic," Quinn replied.

She laughed.

"Let me see," she said. "You were thinking about your piece on the ghost hunter."

"Not quite," he said.

"Well, why else were you smiling?"

"I don't know," Quinn said. "Was I smiling?"

"A little. It made you look a little mischievous. It was cute."

"Well, cute is good," Quinn said.

They neared the hotel and walked in silence up to the door.

"You don't always need to walk me back," Kate said. "I can handle myself. Remember, my dad was a cop."

"I know," Quinn replied. "But the way I look at it, you and I are in this together, whatever the hell is going on. And it doesn't hurt to travel in numbers."

"Well, maybe I should be walking you home then," she said and smiled.

"Maybe next time," he said.

"Sure. And thanks."

"Anytime," he said.

The agony of the moment was nearly killing Quinn. A voice in his head was shouting for him to kiss her. Just move closer in and kiss her.

But he couldn't. A thousand what-if scenarios played in his head. What if she rejected it? What if she gave him the "Let's just be friends" speech? Or maybe he was most frightened by the prospect of her kissing him back.

You are not in high school anymore, Quinn O'Brion, the voice said. You are damn near 30 years old. It isn't like you haven't done this before.

And maybe that was it. He had done it before and look how it had ended. Sharon, the very old-fashioned Geraldine, and Meredith. All had started well and ended up...

"Goodnight, Quinn," Kate said, as she leaned in and kissed him on the cheek.

"Goodnight," he said.

She walked to the door.

Quinn walked home thinking dark thoughts about himself. Fortune favors the bold and he had run scared. She liked him, right? He liked her, right? It was a simple thing then to kiss her and see what happened.

But he wondered if the weight of the past was too much. Or was it something else? Was it that he felt so damned unstable lately—the nightmares, hearing horse-hoofs and constantly fearing what was around the corner?

I'm going crazy, he thought. *That can't be good for a relationship.* Quinn laughed out loud. That seemed to be a gigantic understatement.

It wasn't like he was the only one with baggage either. Her mom had been killed and she was out for revenge on a person who might or might not still be around. Granted, compared to him she appeared stable enough.

But what was he supposed to do? Just pretend he did not feel an attraction because he did not think this was a good time? Maybe that would be a smart thing to do, but it was not what he wanted to do. He needed some kind of positive sign on the horizon to keep him from giving up altogether—maybe that was true for her too.

We are afraid to be alone and scared of what happens if we're not. Hadn't he read that somewhere? Some English poet? Crowley—that was it. He only vaguely recalled the whole poem, but that line had stuck with him.

As he walked up to his own door, it came to him again:

We are afraid to be alone and scared of what happens when we're not.

It was too much. Maybe tomorrow would be a different kind of day. One where he didn't spend all day thinking about murderers and fictional ghosts.

Tomorrow will be different. The nightmare could end—the cloud above him might lift.

When Quinn woke up the next morning, he felt relaxed and ready to face the day. His optimism last night seemed to be right.

The nightmare had lifted.

But it had really only just begun.

Chapter 12

"Where will you find ghosts? Forget the cemetery. There are nothing but corpses there and believe me—those are very different from ghosts. By far the most common place to find spirits is in funeral parlors or battlefields. But it isn't the dead that cause them to reside there, rather the living. Most ghosts are nothing but imprints, a memory left behind that occasionally plays itself back. But those imprints are caused by the most powerful energy force in the universe—emotion. Enough of it in a concentrated place and there is no telling what might happen."
—Terry Jacobsen, "The Truth About Hauntings"

This is what it feels like to die.

His lungs were screaming for air, his legs begging him to stop running. Behind him there was a steady drumbeat of a horse rapidly gaining on him, one that was desperate for neither oxygen nor rest. In the still cold air, he could hear a ringing, the sound of a sword torn from its scabbard and held aloft. In a moment, it would begin its arc downward with a near-silent swish and its steel would rend his flesh. There is no escape, nor hope of it. He was finished.

Quinn couldn't stop his mind from racing even as he continued to run, despair filling him. He fought the urge to give up and kept running.

Just as the horse seemed to be on top of him, he darted suddenly to the right, jumping off the road and stumbling down the soft red clay that covered the hillside. Behind him, he heard the rider stop the horse briefly and turn.

Quinn kept himself moving as he came to the bottom of the hill. He dove into the forest, desperate to put distance between him and his pursuer. The trees were a thick knot of pines and as he ran he could feel their dead branches slicing into him.

He was cut, bruised and shaken, but he kept running. There was no time to stop, barely time to breath and he prayed he could find the right direction. He couldn't think with the sound of his heart pounding.

The moon's light was obscured through the dense forest, but Quinn pushed on toward what he thought must be north. North was the bridge and his only hope for safety.

Behind him, he heard the crash of the horse coming through the trees. Quinn didn't know how that was possible. He only moved forward, hearing the ever louder sounds of something large hacking its way through.

He chanced a brief glance back. He could make out a shape moving preternaturally fast toward him.

There had to be a way out. Quinn jerked himself to the left, crouching low to the ground to avoid branches. He tripped and his hand fell onto a large branch as he tried to stop himself from falling. He stifled a scream and kept running.

The bridge. He had to reach the bridge. He plowed on before reaching a small clearing in the woods. He looked behind him, but he didn't see anything. Worse, he heard nothing. The night was silent.

Where the hell was it? He tried to be quiet and just listen. But he could only hear the sound of his own breathing. There was nothing alive out here, only an endless parade of dead trees.

"Hey Quinn," a voice said.

Quinn screamed.

He had no idea where the voice was coming from. He looked around the clearing and saw nothing.

"Over here," the voice said, and it sounded like it was behind him.

He whirled around but there was nothing. Just the dark forest all around him, fencing him in. All of this felt familiar, very familiar, but something was wrong. He was supposed to start running toward the bridge.

He turned to leave.

"Please wait a minute, Quinn," the voice said, coming from behind him again.

He turned and this time there was someone. A man stood at the edge of the clearing. He was dressed in a black suit, as if he had been to a formal dinner. But Quinn could not take his eyes off the man's face. He had piercing blue eyes, which reminded him of someone. But the eyes demanded control. They demanded he pay attention.

The man came forward. Quinn tried to step back and found he couldn't move. This isn't right. I'm supposed to run for the bridge. The horseman is supposed to chase me. There is no man here.

"I am sorry to interrupt," the man said.

There was nothing wrong with the man's appearance. He shouldn't have been intimidating in the least. He appeared to be Quinn's height and approximate build. He looked older and his face bore a small scar. But Quinn was afraid. He was almost as anxious to run away from the man as he had been from the horseman.

"What do you want?" Quinn asked. He couldn't run, move, or even look away. He felt trapped.

"What do I ever want?" the man asked. "To make a deal."

"No," Quinn said. It was automatic, reflexive. There were no good deals with this man. He knew it in his soul.

"Come now, Quinn," the man said, and his voice was gently chiding. "You didn't hear me out."

"I don't need to," Quinn said. "This is just a dream."

"No, it's a nightmare, but I grant you your point," the man said and he continued staring at Quinn. His eyes bore right through him. "I'm not here to help with that."

"Then what's your deal?"

"Well, you will have to learn to deal with your *cennad* on your own," the man said, and Quinn had no clue what he was talking about. "I can't help you there, even if I wanted to. We all have to face our fears by ourselves."

"What do you mean? Who are you?"

The man waved his hand as if it was unimportant.

"Not the point and it doesn't matter, at least not yet," the man said. "I've come to offer help."

"Somehow I know I don't want help from you," Quinn said.

"Only because you aren't thinking clearly," the man said. "Let me tell you how it's going to go. If you leave now, you will wake up as you always do and remember nothing but the usual nightmare. And when Lord Halloween comes after you and Katrina, he will kill you."

"Are you Lord Halloween?" Quinn asked.

The man laughed at that, a full-throated belly laugh.

"No," he said. "I'm something much worse."

"Then why are you helping me?"

"Let's just say I've been in your shoes before," he said. "And I'd like to move this little game forward. As it is, I'm a little worried my two favorite players are going to be taken off the field before we can really get moving. Lord Halloween knows all about dear Trina, Quinn, and he knows you love her."

"Wait a second, I mean..." Quinn started. "I just met her."

The man shrugged.

"I know what I know," the man said. "And what if I told you she feels the same way? What if I told you she is right now having a dream about you—and it's not this kind of dream. She'll wake up blushing, I promise you that."

"How do you know this?"

"I know a lot of things, Quinn," the man said, and he began walking around him slowly in a circle. Quinn had no choice but to follow, slowly turning around him.

"Here's the deal," he said. "You won't remember much, but keep this in mind. Don't leave Trina alone, even while she sleeps. She doesn't think she trusts you, she will try to keep you away, but she is in grave danger. She isn't the only one, though. Lord Halloween will come for you first."

"Why?"

"Because it's his way. He has already been tracking you two and you have no clue who he is."

"Tell me, if you know," Quinn said.

"Oh, I know," the man said. "But as with our nightmares, there are some things you have to face yourself. I can't give the whole game away. I will give you a hint, if you accept my deal."

Quinn hesitated.

"What's the deal?" he asked.

Suddenly Quinn found he was free to move again.

"That's better," the man said. "A little bit more civilized, I think. Now you are ready to hear. Your only chance to beat Lord Halloween is by embracing what you are. You don't understand what I'm saying and that's okay. When the time comes, you will know. You are far more dangerous than your opponent. He is, at his core, just a man."

The man walked behind him now. Quinn looked up at the moon above and noticed its light wasn't white anymore. It had turned slightly red. A dark maroon moon hung over the sky.

"It's never been like this before," Quinn said.

"No," the man said. "And this is just the beginning. Lord Halloween is a man, but you are something else. Are you scared now?"

And Quinn knew he should be. He could still hear a horse out in the woods somewhere, waiting for him. But suddenly the horse didn't seem to be his enemy. It was calling to him. He could imagine being on the horse, riding through the black darkness, a blood moon guiding his way.

"That's it," the man said. "You can be so much more, Quinn. You can be the thing others are afraid of. You can be the nightmare that lurks in the shadows."

And Quinn felt power surge through him. Suddenly, he could sense everything around him. He could count the pine needles on the ground, hear the wind whistling through the branches, the worms in the earth. This was his time. The horse was coming for him, but not to harm him. To pick him up. To set him free. This was what he was born for.

"What do I have to do?" Quinn asked.

"It is your only chance to save Katrina, Quinn," the man said. "Embrace what you are, or I promise he will gut, torture and kill you both."

"What do I have to do?" Quinn repeated.

"Follow your instincts," the man said. "If you get another chance to kiss Katrina, take it. Don't hesitate. Face your fears. If you succeed, you will be offered a gift. Take it. It's not free, you will find that out in time, but it is yours to take. Use it."

"How?"

"You'll know when the time comes," the man said.

"What's in it for you?" Quinn asked.

The man smiled. It was a cruel smile, the smile of someone who has lived for centuries and watched countless innocents fall into darkness.

"Everything," he said, and that was the only explanation Quinn was going to get.

He shivered.

"I don't know," Quinn said. The urge to say yes had been overpowering, but he faltered. Whatever he was being offered wasn't free—the man had said so himself—and Quinn wondered if the price was too high. What he had experienced didn't feel like something good. It felt like a weapon, one that would corrupt him.

The man took a step forward.

"You don't have to make a decision yet, Quinn," he said. "All I wanted was for you to consider the deal. And understand this: there is no other way to save her than to take what will be offered to you. If you don't want her to die like her mother, this is the only way."

Quinn knew he was being manipulated. How many sources did he work with that tried to push you in a certain direction? This pitch was as subtle as a brick to the head.

"What's your hint? How do I find him first?" Quinn asked.

The man looked at Quinn a long time and he looked satisfied.

"Not every victim of Lord Halloween is among the dead, Quinn," he said finally. "Your girlfriend is one, but there are others. Look for the one that he trusted."

The man turned to walk away.

"Wait," Quinn said. "That's not enough."

Without turning back, the man headed into the forest. Before he disappeared, he said one more thing. "Look for the one like you."

Then he was gone, leaving Quinn standing in the forest. He looked at the moon. Had he thought it was red? It was now just a pale orb hanging in the sky. Quinn shook his head. Had he been talking to someone? Where was he?

He heard a sound in the darkness, a horse neighing. Then he remembered. The horseman. He had to run, he had to get out of here. But he paused on his way out of the clearing.

He couldn't shake the feeling that something different had happened, something new.

It didn't matter. The road was ahead. He had to make his way back. He had to reach the bridge, or die trying.

He moved closer to a patch of moonlight and saw that it looked like a way out of the forest—a break in the trees and then a hill beyond. He moved silently towards the clearing. He paused and looked around him. Nothing stirred.

When he moved into the light, he could see the road lay in front of him. Emerging carefully, he glanced in both directions looking for any sign of the horse. But there was nothing, except long shadows cast by the moonlight.

He could stay here, but it was possible the Horseman had gone back. Maybe now was his only chance. He knew the bridge was to his right. It couldn't be that far. With an effort, staying close to the forest on the far side of the road, Quinn started jogging as quietly as he could.

With every step, he started to feel better. The overwhelming presence of his pursuer was gone—that feeling like somehow he was just behind him out of sight. Maybe he would be free this time. Maybe he could reach the bridge.

He saw it now, far down the road. It was approximately a half-mile away—a few minutes, he thought. That's all I need, Quinn thought, a few minutes.

He gathered up his remaining energy and started to run. It was a dead run, with all the energy he could manage. With every step, the bridge was closer.

That's when it happened. The pounding of hoof beats exploded out of the forest behind him. Quinn didn't dare look, he just kept running. Somewhere behind him he could hear the horse kicking up the clay as he pounded his way toward the bridge. A dark hollow laugh echoed high above the trees and Quinn's blood ran cold.

One minute, he thought—I'm so close this time.

But he knew he wasn't going to get it. The horse's gallop sounded ever closer, a noise that was pounding into his brain with every step. The laugh rang out again as Quinn stumbled.

The horse was on top of him. Quinn could hear the blade come out of the Horseman's sheath. Could hear it positively ringing in the cold fall air as it began its stroke. And Quinn knew where it would be aimed. He could almost feel the blade as it approached his neck.

He could see the bridge, only yards away. But he wouldn't make it.

Quinn knew he was a dead man.

He knew what it felt like to die.

When he woke up, he was screaming.

*****

Friday, Oct. 13

Quinn came in early in the morning and was again one of the first in the office. He felt tired and worn down but forced himself to start working. It was the only way to get his mind off the nightmares. He checked off several ideas on his agenda. He had to keep following up the Kilgore murder, had to write up that piece on Terry and...

Talk to Buzz, he remembered. See if Buzz could think of anything that happened in the *Chronicle* building.

After a moment, he found a note stuck to his desk keyboard.

"Don't forget about the dog story," it read.

Quinn crumpled it up and threw it in the trash. He didn't even look at the signature—a loopy giant H. The dog story? He had written the lead of the paper this week and Helen was still forcing a story about dog shit. It was enough to drive you nuts.

He was also surprised to find his voicemail light blinking. Surely Helen hadn't decided to leave a voice message as well?

But it wasn't Helen. Instead it was a message from an old source of his asking for a meeting.

Quinn wondered what it meant. Why was Dee calling him now?

He would have to wait until school was out to go meet him, so he spent the remainder of the day working on his Terry story and making calls to find an update on the Kilgore case.

He barely saw Kate, who came in before lunch, but then was off again. Janus told him it was for some profile that Laurence wanted.

At about 2:00 p.m., Quinn left to head over to Loudoun County High School.

Janus grabbed him on the way out.

"You need me to come?" he asked.

"Nah," Quinn said. "A source asked for a meeting. Don't know what it's about. I'll be back in a minute."

Quinn shook his head as he walked down the stairs and out the back door of the building, glancing into the printing press room as he passed by.

He arrived at Loudoun County High School near the edge of town five minutes later. He tried to imagine what it would have been like to go there, but couldn't. The building was smallish and dull-gray, with a football field and bleachers not far behind it. It had little to distinguish it from countless other schools.

Quinn walked around the edge of the parking lot and entered a back door. Technically he wasn't supposed to go into the high school, not after the story he had written last summer about its growing marijuana problem. But he also had recently written a glowing profile of the policeman on duty at the school and figured that would ease any complications that might arise if he were caught. It was also after school hours and he thought it unlikely anyone would spot him.

Dee was in the appointed place.

"What's up?" Dee said, leaning against a locker near a science lab.

"You called and I came," Quinn said. "How have you been?"

"I've been all right," Dee said. "But I've got something to tell you. It's important."

Quinn nearly laughed. Dee somehow always had a serious look on his face, like any minute the sky was going to collapse on top of him. Quinn liked him, but it was damn hard to take the kid with anything but a grain of salt.

"Sure, what is it?" Quinn responded.

"Not here, man," he said and gestured inside an empty classroom.

Quinn sighed. This was probably a waste of time. When they got into the room, Dee shut the door.

"I can't be seen talking to you," he said.

"The marijuana article was over a year ago, Dee," Quinn replied, smiling. "I'm sure they've forgotten about it."

"No, it isn't that," Dee said. "They haven't forgotten about it either, but that ain't the point."

"Then what is?" Quinn asked.

"I know something about that murder," Dee said, still looking nervously at the door.

"Mary Kilgore?" Quinn said, suddenly taking the entire conversation a lot more seriously.

"Yeah, the chick from Middleburg," Dee said.

"What do you know, Dee?"

"Like who killed her, man," he said.

"Everybody knows that," Quinn said. "The police arrested her husband."

"It wasn't him, man," Dee said. "No way it was him."

"Look, Dee, just calm down and level with me. What the hell are you talking about?"

"I saw him," Dee said. "Two weeks ago. Jacob and I saw him."

"Saw who?"

"The guy who killed that woman," Dee said. "He was dressed up, but I'm sure it is the same guy. I'm sure of it."

"How do you know he did it?"

"Shit," Dee said. "I've seen some weird things in my time. But I saw this dude try to take Jacob's head off."

Quinn was lost.

"Just tell me what you saw," Quinn said. He wasn't sure if Dee knew anything at all, but the kid was obviously nervous. He sure thought he had something.

"Jacob and I were out near Purcellville the other week," Dee said.

"When?" Quinn asked him.

"A week ago Saturday, I think," he said.

"You were scoring some dope?" Quinn asked.

"Shut up!" Dee said fiercely, looking at the door. "These walls aren't exactly soundproof."

"Sorry," Quinn said.

"Yeah," Dee muttered. "We were out there, doing business, when we heard something coming. We couldn't tell what it was at first."

"Where were you?"

"Out along Gallows Road near..." Dee said, looking irritated by the interruption.

"A good place to stay out of the way," Quinn said.

"Yeah, yeah," Dee replied. "We thought maybe it was a cop, or something. We didn't know what to think. Then I figured it out—it was a guy on a horse. You could hear the sound all around you, man. It sounded like it was hell bent for leather."

"A horse?" Quinn asked and felt his throat constrict. Almost immediately, his palms started to sweat. Dee didn't notice.

"It was a horse all right," Dee said. "You could see him coming down the road, riding like the wind."

"Could you see who it was?" Quinn asked.

"Are you kidding, man?" Dee asked. "It was the dead of night—and you see some crazy fucker riding straight at you. How likely is it you're going to get an ID?"

"What was he dressed like?"

"Dressed like?" Dee asked, his face knotted up in frustration. "You aren't getting it."

"Getting what?"

"Let me finish my goddamn story and you will," he replied. "It was like nothing I've ever seen, man. The rider had this huge cape and the horse looked... demonic, you know? I could see his red eyes staring right at me. I thought for sure I was going to lose my head."

"You panicked?" Quinn asked, growing more uncomfortable by the second.

"No, I mean it literally," Dee replied, looking straight at Quinn. "This dude had no head. He was dressed like the Headless Horseman. You know, the one in that movie?"

Quinn felt like he had been punched in the gut. His throat closed in and he had trouble pulling in oxygen. He nodded only briefly as Dee continued.

"He just ran right past me, but I thought I was a goner," Dee said. "I was seriously toast."

"Jacob?" Quinn croaked.

"Jacob was fine," Dee replied. "But I think the guy may have tried to take a swipe at him. He was so close, it looked like he ran through him. Jacob shit himself, I know that. But he didn't lose his head."

Dee stopped and looked at Quinn strangely.

"You feel okay, man?" he asked. "You look like you're going to be sick."

"I'm fine," Quinn managed, still feeling like his head was spinning. "What did you guys do?"

"Do?" Dee asked. "Jesus, man, what do you think we did? We ran like hell after he left."

"So you didn't see where he went?"

"We didn't exactly stick around to find out what the hell was going on."

"Then what makes you think this horseman killed anyone?"

"What makes me think it?" Dee asked. "Christ, man, I thought you were smart. You asked all those questions when you wanted to do your dope story, made the school look bad.

"You seemed pretty crafty. Where is your head now? Stuck under a rock? When a dude dresses up like the fucking Headless Horseman and then somebody dies with their head no longer attached to their body, it doesn't take a genius to put two and two together, you know?"

Quinn still felt short of breath.

"But maybe it was the husband..."

"Maybe, if he liked to get all dressed up," Dee shot back. "You telling me there is some killer out there *as well as* some motherfucker dressing up like a ghost? Because I'm not sure what bothers me more. The idea that some son-of-a-bitch is out there taking people's heads off, or the fact that he is just one of two psychos in the area. It's the same guy, man. It has to be."

"Why haven't you gone to the police?" Quinn asked.

"Oh, well, I'll just go fucking do that, won't I? 'Hey, Sheriff Brown, you know when I was buying drugs from your son, he and I just happened to see some whacked out motherfucker dressed up like a guy from that Johnny Depp movie?' I'm sure they would give me a fucking medal for that, don't you think?"

"I see your point," Quinn replied, reaching in his head for something intelligent to say. But all the knowledge had been sucked out somehow. One line kept repeating itself: The dream is real. The dream is real. You thought you heard him the other morning. You were right. He's real. The Headless Horseman is real.

"Jacob hasn't talked about it, man," Dee said. "I wasn't going to mention it again, but after the murder... I tried to get him to speak up, maybe say something to his Dad. But he..."

"Jacob's a shit," Quinn said. "He doesn't give a damn about anybody but himself."

"Amen," Dee said.

"I should have printed his name when I had the chance," Quinn said to himself.

"You did that, you wouldn't be in this county anymore. They would have run you out. You were cool, man. You had to play it cool. You know I appreciate that. My guys did too. If our names had been in the paper... Anyway, you have to pull your head out of your ass on this one. Because there is some serious freaky shit going down."

"More than you know, Dee. More than you know."

"Seriously, you look like you need a doctor," Dee said.

"It's nothing."

"Look, I don't want Jacob to know nothing about this," Dee said. "But I felt like I had to tell somebody."

"Thank you, Dee," Quinn replied. "I really appreciate it. I do."

"Do you?" Dee asked. "You look more sick than excited."

"Let's just say you caught me off guard," Quinn replied.

"But you believe me, right?" Dee asked.

"I believe you, Dee. I wish I didn't, but I do."

"Good," he said. "Look, I've got to split. I'm done with this, okay? I told you, my conscience is clear. So don't have no cops show up and ask me about it, okay?"

"It's off the record, don't worry," Quinn said.

"Alright man," Dee said and shook his hand. Two seconds later, he was out the door.

Quinn sat down in one of the chairs. He needed to think. Someone had actually seen the Horseman. He couldn't believe it. Although Dee was a pot smoker, he wasn't a liar and wasn't inclined toward making stuff up. During the whole weed story, he had been one of the few reliable sources of information.

Quinn put his head in his hands and stared at the desk. So it was real. The dreams had been forecasting something, just as he feared.

A voice from the darker part of his mind piped in: What did you think was going to happen? Did you honestly believe it was going to go away? That it was all in your head?

He hadn't, Quinn realized. He had felt this sense of dread all month and it had been increasing every day. When he heard about the murder, it only confirmed what he had seen coming all along.

Hadn't he slipped up and said something about the Horseman to Gary when he called? But he hadn't connected the Horseman with the killing. Maybe it was that serial killer or maybe someone who knew the woman. But he hadn't thought of it. It was just a dream. But what if it wasn't? Quinn kept wondering what he was going to do.

The Headless Horseman was riding in Loudoun. His nightmare was real.

*****

Kate came back to her desk, sat down and sighed. She loved being a reporter, but she wondered how she was going to turn that particular business story into a good profile. It bored her, it bored Josh in photography. She had to face it—it was just boring.

She looked around the room for Quinn to commiserate with, but only Alexis and Helen appeared to be there.

With a start, she realized that her voice message light on the phone was blinking. She had not noticed.

She picked up the phone and dialed in. The voice on the other end surprised her.

"Trina, this is Sue Redacker," the woman said and Kate bristled at the sound of her old nickname. "Johnny needs to talk to you. He said as urgently as possible. But he was a little worried to leave a message himself."

Mrs. Redacker named a time and place and Kate started to worry.

Since she had pressed Johnny Redacker for information, she had begun to wonder more about him. At first she had trusted his intel about the Kilgore murder, but the more she thought about it, it felt wrong. He had so many details about the case—almost as if he had been waiting for someone to ask.

One hour later, she pulled up in Quarry Park near Ashburn Village. Clearly he had picked the spot because it was remote—very few people came here because it was off the beaten track.

Johnny was waiting in his car when she pulled up.He got out and they shook hands formally. This was the first time they had actually seen each other in years and he seemed to be appraising her.

"Your father told me you had turned into a beautiful woman, but I thought he was just giving the usual proud Dad speech," Redacker said after a minute.

"Dad has been known to exaggerate," Kate said.

"Well, not about that," Redacker replied.

"Thank you. So, what's up? I assume this is not a social call."

Redacker shook his head.

"Look, you have to understand that I thought I was telling you the truth," he said.

"About Mary Kilgore?"

"Yeah," Redacker said. "I would never have deliberately lied to you, but..."

His voice trailed off. Kate looked over the park area, which felt bare. It was just a field and a few benches.

"But what?" she said.

"Look, they were quite clear," he said. "Brown called the guys in and told us what had happened—about Don Kilgore and the marriage troubles.

"How the arrest was going to take place. He said there would be rumors floating around, that maybe it was something else..."

"Someone like Lord Halloween," Kate said.

"He didn't say that exactly, but that was the gist," Redacker said and glanced around nervously. "He said we should tell anyone—anyone—who asked all about Don Kilgore. He said he didn't care if that got out, but he didn't want any false rumors going around."

"And you weren't suspicious?"

"Of course I was," Redacker said. "I'm no rookie. It's just— he was so adamant. Said he wanted to keep everyone in the loop. I knew something was wrong with it, but I never thought..."

"You never thought he would lie?" Kate asked. "Come on..."

"I know, I know," Redacker said and sat down at one of the benches. "I know it seems stupid. But it isn't like it used to be in the old days. And when you called..."

"You didn't know if you could trust me?" Kate asked.

"Maybe that was it," he said and shook his head. "It just caught me off guard. And I didn't know what to say. All I had was a vague feeling of unease. I didn't know anything specific."

"And now you do?"

"There is no case against Donald Kilgore," he said. "Brown must have known it. The marriage problems were real enough, but the guy was half-way across town with another woman at the time of his wife's death."

"And you know that?"

"Not officially," he said. "But there is no way the case against Kilgore will stand up in court. Some of the stuff we gave your reporter, it wasn't... It wasn't for real. I'm pretty sure Stu made some of it up."

"Jesus," she said. "That could get him fired. False arrest, falsifying documents..."

Redacker waved his hands in the air.

"Do you think that matters?" he said. "You'll never nail him down. Who gave the reporter the documents? Would he turn his source in? Stu isn't a brilliant guy, but he is far from stupid. If you try and come after him, you won't get far."

"Why the deception?"

"I think you know."

"I need you to tell me," Kate said. "This isn't something to just assume."

"We don't know anything for certain," he said.

"Just tell me what you do know," she said.

"Mary Kilgore? Let's just say she didn't seem like she was murdered in the heat of passion."

"Give me details," she said.

"Look, I don't think..."

"Details," Kate said.

Redacker put his hands up.

"Don't say I didn't warn you," he said.

"Consider me warned."

"She was killed slowly," he said and looked away from her. "Whoever did it had at least basic medical training and knew how to cut someone without killing them. The doctor couldn't be positive, but all indications are that he started cutting while she was still alive and conscious."

"Jesus," she said.

"I'm sorry," he said.

"Sorry that I know the truth?" she asked. "I asked you. Goddammit, I asked you if it was him. And you lied straight to me."

"Kate, it wasn't that simple," Redacker said.

"It seems that simple to me," Kate said.

"We still aren't sure it is Lord Hal..."

"Bullshit!" she said and stood up. "How can you sit there like that? One person is dead. I don't know where he has been or what he has been doing, but he is back. I knew it."

"You can't know that," he said. "Your dad and I think it was really Holober. This could be a copycat."

"It's not," she said.

"You don't know," Redacker replied.

"I feel it, Mr. Redacker," she said. "Call it an intuition or superstition, but I feel it. And you do too. You don't believe this for a second. I know you don't. I doubt my Dad does, either. But you are so anxious to fool each other and yourselves..."

"Maybe that's why I told you what Brown asked us to," he said. "I just..."

"You don't want it to be true," she said and looked across the field. A cold wind blew across it—she crossed her arms and shivered. Winter was coming, you could feel it in the air. "Did you find a note?"

"Brown and Stu said Donald Kilgore was just trying to throw us off the track," he said. "He was trying to make it look like Lord Halloween."

"Do you think that's true?" she asked.

He paused. "No," he said.

"What did it say?" Kate asked.

"I don't know," Redacker said.

Kate turned and stared at him.

"Mr. Redacker, I need to know I can trust you," she said. "I don't have many allies here. And I can't trust you if you keep lying about this. I know you are trying to protect me, but you can't. I'm older. I chose to come back here, remember?"

"Why? Your dad would freak..."

"You can tell him what you want, but you're right, he would freak," she said. "But I'm not leaving. Things are just getting started."

"But that's crazy. You don't need to be here. If the guy is out there, we will catch him," Redacker said.

"You didn't before," she replied.

"You know we tried," he said.

"But it didn't really cut it, did it?" Kate said. She felt her fingers twitch and gritted her teeth. "I need to know I can trust you. Can I?"

"Yes," he said, but he put his head down.

She wondered when the change had happened. Kate had always looked up to her father and her father's friends. They had seemed so strong and commanding when she was young. Now Redacker appeared old and frail.

"Then tell me what the note said," she said.

He lifted his head.

"It didn't say much," he said.

She waited for him to continue.

"It was a small post-it note on her chest," Redacker said. "It said, 'Did you think I would stay away forever? I will be making up for lost time. LH.'"

"That's it?"

"That's it," he said.

"Not very frightening," she said.

"He had it attached to her with a carving knife," Redacker said.

"Any prints?"

"What do you think?"

"He never left any before," she said. "He seemed familiar with police procedure."

"Exactly," Redacker said.

"And you really believed it was Donald Kilgore? That he stuck a knife through his wife's chest?"

Redacker looked down.

"Is that it?" she asked. "Is that all?"

"That's all I know now," he said. "I..."

The radio in his car squawked for a moment.

"Hang on," he said and walked back to his vehicle.

"Yeah, I'm out in Ashburn now," she heard him say. "Yeah, I can head over there. No problem. Five minutes."

He walked back to her.

"I've got to go," he said. "I'm sorry about before. And maybe we're wrong..."

"Just be honest with me," she said. "If not for my sake, then for my mother's."

Slowly he nodded.

"Okay," he said. "I promise I'll do the best I can."

"What's your call?" she asked.

"Not sure," he said. "Some lady wants us to check out her friend's house. She said her friend was visited by the police last night and she hasn't been able to talk to her since."

"Was she visited by police?"

Redacker shrugged.

"I'll check it out," he said. "Usually it turns out to be nothing. I should get over there. Are we okay?"

"Yes," she said. "Just remember your promise."

"I will," he said and walked back to his squad car.

She watched him go. She idly brushed her hair out of her face. She would have to go back to work soon. But she saw her hands were shaking.

Now she knew. Suspecting was one thing, but now that she knew, it felt all the more real. But what had she expected?

It was irrational, but she knew it wouldn't be long before Lord Halloween figured out who she was. He had a county filled with people to target, but Kate would be on the list, she was sure of it. So she wasn't going to wait around for that to happen. She had to find him before he could find her.

Chapter 13

Saturday, Oct. 14

Quinn was startled by a loud pounding on his door. He glanced at the clock. It was barely past 5:30 a.m. The pounding became more insistent.

He got up and moved cautiously to the door, wearing only his boxers. He was not sure what to expect. Maybe it was Janus or Bill with some story.

He had no peephole at the door and briefly wondered what to do.

"Who is it?" he called out.

The pounding stopped.

"It's Kate," a voice came back.

Quinn opened the door and she walked in.

"Get dressed," she said, practically ordering him. She breezed past him and went into the kitchen. "You have any coffee?"

"What's going on?" he asked.

"Something bad," she replied. "Throw on some clothes. We need to get moving before time runs out."

"Should I call Janus?" he asked.

She thought briefly about it for a moment.

"You might want to," she said.

"Do I have time to shower?" he asked.

"No," she said simply and opened the refrigerator. "Can I have this Mountain Dew?"

Quinn waved at her to do what she wanted. He was so tired he forgot to be embarrassed about his lack of clothes.

Instead he stumbled back into his room and pulled on jeans and a long-sleeved shirt. He brushed his teeth, but didn't even take the time to comb his hair.

He came back out to the kitchen.

"Where are we going? Jesus, have you already had the whole thing?"

Kate appeared to be holding a nearly empty bottle of soda.

"Anxiety makes me thirsty," she said.

"Yeah, and all that caffeine should really calm you down."

Quinn picked up the phone and dialed Janus, who answered like he had been awake the whole time.

"What's up?" he asked.

Kate gave Quinn directions, who relayed them to Janus. Then the two of them were out the door.

"I got a call from my source," she said as they walked to his car.

"Who is?" he asked.

She didn't answer.

"Jesus, Kate," Quinn said. "Are we on the same side or not? It can't be a state secret."

"Johnny Redacker," she said.

Quinn whistled.

"He's pretty high up in the department," Quinn said. "He might have even been sheriff if it hadn't been for that incident in Stone's Creek."

"I know," she said.

He started driving.

"Before I get there, can you tell me what is going on?" he asked.

"I'm not sure," she said. "But we had a talk yesterday. He admitted the Kilgore murder wasn't done by her husband."

"Shit," Quinn said. "I'm not shocked, but still. Is it something we can use?"

"You know, I didn't even think about the paper," she said. "I was more worried about me."

"Okay," he said. "But that still doesn't tell me why we are heading out before 6 in the morning to a house in Leesburg. Who lives there?"

"A woman named Mary Louise Fanton," she said. "Evidently she disappeared Thursday night."

"A victim of the Horseman?" Quinn asked.

"The who?" Kate said and looked at him funny. "The Horseman?"

Quinn shook his head.

"Sorry, never mind," he said and wiped his face with his hands. "It's early. I meant Lord Halloween."

Kate continued to stare at him for a moment.

"I don't know," she said. "All I know is I got a call this morning from Redacker. He told me I needed to be out at the house as soon as possible."

"But why is he helping you now, if he lied to you before?"

"He promised he would," Kate replied. "He is a man of his word."

"People who keep their word don't lie in the first place," Quinn said.

"Well, I don't think he is lying now. Something in my gut," she said.

"If the woman is missing, what are we going to find at her house?" he asked.

But by that time they were nearing the neighborhood. Quinn pulled onto the street and then pulled the car over alongside the curb.

"We aren't there yet," she said.

"I know, but we can't exactly drive up if the cops are all around it, can we?" he asked.

A second later, Quinn saw Janus pull up behind him.

The three of them cut between two houses and ducked into the woods, approaching the house slowly. Kate seemed to be chomping at the bit to go faster, but both Quinn and Janus persuaded her not to rush ahead.

As they approached, they could see numerous cop cars out front. Janus pulled out his camera and started shooting, stopping every few feet to take a photo. Quinn counted six cars near the front.

"Hell of a missing persons case," he said.

"Is that what this is?" Janus asked.

"A lady disappeared from here Thursday night," Kate said. "Her friend said a cop showed up and asked to use her phone. And the friend hasn't heard from her since."

"But this is a lot of people to have crawling around here, isn't it?" Janus asked.

They quickly counted. Quinn saw at least 12 cops around the house and also saw some movement over in the woods. The police had put up ropes in front of the house marking it as a police scene.

"They found something in there," Kate said. "It's the only way to explain all this."

"A body?" Quinn asked.

"Maybe," she said. "But I would think they'd be more subtle."

"How did you know about this?" Janus asked while Quinn was on the phone.

"It's a long story," Kate said.

"You seem to know an awful lot about this place for someone who is new to it," Janus said between drags.

"Haven't we covered this already?" Kate asked.

Janus held up his left hand.

"Relax," he said. "I'm no fucking rat. I just enjoy shaking people up a little."

"I had noticed that," she said.

"My mum said it's my mission in life," he said.

"What is?"

"To annoy people to death," he replied and grinned. Janus pointed over in the woods directly behind the house.

"There are a bunch of guys out there," he said. "What the bloody hell is going on?"

"They are looking for something," Kate replied.

"But if they are looking for a person, how come they aren't calling out?" Quinn asked.

"Because they know that person isn't alive," Kate said.

"What would make them so sure?" Janus asked.

"If they are looking for a person in pieces," Kate said.

"Oh, I like her," Janus said. "She's just brimming with positive thinking."

They moved closer to the house. Janus took shots of cops in the woods and more of them roping off the house. So far, no one had noticed them.

"Let's see if we can get a look inside," Kate said.

"We'll get caught," Janus said.

Kate shrugged.

"So?" she said. "I'm not exactly intimidated by them."

They approached the house slowly, but the cops' attention still seemed focused elsewhere. They came at it from the side, hoping to get a look in the den window.

They had nearly reached the window when cops started shouting. All at once, five officers stood around the three of them.

"Hiya blokes," Janus said. "Do you have any donuts? I'm really famished and this seemed like the best place to grab a bite."

The cops started throwing questions at them. Who were they? How did they get here? What was with the camera?

Then a voice cut through the rest.

"Janus, I should have known," he said and the group parted to let an officer come through.

"Stu, how are you?" Quinn asked.

Stu looked at him warily.

"Let me see your camera, Janus," he said, turning away from Quinn.

"I really don't think that is a good idea," Quinn said.

"Why not?" Stu asked. "I wouldn't want to have to call you guys in for questioning. But if I were to have the camera for a minute..."

Janus busted out laughing.

"Oh, that's a great threat," he said. "I'm fucking quaking, aren't I?"

The cops around them seemed to be growing angrier.

"Give me the camera, Janus," Stu said.

"You'll have to pry it out of my cold dead hand," he responded.

"What do you say, Kate?" Quinn asked. He pulled out a notebook and pen from his jacket and started writing. "Let's see... 'When reporters approached the house, the officers became extremely anxious and threatened to take away a photographer's camera.'"

"Now hold on," Stu said.

"Honestly, Stu, do we look stupid?" Quinn asked.

"Well, we might actually look stupid," Janus said. "We just aren't."

"There is no way you can force that camera out of his hands," Quinn said.

"Are you going to accidentally break it or something? I would think you would know by now how to treat the press. But if not, let me give you a tip: Stop being an asshole."

"That's it," Stu said. "You three are all coming with me."

"Right, throwing us in jail will improve the sheriff's reputation in town?" Kate asked.

"Let me put it this way," Stu said. "You guys are at a crime scene. You are interfering with police business. You've been taking unauthorized photos."

"Unauthorized?" Janus asked. "Since when is a newspaper photographer taking photos of a crime scene unauthorized? Give me a fucking break."

"Look, you little English shit," Stu said. "I've had it with you. All of you. You're coming down to the station."

Kate pulled out her own notebook and started writing everything down.

"First of all, I'm not fucking English," Janus said. "I'm Welsh. There is a huge difference. For example, you are probably English by blood. It's the only way to explain your looks. And blind stupidity."

Stu crossed over to him.

"Gentlemen," Quinn said. "This is getting a bit ridiculous, don't you think?"

"Another time, Janus," Stu said. "You and I should have a man-to-man talk."

"Cut the macho bullshit," Kate said. "If you want to have us down at the station, we are happy to go."

"We are?" Janus asked.

"Sure," Kate said. "But we want a meeting with Sheriff Brown."

"It's just past six in the morning..." Stu said.

"I'm sure he is in," Kate said. "You just tell him we want to talk."

"Lady, whoever you are, there is no way he will talk to you," he said. "If you think you can trespass onto a crime scene and then win yourself an exclusive interview, you've been drinking from the same water as these two."

"Just tell him we want to talk about the message found inside the house," Kate said and pointed.

Stu looked at the cops around him. He paused for a moment and licked his lips.

"What message?" he asked. "We don't know what you are talking about."

"Did you think I would stay away forever?" she said.

Stu's jaw practically came unhinged and he stood there for a moment with his mouth open. Janus grinned at Quinn.

Stu stood still, until finally he sent the other cops away.

"I don't know what you are talking about," he said finally.

"Sure you don't," Kate said. "Now how about that meeting?"

Stu pushed his tongue out to his cheek and considered.

"I'll see what I can do," he said.

*****

Brown was waiting for them in his office.

"This is ridiculous," he said, before any of them sat down. "I will not have members of the press interfering in police business."

"And what, exactly, did we do?" Janus asked.

"You were trampling all over a crime scene," he said. "You were attempting to enter a residence..."

"We attempted to look inside," Quinn said. "There is a difference, you know."

"Is there?" Brown said. Stu shut the door behind them. "I want you three to know I'm lodging a complaint with your editor."

"Go ahead," Quinn said.

He picked up his notebook and started writing in it.

"What are you writing down?" Brown demanded.

"This conversation," Quinn replied. "I need to record it for my article."

"You are not going to write an article about any of this," Brown said.

"So you're the editor now?" Janus asked.

"This is ridiculous," Brown said.

"Call it whatever you like," Kate said. "The return of Lord Halloween is big news."

Brown appeared more flustered than ever.

"That is patently absurd," he said.

"Is it?" Kate asked. "You lied to us about Mary Kilgore. Her husband was off with another woman at the time of her death. And he didn't stick a knife through her chest with a note on it."

"You're talking nonsense," he said.

"It ought to be pretty apparent I'm not, Sheriff," she said. "I know a lot more than you think I do. We knew about Fanton, didn't we? We know about the note on Kilgore's body and I know about the note in the house today."

"How could you possibly know that?" Brown demanded.

"You covered up Mary Kilgore's murder and I bet he didn't like that one bit, did he?" Kate continued as if she had not been interrupted. "So he's going to make damn sure nobody misses the point now. The man likes his publicity..."

"He's dead," Brown said. "Holober's dead."

"Come on, Sheriff," she said. "Do you think people will still believe that when news of Mary Louise Fanton's death is released? Do you think you can just hide in denial, watch the bodies pile up and hope no one will notice?"

"There is nothing to deny," he said.

"Do you really believe that?" she asked. She stared at him for a moment. "My God, you really do, don't you? Then what? This guy is just a copycat?"

"It's possible," Brown said and then shut his mouth. "Never mind. The point is we don't know Ms. Fanton has been murdered."

"But I'm right about the note, aren't I?" Kate asked. "It referenced the earlier one. We've done our research. What he wants is publicity. If you deny it to him, it makes him madder. And people will be walking around unprotected."

"What you are suggesting would start a panic, mass hysteria," Brown replied.

"Sheriff, people have the right to know," Kate said. "If you tell the truth, panic may come, but at least people will have a fighting chance to defend themselves."

"By locking themselves away again?" he asked. "By instilling a curfew? I'm not going to let this happen again."

"If that is what it takes," she said. "But you can't just bury your head in the sand. It will only get worse."

"How in the hell could it get worse?" Brown asked.

"Your family, Sheriff, how safe are they?"

"How dare you?" Brown yelled. "That sounds like a threat."

"He's killed cops' families before—remember?" Kate said quietly.

Brown paused for a moment.

"My family is perfectly safe," he said, but he paused for a moment. "This is absurd. Just go. Get out. If you print any of this, you'll regret it. It would be irresponsible to cause this kind of panic.

"And I'm going to call your editor," Brown added as an afterthought.

"Call away," Kate said. "At the very least, we have a missing persons case. And how much longer is your story on Kilgore going to keep? How much longer before someone finds out that you faked documents?"

"You're crazy, you know that," he said. "You come in here with a lot of guesses and no facts. You make false accusations so you can get a headline. I don't play that game. This is a police investigation. I have nothing more to say."

"Did you think he would stay away forever, Sheriff Brown?" Kate said as she turned to leave.

"Get out. Now."

And the three of them walked out.

*****

When they got outside the building, Quinn and Janus both stared at Kate.

"That was amazing," Janus said. "I thought I would be the one to piss him off, but good Christ..."

"Are you okay?" Quinn asked and started to touch her shoulder.

She shook her head.

"Far from it," she said and stepped away from him. "Because of Brown, that bastard got away. And now he is living in some dream world while the body count is increasing. It's just two now, but there will be more. There may already be more. Each second we waste..."

"I know," Quinn said. "I know. But what if it isn't the same guy? What if it is some kind of copycat?"

"It's not," Kate said. "I feel it. I just have an instinct about this."

Quinn thought about telling her Dee's story, but dropped it. He would sound crazy.

They had a real demon to pursue. He couldn't focus on phantoms. But Dee saw it...

Quinn pushed the thought away.

"I believe you," he said.

"Good," she said. "Let's get in touch with Kyle and find out what he can get from the police. By Tuesday, Brown will be having a press conference."

"How do you know?" Janus asked.

"Because Lord Halloween is not subtle," she said. "Fanton is probably dead and if they haven't discovered her body yet, they soon will. And it won't be in an obscure place. It will be out in the open. He will make sure no one can miss it this time."

"I hope you're wrong," Quinn said.

"Me too," she said.

But she wasn't.

LH File: Letter #7
Date Oct. 19, 1994
Investigation Status: Closed
Contents: Classified

Mr. Anderson,

You see now the price of ignoring my wishes, don't you? You can't say I didn't warn you. For this to work, I have to live in people's minds. They have to see me everywhere. They have to fear me when they take out the trash, or close their eyes in the shower. They are doing that now, I know, but it would have been so much easier—for both of us—if you had just listened to me the first time. But you didn't.

No, you played along, didn't you? When the police told your editors what to do, you just did it. They wanted to keep me under wraps. That's the way it's always been with fear. Some people think they can just wish it away. But what you fear is always out there, Mr. Anderson. It's always lurking behind your home, waiting for a moment to strike.

And I struck. You've seen just a taste of what I can do. There are eight bodies, but I'm just ramping up speed. I'm sorry about your girlfriend, I really am. Had you had sex yet, Mr. Anderson? I knew you were only just dating, after all. It would make me feel better to know that you had a chance to fuck her good and proper. Such a pretty girl.

I didn't touch her, rest assured. Rape is so very pedestrian and then you get the feminists claiming all sorts of things about you, your mother and your local priest. But she had lovely brunette hair, those soft, dewy brown eyes and that figure. Oh, that figure was exquisite.

I have to say you were aiming up. Good for you! You have to always have ambitions in life—God knows I did. You can't accept where other people would put you. So she was out of your class, you made a play and—voila!—you did it. You scored.

Of course, you also killed her. You do know that, right? She wasn't on my list. Oh, who am I kidding, what list? But I didn't have my eyes on her until you made me angry. I could have killed you, but where's the fun in that? Besides, I can get around to that any time I want, Mr. Anderson.

She didn't call your name—I don't want you beating yourself up about that. That could have been because I cut her throat and she was choking on her own blood, but you can never really tell, can you? She had a lot of blood too, Mr. Anderson.

It's true she suffered a lot, but I will give you one passing comfort. She died well. So many don't. There's the screaming, the crying, the begging, the carrying on. As if I would stop. As if I would consider it. Please. But not your girl. She just sat back and took it. She accepted her fate. Hey, maybe she even wanted it, right? Some people are really sick in this world.

So where are we? Oh, I imagine you're a little upset and you think you won't do what I ask you to. We can play it that way if you want to. But there are other people you are close to, Mr. Anderson, and you can't possibly protect them. So let's do this my way from here on out and everyone can go home happy. Well, everyone except your little girlfriend. She lives in a box now and I don't think happiness is on her agenda.

I want a full page spread. I want my name in bold face type. I want it to be all about me. You've had a run of good victim stories. Well, they're done. It's all about me now. Where am I going to strike next? Are your children safe? Why can't the police stop me?

That's what I want and that's what you'll give me.

Yours Truly,

Lord Halloween

Chapter 14

Wednesday, Oct. 18

Quinn stared at the headline for almost five minutes.

"Woman murdered in Leesburg," it said.

It was simple enough, but it didn't begin to tell the story. In fact, it looked too much like last week's headline for his comfort.

But it wasn't like last week, at least not to him. They had found Fanton's body on Monday. As Kate had predicted, it was hard to miss. Fanton's body was dumped sometime late Sunday night outside the courthouse. It had not been noticed until early the next morning. Though the police tried to play it down, the news traveled fast.

By Tuesday, there was a press conference. Few details. Unexplained murder. Brown denied a persistent rumor that Fanton's head had been mailed to police headquarters. He suggested people were trying to panic the populace. Brown squashed any implication that it could have been the same murderer as a week before. He denied rumors of notes found on both bodies.

For now, at least, it appeared many people believed him. No businesses shut down. *The Washington Post* put the story on the front of their Metro section, but even they didn't bump it to A1 status. On the surface, things seemed normal enough.

But Quinn sensed it all around him. By this morning, people were at least openly talking about the possibility that their long-lost murderer had come home. It had started. A few more bodies and panic would be close at hand. He put his head on his desk. The bottom of their story made mention of a serial killer 12 years ago, but it didn't attempt to draw any conclusions. There was no need.

"He won't like the fact that he isn't mentioned," a voice said behind Quinn.

Quinn practically jumped in his chair. He turned around to see Buzz watching him.

"I didn't see you come in, Buzz," Quinn said.

"I like to make a stealthy entrance," Buzz replied. "I don't like people to know I'm around."

"Is that where you are at staff meetings—lurking in the corners?" Quinn said.

"Sometimes," Buzz said.

"Anyway, what are you talking about? Who wasn't mentioned?"

"The story," Buzz replied. "You refer to Lord Halloween's murders, but you don't mention his name. He won't like it."

"Well, I guess he can always write a letter to the editor," Quinn said, hoping for a laugh. "'To the editor: I may be a psychotic madman, but I would appreciate your using my full name.'"

Buzz didn't laugh.

"You think this is funny?" he said. "It's not. He has ways of making his wishes known and though they involve notes, they aren't exactly publishable."

"I'm just kidding around."

"He isn't a joke," Buzz said.

"Look, even if the guy wanted his name printed, that's a reason not to do it," Quinn said. "We don't pander to madmen."

Buzz waved his hand in disgust.

"Spare me the good journalism speech," Buzz said. "If you don't print his name, you wind up dead. You aren't much good to anyone then."

"Why are you so obsessed with him anyway?" Quinn asked.

"Who wouldn't be?" Buzz asked. He looked around him. "He is ruthless, inventive, creative and intelligent. If you don't study up on him, he might catch you napping."

"I've done my research," Quinn said.

"Have you really?" Buzz asked. "Then I'm surprised you didn't mention his name."

"It wasn't me, it was Kyle," Quinn said. "He wrote most of it. I even suggested putting the nickname in there, but he thought it was too 'provocative.' This from a guy who thinks wrestling is high art."

"Yes, well, as I said, he has ways of making his point known," Buzz said.

"I know, like mailing a head to Sheriff Brown," Quinn said. "I'll be careful."

"You'll be dead," Buzz said.

Buzz started to walk away before Quinn remembered. He burst out laughing and Buzz looked confused and then angry.

"No, Buzz," Quinn said. "It's a line from *Star Wars*, remember? Luke says, 'I'll be careful' to some dude in the bar and then the guy says, 'You'll be dead.'"

"It's not funny, Quinn," Buzz said. "It isn't like he hasn't targeted reporters before—ones just as talented as you."

"Hold up a second," Quinn said. "What reporter did he target?"

But Buzz was starting to walk away in disgust. When Quinn caught up with him, he wheeled around.

"Everyone likes to make fun of me," Buzz said. "You say I'm paranoid. And I am. But did you ever think I have reason to be? Tim was just a young reporter when he started here, but he was amazingly talented. I was a little envious, actually."

"Tim?"

"Anderson," Buzz said. "He came in just like you.

"Left college, wanted to write. Worked on the sports desk for two years and started doing general assignments. About a year before Lord Halloween showed up, Laurence moved him to the crime beat. And he was great at it."

Quinn wasn't laughing anymore.

"What happened?"

Buzz paused. He had a far away look on his face as if he wasn't just remembering being back in 1994, but he was actually there.

"He started getting letters," Buzz said. "I'm not sure when. It could have even been before the first murder."

"What did they say?"

"I don't know," Buzz said. "Nobody here knows but Laurence and Ethan. Tim only ever shared them with those two."

"But they were from Lord Halloween?"

"Oh yes," Buzz said. "Most definitely."

"Do you know anything about what they contained?"

Buzz shook his head.

"Don't you think I wanted to know?" he asked. "I tried everything I could to get a copy, or see if Tim would talk. But the letters were promptly handed over to police. Ethan said we could never publish them."

Quinn got a bad feeling in the pit of his stomach.

"Lord Halloween didn't approve?"

"No, he didn't," Buzz said. "I know that..."

His voice trailed off. He was staring into space.

"You know that what?"

"Tim begged to publish those letters, Quinn," Buzz said. "I don't mean he asked, I mean he literally begged. Laurence and he had giant fights about it, but..."

"Laurence just did what Ethan wanted."

"Same as it ever was," Buzz said, and nodded.

"What happened to Tim?"

"I really don't know," Buzz said. "One day he just didn't show up for work. You won't find him on any official list of Lord Halloween's victims. But I know he's dead."

"Why? Maybe he just freaked and ran away?"

"You couldn't keep a guy like him away from writing," Buzz said. "He was born to do it, just as you were. He had a great beat and was a star reporter. He wouldn't have left."

"Sometimes people do funny things when their life is on the line," Quinn said.

"He angered Lord Halloween," Buzz said. "Then he disappeared. You tell me what is more likely. That is one killer with a lot of follow through."

Quinn thought of the blood in the basement, the reports of a ghost in the building. Maybe Lord Halloween killed Anderson here and hid the body? He shivered at the thought of someone lying down in the press room, screaming for help. But if the press was running, there would have been no one to hear. He could have died surrounded by people that might have helped him, but just couldn't hear him.

"I need those letters," Quinn said. "If Lord Halloween is back, I need to know more about him."

Buzz looked at him.

"The police have all of them," he said. "Technically."

"What do you mean, technically?"

Buzz looked around the office. There was still no one around. He leaned into Quinn's face.

"I think Laurence kept copies," Buzz said. "I don't know for sure, but I saw him copy one of them late at night. Ethan would not have approved. But he doesn't keep them in his office."

"How do you know?" Quinn asked.

Buzz smiled and shrugged.

"You broke in, didn't you?" Quinn asked.

Buzz shrugged again.

"Still, if he copied one..."

"There's a good bet he copied others," Buzz said. "Stay on your toes, Quinn. If Lord Halloween writes you a letter, I would make your own copy first. And I'd print it."

"If they let me," he said.

With that, Buzz walked off again. Quinn went back to his desk and sat down.

He put his head in his hands. When he looked up, Kate was staring at him. She looked pale, almost sick. He wasn't sure when she arrived. He got up and walked over to her.

"What's wrong?"

"I didn't sleep well," she replied. "I feel like I haven't slept in days."

"I know the feeling," Quinn said. "When I do sleep, all I have are nightmares."

"Believe me, I understand," she said. "What was that little pow-wow about?"

Quinn filled her in on the brief and tragic career of Tim Anderson.

"So he's the blood in the basement?" she asked.

"It's a good guess, but it isn't conclusive," Quinn replied.

"We need those letters," she said.

"But how are we going to get them?" Quinn asked. "I doubt Laurence will admit he has them—if he even still does."

"We can find a way," Kate said, and Quinn did not like the look on her face. Not one bit.

"We don't have a lot of time," he said. "If it is Lord Halloween, he'll make another move soon. He'll want more attention then he got here. And it's less than two weeks to Halloween."

Rebecca stood at the door of the conference room and called everyone into the staff meeting. Both Kate and Quinn went inside.

*****

That afternoon, Kate, Janus and Quinn sat in the coffee shop down the street.

"You want to do what?" Quinn asked. "Are you insane?"

"Well, can you think of a better way?" Kate asked.

"Than breaking into Laurence's house?" Quinn responded. "We could just ask him, you know."

"And he'll deny they exist," she responded. "You've got exactly one person who saw him making a copy—and that's Buzz. Is he the most credible source?"

"How do we know they are even at his house?" Quinn asked.

"Because they aren't in his office," Kate responded.

"How could you possibly..."

Quinn's voice dropped off. He looked at the two of them. He had wondered why Kate had insisted on bringing Janus along. And now he knew. Only Janus would have been crazy enough to go along with this plan.

"You broke into his office, didn't you?" Quinn asked, looking at Janus.

"Broke in is such a strong term," Janus said with a smile. "I prefer active investigatory intrusion."

"Are you two nuts?" Quinn said. "He is your boss. Your boss. If he had caught you, you both would have been fired. "

"I had a cover story," Janus said.

"Which was what?"

There was a long pause.

"I needed a stapler," Janus said.

Quinn put his head on the table and softly but repeatedly banged it against the ceramic stone. It felt strangely soothing. My job will be the first thing to go, he thought. He looked up and they were both staring at him. Janus at least had some vaguely apologetic look on his face, as if he were aware that some line had been crossed. Kate, on the other hand, just looked determined.

"And is that going to be your cover story when we break into his actual house?" Quinn said. "When the police show up, we're going to tell them that the three of us really needed staplers?"

"No, I was going to go with we all were tweaked out on ecstasy and thought we were throwing a party there."

Quinn returned to banging his head on the table.

"It's the only way," Kate said.

"The only way?" Quinn asked, and laughed. "Again, we could ask him. I'm just throwing out a crazy idea that instead of breaking into a house—a home I might add that we don't even know has the letters, much less where to find them—we could just confront him and demand he give over the letters."

"And when he says no?" Kate asked.

"Have you met Laurence?" Quinn said. "He doesn't say no. Traveling salespeople probably come from miles around because he is physically incapable of saying no. If he were drowning, he wouldn't say no to more water."

"I don't think so," Kate said.

"I've known him for years," Quinn said. "You've known him for like 20 minutes. Come on."

"She's right," Janus said.

Quinn pointed his finger at Janus.

"You just want an excuse to break in somewhere," he said. "You've been wanting to do that for ages. Remember that Cascades bar?"

Janus just shrugged.

"She's right and you know it," he said. "Laurence can't say no, but he can pretend the letters don't exist. And that's what he'll do."

"We are taking way too much on faith here," Quinn responded. "That he really did copy the letters, that he has kept them all these years, and that they are sitting at his house."

"We have to start somewhere, Quinn, or are we just going to be wait for Lord Halloween to find us?" Kate said.

"What if they tell us nothing? They didn't tell the police much, did they?"

Still, within two hours, Quinn found himself along with Kate and Janus outside of Laurence's house. He had a modest enough place just outside Leesburg. Quinn didn't know for sure, but he thought Laurence must have moved recently. The house looked relatively new and had that cookie-cutter look that most of the developers were going for.

The nice thing about the outskirts of Leesburg was that they had so much surrounding woodland still left. The three journalists positioned themselves in Laurence's back yard and scoped out the house.

"It's all dark," Quinn said.

He thanked God it was October and the sun was starting to go down so early. Somewhere he could hear a dog bark and he hoped it wasn't making noise because of them—or that Laurence owned it. At least now they could lurk around without anyone seeing them. Quinn couldn't see why Lord Halloween enjoyed that aspect of his work.

Instead of feeling invisible, he was worried any minute he might be seen or, knowing Virginia residents, shot at.

"So who's going in?" he asked.

He shouldn't have bothered. Once they confirmed that Laurence wasn't home yet, Janus was already moving to approach the house.

"Does he even know where he's going?" Quinn asked.

Kate shrugged.

They watched Janus approach the backdoor. It was a nice double door opening out to a patio. Janus tripped a motion-detecting floodlight, but clearly didn't seem worried about it. He stood there, standing out.

"This isn't going to work," Quinn said.

"Could you please try and be a little positive?"

"Well, I didn't bring up the part where we all get fired and go to jail. I thought that was pretty positive."

Janus had pulled something out of his pocket—Quinn at first thought it was going to be his lighter, the one he carried with him everywhere. Instead it appeared to be a tool of some kind. He was using it on the door. Within seconds, the door came open.

Quinn braced himself. If there was an alarm, this would be when it was triggered. After the attacks by Lord Halloween, most Loudoun residents had bought an alarm. But he heard nothing. Instead Janus gestured back at them.

Seconds later, Quinn and Kate were through the door. The house looked nice considering he knew how little Ethan Holden paid anyone. It was possible Laurence was paid more money than most, but he doubted it. Laurence wasn't a tough negotiator and it was hard to imagine Holden ever willingly parting with cash when he didn't absolutely have to.

"Let's spread out," Kate said. "The shorter time we're here, the better chances we have."

"Nothing ever went wrong with *that* plan," Quinn said, but Janus and Kate had already split up.

Quinn decided to stick to the back. He walked through the dining room, which looked totally bare except for a table, and then briefly stopped in the kitchen. He doubted Laurence would have any files in there. As he turned the corner, he saw a door to the basement. He felt like he was in a bad horror movie. Don't go in the basement, he told himself. But didn't that seem like a better place to hide files?

Slowly, he walked down the steps, taking care not to trip in the dark. When he got to the bottom, he fumbled along the wall until he found a light switch and turned it on. He hated turning on the light—what if Laurence came home—but had no choice. Without it, he was effectively blind.

The basement wasn't as dank or scary as Quinn had feared. It was largely bare, however, with a big TV and a stationary bicycle on the far side of the wall. It didn't look like either had been used recently. But feeling the urge to be thorough, he walked to the back of the room and found another area off to the right.

The room was an almost identical replica of Laurence's office at the *Chronicle*. Two desks were pushed together and an older-looking computer sat at the direct center of one of them. He flicked on another light to get a better look. Bingo! Two filing cabinets sat by the far end of the room—just like at the office. He was just about to shout upstairs to the others when he heard something that made his blood stand still.

The front door had opened.

He couldn't move, he couldn't breathe, he couldn't think. He was a journalist—trained for stressful situations—but Quinn could see getting fired, possible jail time and the end of everything he had tried to build here. What paper would hire him now? He would be a part-time criminal. Maybe he could convince Laurence not to press charges. He could just walk upstairs and admit it.

He heard footsteps as someone walked in the house. From the sound of it, it was probably two people. He heard voices, even giggling. Quinn had to do something.

The files, a voice in his head said. Get the goddamn files. If he was going to go down, he shouldn't be standing around waiting for something to happen—he should act.

His eyes darted to the filing cabinets. Please don't be locked, he thought, as he heard more talking upstairs. How long until Kate gets caught? What about Janus?

Focus, he thought. Focus on what you are here to do.

He examined the filing cabinets and tried to pull them out. But as he feared, they were locked.

"Shit," he said under his breath. "Motherfucking piece of shit."

He looked around the room. Keys, keys, there have to be keys somewhere. The desk was bare. Near the computer was a series of newspaper clippings, laid out in an unusually neat pattern. He opened the drawers and started looking through. How long before they notice the light is on downstairs? How long do I have? There were pins, pens, notepads, paper clips, staples, a letter opener, highlighters and every kind of other junk in the first drawer. The second drawer was filled with random stuff as well, as far as Quinn could tell. There were papers in there, but nothing else.

There's no key here, Quinn thought. He should run now. Just get out of there while he could. But this would be his last chance. He wasn't going to get another shot at this. And if Laurence caught even a glimpse of him, he would know it was Quinn.

He could hear the voices talking upstairs, moving around a little. It sounded like they were in the kitchen—he could hear glasses clinking.

"Shit," he said again.

His eyes searched the room. He returned to the filing cabinet and gave it a good look. It looked like solid oak, but the lock

181

was very small. Maybe it wasn't that stable. He could see the piece of metal through the opening slat holding the drawer shut. If he had something flat, small and hard, he could maybe move it without a key. His brain was working on overdrive.

The voices had stopped talking and he could not hear anything upstairs. He didn't know where Laurence and his friend were, but they could be anywhere.

The letter opener, Quinn thought. He moved back to the desk, pulled open the drawer and grabbed it. Please let this work. He slid the letter opener into the slat and tried to push the latch. At first there was nothing and Quinn thought it was over, but then it gave way slightly. He pushed a little harder. It was resisting him, but also moving.

Above him, he could hear people moving and voices again. It didn't sound like anyone had been caught—maybe Kate and Janus had gotten out already. But the footsteps sounded like they were coming towards Quinn. He could almost make out what the people were saying.

The lock gave way. One minute it was resisting slightly and the next it had slid all the way into the drawer. He'd done it. He pulled open the drawer and looked at a series of files. At first he couldn't make out what he was looking at. On each file was written a name—and there were at least two dozen files. They meant nothing to him until he saw one near the front: "Mary Kilgore." The murdered woman.

He pulled it out. In it was his newspaper article on the murder and even the metro article from the *Post*. A headshot also fell out. Until that moment, Quinn hadn't known what she looked like. She looked in her early fifties. Her hair was dark, but Quinn had a feeling it was colored. She had been pretty once, but in the photo she just looked tired. Her smile looked forced, as if she didn't have any reason to be smiling. Quinn put the photo back in the file and returned it to the drawer.

He looked at the other names until one jumped out at him: Sarah Blakely. It was Kate's mom. He looked more carefully at the names now and could see he recognized many of them: they were all victims of Lord Halloween.

Laurence had an entire drawer filled with information. Had he also done his own investigation? He didn't have time to think about it. The footsteps now sounded like they were at the top of the basement stairs. He heard a voice as clear as day.

"Just one second," Laurence said.

He started walking down the basement steps.

"I didn't think I left the light on down here," Laurence said to himself.

Quinn was finished. In five seconds Laurence would be down the steps and it would be over. Instead of his life flashing before his eyes, Quinn saw his career flash before him. Starting as a cub reporter working sports, trying to learn the ropes, then finally working his way up to general assignment. It was over. It was all over.

At that moment, the doorbell rang. Laurence paused on the steps, turned around, and walked back up them. Quinn nearly shouted in relief. His heart was racing. Whatever chance he had just been given, he took it. He looked back at the files and frantically searched through the names until he found the one he wanted: Tim Anderson.

He grabbed the file. It was clearly one of the biggest. Quinn didn't read it. If the letters weren't here, they weren't anywhere, and now was not the time to check. As an afterthought, he grabbed the file on Blakely as well—and shut the filing cabinet as gently as he could.

Hoisting the files under his one arm, he began to creep up the stairs. Whoever had rung the doorbell, he just hoped they would keep Laurence busy. At the top of the stairs he stood and listened.

"I just thought it was worth bringing to your attention," a voice said. With shock, Quinn realized it belonged to Janus. He had been the one to ring the doorbell. He must have snuck out of the house and gone back around to the front.

"You really think he's harassing her?" Laurence asked.

"Well, I don't know that it's risen to that level yet," Janus said. "But between you and me, he hasn't had a good date in a long time and the way he looks at her—well, frankly, it makes me uncomfortable. I can only imagine how I would feel if I were a new reporter."

What the hell was Janus even talking about? Quinn knew he was just creating a diversion, but the conversation sounded...

"I'm worried about Quinn," Janus continued. "I really am. He's been acting all paranoid lately, and he had that run-in with the police. You should have heard him. He was downright disrespectful to the police—Kate and I were shocked.'"

Oh, fuck, Quinn thought. He wanted to go out there and set the record straight and realized with a start that he had broken into this house. It was now or never to get away.

He walked toward the kitchen and heard someone open the refrigerator. Laurence wasn't alone, he should have remembered. Whoever it was wasn't rushing out to meet Janus, though. Quinn couldn't go that way.

Instead, he went the other direction. He was near Laurence's living room. He crossed quickly in the dark through the dining room. He hoped whoever was in the kitchen didn't move.

"I just really wanted you to know about it," Janus said.

"Well, thanks Janus," Laurence said. "I'm very glad you brought these concerns to me. Rebecca and I will talk to Quinn first thing in the morning."

Quinn was about out of time. He moved carefully but quickly through the dining room and to the back door. From there he could see into the kitchen and was surprised to see Rebecca standing in it. She was clearly listening to Laurence's conversation, but did not appear eager to give herself away. If she looked away now, she would see Quinn.

He quietly opened the door and backed out of the house. The floodlight was still on, but Rebecca was looking the other direction, toward the front door. Quinn backed across the lawn. He had to be sure he wasn't seen. As soon as he was out of the light, he turned and ran across the back yard, grasping the files in his hand to keep them from falling out.

When he got to the rendezvous point, he stopped.

"You made it," Kate said, and Quinn nearly screamed. He hadn't seen her in the dark. "Janus and I knew you were still in there: he hoped to create a diversion."

"Well, he did that, although I think he was saying I was stalking you."

"What?" Kate asked, but her eyes were on the folders under Quinn's arm.

"Did you find something?" she asked.

Quinn nodded. "He has files on every victim of Lord Halloween, Kate."

He handed the files over to her.

"That's Tim Anderson's," he said.

The next thing he knew Kate had kissed him again. It was brief—all too brief—but it felt great. She let him go.

"Fantastic," she said. "Let's get out of here."

"What about Janus?"

"What about me?" Janus said, appearing from nowhere. Both Kate and Quinn jumped.

"What the hell were you doing back there?" Quinn asked.

"Saving your ass," he said. "Now let's get gone before we have another little incident."

*****

Kate and Quinn sat in Quinn's apartment, each of them drinking a Coke. It was late, they should be sleeping, but instead they were sitting with a raft of paper. The file on Anderson had been thick. In it were stuffed Anderson's articles from the murders: a profile of a kid that was murdered, reports on the police investigation, and a big blow up piece that read, "Who is Lord Halloween?" Below the headline was the deck: "And why can't the police stop him?"

Quinn glanced through the article. "The police investigation appears crude, inept and ineffective—and the killer undoubtedly knows it," one article read. "While police routinely try to contain information about a case in order to confront a suspect with evidence unknown to the public, they have also attempted to bury information that could be vital to the citizens of Loudoun County. The police concluded there was likely a serial killer in the area three days before the death of Trudy Pharaoh on Oct. 16, yet refused to acknowledge as much until after her death and those of two other people. Critics charge the police have put the public at risk and are no closer to identifying a suspect in the case."

No wonder the cops hate us, Quinn thought. Not that what Anderson wrote was untrue, but still, it was harsh. If the police had told everyone there was a serial killer in town, how long before panic set in? As it was, when people had figured it out, the reaction had been over the top. A curfew and a ban on Halloween and related activities had been just the beginning. Then again, weren't the police making the same mistake now, denying that the deaths of Fanton and Kilgore were related?

"Fascinating," Kate said. "Lord Halloween really had a yen for Anderson. Look at these."

She produced a stack of paper and handed them to Quinn. He started reading from the top of the stack: "Some of what I tell you will be lies. I don't mean to get us off on the wrong foot, but I thought I should make that clear from the outset."

"He wrote about ten letters, it looks like," she said. "Though not all of them appear to be here. We are at least missing letters four and six."

"What do they say?"

"You should read them, but they are quite the ego trip. It turns out Lord Halloween was apparently an anti-development pioneer—way ahead of his time. It's all about stopping change, and yadda, yadda, yadda."

"Maybe he's part of the anti-development team now?" Quinn asked. "One of the people trying to preserve Phillips Farm, for example."

"I don't think so," Kate said.

"Why not?"

"I think it's all a show," she said. "I think he was trying to give a motivation to Anderson that would be somewhat sympathetic—however crazy—to people who read his stories. He's like an eco-terrorist on steroids. But I don't think he meant a word of it."

"He might have meant some of it," Quinn said.

"Everything about these letters is over the top," Kate said. "Just like the man himself, I assume. I think 'Lord Halloween' itself is a put-on, a sham, something designed to scare the kiddies. The man behind it probably thinks it's all in fun."

"Then what's the point of the letters?"

"To establish a mythos," she said. "To create buzz around him. He's not just a killer. He's a serial killer bent on destruction and chaos. But my point is, he feels about as real as a comic-book villain. Yes, he kills people, but the whole, 'she screamed delightfully' while she died."

"The editor in me noted that you can't really scream delightfully," Quinn said.

"Exactly," Kate said. "It's a put-on. He's trying to make himself bigger than he is, some kind of arch-fiend. He's not. He's just a guy who gets off on killing people. That's it."

"But he also seems to want a certain kind of press," Quinn said, flipping through the letters.

"Yeah, that's the other point of the letters, I think," Kate said. "It's about control. He's trying to get around the police muzzle about his existence and using a reporter to do it. When the reporter doesn't do it..."

"He kills him," Quinn said.

"Very likely," Kate said. "Though that last letter has thrown me a bit. Maybe it was meant to throw other people, I'm not sure. But one letter seems to imply he killed Anderson's girlfriend. That's a place we ought to start looking. Who was she? Did she work for the *Chronicle*? It's too bad you couldn't steal more files."

"I've had another disturbing thought," Quinn said. "Why does Laurence have all those files anyway? If it were Buzz, I wouldn't think twice..."

"I wonder if it's him," Kate said.

"Him?"

"Maybe Laurence is Lord Halloween," she said. "This is his way of tracking his victims, enjoying the thrill."

Quinn laughed out loud.

"You aren't serious?" he said. "Have you met Laurence? There's no way. He can't even stand up to Rebecca."

"So maybe he acts out in other ways, Quinn," she said. "You don't really know people: not ever. Maybe he's just a nice guy on the surface and underneath..."

"No way," Quinn said. "I just don't see it."

"I hope you're right," she said.

She looked at her watch. It was past three in the morning.

"I should get back to the hotel," she said.

"You can stay here," Quinn said.

They looked at each other. For a brief moment, Kate saw the Tarot card lying on Madame Zora's table: a man and a woman with the Devil standing between them. But she was far too tired to be thinking that way.

"I'll sleep on the couch," Quinn rushed to clarify. It was good that Janus had already gone home. He would have mocked Quinn—in front of Kate, no doubt.

She was also too tired to argue. She nodded. He rushed off to get towels and generally get his room in order. Within fifteen minutes, they were both asleep.

LH File: Letter #8
Date Oct. 23, 1994
Investigation Status: Closed
Contents: Classified

Dear Tim,

I think it's about time we used each other's Christian names, don't you? That last article—that was what I wanted all along. Was that so hard? The police are inept, no one can find me, and I'm killing with impunity. If that doesn't frighten the huddled masses, I don't know what will.

I confess I thought our partnership was a failure, but here we are, finally working together. I'm sure the police are thrilled. Maybe you don't want to hand this letter over? Just a suggestion, but how long do you think it is before they begin to suspect you? Think about it: Maybe you're just a reporter who wants attention. Maybe you're writing these letters to yourself. You could even have multiple personalities and not know it. Sure, it's crazy, but the police are desperate, Tim. How long before they go looking for a scapegoat? Hey, it can even be the same reporter that called them names. Think of how excited they would be.

Is your blood pumping yet, Tim? I could help them, you know. I know where you live, I know where you eat, I know everything about you. I've even been in your room while you slept. Bet you didn't know that, did you? I came to kill you, but thought better of it. You're good at what you do. I'm good at what I do. There should be room in the world for two people of talent, don't you think?

But our time is fading. By Oct. 31, my time here will be up— at least for this year—and you... You could be in jail. Or dead. Or just mentally unhinged. Part of this is up to you. Your next article should hit the police even harder. They have suspects, I will tell you that. My favorite is Charles Holober, a paranoid schizophrenic that lives in Ashburn. The guy keeps dead fish in his drawer, Tim. He's married, but there are all kinds of domestic trouble. He even cut her.

Or there is always Mike Taylor down in Sterling. He's been arrested for armed burglary twice in the past 10 years, so he knows how to get into houses. He could be their man.

This county is filled with sickos and psychos, fools and fall guys. They'll find someone that fits their bill. It won't be me, but I can pretend, Tim. I know a lot about pretending.

And so do you, it seems. I've seen your brave face to the public. I also know how you begged your bosses to help you. But you are starting to feel it, aren't you? The burn, the weariness, the feeling that it will all be for nothing. She's dead and you can't bring her back. This story is making your career, but the price you are paying is your soul. Do what I want and you are nothing but a hack. Refuse me and you are nothing but a corpse.

So let's go out with a bang, shall we? Hit the police even harder, Tim. Pull no punches. Waste no ink. Let's see what you really are.

Yours Sincerely,

Lord Halloween

Chapter 15

Thursday, Oct. 19

Quinn and Kate were careful not to walk into the office at the same time, lest they start any rumors. Quinn had rustled up some breakfast, drove them both to Starbucks, then let Kate arrive a good 15 minutes before he walked into the office.

Still, as soon as he walked through the door, he could see Janus smirking. He caught Quinn near the vending machine where, after finishing his overpriced espresso, he was heading for a Coke.

"So how did it go?" Janus asked. "You noticed I got out of there pretty quickly. I was hoping maybe a little adventure got the blood pumping and you two…"

"Please silence the porn movie in your head," Quinn said. "We were exhausted. We went to sleep."

"Yeah, but she stayed over right? You cuddled a little bit, right? Right?"

Janus stared at Quinn for a moment.

"You didn't even cuddle, did you? Seriously, dude, everything was right. There was action, drama, a hint of romance—this always works."

"In the movies, Janus," Quinn said. "In the real world, these things tend to tire you out."

But in the back of his mind, he wondered if that was true. They were both exhausted, but hadn't he continued to feel that spark during their evening together? Should he have made a move? He remembered something then, a voice saying, "Don't hesitate." Who had told him that?

"Thanks so much for bringing this up," Quinn said.

Janus clapped him on the shoulder.

"Next time, make a move," Janus responded.

"Make a move on what?" Kate asked, walking up to them both.

Quinn had to give Janus credit. If he had intended to embarrass Quinn, he could have easily done so. Hell, he could have simply let an awkward silence reign. Instead he immediately said, "He should have grabbed more files when he had the chance."

"Come on, he did great," Kate said. "I thought we weren't going to find anything."

With that, the three of them returned to their desks and began to work. They had divided up their investigation into Lord Halloween. Kate was cross-referencing previous victims with their addresses and occupations in an attempt to figure out if any had been killed in the *Chronicle* building and if any were connected to Tim Anderson.

Quinn, meanwhile, was interrupted by Laurence to have a brief conversation in his office about the company's sexual harassment policy. Glaring at Janus when he finally returned to his desk, Quinn started looking through old clips of Anderson's and doing some Internet research to find out if the reporter was still alive. One thing was clear: Anderson was not on the official victim's list. He wasn't even officially labeled missing. So whatever had happened, no one had made it public.

Since neither was supposed to be doing their investigation during work hours, they both also had to keep handling their normal workload, with Quinn writing up his story on the ghost hunter while Kate finished off the piece on Madame Zora.

After a few hours, Quinn was growing increasingly frustrated. He had gone to the library and managed to find microfiche on the *Loudoun Chronicle* and read Anderson's work. Quinn thought it was some of the best writing he had ever seen.

Anderson should have easily made his way beyond the *Chronicle* to the *Post* or even *The New York Times*. But in a search of LexisNexis later, Quinn found no by-line by that name or others like it. Assuming Anderson was alive, he hadn't kept writing—at least not under his own name.

He was probably dead, Quinn thought. But something about that last letter from Lord Halloween made him wonder about that. The letter had said Anderson passed some kind of test. It had warned him to leave, but it hadn't threatened to kill him. Additionally, Lord Halloween was anything but subtle. If he had killed Anderson, wouldn't he have left a calling card? He did with everyone else.

But if Anderson had left, where had he gone? What was he doing? And if it wasn't his blood in the basement of the building, whose was it?

An idea popped into Quinn's head. He got up suddenly from his desk and wandered over to where Alexis was.

"Alexis, I was wondering if you could help me out?" he asked.

"Sure," she said, turning in her chair to face him. "What's up?"

"That story you did a couple months ago on how teachers are cracking down on kids who use the Internet to copy term papers," Quinn said. "You mentioned someone was selling software to help catch them. How did it work?"

Alexis was clearly excited. She often felt like she was considered the unimportant part of the paper, but clearly Quinn was reading her work. It mattered to him.

"It's sold over the Internet," she said. "It's just software that detects patterns in a document and looks for it elsewhere. So if a kid copied a term paper from the Internet, it would catch that immediately."

"But could it also find phrases? Something that literally wasn't the same exact document?"

"Yes," she said. "At least, I think that's the idea."

"Great," Quinn said. "Where can I buy it?"

*****

Kate and Quinn met again for dinner that evening and he had trouble taking his eyes off Kate. When he showed up at the hotel, he hadn't been expecting her to dress up. But she came downstairs looking amazing. He had suddenly felt embarrassed about his own appearance.

He chose the King's Court Tavern right near the center of town and Quinn was surprised when Kate asked for a romantically lit table in the far corner. Then he figured it out: it was much better to discuss their investigation without being overheard. When the waiter had finished taking their drink orders, Quinn started.

"So I did some digging," he said. "Thomas Fillmore."

Kate gave him a blank look.

"Should the name mean anything to me?"

Quinn looked around to ensure no one else could hear.

"That's Tim Anderson," he said. "He goes by Thomas Fillmore. Lord Halloween let him live."

"How the hell do you know that? And why does that name sound familiar?"

"Let's start at the beginning. I think Lord Halloween let Tim go, but also told him to get lost. So he does. But where does he go? And what is he going to do?"

"He could go anywhere or do anything," Kate responded.

"Go anywhere? Yes. Do anything? I don't think so," Quinn said. "If you looked at his writing, it's exceptional. I think I'm pretty good, but this guy was much, much better. I'm sure Lord Halloween put him off journalism for some period of time, but in 12 years, is the guy liable to give it up altogether?"

"He could go into PR," she said.

"Not a guy like this," Quinn said excitedly. "This is his talent. I've met people who are good at a couple things, but never one who is exceptional at more than one. Frankly, I don't know what I would do if I left journalism and PR is not a viable option for me. So wherever Tim went, it's a safe bet he's a reporter."

"And Fillmore is a reporter?"

"He's now the editor of the *Bluemont Gazette* in West Virginia," Quinn said.

"Hasn't that paper won a few awards?" she said.

Quinn put his finger to his nose. "Bingo," he said.

"There are more than two good writers in the world," Kate said.

"I paid $30 to buy some software that helps track down kids that are cheating in school. You know, they don't write that paper on *Great Expectations*, but instead just download it from the Internet? The software tracks phrases, even writing style, to help a teacher figure out if something is plagiarized. So it also can be used to scout through newspaper articles looking for someone who is ripping off someone else. If that's true, Fillmore is the biggest copycat of Anderson I've ever seen."

"How so?"

"Every writer establishes a style and we tend to fall back on the same turns of phrase, over and over. Anderson was dramatic but concise. In 1994, he wrote a story about the victim of a shooting that started: 'Violence was the thing that Carlos Ramirez fled from in El Salvador to start a new life in the United States, but it caught up with him on Friday night.' In 2003, Fillmore wrote this: 'Violence has been a factor in the life of Harry Davids since he was a teenager, but it finally caught up with him on Saturday night.'"

"Not conclusive," Kate said, but she was looking excited.

"No, but do you know how many matches I had by loading up Anderson's old articles into the software? Throughout the country, I got as many as two hundred to three hundred hits on a single reporter using the same kinds of phrases. That's not that weird, because not everything is unique. With Fillmore, that number is two thousand, five hundred and sixty-one. That's how many hits come out. Call it a writing signature."

Kate looked up at him.

"Quinn, you are a genius," she said. She leaned across the table and kissed him again. This time, the kiss seemed to linger for a second or two longer.

"Where is Fillmore now?"

"Still sitting in Bluemont, less than two hours' drive," Quinn said.

"Why wouldn't he go further away?" Kate asked. "I would think he'd be in New Zealand by now."

Quinn paused. "You are a fine one to talk," he said.

"But I'm..." she stumbled. "Actually, it's a good point. I don't know why I'm here either."

"Maybe he just couldn't get away," he said.

"Or maybe he's Lord Halloween," Kate said.

Quinn whistled. "What makes you say that?"

"Come on, he writes letters to himself, that's not so hard," Kate said. "One of the last letters even suggests as much."

"He's drawing attention to himself," Quinn said.

"And Lord Halloween lived for that," Kate said. "Anderson is a key to this puzzle. There is no doubt about it. Either he is Lord Halloween, or there is something very specific he wanted from Anderson."

But Quinn remembered something he couldn't quite place. Hadn't someone told him to look "for the victim that still lives?" For the life of him, however, he couldn't place who had told him that.

He had a hunch that Fillmore wasn't the killer, however.

"Either way, it sounds like a field trip is in order," Quinn said.

"Agreed," she said. "You have weekend plans?"

"I do now."

*****

After dinner, Quinn prepared to walk her home again.

"I need to stop by work first," she said as they got outside. It was just around the corner from the restaurant.

"You'll be back there again tomorrow," he said.

"I know, but I left some stuff I wanted to read over tonight," she said. "Fillmore still sounds familiar to me. I want to look at some of my research and see if I've come across the name before."

They arrived at the *Chronicle* and Quinn pulled out his key.

The office was dark and seemed foreboding at night. Neither Quinn nor Kate mentioned it, but both hurried through the reception area, past the advertising section and into the editorial room.

Kate stopped.

"Did you hear something?" she asked.

"You're kidding, right?" Quinn replied. He looked around. All the offices were dark, lit only by a faint light from the front reception area. "Let's grab your stuff and get out of here. I don't want to be more creeped out than I already am."

They paused a moment, heard nothing and she headed for her desk. She started rustling around.

"Quinn, turn on the light on my desk, will you?" she asked as she opened up her file drawer.

Quinn fumbled for the switch on the desk, found it and flipped on the light.

He glanced at the computer area and saw some print-outs on the left-hand side. There was a post-it note stuck to one.

He picked up the stack.

"Is this it?" he asked. "It looks like you labeled this stack."

He held up the stack to the light and froze.

The note wasn't a label.

"I don't think I labeled it," she said, shutting the file drawer and looking up at the papers.

"Oh my God," he said.

She read the note over his shoulder.

"He was here," she said. "And he knows."

The post-it note was simple: "See you soon, Trina."

Both of them looked at each other and then around the office.

"He could still be here," Quinn said quietly. "We should get out of here. Right now."

She grabbed his arm and reached into her purse. She pulled out a gun.

"Fuck," he said. "I didn't know you..."

She put a finger to her lips and the two carefully moved back toward the front door. They moved slowly, waiting for any sound, and she held the weapon out in front of her. They passed through the advertising section and Quinn thought he saw movement on the side.

But when he looked again, it was only his shadow on the wall.

Quinn looked to the front, while she kept an eye out behind them. Quinn felt like they were moving too slow. He fought down the urge to grab her and bolt toward the door.

At the reception desk, both jumped as the phone at the front rang. Kate pointed the gun at it.

"It's past 10 o'clock," Quinn said. "Who the hell would be calling?"

"Pick it up," Kate said.

"I don't think that's a good idea," he said.

"Pick it up," Kate said.

Quinn slowly reached over the desk and did so. He stared at the receiver and picked it up.

"*Loudoun Chronicle*," he said. "Hello."

There was no answer. At first, he wondered if it was a hang up. But then he distinctly heard the sound of breathing on the other end.

"Who is this?" he asked.

No response.

He walked around the desk and looked at the phone more carefully.

He dropped the phone, grabbed Kate and the two of them ran out the door.

"What did he say?" Kate demanded, still holding the gun in her hand as they ran down the street.

"Nothing," Quinn replied.

"Then why are we running?"

"It was an internal call," Quinn said. "He was in there."

Quinn and Kate fled into the darkness.

Chapter 16

Friday, Oct. 20

Quinn woke up stiff from sleeping on the couch all night. He looked at the clock. It was barely past 5 in the morning. He was not surprised.

Last night's adventure had him so wired he had taken more than three hours to fall asleep. And even in his dreams, he seemed to be keeping a close eye on the door.

Kate was in his bedroom—the two of them having mutually decided that it was best to stay together. Quinn wasn't sure to whose advantage that was. She had a gun and seemed to know how to use it. Of course, she was also the one being hunted.

The note had felt like a jolt to his system. He could only imagine what it felt like for her. The guy knew. Somehow he knew who Kate really was.

He kept turning the possibilities over in his head. The first was that Lord Halloween could have just seen her at some point, recognized similarities and done some research. That seemed implausible, however. How would you recognize someone after 12 years out of the blue, especially when they were a kid when you saw them last?

The second was that someone Kate had told had passed that information along to someone else. Or perhaps she had told the killer himself.

But Quinn knew that was a limited few, of which he was one. Since he knew he hadn't done it, he mentally marked himself off that list. He would just have to hope she did that too.

Janus clearly suspected Kate had a history here, Quinn considered briefly, but pushed the thought to the back of his head.

For starters, Janus was his best friend and incapable of being a murderer. A pain in the ass, yes. But he was no psychopath.

But how, he thought, do you know anyone for sure? He supposed the real murderer had friends he must hang out with, people he must know. Did they suspect? Quinn doubted it. Whoever did this kept that part of himself buried. And it was possible it was so buried the killer didn't know himself. Quinn had heard of people with multiple personality disorder, ones who weren't aware of what their other personalities did.

Even aside from that, Janus was not a logical suspect. Janus was... what? 30? 31? If he was the same murderer from more than a decade ago, he would have to have been killing as a teenager. Possible, but likely? Sure, there were kids in schools who started shooting people, but this was a different deal. This was vicious murder of a very personal nature.

Quinn sat up and rubbed his eyes. Maybe it was the lack of sleep. Could he really calmly be assessing whether his best friend was a killer?

He got up and walked the few steps to his kitchen. It was a mess, of course.

If he had known Kate would stay the night again, he might have cleaned up.

But the idea had never occurred to him. Not in the end-of-a-date romance kind of way and certainly not this one.

He idly fixed himself a cup of coffee, still keeping one eye on the door.

The guy could have followed them back. A worse thought suddenly occurred to him. If he knew who Kate was, he undoubtedly knew who Quinn was. And almost certainly knew where he lived.

Quinn would have to find someplace else to stay, he decided. They both had shied away from Kate's hotel, but Quinn wasn't sure why. They had hardly discussed it.

Quinn thought he heard a noise and paused for a moment. It was a soft clicking coming from his bedroom. It took him a minute to recognize the sound—someone was typing. Kate must be using his computer, he thought. He walked down the hallway and paused outside his door to be sure.

The typing stopped. Quinn waited and heard nothing.

He thought about tapping on the door, but decided he was imagining things. He turned to walk away and then the typing started again.

He cautiously opened the door.

Kate sat there fully dressed at his computer.

When the door opened, she practically jumped out of the chair.

"Quinn," she said.

"You couldn't sleep?" he asked and moved over to look at the computer. She hurriedly was closing windows on the screen. But Quinn caught a brief look at one.

It took him only a moment to figure out what was going on.

"Either you are now hiding your secret love of Internet porn, or you've been doing research—on me," he said.

Kate looked at him for a moment. He wondered if she had slept at all. She was dressed in the same clothes from last night.

"What makes you say that?" she asked.

"I caught a glimpse of my old paper on the screen as you were shutting down," he said. "Plus, you just look guilty."

Kate studied him for a moment more.

"I was doing research on you," she said finally.

Quinn sat down on the bed.

"Let me guess," he said. "You were trying to figure out if I was the killer? Or if I might be in league with him at any rate?"

"You were the only one I told, Quinn," she said. "I told you who I was and nobody else. So if he now knows..."

Quinn nodded.

"That's logical," he said. But he felt like he had been cold cocked nonetheless.

"It isn't that I think you're him, I just..."

"Had to be sure," he finished.

"Yes," she said.

"And are you?"

"Am I what?"

"Sure?" he asked.

She looked back at the computer screen briefly and laid her palm on the desk.

"No," she said. "I found nothing in there that helped me."

"I thought not," he said.

"I have to say—you are taking this pretty calmly," she said.

"So is that a strike for or against me?" he asked, with an air of resignation.

"I don't know," Kate replied.

He leaned on his knees.

"It hurts a little, you know," he said. "I have all this... I don't know. Since you came here and I met you, I've felt... Oh screw it."

He ran his hands through his hair. He was tired. She was paranoid. What was there to say?

"You felt what?" she asked, but she looked away from him.

"A connection," Quinn replied. "Like you and I were supposed to be together or something. I don't know how to explain it."

"I know you think you know me," she began.

He cut her off.

"That's just it," he said. "I don't think I know you at all. I just know I want to. But I can't do that if you don't trust me."

"I think you will agree our circumstances are a little different," she said.

"Of course," he replied. "And probably if I were in your shoes, I wouldn't trust anybody either. But I don't know how to convince you. I've been as honest with you as I know how."

Kate sighed.

"Here's the thing," Kate said. "How do you know another person really is who they seem to be?"

"You don't, you just..."

"No, no, don't answer quick," she said. "People can't see inside each other's heads. Everyone knows that. But think about how much people really don't know about their friends and their family. Read the papers. Read our paper. How many child molesters? Rapists? Bullies? Killers? How many of them have families who just see them as friendly old John or Joe?"

"I know," Quinn said.

"People don't even know themselves. Husbands and wives cheat on each other and even they can't explain it. They betray, they lie, they steal and sometimes feel like they are watching someone else do these things. Behind each person, there is a monster. A thing that lurks deep in their brain and slithers out every once in a while."

"That's not true," he replied.

"It is true and you know it," she said. "Everyone knows it. I've learned the hard way. You can't trust anybody. You can't even trust yourself."

There was a long pause between them.

"I don't believe that," Quinn said finally. "I believe you can trust people."

"But who, Quinn? How can you be sure?"

"I don't know," he said. "It's a risk..."

"Let's take it out of the hypothetical," Kate said. "How do you explain how the killer knows who I am? Let's assume it isn't you. Then how does he..."

"There are a few possibilities I was running over in my head," he said. "For starters, what about your dad's friend? The cop."

She nodded.

"I've been trying to do some research on him as well," she said.

"He's a possibility?" Quinn asked.

"I don't know," she said. "He is one of my dad's best friends. I find it hard to believe..."

"There is another possibility," Quinn said.

"Janus?" she asked. "I know. He could have figured it out."

Quinn did not know if he wanted to scream or laugh.

"This is insane," he said. "We are paranoid. I thought about it. I want you to know that. I really considered Janus. It's a possibility, but I don't think so. He would have been really young the first time around."

"Still possible, though," she said.

"Very unlikely," he replied. "Or there's the paper."

"Do they all know?"

"You blew up in a room full of reporters," he said. "You could have made someone curious."

"So one of the guys could be..."

"Or one of the women," Quinn said. "Or they could be working with him. Anybody could have been curious and dug a little."

She put her head in her hands.

"I knew this would happen," she said. "I just knew he would find me."

"He hasn't found you yet," Quinn said.

"How do you know?" she asked. "He could be here right now, waiting outside the door. He could be anyone—even you."

"I'm not him," Quinn said.

"I know, I know," she said, and then she laughed to herself. "But how do I really know? How can I trust anybody?"

Slowly, Quinn reached across and took her hand. She pulled it away.

"I'm sorry," she said. "I want to trust you. And I do..."

"But only so far," he finished.

"Yeah," she said. "I'm sorry. But I'm on my own here. He's hunting me, not you."

Quinn sighed and lay back on his bed. What was he supposed to say? How do you really know somebody else? There has to be some leap of faith, but what if you're wrong?

He raised himself up again and looked at her.

"I believe in you," he said. "I know it sounds corny. But I don't think you're going to be beaten by this guy. He may know who you are, but other than that, he knows nothing else about you."

"Like what?" she asked.

"You're not a scared little girl anymore, Kate. You're not the girl he saw. Don't let him put you in that position. You grew up. You're smart, capable and tough."

"Plus I have a gun and know how to use it," she added and smiled a little.

"There is that, yes," Quinn said. "You'll beat him. We'll beat him."

"I hope you're right, Quinn," she replied and the smile faded. "I hope you're right."

"Any news?" Janus asked when Quinn and Kate arrived at the *Chronicle* in the morning. Quinn was used to having most of the newsroom to himself, but he noticed Kyle, Buzz and Laurence were already there too.

"Hello," Janus said again, as Quinn stared at the Coke machine in the kitchen. "Any news?"

"What news?" Quinn asked, and suddenly he was reluctant to share too much information. "Not much help in the files, I'm afraid."

"Christ, you are bloody stupid," Janus said. "Not about that."

Janus glanced meaningfully in Kate's direction, who was already sitting at her desk.

"Oh," Quinn said and sat down. God, he was tired. "Not much."

"Not much?" Janus asked. "Dude, you guys came in together. And unless I miss my guess, this is the second day in a row where that's true. Plus you look totally knackered. So what kept you up all night, eh?"

"Not what you think," Quinn replied.

"So she didn't stay with you?" he asked. "I mean, it's early in the morning..."

"She did, but..." Quinn said. "Let's just say she came by to grab some stuff here last night. What she found was not exactly the stuff of romance."

"What?" Janus asked, sitting down in the chair across from him.

"A note from everyone's favorite serial killer."

"What?" Janus asked. "Are you fucking insane? Shouldn't the police be here then? What did they say when you called them?"

Quinn shook his head.

"We didn't. It would raise more problems than it would solve."

"That's the stupidest thing I've ever heard," Janus said. "You have to tell them. What if the guy left fingerprints?"

"He never does at murder scenes. Why would here be any different?"

"But you don't know, Quinn."

"I know that if we bring the police in, nothing good will come of it," Quinn replied.

"If you keep this a secret and they find out later, nothing good will come of that either," Janus said.

"Maybe. But some things are better left not broadcast."

Quinn was not sure why he and Kate had agreed to keep it secret. After all, the one person whom they did not want to find out her identity clearly already knew it. But there would be questions from Sheriff Brown, not exactly what either of them wanted at the moment.

"So he left a note?" Janus asked.

"He did," Quinn replied. "So she stayed at my place just in case he figured out where she lived."

"Where does she live?" Janus asked.

Quinn stared at him a moment.

"What makes you ask now?"

Janus' eyes widened.

"Are you crazy?" Janus said. "What—you think I might be behind this?"

"I don't know who's behind it, Janus."

"Well, it bloody well isn't me. And you should keep your paranoia in check."

"Just because you are paranoid does not mean they are not out to get you," Quinn replied.

"Come on, Quinn, you can't be serious," Janus said. "You know I could never do any of this. I was just being fucking inquisitive. Like reporters are supposed to be..."

Quinn lifted his hand.

"I don't think you did it," Quinn said.

"Good," Janus said. Then a long pause. "Why?"

"Just my intuition," Quinn said and got up to leave.

The two walked out of the kitchen to see much of the newsroom now in motion.

Nearly all the reporters were at their desks, even Buzz, who made it a habit never to be around when anyone else was.

"Big crowd today," Quinn said. "And early, too."

"Not hard to see why," Janus said.

Quinn looked at him.

"If there is a killer on the loose, would you want to be sitting at home alone?"

Quinn looked over at Kate who was working the phones.

"No, I wouldn't," he said.

*****

Though all the reporters were at the office, most of them were stuck with little to do. Friday was a slow day in their news cycle, the day they were supposed to kick back, check with sources and plan for the next week's paper.

Kyle was the only reporter who was busy.

It was a hard thing for Quinn not to resent. Since crime was Kyle's beat, he had taken over much of the investigation into the recent murders. Around noon, he loudly mentioned to anyone in ear shot that there was another possible killing in Lovettsville and had to run to check it out. It turned out to be nothing but a wild goose chase, but it was clear the guy was in his element, having fun. He was on the phones all day checking in with people.

And Quinn had nothing. He had found Tim Anderson—maybe—but he couldn't go out there today. He worked the phones all day hoping to get some new information on the murders, but he got nowhere. His police sources were terse, barely even polite, and he felt like he was spinning his wheels.

Quinn watched Kyle stand up and, much to his surprise, the mustached reporter came his way.

"Quinn," Kyle said. "I was hoping for some assistance."

Quinn's jaw practically hit the floor. That had simply never happened before. Kyle hated help. He didn't seek it and he didn't want it.

"I know, I know," Kyle said. "It's unusual for me to ask."

Unusual? Try unprecedented, Quinn thought.

"But there is a lot going on here and I can't keep up with all of it."

"What can I do for you?" Quinn asked. It came out sounding more excited than he meant it to.

"I'm chasing down too many leads," Kyle replied. "There was the Lovettsville thing and I keep getting calls from people who think they may have seen something. There are just too many to keep track of and I'm already thinking I could be here all night every night for the next week. I thought maybe we could divide some of it up and you could help with the legwork."

Quinn sat stunned.

"You want to be a team on this?" Quinn asked.

"It's too much for one person," Kyle said. "I figured rather than getting beaten by the *Post*, it would be smarter to get help."

"Sure, Kyle," Quinn said. "You know I'm happy to help."

And with that, the two of them sat down and went through a list of more than a dozen phone calls. If he had not already known the panic was coming, Quinn could see it now. It was just a trickle of course, but one more murder would send everyone over the edge. There were calls from all over the county. They divided up the list of leads, with Kyle even allowing Quinn to pick a few. Quinn was still amazed at the sudden shift in Kyle's behavior. This was a guy who usually wanted the biggest story all to himself. Quinn had been free to pursue his own leads, but the idea that Kyle might share his own tips had never crossed Quinn's mind.

Maybe Rebecca or Laurence had talked to Kyle, he thought.

By afternoon, he was half-way through his list. For the most part they were dead ends: people who heard vague noises outside their house at night and a couple who thought their neighbors, whom they had never liked, were the killers. Quinn would have preferred to go in person, but there were simply too many leads.

It was the seventh or eighth call that sounded different. It was something in the guy's voice that did it for him. He sounded too calm and kept apologizing for bothering anyone. Panicked people didn't do that. They insisted that it was something serious and demanded attention.

Quinn called Janus and asked to meet him in a neighborhood on the outer edges of Leesburg.

On his way out, he stopped by Kate's desk. She was busy looking things up on the Internet—Quinn couldn't immediately tell what. He knelt down beside her.

"I have to meet Janus out near Rudolph Street," Quinn said. "You okay here?"

She turned to him and Quinn momentarily wanted to step back. He felt like he was looking at a stranger. Her face was impassive.

"I'm okay without you, you know," she said.

Quinn held up his hands.

"I never implied anything else," he said. "It's just..."

"I'll be fine," she said.

Quinn didn't want to draw attention to them. He looked at her for a moment more and then headed out the door.

It was about a 10 minute drive to the house of Tony Comizio, a big burly guy who should have a voice like Arnold

Schwarzenegger's, Quinn thought. Instead, his voice was almost too soft.

"I should have called the police maybe," Comizio said, and Quinn had to inch closer to hear him. "But I know a couple of guys over there and I didn't want them making fun of me."

Janus pulled up in the driveway behind them.

Quinn motioned to the car.

"That's my photographer. Why would they make fun of you? You said on the phone you found something."

"It's probably nothing," Comizio said. "You guys can come out and see. I'm probably wasting your time."

Janus looked at Quinn quizzically as he walked up and Quinn shrugged. He was beginning to think Mr. Comizio had self-esteem issues.

They followed Comizio around back. The house was a nice large, brick colonial. It was in a good subdivision but backed up on a forest. In a few years, Quinn knew these beautiful woods would be gone, plowed down to make way for a new subdivision. But for now... it was nice.

"It's back here," Comizio said. They walked to the back of his yard and followed him as he disappeared into a copse of trees.

Quinn was amazed at how fast civilization seemed to disappear here. One minute he had been driving through a pleasant suburb and now all he could see were trees. Comizio stopped at the top of a hill and looked down a steep slope.

"It's down here," he said. "Watch your step."

Janus nearly fell, but grabbed a branch to avoid sliding. The three of them carefully worked their way down the slope.

"It's wild back here," Quinn said.

"We're on the old Phillips farm now," Comizio said.

"Right," Quinn said. He knew more than he wanted to about this place.

"Some developer wants to pay a fortune for it," Comizio said. "It's a huge space. About 60 acres of prime Loudoun land."

They continued walking for a bit. Normally Quinn might have loved the opportunity for a walk in the woods. But he still felt jumpy from last night and had a strange feeling that someone was watching him.

"What do you think about the development deal?" Quinn asked.

He was not sure he cared that much. But it was a conversation and Janus was being oddly silent.

"Well, I guess most of us are against it," he said. "I mean, it's historical land, isn't it? That fantastic dirt road, you know? George Washington used it. And they keep that covered bridge in great condition. Well, the Phillips used to at any rate. It's a little worse for wear now."

"Right." But Quinn didn't have any idea what he was talking about. The feeling in his stomach had gotten worse. He felt queasy and the sense of being watched was stronger.

"You know the one, right?" Comizio asked. "People still use it occasionally to get out to Waterford, especially during the craft fair like the one last week. You have to go slow, of course, but people still use it."

Quinn now remembered the bridge, but couldn't remember taking it. He also couldn't remember the last time he was in Waterford.

"Right," he said.

"We're almost there," Comizio said again, as they walked up a short hill.

"I'm bloody out of shape," Janus said finally. "I mean, I'm doing okay. I'm pretty sure Bill would have keeled over already. But still..."

"I started hearing it about a week ago," Comizio said as they came to a clearing. There was a small, narrow field in front of them.

"Hearing what?" Quinn asked.

"Horses," Comizio said quietly.

Quinn's heart skipped a beat.

"Multiple horses?" he asked.

"I don't know," Comizio said. "Believe it or not, you can hear a lot from the house. But the first night I thought I was dreaming."

"What did you hear?" Quinn asked. He felt like he had to concentrate just to get the words out. Now he knew why he felt so terrible. The field, the woods, everything had a familiar feeling. In his head, he turned over Comizio's words again. The road. The bridge. He felt like he wanted to run.

"It would be in the middle of the night," he said. "I mean— it's impossible to ride at that speed in the dark, especially through here, you know?"

"Yeah," Quinn said.

"So I thought I was just imagining it," Comizio continued. "It was the same thing every night. I would hear it at one o'clock one night, then two hours later. It was a little freaky."

"I bet," Janus said.

"I'm sorry again, guys," Comizio said and looked down at his shoes. "This probably has nothing to do with what you are working on."

"Why did you think it did?" Quinn asked.

"Because I thought I was crazy, right?" Comizio said. "Then I came down here and started seeing stuff, too."

Comizio walked forward a bit and pointed at a patch of mud near the edge of the field. Quinn did not even have to look. There were hoof prints in the mud.

"That was the first thing," Comizio said. "Then it was other stuff."

"What other stuff?" Janus asked.

Quinn could not move. He felt his heart pounding. He wanted very much to run or stay immobile. He could not decide.

Comizio and Janus appeared not to notice.

"Look up here," Comizio said. He and Janus walked over to some trees near the edge of the field. Quinn couldn't hear them anymore.

"You coming, Quinn?" Janus called back, but without looking.

Quinn did not know how he could. I won't be able to take it, he thought. Last night a very real killer had been in the same room with him. He might be watching him even now. And now this guy was seeing Quinn's phantom. Something that should not be real. I can't take both of these things, Quinn thought. I'll lose my mind.

"Quinn?" Janus called.

With tremendous effort, Quinn moved forward. He walked stiffly across the distance and could feel his legs wanting to break into a run.

"What?" he asked. His voice came out as a whisper. Janus looked at him for a minute.

"What?" Quinn asked again.

"Cuts in the tree," Janus said. "Look at the limbs on the right side."

Quinn looked down the right side of the field. Branches hanging over the right side were broken, as if something rode through them.

"Someone has been riding up and down the field," Janus said. "Apparently in the middle of the night. And look at this."

Janus pointed to the tree in front of them. There were a series of cuts on it. Quinn knew what kind of instrument had done the cutting: a sword. The Horseman had been here.

"I think it forms a word," Comizio finally said.

"Really?" Janus asked. He looked at the tree harder. "Is that an S?"

Comizio nodded.

"It took me a bit," he said. "But I figured it out. Or at least I think I did."

Before he could say it, Quinn knew what the word was. He did not know how or why.

"Sanheim," Quinn said.

Comizio turned in surprise.

"Yeah," he said. "But it took me a couple of days to figure that out. You have to step back. How did you even see it?"

"Sanheim?" Janus asked. "That's just another word for Halloween."

"What?" Quinn asked, suddenly turning to Janus.

"He's right," said Comizio. "I looked it up on the Net. It's similar to the spelling of the Celtic word for Halloween. He was the God of Halloween, I think. All these Christian groups are going on about how Halloween is a pagan festival and stuff. They keep using his name. That's why I thought you guys would want to see it. Because of that killer. I've only lived here six years, but I've heard the stories. Lord Halloween, right? Isn't that his name? It wasn't in the paper, but I thought..."

"That's his name," Quinn said. He stared at the word on the tree. It should mean something to him, but it didn't. Or it did, but he couldn't remember it. It was like having something on the tip of your tongue, but not being able to say it. He knew the word, but why? Was it in his dream too? Everything else about this place was so familiar.

"Right," Comizio said. "So I thought this was the God of Halloween, right? The killer calls himself Lord Halloween? It can't be a coincidence, right? Maybe the killer has been out here, riding around. I know I must sound pretty stupid."

"It doesn't sound stupid at all," Quinn said.

"I'm glad to hear you say it," Comizio said. "Should I call the police? I mean, I didn't want to if it was a waste of time. I know those guys are busy."

"You might want to," Quinn said. "They might not get it, but it can't be a coincidence. I talked to someone else who thought they saw a horseman late at night, too."

"Really? Oh, thank God, I thought I was going crazy." Comizio was visibly relieved. "I thought maybe you guys would laugh at me."

Quinn stared at the word in the tree. The hunt for Lord Halloween had pushed a lot of what Dee said out of his mind. He had been focusing on something real. But this was something different, he could just feel it.

"Are you okay?" Comizio asked. "I mean, you don't look great."

"I'm fine," Quinn said. "Janus, why don't you take some photos? See if you can get the word in it."

"Right," Janus said. "I actually forgot."

"So you think I should call the police then?" Comizio asked. "To be honest, you are kinda weirding me out, too, you know? You keep staring at that thing."

Quinn wrenched his attention away for a moment.

"It's just unusual," he said. "Yes, you should call the police. And one other thing."

Quinn looked around him. He still felt watched and he felt that every minute pretending to be okay was a tremendous effort.

"What?" Comizio asked.

"Move," Quinn said. "Pack a suitcase, take your stuff and get the hell out of here."

Comizio stared at him for a moment.

"Are you kidding?" he asked. "I mean, it is weird, but I'm okay at handling myself."

"Not at handling this," Quinn said. "If it is Lord Halloween, no one tangles with him and lives. And it could be something different but I don't think you want to find out. Because if it is, I think that would be just as bad. Honestly, I think it could be worse."

Chapter 17

"When they found me, I was unconscious. At first they believed I had something to do with it. As if I alone could harm 100 people or make them vanish into thin air. I knew the truth, I told it to them. But they would not believe. They still scour the countryside for those that can never be found. I have been left behind as an emissary. The Prince of Sanheim has come. His time is at hand."
—Horace Camden, "The Prince of Sanheim"

Saturday, Oct. 21

Quinn stared at the clock. If he had fallen asleep at all, in his dreams he had still seen the clock. But he wasn't sure he had actually fallen asleep. It was too risky. He could not afford to dream about the Horseman anymore.

He and Kate had barely spoken in the evening. She was still sleeping in his bedroom and he was out on the sofa again. There was an unspoken assumption that his place was somehow safer. Quinn wasn't sure why. Maybe it was just that his place was better stocked with food.

But he and Kate didn't feel like partners anymore. She seemed angry again last night and Quinn was reasonably sure she had barricaded her door before she went to sleep. So either she still didn't trust Quinn or she didn't care if the killer got him first.

He was not sure he blamed her. After going to Comizio's house, nothing seemed real anymore. He felt like he had gone crazy—like this is what it felt like. He didn't tell Kate. She had hardly been in a talking mood, for starters, but mostly he just could not bring himself to.

What was he supposed to say? She had a real problem—a madman with a penchant for carving his victims was after her. And what was his problem? A phantom Horseman from a fictional story? One that has lived in his dreams for years and now appeared to be stopping off for a little tree graffiti? If he was trying to convince Kate he could be trusted, somehow he didn't think that story was the place to start.

But what was he supposed to do? There was nowhere to run and nothing he could say to anyone. Janus had tried to talk as they walked back from Comizio's place, but Quinn could not bring himself to say any of this out loud. It was too nuts.

Quinn's reverie was interrupted by screaming. Acting without thinking, he was out of the sofa bed and ran toward where Kate was sleeping.

He collided with the bedroom door with a thud. He started pushing on it as hard as he could and then backed up to launch himself at the door. It worked well enough and Quinn thought wryly that it was not much protection against any real intruder.

His dresser had been placed behind the door and had now tipped over. He got his door open just far enough and then squeezed his way through.

The screaming kept coming. Quinn could hardly see. He tried to flip on his light to see what was happening, but missed the switch. He didn't pause, but kept running to the bed. Other than Kate, though, there was no one there.

She was screaming in her sleep. He grabbed her arm and her eyes flew open, but she kept screaming for a moment. And then she stopped suddenly.

"Kate," he said, as gently as he could. "Are you okay?"

She didn't respond, but just stared at him for what felt like several minutes. She looked like a person in shock.

Quinn instinctively moved closer to her and put his arm around her in a kind of half hug.

"It was a dream," he said. "It was just a dream."

Her eyes followed him carefully, watching him as if he were about to do something suddenly.

"It's okay," he said, and tried to smile. "It's okay. You were screaming in your sleep. I came in to wake you up."

Her eyes drifted to the door. Enough light was peaking through the doorway that Quinn could now see his dresser on the floor. It flashed through his mind that he was glad he had gotten the furniture for free from an old friend. Otherwise he might have been sorry to see it so abused.

"Are you okay?" he asked, and sat up looking at her.

"Yes," she said finally, with what seemed like a tremendous effort.

"What were you dreaming about?" he asked.

She shifted her eyes away from him and back to the door.

"The door is open," she said. She sounded like a robot.

He looked back that way.

"I know," he said. "I'm sorry. I had to break in because you were screaming in your sleep."

"Oh," she replied, still with a strange monotone quality.

And suddenly it clicked.

"You're still sleeping, aren't you?" he asked. He had heard someone talking about this once. Some people could carry on entire conversations in their sleep. It explained why she had that strange tone of voice and it took so long for her to answer.

She didn't respond.

"Okay," he said. "I want you to put your head back down on the pillow and close your eyes. Okay?"

She seemed not to hear him.

"Kate?" he asked. "You need to go back to sleep. You need to get rest."

"You should shut the door," she said.

"I promise I will when you go back to sleep," he said and ran his hand through her hair in the hopes of calming her down.

"You should shut the door now," Kate said again, still in the eerie voice. "My mom says he is coming."

The hairs on the back of Quinn's neck stood up. Suddenly the room felt colder and he looked at the door too.

"She told you that just now?" he asked.

"Uh-huh," she said. "She said he has been watching us."

"When will he come?"

"My mom says soon," Kate said. "You should shut the door."

"I will, Kate," he said. "I'm going to go back over there and shut the door on my way outside. I'll be outside and I won't let anyone through. If you need anything, just shout... again."

"No," she said simply. "Stay here. You should stay here in case he gets in."

Quinn paused for a moment. He was freaked out now, too, and somehow being in a smaller place with only one small window seemed safer.

"Okay, Kate," he replied. "I'll shut the door and I'll be right over there."

He pointed at the computer chair. He got up and shut the door, then wrestled for a minute with the dresser to right it again in front of the door. He was not taking any chances. It took a minute for his eyes to get used to the dark, but when he looked back at Kate, her eyes were closed. She was sleeping again.

Quinn sat down in the chair and waited.

*****

"How did you get in here?" a voice asked.

Quinn woke up with a start. He felt disoriented and it took him a while to figure out what was going on. He was in his room and he realized that somehow he had fallen asleep.

"What?" he said groggily.

Quinn looked around. Kate was sitting up in bed (his bed) and looking at him.

"How did you get in here?" she asked again. She was looking at the door, which still had the dresser propped up against it. "I never heard you get past that. The noise should have woken me up."

It took Quinn a moment to remember everything. He was surprised he had fallen asleep. One moment he had been waiting for something to happen and then... nothing. And he appeared to have slept pretty deeply too. He wiped some drool off the edge of his mouth.

"You were screaming," he said. "You started screaming and I busted down the door enough for me to get in."

"I don't remember that," Kate said. Her tone sounded accusatory.

"Well, that's not my fault, is it?" he snapped back at her. She had acted like this all the previous evening—cold and distant. On the one hand, they were together and supposed to be partners in this mess. But he felt like he was just dead weight in her eyes. He was simply an obstacle the killer would have to mow down before he got to the real show.

"I didn't..." Kate said and stopped. She took a deep breath. "I just meant, what happened? Why was I screaming?"

"I'm not sure," Quinn said. "I thought I woke you up, but you were sleep walking. Well, not walking. I guess sleep talking. You stopped screaming at any rate and we talked for a little bit."

"What did we say?" Kate asked.

"Look, is that important?" he replied. "You had a bad dream. You kept looking at the door and telling me I needed to close it. So I said I would on my way out and you said I should stay here. So I fixed the dresser back up against the door and stayed here.

"I just thought it was safer that way. What is the point of one of us staying in a boarded-up room and the other one left outside it?"

"I put it there because..."

"I know why you put it there, Kate," Quinn said. He suddenly didn't feel like playing nice anymore. "Because either you don't trust me and think I might kill you, or you don't care what happens to me out there."

"That's not true," she said.

"It isn't? So if I had started shouting for help out there, how fast could you have been out there with your gun? How long do you think it would take for somebody to kill me? Jesus. If we're supposed to be safer together, then let's be together. But instead you want it both ways. I'm out guarding the main door, but if he makes it through there, then at least you get some time to prepare before I'm out of the way."

"Quinn, I..."

"Look, I know you are scared," he said. "I understand that. But I'm scared too. I know this guy is gunning for you, but do you really think he is going to stop and have tea with me when he finds us? I'm staying near you because I want to help. But between yesterday's 'I don't need your help Quinn' and physically locking me out of my own room, what the hell am I supposed to think?"

He was really angry now and knew he should drop it. She had been through a lot and it wouldn't help if he blew up at her. But damn if he didn't feel better.

Quinn got up and walked over to the door, taking a minute to work the dresser out of the way.

"Either trust me or don't," Quinn said, more quietly this time, as he opened the door. "If you can't trust me, then take shelter somewhere else, because then I'm just one more thing to worry about."

He walked outside. And stopped dead cold when he saw the note.

Right on the outside of the door was a small post-it note. It simply had one word on it.

"Almost."

*****

Fifteen minutes later they had checked the apartment with her gun and satisfied themselves that there was no one else there. The front door had clearly been forced from the outside. If Quinn thought he would have satisfaction from finally having proof that he wasn't involved, he didn't feel it. Instead, he concentrated on the fact that if not for Kate's nightmare, he could have been dead. Likely would have been.

Of course, he had been awake in the living room. Maybe he would have been awake when the guy came through the door. But he didn't feel like it. He felt that somehow the guy must have known when he was sleeping. Even after checking every nook and cranny of the apartment, he did not feel safe. Would the guy hit them on the way out the door? Would he be waiting in Quinn's car?

Kate, for her part, appeared better than she had been for several days. She checked the apartment with a strange calm that Quinn was grateful for, since he was definitely lacking it. For the only time he could remember, Quinn was glad he had few rooms— and fewer places to hide.

"We can't come back here," she said finally. He nodded and they packed quickly. Their visitor was in all likelihood gone, but how could they be sure of anything?

Five minutes later they were at the car and after Quinn first checked the trunk and back seat carefully, they climbed in. He felt like he was being watched from somewhere and knew that was probably right.

He started driving with no real direction in mind.

"Where to?" he asked when they pulled onto Route 7.

"We need to check the hotel," she said.

"That's not a safe place," Quinn replied.

"I agree, but I should pick up some stuff before we hit the road."

"And where, exactly, are we going to go?"

"For starters—Bluemont," she said.

"You can't be serious," Quinn said.

Kate just stared at him, raising her eyebrows.

"Okay, apparently you can be," Quinn said. "Even if I got the right guy, how's that going to help?"

"It's a lead," she said. "And besides—we have to find Lord Halloween before he finds us, again. Wouldn't you rather be on the offensive?"

"Couldn't we just run?" Quinn said. "We could just take off, you know. We don't have to stay here. He can't follow us forever."

"I've done that, remember?" Kate said. "You run now and it'll never end."

"That's all well and good, but this is serious," he said. "They say that in the movies all the time, but this is real life. Couldn't we live with a few phantoms over our shoulders?"

She shook her head and put her hand on his shoulder.

"If you want, go ahead," she said. "But I'm through running. I told you—there is not a day that goes by that I don't think of him. I'm not going to keep going like that, even if it means I'm dead. Besides, I think he is underestimating us."

"You do?" Quinn asked. "No offense, but we got caught with our pants down back there. He walked in right under our noses."

"But we are still here, Quinn. We are still here, aren't we?"

"Forgive me if I don't feel that much better," he replied. "That seems like blind luck."

"You are thinking of it all wrong," she said. "He has had the advantage from the beginning. There is no surprise. He knows who I am. He knows who you are. We don't have that luxury. We can't follow him home. But he has given himself away too. I don't think he came here meaning to scare us again, Quinn. I think he came ready to kill."

"And let me get this right—this makes you feel better?"

"It does," she said. "Because he failed. And he proved to me one thing—you aren't helping him."

"How can you be sure?" he shot back. "Maybe I went outside, forced the door open to look like a break-in, left a note, broke down your door, then put it all back up again."

"Why would you do that?" she asked.

"I'm honestly not sure," Quinn said. "So that you'll be lulled into a false sense of security and trust me? I admit it's a reach."

"Yes, a bit too far," she said. "The only reason he would do all that would be to kill me at my most vulnerable. But you've already seen me that way."

"When?"

"Last night," she said. "You could have killed me then."

"Well, you were kinda awake," he said.

"Not enough," she said. "I'm sorry I blocked the door, but the other night, I couldn't sleep at all. I kept wondering what if. What if you are working with him? What if you are him? What if..."

"I get it, I get it," he said.

"But if last night was a test, you passed. I never heard that dresser come down and I never saw you put it back up either. We were locked in a room by ourselves—so much so that he must have thought he could not get through without waking both of us up. I don't think this guy plays the kind of psychological game where he pretends to be my boyfriend and then murders me. I think if he had the chance to kill me—just one chance—he would have taken it."

"Why? He seems to enjoy playing with his prey."

"No, I think I figured out what he wants," she said.

"Which is?"

"He wants a story," Kate said.

"He is a story," Quinn said. "He is all anybody talks about."

"But talk is the right word," she replied. "So far nobody has put his nickname in the paper. People might be talking, but there is no real mention of him."

"He will get it soon enough."

"I agree and I think he knows that too," she said. "But I think he wants the story to be about us."

"You and me?"

"Me and him," she said. "I think he would have killed us last night and left a note about who I was. That would have been a two-for-one—it would have proved to the police he is Lord Halloween and it would have splashed the story right on the front page with his name on it. It also would have been a sad story, with pictures of me and my mother and interviews with my dad. And details about how I concealed my identity."

"You have it all worked out," Quinn said.

"Believe me, so does he. That's why I caught his attention. He might be taking down some other people to add to his body count, but I think he intended to make me his official grand entrance, so to speak."

"Well, he came close."

"But that's just it—close, but not close enough," she said. "And I don't think he thinks very highly of our ability to protect ourselves."

"Well, we have one thing in common," Quinn said.

"That's going to change," she said. "I've been giving this a lot of thought. But one problem was my own doubt."

"In what?"

"In who?" She re-phrased his question. "I doubted you. But I'm going to take that leap of faith you suggested. From this point on, we are in this together."

Quinn laughed.

"From this point forward? I've been there," he said.

"Well, now I'm there too," she said.

They drove to the hotel.

*****

They had barely crossed the lobby before a manager began approaching them. Dressed up in a tight, vaguely Victorian-era version of a tuxedo, he was clearly angry.

"We've been trying to reach you, madam," he said, giving Quinn a glance that suggested he thought very little of him as a dresser or a person.

"You've had my cell phone," she said.

"Well, your boyfriend said you changed it," the hotel manager said. He looked meaningfully at Quinn.

Kate looked confused and glanced at Quinn, who shrugged and indicated he had no idea what was going on. Secretly, however, in the middle of one of the biggest scares of his life, he was pleased. The manager had said boyfriend and Kate had assumed—just assumed—he was referring to Quinn. Maybe that meant something or maybe it didn't, but he was still damn glad to see it.

"He gave us your new phone number," the manager said, but the glances between Kate and Quinn had unnerved him. The bluster and outrage building in the hotel employee appeared to be fading. Something was not going according to his plan.

"And you didn't think to try the old one?" Kate said. "Who, exactly, did you say said this?"

"Your boyfriend," he replied, sounding less angry. "He called from your room."

"And was I in it?"

"Well, I assumed you were," the manager said, and anger had clearly been replaced by something else: defensiveness.

"Why were you trying to reach me?" Kate asked calmly.

"Your room. It was left in an unacceptable condition," the manager said, but he was looking around him now. Quinn thought he looked like a man searching for back up.

"I see," she said. "And did it ever occur to you that my 'boyfriend' may actually have been an intruder? That maybe, just maybe, he wasn't with me at all?"

"No, that did not occur to us," the manager said. "He seemed so confident, like he was supposed to be there."

"I want to see the room," Kate said.

"I don't think that's such a good idea," the manager said, clearly wishing he hadn't started the conversation to begin with.

"It's my room—I paid for it," Kate said.

She started walking very calmly toward the elevators.

"Madam," the manager said. "Madam, I can't allow that."

"But you can allow a total stranger in my room?" Kate said. "How did he get in there anyway?"

"We assumed you let him in," the manager said. "I think now maybe this is a police matter."

"You may be more right than you know," Kate said. "Which is why I want to look at the place before they get here."

"I can't allow that," the manager said.

"What's your name?" Quinn asked. He pulled out a pad of paper and started writing.

"Eric Hoffman," the manager said stiffly. "I have the full backing of the hotel's owners, I can assure you. There's no use trying to intimidate me."

"I'm not trying that," Quinn said evenly. "Just wanted to know your name for the paper."

"The paper?"

"We work for the *Chronicle*, Mr. Hoffman," Quinn said. "I work on the crime beat. And this is a crime. I'm sure a lot of people will be interested in your security standards."

"Or you could just let us in and we'll keep your name out of it," Kate said.

The manager paused and considered. It felt like forever, but he finally gestured toward the elevator.

"But my name is not to be anywhere near this story," he said.

They rode the elevator in silence and Kate walked quickly to her room once it stopped and opened. If she was nervous, she didn't show it. Quinn almost wondered if she would grab her gun, but she didn't even pause when the manager opened the door.

"Dear God," she said as she walked in.

The room was a disaster. Virtually every piece of furniture had been overturned. The table lamp lay on its side with the light bulb crushed into the carpet. The bed's mattresses had been taken off the bed frame. One lay against the wall and the other was strewn halfway on the bed. The coffee table had been shattered as if someone had fallen on it. Quinn glanced into the bathroom and could see shards of mirror lying on the floor.

"You see why we were upset," the manager said.

"You thought she did this?" Quinn said.

"We thought... the man said... he told the front desk there was a bit of a party. We didn't hear much, so we didn't think about it. It wasn't until the next morning..."

"How could you not hear this?" Quinn asked.

Kate started walking around. Her clothes had been removed from the drawers and were strewn all over the room. There was a bra hanging from a light fixture and three panties laid out in a row on the bed's headboard. Kate made no move to pick anything up.

Instead, she appeared to be looking for something.

"Watch out for the broken glass," Quinn said. He wasn't sure what she was looking for.

"We need to call the police," the manager said.

"In a minute," Kate said. "You and I need to talk first."

"Talk about what?" the manager said. He sounded nervous. He clearly had assumed Kate would pay for damages and now had stumbled onto something quite different.

Kate didn't answer. Instead she scoured the hotel room floor, stepping over a pair of pants and a blouse. Quinn was about to ask her what she was looking for when she leaned down and scooped a piece of paper off the ground. She read it, crossed the room and handed it to Quinn.

"I'm going to kill you slowly, Trina," the note read.

"What's it say?" the manager asked.

Neither one of them responded.

"Here's what we're going to do," Kate said. "I'm going to cut you a deal."

"Cut me a deal? We have insurance. If you don't know the gentleman who did this..."

"Oh, I know him," Kate said. "Lord Halloween did this."

The man audibly gasped.

"How can you say such a thing?" the man said. "That's libel. I'll sue."

"First of all," Quinn said, "It's slander, not libel. Libel is printed and we haven't done that yet. Second of all, it's also true."

"You're going to make two copies of the hotel security feed for the past several days," Kate said. "One copy goes to me and the other goes to the police."

"Why would I do such a thing?" the man said. "I'm not giving anything to reporters. If the police want them, we will of course cooperate."

"You want to help me," Kate said, and she smiled. Quinn thought she was beautiful, but the smile looked cold and ruthless. "Because if you don't, I'm going to put this on the front page of the *Chronicle*: 'Lord Halloween Strikes Leesburg Inn.'"

"The police will do that anyway," the manager said, but he sounded doubtful.

"Please," Kate replied. "The police want to cover this up even more than you do. But as you say, we're reporters. I would be more than happy to write in detail of how the hotel security let a psychopath into one of their guest's rooms. Do you know how fast business would dry up?"

"I'll tell everyone you threatened me," the manager said.

"Say what you want," Kate said, and smiled again. If anything, it looked more cruel than before. "No one will believe you. You will just be trying to protect yourself. They'll be too busy running away from here and your bosses will be too busy trying to find someone to blame. And it won't take them long to find someone, will it?"

The manager stood and stared. He looked at Quinn, who just stared back

"What do you want?" the manager said.

"The security feed," Kate said. "Just a copy—same as the police get—we're not trying to interfere, after all."

"To do what with it? Put it in the paper?"

"We're going to do you a favor," Kate said. "If the police don't mention you, we won't either. The minute they go public with this, we can't help you. But if they cover up this incident, you're home free. We'll just use the tapes for research and nobody needs to bring this up again."

Quinn could see the manager turning it over in his mind. It was a trap and he knew it. If he didn't cooperate, he would be looking for a new job by the end of the week. If he did, there was no guarantee it would help him much.

"Your call," Kate said. "Take a risk and you might get lucky. But if you don't play along, I assure you this place will be out of business by Christmas."

The manager turned and looked at the room.

"Why do things like this always happen to me?" he said. Without looking back, he turned and walked out of the room. Very quietly, as he passed Quinn, he motioned for them to follow him.

Twenty minutes later, Kate and Quinn were handed copies of the tapes covering the entire week.

The manager had regained his officious tone.

"You breathe a word of this and I will sue you," he said.

Kate nodded but waited till they were at the door to respond.

"The police are going to want to question me," she said. "Tell them I'm staying with Quinn O'Brion. And one other thing..."

"Yes," the manager said. In his head, he was beginning to see a way out. The police would come and they would stay quiet. And these reporters—who were they, really? They would stay quiet or face a lifetime of litigation. Eric Hoffman was back in control again.

"You missing any personnel?"

The manager stopped in his tracks. The blood drained slowly from his face.

"When did she disappear?" Quinn asked.

The manager didn't respond. He didn't have to; his face said it all.

"You might want to tell the police about that too," Kate said.

And with that, the two were out the door. Eric Hoffman went back to his desk a broken man.

*****

They had gone shopping. That was the thing that Quinn couldn't believe. They were being chased by a psycho and they had gone shopping.

Quinn could see it was necessary. Kate simply hadn't wanted anything left for her at the hotel and he couldn't blame her. The police would probably be rifling through her things by now anyway.

So they had spent two hours in the Leesburg outlet malls just outside of town, jumping from one store to the next. Quinn—who hated shopping above all else—actually found himself enjoying it. For one, it was such a normal activity that it was easy to forget they were under imminent threat of death. The day was bright, the sun was shining and hundreds of people were with them. The night before felt like a bad dream.

The other thing that was hard to miss was how much Quinn felt like Kate's boyfriend. He waited outside the dressing room with the other boyfriends and gave a thumbs up or down anytime she came out with something new. Granted, some boyfriends got to go inside the dressing room, but Quinn wasn't complaining. He just enjoyed being with her.

And it was then that he finally knew it: he was in love with her. He had only known her a few days, but it felt like forever. She had literally left him to die in his own apartment because of her trust issues and he didn't care. He looked at her and everything was better. He was with her and everything was right. Had he ever been in love before? Quinn had thought so. He had believed he was. But that felt like a pale imitation of what he was going through now. And he knew it was real because of this: Quinn was in real danger. Kate could very well—almost certainly would—get him killed. And he didn't care. The thought of abandoning her, of running from her, was unfathomable. He would never do it. He would die for her.

"What are you smiling about?" Kate asked him as she showed off her latest pick of clothes.

"Nothing," he replied, and wiped the smile off his face. He was going to die, but he was in love. He didn't feel alone anymore.

Within ten minutes, they were back in the car. If Kate was scared, Quinn had trouble seeing it.

"He could have followed us out here, you know," Quinn said.

"That's true and he could follow us now," she replied. "But I don't think so. He has other plans than just me and he can't afford to watch us all day. He can't be everywhere at once. Besides, let him watch me. Let him see me not cowering in front of him. That will frustrate him more than anything else."

"So where are we off to?" Quinn said.

"Same plan as before," she replied. "Bluemont."

"The police are going to want to see us," Quinn said. "After the hotel and everything."

"They can wait," she said. "Their job will be to cover this whole thing up. I'll talk to them when we're ready."

They headed out on Route 15, heading south. The drive was less than two hours away, but the further they got away from Leesburg, the better. It felt safer.

Chapter 18

Saturday, Oct. 21

Bluemont was bigger than Quinn expected. He had thought he would find a small, dusty town. Instead, it was a medium sized town in the shadow of the Blue Ridge Mountains. The town's business had clearly once been coal mining, which explained why it had grown so much. Now it looked like it also catered to hikers of the Appalachian Trail and other tourists.

Kate and Quinn pulled into the biggest hotel and made a reservation. From there, they went to find the *Bluemont Gazette*. Unsurprisingly, the building was closed because it was a Saturday. It was a small office. Quinn doubted more than five people worked there.

They hit the streets. They stopped into a bakery, whose owners said they didn't know anyone at the paper and had never heard of Thomas Fillmore. They dropped by a hardware store where the owner said the same thing. By the time they hit the grocery store, they knew something was up.

"Never heard of him," the lady at the customer service desk said. "I know most everyone in town, so maybe you are in the wrong place."

"You know anyone at the *Bluemont Gazette*?"

"That old rag?" she said. "I'm surprised it hasn't shut down."

Quinn and Kate looked at each other. The woman's face was beet red, she wasn't looking them in the eye and she seemed extremely nervous.

Quinn leaned in conspiratorially.

"Can I tell you a secret?" he asked the woman. He glanced at her badge. "Ms. Hawkins?"

"Well sure, honey, but everyone calls me Midge," the woman said.

"I don't want anyone else to find out about this," said Quinn. "But Katrina here... well... she has a very special reason for finding Mr. Fillmore."

"I told you I don't know any..."

"I heard you, but I thought if you knew why we needed to find him, you might be a little more sympathetic to our plight," he said. "Maybe it would jumpstart your memory."

Quinn hurried on before she could interrupt.

"Katrina here used to live in Loudoun County, over in Virginia," he said, and Midge nodded as if she understood. "Well, her parents went through a nasty divorce when she was just a little kid and she never really knew what broke them up. Her mom, God rest her soul, was recently diagnosed with cancer and told her the truth: Katrina's birth was the result of an affair. Now she wouldn't tell her who, but she found these old letters up in the attic and eventually found out that Thomas Fillmore was her father. Apparently, he left Loudoun about 12 years ago. Katrina is desperate to find him before her mother dies. He was the one true love of her life."

Kate was looking at Quinn with an expression that mixed awe with disapproval. She was impressed how easily he could lie, but a little disturbed by it as well.

"Please, Ms. Hawkins," Quinn paused awkwardly. "Midge, we need your help. I know Mr. Fillmore is a private man."

Midge Hawkins looked around the store to see if anyone else could overhear them. She leaned in closer.

"You don't know the half of it," she said. "He is the most paranoid man I ever met."

"So you know him?" Quinn said. "Fantastic, Ms. Hawkins. Could you help us, please?"

Quinn took Kate's hand and gave it a squeeze.

"It would mean so much to us," he said. "We were fixing to get married soon and..."

Kate squeezed his hand sharply. He was putting it on a little too much for her taste and she worried it would spook Midge Hawkins. Instead, it worked like a charm.

"Well, I never could be one to stand in the way of love," she said. She grabbed a piece of paper and scribbled something on it. When she slid it over to Quinn, he saw with relief it was an address.

"Thank you so much, Ms. Hawkins," Quinn said. "God bless you. Really. You don't know what this means to us."

He put his arm around Kate and she tried not to look alarmed. How in the world this worked she had no idea. She would have seen it was an act after about five seconds. But Midge Hawkins was beaming from ear to ear.

"Now don't tell him I said anything," she said. "I don't know what he'll do, but please keep me out of it."

"Mum's the word," Quinn said, and made a zipping motion across his lips. "Thank you so much."

They turned and walked out of the store, walking quickly back to the car.

"Don't you think you laid that on a little thick?" Kate asked when they were safely in the car.

"Did it work?" he asked.

"You have a way with people, I'll give you that," she said. "Is that your reportorial style—lying?"

"Not generally, no," he said. "But the old puppy-dog, I-just-need-some-help works particularly well on a certain kind of female, namely older women who are reminded of their sons or grandsons."

"You're kind of evil, you know that?" Kate said.

Quinn smiled. "Yeah, but I bet you dig that about me."

Kate looked away, but he was right. She did dig that about him. In fact, her feelings toward him had moved 180 degrees in just a day. Now that there were no doubts about whether he was working with Lord Halloween, she kept thinking about him. The Tarot card flashed through her mind again, but she realized now she liked him—a lot. She was very glad he was her partner in all of this.

After fifteen minutes sorting out directions, they found themselves heading toward what they hoped was Tim Anderson's house. The house was further out than they suspected and they drove at least 20 minutes before they came to a remote dirt road. There was no mailbox to mark the location and barely any sign anyone lived there at all.

"I hope this is right," Quinn said, as he turned down the road.

Far in front of them they could see a house in the distance. It didn't look like much. Just a small trailer parked directly at the end of the driveway.

"He's paranoid all right," Kate said. "He's designed this to make sure he can see whoever is coming. He's got to be our guy."

"I just hope he's useful," Quinn said. "If he knew who Lord Halloween was, he probably would have mentioned it by now."

"We need more information, more context," Kate said. "We've read the letters, but I feel like there is more there. For some reason, Lord Halloween left this guy alive. I need to know why. If he's a reporter, he also likely saved some of the good stuff."

"The good stuff?"

"You know, the stuff you can't print? The stuff that's half rumor or part speculation. That's the information we need."

They got to the end of the road, parked and got out. That was when the gunfire started.

*****

Kate and Quinn both dove behind the car as a series of gunshots dug up dust all around them.

"Get the fuck off my property!" a voice shouted.

More gunshots rang out. Quinn suddenly felt like he was in a war zone. He heard bullets slam into the ground all around the car. He actually started to laugh and Kate looked at him like he'd gone crazy.

"What the hell are you laughing about?" Kate asked. She wondered if Quinn was finally cracking due to the stress.

"I have the best time with you," he said, smiling. "A madman broke into my home and tried to kill us both, and now I'm getting shot at. Believe it or not, I actually had a normal life before you came along."

"Well, it's not my fault," she said. "You picked the wrong county to live in, Quinn."

It took them a minute for them to realize the gunfire had stopped. They didn't dare move.

"He could be moving to get a better position on us," Quinn said.

"I don't think so," Kate said. "Whoever is shooting at us is an expert marksmen. He didn't hit the car once from what I can tell and he's shooting in such a way that there's little danger of ricochet. He doesn't want to kill us, just scare us."

"Speaking personally," Quinn said, "It is working."

"We just want to talk to you!" Kate yelled.

The gunfire started again, hitting the ground on both sides of the car.

"I'll take that as a 'no,'" Quinn said.

The gunfire stopped.

"Just go," the voice said. "I don't want to talk to any reporters."

So he knows who we are, Quinn thought. He wasn't surprised. Midge or one of the other people they talked to must have phoned ahead. He probably knew exactly why they were there. Which meant something else: he really was Tim Anderson.

Kate stood up and walked around the car. Quinn jumped up to stop her.

"What are you doing?" he said, trying to grab her to drag her back behind the car. She shook herself loose.

"You aren't going to kill me," Kate yelled.

A single gunshot rang out and a puff of dirt flew from the ground just by her feet.

"I will if I have to," the voice called back.

Quinn tried to look at where the shots were coming from. He could just make out a shape behind an open window and something black, metal and ominous sticking through it.

"We're not here for a story about you," Kate said. "We're here for what you know."

"I don't know anything about him!" the voice said. "You're wasting time and putting me in danger."

"You've always been in danger," Kate said. "I have to find this guy."

There was laughter inside the house. It sounded old and bitter.

"For what? A story? Because you want to play junior detective? Give me a break. You guys look about twelve."

"My mother was Sarah Blakely," Kate said.

Quinn stood beside her waiting to see if they would get shot. At least it would be quick—he hoped it would be quick. If Lord Halloween found them, it would undoubtedly be a slow death.

There was a long pause.

"I just want to talk to you," Kate said. "He's hunting me again. I need to stop him."

"You can't," the voice called back. "No one can."

"Then I'm dead already," Kate said. "So you can at least talk to me."

There was another long pause. They waited for what felt like an eternity. Quinn thought he saw the shape by the window move and then the front door opened. A man walked out, about Quinn's height with mouse brown hair. He was unshaven and looked older than the early forties that he was. Both Kate and Quinn walked forward.

The man looked tired. He wore old jeans with holes in them and a white t-shirt that showed off his beer gut. The rifle he carried in his hand added to the overall impression that he was little more than stereotypical white trash. But his eyes were a dark brown and he seemed to be looking everywhere at once, his eyes darting this way and that. It was unsettling and Quinn thought it made him look crazy. Which maybe he was.

The man laid the rifle near the steps and walked towards them. He looked like someone who expected them to try and attack him at any second.

Kate stuck out her hand and the man almost flinched.

"Nice to meet you, Mr. Fillmore," she said.

"Please," the man said. "You already know who I am. The name's Tim Anderson. And this is the last time I will ever introduce myself this way. Shall we go inside?"

*****

The inside was cramped and dirty. Kate and Quinn sat in the living room looking at the sole decoration in the house: guns. Every different type of assortment hung on the wall. Quinn wondered if ammo was nearby and wouldn't have been surprised if it was.

Anderson sat down.

"I wasn't into guns before I met Lord Halloween," he said. "But afterwards... Well, it seemed like a good idea to be prepared."

Kate nodded.

"I got my first gun as soon as we moved," she said. "After my Mom died. My Mom had never really wanted me to be trained on a weapon, but after she was gone, well, my Dad thought she would understand."

Anderson nodded.

"How did you find me?" he asked.

"Tracked your writing style," Quinn responded. "There's an Internet program..."

"The one Alexis wrote about?" Anderson said.

"Yeah. You still read the paper?"

"Every week," he said. "I have to."

"It would be your first sign that he's returned," Kate said.

Anderson nodded again.

"I'm going to save you a lot of trouble," he said. "I don't know who he is. If I did I would have told the police or died trying to kill him myself."

"I know," Kate said. "But I think his interaction with you is critical. The letters tell a part of the story, but not all of it makes sense. Why not use his nickname earlier? He claims he killed a girlfriend of yours and then he let you go. I never knew he let anyone go."

Anderson sighed and waited.

"I'll start at the beginning," he said. "The *Chronicle* was my home and I loved it. I worked every day and had very little social life. In those days, I was a rising star. Laurence let me do whatever I wanted and once I started winning Virginia Press Association awards, Ethan let him pay me closer to a living wage. I was a big fish in a little pond and I liked it. I didn't expect to be there much longer—maybe a couple more years—before I would try my hand at the *Post* or one of the dailies just outside D.C."

"Then Lord Halloween showed up," Kate said.

"I thought the first letter was a joke," Anderson said, and he wasn't looking at them anymore. He was staring at the window as if lost in memory. "'Some of what I tell you will be lies.' He had said it himself. I thought it was some kind of prank that Buzz or Kyle had created."

"They both worked there then?" Quinn asked.

"Buzz did," Anderson replied. "Kyle was actually working for the fire department at the time, but he desperately wanted to be a reporter. He was always hanging around the paper, wanting to know the latest scoops. He asked me to help get him a job, which I did, albeit unintentionally. I left. Anyway, those guys were both known for a practical joke or two, so I thought this was a good one. I thought it was sick, don't get me wrong, but I didn't take it seriously. I did what any good reporter does, however. I checked out the scene myself.

"Up until the moment I found her body, I still thought it was a setup. Just where he told me, there was an easel set up and painting equipment. And I kept thinking, 'Wow. Someone went to a lot of trouble to make this joke work.' I walked around the park, looked at the painting, which was quite good, and was just about to get back in my car when I saw it. There was a clump of forest just outside the clearing and I saw something glinting in the sun. It was a paintbrush. So I went over to check it out and the body was just ten feet away. There was blood all over the ground and the number of flies buzzing around her was incredible.

"I didn't know they could be that loud—or there would be that many. I vomited into the bushes. I had never seen a dead body and I simply couldn't look away. It wasn't like the movies. I kept looking at her face, which looked frozen in agony."

"What did you tell the police?"

"Everything," he said. "I knew if I didn't it would look suspicious. I knew enough not to contaminate the crime scene, drove to the office, gave the letter to Laurence and we called the police together.

"Showed them the letter, which they promptly took, and they went to find the body. I spent a full day being questioned by them. I think many of the cops thought the letter was a ruse—that the woman was somehow my girlfriend and I had just created an elaborate scheme. I don't think they seriously considered that it was for real. Well, not until the second letter."

"Did you check that out ahead of time too?" Quinn asked.

"No," Anderson said. "That time I just called the police. I had no choice. They had ordered Ethan Holden not to publish the letters and I was to hand them over as soon as they came in. I wasn't even supposed to read them first."

"Ordered him not to publish?" Quinn asked. "They can't do that."

"That was what I said," Anderson responded. "In the early days, it was all about journalistic integrity to me. We had a duty to warn the public, we had a responsibility to give information to the readership. And hell, it was a good story, right? It wasn't the primary motivating factor, but I'm not saying I didn't know that."

"But Laurence wouldn't do it?"

"The problem wasn't Laurence," Anderson said. "It was Ethan. He would rant and rave about not being a puppet to a madman. He saw it as a noble thing that we weren't publishing the letters. For a while, we didn't even use the nickname. I couldn't change his mind. I actually thought about giving the letters to the *Post*, but I was being watched too carefully. As soon as I got a letter, I would show it to Laurence, he would make a copy, and we would give it to police. But the cops got wise to the act. They got a couple of the letters before I could even see them."

"What happened?"

"If you've seen the letters, you know," Anderson said. "He got angry. He didn't get the publicity he wanted and I wasn't doing my job.

"I managed to sneak a few things into the early articles so that he didn't feel like I was totally ignoring him, but I didn't see it as my job to do his bidding. I didn't really think he would come after me. It sounds stupid now, but I was a journalist and we view ourselves as protected. I could cross crime scene lines, ask rude questions to important people—we are observers of the world, not participants."

"But Lord Halloween didn't see it that way," Kate said.

"No," he said. "First there were the phone calls. They started in the evening. Just someone calling and then hanging up. I could never hear anything but breathing. But the calls started coming in the middle of the night. I kept my phone on in case there was some kind of emergency and at first I didn't want to turn it off, but eventually I had to. There was no pattern to them. He could call you at 1 a.m., then fifteen minutes later, then wait two hours. But I wasn't sleeping well. I wouldn't be able to go back to sleep and when I finally did—the phone would ring."

"He was trying to harass you, put you off guard," Kate said.

"Exactly," he said. "It struck me as a militaristic tactic, really. It was strategic. He didn't want me to be thinking totally clearly. And then I started to feel watched. When I went to the grocery store, I would feel like someone was following me. I would park my cart, walk over to get milk and come back and find some of the things I thought I had bought weren't there. I know it sounds crazy, but do you have any idea how unnerving that is? He's messing with my fucking shopping cart in the middle of a store and I don't catch a glimpse of him? And then I was doubting myself. Did I really buy that guacamole? It only happened a few times—but it happened, I know it did. The last time my entire cart was rammed into a store display. The manager thought some kid did it, but I knew. Of course I knew.

"And it got worse. He bled into everything. I would be at the book store and books would start falling off the shelves around me, just barely missing my head in one case. No one ever saw anything and I just seemed crazy. Maybe I was crazy, I don't know. I saw him everywhere in everything. I couldn't be anywhere anymore without a clear line of sight. I moved my desk to a far wall so no one could sneak up behind me. I bought four extra locks and a security system for my apartment—this was before the real rush on that stuff occurred. I was afraid to shower or play music or watch TV or do anything that made any noise."

Anderson was shaking then, not looking at anyone. He was slightly rocking back and forth as if trapped in a memory.

"And then Carrie..."

There was a long pause. Quinn wondered if he would start talking again and then Kate quietly said, "Carrie Sterns?"

For just a moment, the spell was broken and Anderson looked up.

"Yeah," he said. "Victim number nine to you, isn't she?"

Kate shook her head. "You should know better."

"Right," Anderson said. "Your mother."

"She was your girlfriend?" Quinn asked.

Anderson laughed. Once again, Quinn was struck by how little warmth or humor was in that laugh.

"No," Anderson said. "That was the thing. She wasn't. She was just a girl I knew in the advertising department. She was pretty and I liked her, but we had only gone out once after work. It wasn't a serious thing and we didn't even kiss. She was so sweet, though. The reporters never mixed with the advertising staff, but she was an exception. Everyone loved her. She was nice and thoughtful. She remembered birthdays. I at first thought she was flirting with me—that's why I asked her out—but I realized later she was that way with everyone. She was one of those people that make you think the world is better and brighter than it is."

"And he murdered her," Kate said.

"No," Anderson said forcefully. "He butchered that girl. Murder is too nice a word for what he did. He tortured her. I saw the police report. It took hours for her to die. Hours in which I'm sure she begged for God, or the police, or anyone to come find her. Hours in which she was lying so near other people that if they had only heard her, they could have saved her."

"She died by the printing press," Kate said.

Anderson looked surprised.

"How could you possibly know that?" he asked.

Kate shook her head. "Does it matter?"

"Yes," Anderson said, and his eyes looked shrunken and hollow. "It matters to me. That girl's death is my fault. I didn't cut her face up or make small incisions on her body to allow the maximum amount of blood drain without letting her die quickly, but it's my fault. He killed her because I didn't do my job. He killed her because I didn't give the public all the information it deserved. He killed her because I listened to the cowards and the fools who say they have control, when they control nothing! All they wanted is to control information.

"Did they try to find the killer, or did they just hope he would go away? They were powerless to stop him and they did everything they could to make it seem like they were in charge, but he was in charge. I broke the rules and a sweet, pretty, lovely girl who always remembered birthdays and everyone loved died in the worst fashion I can imagine. We were all in the building, did you know that? She was dying and calling for help and we were all there! All of us upstairs making changes and doing our jobs and she was begging us to help. But we couldn't hear her. The printing press was running and running and running and it was so loud. She died screaming for help, knowing it was seconds away."

Quinn had the feeling this was something Anderson had wanted to say for 12 years and never had.

"In the letter, he made it sound like you were dating Carrie," Kate said. "Do you think he knew you weren't?"

"Oh, he knew," Anderson said. "It was all just an elaborate trap. I had to spend hours talking to the police about a relationship that simply did not exist. They thought I did it. Once again, they thought I was Lord Halloween. Because why not? They couldn't find any other candidates. Holober was a sick fuck, but he wasn't a serial killer and they knew it. He was just another schizophrenic. They wanted a better candidate. I spent hours with the police. Hours I should have been looking for the real killer."

"What happened? Why didn't they blame you?"

"Holden happened," he said. "He showed up with a lawyer and scared the shit out of them. He got them to seal the records on Carrie's death, too. She was listed as a victim of Lord Halloween, but he convinced the police to keep where the body was found as confidential. He said it was about protecting information that only the killer would know, but I knew better. It was about protecting his precious paper."

"And after that?"

"By then, all hell had broken loose anyway," Anderson said. "The town banned Halloween, trick or treating, you name it. They would have agreed to any demand from Lord Halloween, if he had asked. And I just followed the story. Ethan finally gave me free rein to write about the impact on the town, speculation as to the killer's motives, everything. Lord Halloween was happy with me. He wanted chaos and I gave it to him. I couldn't write about the letters, but I wrote enough. There was sufficient information to characterize the killer and I did it."

"So he let you live?" Kate asked. "You did what he wanted and he let you live."

"Oh no," Anderson said. "With him, there is always something beneath the surface. He set up a final test. You read the hint he gave already; pull no punches. That was about the police, but I pulled no punches with everyone. I am surprised Laurence let me publish it—certainly Ethan was pissed as soon as it came out, so he apparently didn't know anything about it. Go find it in the archives. It was the best piece I have ever written—a sum up of the murders, the town's reaction, the paper's involvement, and the killer himself. And I let everyone have it.

"When we give in to madmen, we lose the most vital part of ourselves. And we have given in to Lord Halloween. We have panicked, turned on each other and lost our way. In a time when we should be united against fear, we have let it run rampant, divided ourselves and given terror a free hand. This man—and that is all he is or will ever be—is a thief. He has robbed us of our safety, our piece of mind and our faith in each other. He has stolen our very soul. And we have let him do this. Where we should stand firm and fast, we have wilted. Where there should be resolve, there was cowardice. For that, we bear some responsibility.'"

"Sounds like Lord Halloween would have loved it," Quinn said.

But Anderson wasn't finished yet.

"'But I do not forget who holds the most responsibility for this month that will never end. It is the man who calls himself Lord Halloween. He preys on the weak, feeds on fear and lurks in the shadows. He does this under the illusion it makes him powerful. It makes him nothing. He is a phantom and nothing more. True, he has held a mirror to our faces and we have been found wanting.

"'But if we have given into fear, so has he. He could have played a part in this world, but he has chosen to hide in it. He strikes at us because there are things he doesn't understand: love, compassion and empathy. They have always been alien to him. He mocks them with his actions, but the truth is something he must know: he envies us. We experience feelings he can't know or express and he hates us for them. He is a creature to be pitied, not feared. He is alone in this world and always will be. When we pick up the pieces of our lives, we will go on loving, caring and empathizing. We can hope we will learn from this miserable experience and stand stronger against the things that would tear us apart. He, however, will be by himself, lost in a world he cannot fathom. I do not fear you Lord Halloween, I fear what you have wrought in us. One day we may bring you to justice, but if we do not, do not think it has not already been meted out. You have been judged and found unworthy.'"

"Damn," Kate said.

"You should have been dead man walking."

"I expected it," Anderson said. "That was published on Oct. 31. And I went home and waited for him to strike. I wasn't going to make it easy. I had bought a shotgun and I sat in a corner of the room where no one could sneak up on me through a window or anything else. I didn't answer the phone, I wasn't going to be baited outside. I just waited. It never occurred to me that he would let me live. Why should he? I had called him out. I had told him who he really was. I had struck him with the only weapon I have, the only one that ever matters: the pen."

"And you remember it word for word?"

"I took a long time to write it," he replied.

"What happened?" Quinn asked.

"At about midnight exactly, a letter was pushed through my door. I watched it come through, but I didn't move. I assumed it was a trick. I would get up, read the letter and he would somehow sneak in behind me. So I sat there for six more hours. I could hear the birds in the trees and dawn was coming. And I thought, 'What does it matter now? He'll get me in the end anyway.' And I got up and read the letter."

"He let you live," Kate said.

"Yes. I realize now it was his way of saying goodbye. He told me in no uncertain terms to get lost, but he also said he was letting me go. I didn't fully believe him, but I suppose the fact that I am still here means he was serious."

"Why?"

Anderson got up and paced around the room.

"You've seen the letter," Anderson said. "I gave it to Laurence, whom I know kept copies. He kept copies on all of Lord Halloween's victims."

"Why?" Kate asked.

Anderson shook his head.

"Laurence was once a reporter, too," he said. "It was a good story. A good journalist keeps all his notes. I'm assuming he gave you those letters from Lord Halloween. I know the police didn't."

"I wouldn't say he *gave* them to us..." Quinn said.

Anderson smiled wanly.

"I didn't feel any relief when I got the letter," he said. "Not then and not now. I had been let go. I didn't escape, he had simply chosen to let me live. And I thought about Carrie a lot. About how she died. I also did what he wanted: I left. I knew then that he was going to lay low. My death would have looked like an accident, but he would have found a way to kill me. So I packed up, handed in my resignation and moved west."

"Why didn't you go further away?" Kate asked.

"The same reason you came back," Anderson said. "Because you are never really free. Would I be safer in Seattle? Maybe. But I didn't know who he was and he could find me, I knew that. Anywhere I went, he could show up and take me out. So there was no point in going far away. I sometimes wonder if he did me no favor by letting me live. I still see him everywhere. I don't trust anyone and the fact that you found me so quickly shows how useless that was. I'm a haunted man, Quinn O'Brion. I don't need to tell Kate this: she already knows. I've been waiting for him to show up for 12 years."

"Do you know who he is?" Kate asked.

"No," Anderson answered. "I had theories at some point, but none of them really held together. I will tell you this: whoever he is, he's connected with your paper."

Kate nodded.

"Why do you say that?" Quinn asked.

"He chose me," Anderson replied. "And at first I was arrogant enough to assume it was about me. But it wasn't. He chose the paper, not the reporter. I find it curious he hasn't sent letters to either of you—what that means, I don't know, but it means something. But I think that paper mattered more to him than the *Post* or *New York Times* or any of it—papers, by the way, that did cover his killing spree. I think it was this: I think the *Chronicle* was his hometown paper. I don't think he went anywhere for 12 years. I think he just laid low. But whoever he is, he knew who you two were long before he started his latest spree. My guess is he knows everyone at the paper."

"Ethan Holden?" Kate asked. "That's who you think it is."

"You're perceptive, I'll give you that," Anderson responded. "Yes, that's been a particular focal point for me. He's a bit old to be running all over town killing people, but you can't rule it out. He shares certain qualities with Lord Halloween: he's arrogant, cold-blooded and deeply in need of a conscience. He thinks he's high minded, but he's not. I watched him encourage Laurence to take stories in certain directions—ones that might sell more papers, but weren't exactly true either. Nothing overt. Nothing you could stand up and take a stand against."

This time it was Quinn who was nodding.

"He's your best candidate," Kate said. "But are there others?"

Anderson responded by getting up and walking away again. When he came back, he held a monstrous file in his hand.

"This is it, the Holy Grail," he said. "As much information as I could collect on everyone. Ethan, Kyle, Buzz, Laurence—even Sheriff Brown is in here. Nothing conclusive on anyone. If you look hard to see if someone's a murderer, you find all sorts of things that could prove you right. But that doesn't mean you are. Most people make mistakes and some are even ruthless, but that doesn't make them killers."

"You're giving this to us?" Kate asked.

"It's yours," he said. "If Lord Halloween kills you, he'll find it with you. When he does, he will know who wrote it. If he doesn't know already you came to see me, he will after that."

"You want a final showdown," Quinn said. It wasn't a question.

"I want it to end," Anderson said. "I've been waiting for 12 years. It's long enough. I won't just kill myself—that's a coward's way out. And I won't go down easy. But I'm through waiting. Either you finish him or he finishes me."

"Thank you for all your help," Kate said.

"How could I refuse you?" he asked. "I met your mother once, working a crime story. You look stunningly like her—same blue eyes and blond hair. She was beautiful. When I saw her, it was to meet your dad. She knew your dad didn't like to talk to reporters, but she couldn't have been nicer to me. I'm sorry for what that man did to her. I'm sorry for what he did to you."

"I'm going to finish him," she said. "I'm going to make him pay."

Kate and Quinn rose to leave. As they were heading out the door, Anderson spoke for a final time.

"Promise me something," he said. "When you find him, don't treat him like the monster he wants to be. He gets off on that. He's just a man. Treat him that way."

When they were in the car driving away, Quinn turned and asked, "What did that mean? Treat him that way."

"He meant he wanted us to kill him," Kate said. "Don't capture. Don't wait for the police. If we get a chance, take him down."

"You think you could?" Quinn asked, but he already knew the answer. He had trouble imagining himself hurting anyone, much less killing them.

"It's not a matter of could," she said. "When I find him, I will."

*****

Kyle paused while cutting onions and waited. He was preparing dinner, but he moved slowly. He kept listening for the scanner to go off.

There would be action again soon—he could feel it. All day he had waited for the call. A new body, a panicked police source, but nothing had come.

He managed to finish making dinner without any unusual scanner activity. He flipped the TV on while he ate.

He turned the channel to find some wrestling, found it and watched it without paying much attention to it.

He still had one ear cocked for any squawk of the scanner.

A loud thud came from outside and Kyle jumped out of the chair. God, he was testy, he thought. It was probably just a package being delivered. Still, he weighed possibilities in his mind, decided it was better to be cautious and moved to the kitchen. He picked up the knife on the counter, still moist from chopping onions.

He looked outside the kitchen window and saw nothing. He could wait here, but Kyle preferred action to waiting. If someone was playing a game, let them come. He would be ready.

He walked toward the back patio and slid open the sliding glass door. He moved slowly and quietly. He thought with some irony that this would make a good story. A very good first-person perspective piece.

Kyle crept around the outside of his house, keeping his eyes peeled for any movement. When he got outside the kitchen, he saw it. The bushes right by the window had been trampled. Someone had been looking in.

He held the knife steady in front of him and kept walking. If someone was here bent on mischief, they would have another thing coming. Kyle had not spent years in the service so that he could be sneaked up on and ambushed.

Kyle came around the front of his house and saw with some shock that the door was open. He cursed himself. Had he even locked it? He should have been more careful.

It occurred to him that his tracker knew he had been running around outside the house. Shit. Now the person was inside and he was the one skulking.

He felt a twinge of anxiety as he crept to the front door. He should be more careful. He could even call the police. But he pushed that thought away. They would mock him for calling them out here if they didn't find anything. He wasn't sure he could take it. No, he would handle this as he did everything else—by himself.

He crept up to his front stoop and slowly opened the storm door in front. It squeaked slightly and made Kyle wish that he had oiled it more recently.

The front door stood wide open. Closing the storm door quietly behind him, Kyle carefully walked in, the knife still at his side.

He tensed with every muscle and listened. He moved to the stairs and walked down into his den.

Slowly, Kyle thought. I mustn't rush. He thought about his gun upstairs, but he had not used it in years. Mostly it had been there for decoration, since Kyle had never fully embraced the weapon.

He pushed himself up against the far left wall and crept ever so slowly forward. He checked behind him, but there was nothing. Moving forward, he edged around and looked beyond the corner, just briefly.

Sure enough, there was a figure sitting in the chair in his computer room.

"You can come out now, Kyle," the voice said, startling him. "I've been watching you for some time. You aren't nearly so clever as you think you are."

Kyle walked around the corner and instantly recognized who sat in the chair. He took a step back in surprise.

"What the hell are you doing here?" Kyle asked. "Don't you know there is a murderer on the loose?"

"Yes," the figure said and chuckled slightly. "I do."

Even though he was draped in shadow, Kyle saw him pull something large from behind him.

"What the hell do you think you are doing?" Kyle asked.

"I think you know," the figure replied.

Kyle realized that the man had a gun pointing at him.

"Jesus, you can't be serious," said Kyle, backing up.

There is a way out of this, he thought. I will not go down like this.

"Deadly," the figure said. "Don't make a move, Kyle. Not even a sound. I knew you would be trouble, so don't think I won't fire first. I'm taking no chances here. But don't worry, that is not what I have in store for you. I want to take my time with this."

Kyle decided that he would have to make his move soon. He gripped the knife at his right side and wondered how quickly he could throw it.

The figure took one step toward him and Kyle made his move. He flung the knife in the figure's direction and darted off to the right. As he started to move, Kyle heard the gun go off.

Nov. 1, 1994

Dear Tim,

    At least you went out with a bang. I want you to understand two things: I fully intended to kill you the other day, but I'm not going do so anymore. You have proven worthy. You were brave when most men would have been cowardly. You signed your name to an article you knew would infuriate me, with the full knowledge that I would end you for it.

    Your words did cut to the bone, Tim. I won't lie. But right is right and sometimes even I have to concede a point. So, congratulations, you get to live.

    There is one condition to this: you have to leave. I don't want to keep seeing you around. Eventually, I'm bound to let my anger get the best of me. It wouldn't be a death at the hands of Lord Halloween—they caught him, remember?—but it would be an untimely accident.

    You have three days. If I see you here again, your death will be so quick, your soul will leave your body before your corpse even hits the ground. Leave Loudoun County to me. Find somewhere else to roam. I'm finished with you.

Sincerely,

Lord Halloween

Chapter 19

Sunday, Oct. 22

"You still awake?" she asked in barely a whisper.

"Of course," Quinn replied.

After visiting Anderson, the two of them had headed back to the hotel room to look through the files. They had tried unsuccessfully to find a VCR to watch the security tapes from Kate's hotel, but the man at the front desk said there were none available. They had pored over the information until they couldn't see straight.

There were a host of suspects in Anderson's file: Laurence, Holden, Kyle, Buzz, Brown, even Johnny Redacker, Kate's family friend. Everyone had been analyzed and dissected by Anderson, but no conclusions had been reached.

They had taken no chances themselves. Kate doubted Lord Halloween was busy following them—he was probably lining up his next victim—but the door was blocked by several pieces of furniture. They had picked a room on the sixth floor—the highest the hotel had—but even the door to the balcony was blocked, just in case Lord Halloween could somehow scale up the walls outside. Kate had also been adamant with staff—no employees were to come in under any circumstances. She had pretended it was for romantic reasons, after which the hotel manager had knowingly winked at Quinn.

But far from making out, they had laid pieces of files all over the bed and gone through them one by one. They had briefly grabbed food and returned to the room. Finally, around midnight, Kate had suggested they sleep. After the night before, Quinn didn't think he could, but they had carefully reassembled Anderson's file, gotten ready for bed and turned off the lights. Before they did so, Kate had put her gun on the table next to her.

But it still did not mean either were sleeping. For Quinn, the problem was two-fold. His dreams were as bad as real life. Chased in the real world, he fell asleep so he could be chased there too. The dreams, if anything, seemed to be even clearer now—if that was even possible.

It was the one thing he had not told Kate about and he knew that was most likely a mistake. After all, it may have something to do with Lord Halloween. But that seemed ridiculous to Quinn. He wondered if Comizio had ever called the police and what they thought. Quinn had talked to Janus yesterday, but per Kate's insistence, had not told him where they were or any details of the night before. Janus did not bring up the horse story, either, and Quinn was more than happy to let it drop. It meant something, but he could not for the life of him figure out what.

If all that were not enough, Quinn had one additional problem, one he knew was neither crazy nor surprising. He had offered to sleep on the floor, but Kate had insisted he did not. It was a queen bed, she pointed out, and stupid that they couldn't share it.

So now Quinn was in a position he might have killed for under different circumstances—he was sleeping with a beautiful woman in a private hotel room and nobody knew where they were. The perfect romantic weekend. He thought of the manager's wink.

Only it wasn't romantic. They were tired, scared and irritable, for starters. Second, they weren't lovers. They had an air of intimacy like people who knew each other for longer than they really had—Quinn supposed being in a life or death situation would do that—but not the kind that a real couple has. They both changed separately in the bathroom and there was not even a kiss on the cheek to say goodnight.

But the only thought that pushed away the Headless Horsemen and a certain serial killer was Kate. While it gave Quinn comfort to think of her and be close to her, it was also highly distracting, even under these conditions. He was determined to be an honorable guy. Now was not the time to bring up conversations about mutual attraction or simply try to start something. Now was the time to plan, to prepare, to strategize—and yet here she was, gorgeous and in bed with him.

Quinn felt like he wanted to scream. If it was not his fear of an imminent and bloody death keeping him awake, it was his sex drive. What a fantastic day he was having.

So when she asked him if he was awake, he found the question downright funny.

"Why 'of course'?" she asked back.

"You know," he said and let it drop. There was nothing to say.

"I'm having a hard time sleeping too," she said.

He turned over to face her. The covers reached just to her shoulders and she was turned on her side looking at him. God, she looked good, he thought. He wondered if she ever did not look good. Even with no sleep, she was still hot.

Quinn laughed.

"I'm sure I can guess why," he said.

She smiled back.

"That and other stuff," she said, not wanting to get into it. Truthfully, she was having thoughts about Quinn too—more than she was comfortable with. There was no denying she was attracted to him and every time she thought about him romantically, that damn Tarot card popped into her head. The devil and lust. She had a feeling like she did not want to indulge any romantic feelings. It would make them both distracted.

Instead, she tried to change the topic.

"I keep thinking that our research has not gotten us very far," she said. "We don't know much more than we started with."

"I know," Quinn replied. "It feels like we have been spinning our wheels a bit. The more I know, the less certain I feel."

"It feels like rats in a maze or something," she replied. "Or bees in a box. He shakes us up and we buzz all around. But then we quiet down and wait for him to do it again."

"Look, it's natural. We are both a little afraid. Okay, not a little."

She sat up in bed. Quinn noticed she was wearing one of his t-shirts. It did nothing to stop his attraction. Her blond hair fell down just shy of her shoulders and she shook her head.

"That's just it," she said. "I'm so tired of being afraid all the time. And now I'm starting to worry that is all that we are—our fears."

"I don't follow."

"For most of my life, fear has been controlling me," Kate replied. "Even before all of this that was true. It seems like the original human emotion. You start out in life scared of the world. Then you're scared of the dark or that your parents will leave you or of being lost in the woods.

"When you are older, you get scared the other kids don't really like you, that you will never fit anywhere, that you will never find the right guy. Then you get a guy and you become scared you will lose him. You raise children and are scared something will happen to the kids. You get a good job, you are scared the bosses won't like you or you won't get that promotion. All through your life, no matter how mature you become, there are a million things to be afraid of. It's the emotion most central to our lives."

"That may be true."

"People always define themselves by their jobs, their families, or God knows what else. But I think they're wrong. I think it is what you are afraid of that defines you, that shapes your behavior and tells you what to think. Call it an existential crisis, Quinn. I am what I fear. What I fear is me.

"And before you say it, I know that this is a weird time to be thinking of this. There are a million things that I should be thinking of and this just isn't one of them."

"Actually, I think it makes perfect sense," Quinn said. He sat up and they faced each other sitting cross-legged. "But I think you are wrong. Our fears are not us. It is like any other emotion. It is what we do with it that counts."

"But that's just it. The other emotions aren't dominant. I think fear is. And I think even when we believe we are controlling it, it is controlling us," Kate replied.

"No," Quinn said. "Look at you. You came back to Loudoun even though it was what you most fear in the world. You didn't run when I asked you to. We are trying to find him before he finds us. You are facing your fear."

"Am I?" Kate said. "Or am I just being stupid?"

"Maybe both," Quinn said. Before she could protest, he continued. "I don't think fear—or any one thing—runs our lives. Sometimes it does. And sometimes it is like the white noise on a TV screen: always there, but you can tune it out. It doesn't matter what we are afraid of. All that matters is what we do about it.

"Take your example, the kid who is afraid others won't like him. That is not the soul of that kid. It is how he responds to it— does he conform to be like the more popular kids or does he face the idea that they may dislike him and be himself anyway? Do you run from your past, from all the horrible things life has dished out for you, or do you do something about it?"

"But even if we win, even if we face down this guy and beat him, I will still be that scared little girl," she said.

"You aren't even that scared little girl now," he replied. "Would she be here now? Could she have come back to Loudoun? And you are already stronger. The minute we admit to ourselves what we fear most and face it, we have a chance—maybe just a small one—to do something about it. And that is very powerful— that we are given a chance to break free of the things that haunt us, to conquer them and be stronger for it."

She smiled and Quinn was struck again by how beautiful she was.

"I'm sorry," he said. "I must sound like an idiot."

"No, you don't," she said. "I'm just wondering how I got so lucky. Of all the people to be stuck with in this... mess, I'm glad it was you."

"Thanks," he said, and desperately wanted to lean over and kiss her. But he didn't. Surely this would be more awkward if he tried something.

"I have one other thing I'm afraid of that I haven't admitted," Kate said and glanced away.

"Come on," he said. "Shoot."

"Okay," she said and took in a breath. "I'm afraid of what would happen if I kissed you right now. What it would mean for us · and this? Whether it would be a terrible idea?"

Quinn needed no more encouragement than that. He leaned over, put his hands on her cheeks and kissed her softly on the lips.

Everything else in his mind evaporated when she kissed him back. Before he knew it, he had moved closer and his arms were around her. For a moment, neither Quinn nor Kate thought about anything else.

When they broke apart, they both took a deep breath and looked at each other for a moment. Then Kate put her hand on the back of Quinn's neck and pulled him down next to her on the bed.

They kissed again and Quinn felt the same current he had felt with her that very first week. Except now it was like he was holding his hand above a live wire and the voltage had been cranked up. He did not know what it meant, only that it felt good.

When they paused for air, Quinn held her for a moment and ran his hands through her hair. They were both out of breath.

"Should we stop?" he said finally, wanting to do anything but stop. "If we keep going, I don't think we'll be able to quit."

"Who says we would want to?"

She gently rolled over on top of him and paused with her face millimeters from his.

"What are you doing?" Quinn asked.

"Facing our fears," she said.

She smiled and kissed him again.

*****

It started off slow. They kissed for what felt like forever: long, wet, lingering. Quinn knew immediately she was the best kisser he had ever known. She broke away from him and sat up. Slowly, he lifted her t-shirt off and began kissing her everywhere.

For the first time in weeks, Kate wasn't thinking about her mother or her wrecked life. She wasn't thinking about anything at all. She reached down and took off his t-shirt. Kate wanted to feel her flesh on his. They lay down together and slowly, all the clothes came off. She wanted this to go on forever, but she didn't know if she could take it. She wanted him, more than she had ever wanted any man in her life. Just when she didn't think she could take it anymore, she briefly pulled away.

"You okay?" he asked, and she loved him for it. His face was flush with excitement, but she knew if she asked him to stop, he would.

He loved her and would do anything for her, even if that meant stopping. But stopping was the last thing she wanted.

She nodded and they began kissing again. Somewhere in the back of her mind there was a warning—a flash of a Tarot card with two lovers staring at each other while the Devil looked on. And a message: "Sex changes everything."

But she wouldn't—or couldn't—stop. They were moving as one and it was like nothing she had ever felt. His touch was electric to her and her entire body felt a surge go through it. This was far beyond sex. Whatever was going on was joining them in more ways than the physical. She could feel what he felt, think what he thought.

Everything was becoming interlinked. As their bodies moved together, she was experiencing memories that weren't hers. A first date with a girl she had never met, an awkward kiss in a college dorm room, the first time he had sex. It didn't frighten her, it was like she was there, like she was Quinn. She saw the first time he saw her in the coffee shop, the way his heart raced, the way he had loved her even then.

This was dangerous. She should be frightened. She could tell that her every thought, every memory, was now inside of him as well. They were moving together faster, but it seemed to last forever. She thought she wouldn't be able to think ever again.

And then it slowly receded.

Quinn was going to speak. He was going to ask what was going on. She knew that and didn't want him to. She didn't want to break the spell. He stopped without her saying anything and pulled away. When he left her, she felt unexpectedly empty.

When he lay down on the bed next to her, she pulled him to her and started kissing him again. It was even better than before. She felt everything he felt, every touch of her tongue. It was like being two people at once. There was no slow build up this time, they just immediately began making love again.

Kate knew they had already lost control. She thought of the Tarot card again and didn't care. She wanted this. She deserved this.

It went on for hours. She loved him, but it wasn't love that was driving them now, it was lust. They knew what the other wanted and reacted out of instinct. They had joined together and could no longer be apart.

Finally, after what felt like forever, they both collapsed back on the bed. He tried to speak, but couldn't. She opened her mouth to say something, but they were both asleep in seconds.

*****

Quinn looked down the dirt road, straining to see anything in the darkness. Next to him, the trees stirred in a passing breeze. The night was cool, but not freezing. He wished he had brought a jacket.

Actually, he thought suddenly, he wished he knew how he was here at all.

"Where are we?" Kate asked behind him and Quinn jumped.

Quinn looked down the road past her.

(*He's coming*)

"I'm not sure," he said. "I think it could be the Phillips' farm road."

"How did we get here?"

Quinn looked at her and shrugged.

"I think this is my dream," he said. "I don't think we are here at all."

Kate frowned.

"Look, I don't mean to pick a fight, but I don't see how I could be in your dream," she said. "Either you are in mine, or..."

Quinn shrugged again.

"It's just that I've dreamt this before," he said. "I'm walking on this road and..."

(*He starts chasing me.*)

"Who's he? Who's coming?" Kate asked. "Did you think that or did I?"

Quinn was confused.

"I don't know," he said. "I don't know what is going on. I've had this dream before, but it feels different now."

He bent down to the road and picked up a handful of dirt. He let the dust run through his fingers and then shook his hand clean.

"This feels more real," he said. "Are we sure we didn't sleepwalk or something?"

(*He's coming and he will be mad that I brought her.*)

"Quinn, who are you talking about?" Kate asked. "I feel something, this... sense of immense dread and I don't know why. What's coming?"

"Never mind," Quinn said and looked up the road. "However we got here, we need to keep moving. The bridge is around the bend."

(*What is going on?*)

"I don't know what is going on," Quinn said. "Wait. Did I think that or did you?"

Kate turned and looked behind her. Her heart was pounding in her chest.

"I think I'm feeling your emotions," she said.

"And what do you think I'm feeling?"

"Terror," Kate said.

"Sounds about right. Look, we need to start walking. We don't have long."

"What is coming for us, Quinn? Lord Halloween?"

He grabbed her hand (*it feels so real*) and they started walking down the road.

"I don't know exactly," he replied. "I don't think they are connected."

He moved a little faster and pulled her along.

But Kate stopped dead in her tracks.

"Kate, look, I will tell you all about it later," he said. "This is the nightmare I told you about, remember? The one that I keep having? But this is the first time you've been in it."

But she was not paying any attention to him. Instead she was staring at the ground.

(*What is it?*) Quinn thought.

"On the ground," she said. "Look at the lines."

She pointed at lines drawn in the dirt. When Quinn stepped back, he realized it spelled a word.

"Sanheim," they both said.

And then Quinn started to hear the sound of horse hooves in the distance, like the beating of a far-off drum.

"We have to go now," he said, and pulled her arm along to make her start moving. Kate looked back at the word in the dust again, but started jogging alongside Quinn.

"Sanheim—I've seen that word in my dreams before," she said to him.

Quinn kept looking behind him.

"You have? But I thought..." (*I was going crazy*).

"You've seen it too?" she asked him, and now she started to glance behind her as well. The sound was getting closer and though she was not much clearer on what was coming, she thought she had some idea.

"Janus and I found it carved into a tree out near Leesburg," he said. "A guy called us out to the Phillips' farm and it was right there in a clearing."

It was with some sickening feeling he realized he was close to that field now. As they ran along the road, the right side opened up to reveal that large narrow field.

(*It's over there. He carved it into the tree with his sword.*)

"It was on the Tarot card," she said. "I was so freaked out by the whole experience I didn't think to mention it. Madame Zora didn't know what it meant either."

"Who the hell is Madame Zora?"

Then he saw in his head a picture of a woman wrapped in fake jewels in a candle-lit room. The psychic, he knew.

"Oh," he said.

Kate looked at him funny but continued to run. Both looked over their shoulders. They were almost past the field now, but still not close to the bridge.

(*Why didn't you tell me?*)

Quinn heard the thought inside his head and didn't know how to answer. He was rapidly becoming too terrified to think.

"You had enough to worry about," was all he said.

"But this could be important," she said. "It could be a clue."

The sound was much louder now and even Kate recognized it—the galloping gait of a large horse, riding as if it had the devil at its heels.

She looked to the forest around her.

"We could go in there," she said, becoming slightly out of breath.

"The woods don't help," he said. "He'll just get ahead of us. We have to beat him to that bridge. We will be safe there."

But the bend in the road still seemed too far away and the hoof beats were getting steadily louder. They seemed to echo off the trees around them.

"What's coming, Quinn?" she asked. "The fear I'm feeling, I can't tell if it is yours or mine or both. But I don't think you would be this afraid of just a horse. So what's chasing us? What's on that horse?"

"See for yourself," Quinn said, as they continued running.

She turned to look behind her and she could now see something in the distance. It was little more than a blur, but it was moving very, very fast.

With a little relief, she saw they were now close to the bend in the road. She and Quinn ran forward, hearing the gait of the horse grow louder with every step. They rounded the bend and Kate felt her spirits drop.

The bridge was still far away. She could see it in the distance.

(*We aren't going to make it.*)

(*I might be able to slow him down, Kate.*)

(*I'm not sure much could slow him down at this stage.*)

She could see details of the bridge, could tell they were getting closer, but now the sound of hooves was everywhere. The bridge was one of the old-fashioned covered ones—long and narrow. She had heard there was one in Loudoun County, but it had fallen into disrepair. It reminded her of something, some story she had been told.

(*The Legend of Sleepy Hollow.*)

Kate looked behind her and stifled a scream. The horse had just rounded the bend and she could see the rider pushing it to go faster. Somewhere she heard a terrible laugh, deep and booming, and it did not sound human.

(*Because it isn't human, is it, Quinn?*)

(*Just keep going. You have to keep going. Even if I fall behind. You will be safe in that bridge. I don't know how I know that, but I do. You have to reach it.*)

She could tell the Horseman was gaining in huge strides behind her and she pushed herself to run as fast as she could.

How could she feel so tired in a dream? The bridge was closer. It was just 50 feet, then 40 feet.

The sound of the horse drowned out everything else. Kate and Quinn looked behind them and immediately regretted it.

The Horseman was no more than 15 feet away—a black rider out of a nightmare.

He was in ancient clothes that looked half-rotted away. A black tattered cloak spread out behind him. In the moonlight, they could see a long saber held in his hand pointed forward—like a cavalry officer on a final charge. Even the horse was frightful, with red penetrating eyes that seemed to flash each time a hoof hit the ground. But the rider's most striking feature was what was missing... He rode with no head at all, with his sword held forward as if it was guiding the way.

The Horseman was now 10 feet behind them. And they were still 20 feet from the bridge.

(*Keep going, Kate. Run as fast as you can.*)

Before she knew what happened, Quinn had abruptly stopped, turned and ducked out of the way of the Horseman before it trampled him. Even as she continued to run blindly forward while looking back, she saw the effect on the Headless Horseman was immediate.

He yanked back on the reins and the horse gave a terrible cry of pain. The Horseman rounded as Quinn stood in the road facing him.

Kate was a few steps from the bridge and stopped.

(*Don't stop, Kate, keep going.*)

"Quinn, what are you doing?" she shouted.

The Horseman paused, turning sideways suddenly. It was almost as if he was unsure what to do.

"Just get into the bridge," Quinn yelled. "It's me he wants."

But suddenly that seemed unclear. The Horseman sat poised between the two, as if deciding which to pursue.

"Come on," she yelled at the Horseman. "I've got five feet between me and the bridge. You scared of a little water?"

"What are you doing?" Quinn shouted.

"I'm not losing you," she said.

"Just get in the damn bridge," he said. "Come on, you headless bastard. Let's get it on."

The Horseman suddenly turned again to face Kate, and before she could move, the horse surged forward. His sword was out and the Horseman closed the distance in mere seconds. Kate cried out and fell in the dirt as she made a desperate attempt to close the few remaining feet between her and the bridge.

But the Horseman was too fast.

He held the sword high over his body. His laugh again echoed off everything and it seemed to Kate that it was in her head as well.

Quinn felt like he watched in slow motion as the sword came down, flashing brightly for a half second, in a swift stroke aimed at Kate's head.

He screamed at the top of his lungs, shouting "No" louder than he ever had before.

For a moment, everything seemed to stop—the blade held in midair, the deadly stroke did not come down. The Horseman halted, laughed, turned to face Quinn and then abruptly disappeared.

*****

Quinn and Kate found themselves awake in their hotel room.

"What the hell was that?" she asked and nearly jumped out of bed.

"I don't know," Quinn replied, and it seemed stupid to ask if she was inquiring about the same dream.

Kate put her hand to her neck and felt the back of it.

"I thought I was finished," she said. "But you stopped him. You defeated him."

"No," Quinn said, as he got out of bed and quickly began pulling on clothes. "I don't think so."

"What do you mean?" she asked. "He stopped."

But she began putting on her own clothes.

"Help me get the chairs away from the balcony door," he said.

"What is going on?"

"It was a trick," Quinn said. "I don't think he could have hurt us in the dream. But I think... I think he heard me for real when I shouted like that."

"I don't understand," she said.

"I don't either," he replied. "But I think he knows where we are now. And I think he will be coming soon."

"Quinn, that's ridiculous, it was only a dream..."

But her voice fell flat. Far away, she started to hear the pounding hooves again. This was not a dream. The Horseman was coming for them.

She ran to the balcony door and the two of them hurriedly removed the furniture in front of it.

(*He's coming for us both now. I'm sorry Kate.*)

(*This can't be happening, Quinn.*)

(*I know, but it is.*)

The horse was getting closer.

"We need to get down to the balcony below us," Quinn said.

Kate saw a picture of them lowering themselves down the balconies. She added her own mental picture of creating a rope with bed sheets.

Quinn nodded.

"That's a better idea," he said.

(*What the hell is happening to us? I can hear what you're thinking.*)

(*Worry about it later.*)

The hoof beats stopped.

Far from feeling better, Kate now felt worse.

"What happened?" she asked.

"He's in the hotel now," Quinn said. "He'll be here soon."

"How, the elevator?"

"I don't know," he said.

She grabbed the sheets from the bed and yanked them off. They opened the balcony door and Quinn began tying part of the sheet to the railing.

"This won't get us very far," he said. "We'll need to scramble down the rest of the way."

Both of them heard a large crash down the hall, clearly coming from the same floor. Impossibly, they heard the sound of hoof beats in the hotel and someone began screaming.

Kate crossed the room and picked up her gun off the side table.

"I'm not sure a gun is going to help against him," Quinn said.

"Maybe, but it beats the hell out of just standing here," she replied.

"True," he said.

The pounding hooves came to their door and stopped.

For a second there was silence. And then the room exploded with noise as a giant force collided with the door. They watched as the door seemed to bend inward and the furniture in front of it shook. But it held.

"He's trying to come through," Quinn said.

There was another moment of silence. Somewhere down the hall, Quinn heard a voice shouting for someone to call the police.

It definitely isn't our imagination, he thought bitterly.

Kate pointed her gun at the door.

Another loud crash came a few seconds later as the horse collided with it again, but this time there was a cracking sound as well. They could see the door begin to splinter.

Kate cocked her gun.

"Come on through," she said. "I'll shoot you, you headless son of a bitch."

The door shuddered again with another large crash.

"That ought to put the fear of God into him," Quinn said. "Be sure to shoot him in the head."

"Well, I don't see you coming up with any better ideas," Kate said.

The door bulged in the middle and there was another loud crack as it began to come apart. The horse made another run at it and splinters flew from the door. The furniture reinforcing it fell over and the horse's nose broke through.

"Well, running away is starting to look like a great option," Quinn said.

Kate stared at the door. Would a bullet even harm the thing?

"Okay, we need to get out of here," she said and headed for the balcony. She holstered her gun and put it into her pants. "Come on, Quinn."

"Where is he?" Quinn said. "The horse is out there, but I can't tell if the Rider is."

"It doesn't matter. Come on!"

Quinn went to the balcony.

"You first," he said.

Kate grabbed the bed sheet and swung herself around the iron railing. In the room, the horse now appeared to have pushed his whole head through the door. She tested the sheet-rope and decided it would probably hold. Using it, she lowered herself to the balcony below.

Quinn watched as the horse continued to destroy the door. It now had most of its body through. But he couldn't see the Headless Horseman. The horse was there, but no rider. He didn't have time to think about it. Instead, Quinn swung his legs around the railing and lowered himself down to the balcony below.

Above, they could hear a loud crashing. The horse was now through. Quinn could hear its hooves on the floor above.

Hanging to the fifth floor balcony, he lowered himself until his feet touched the balcony railing below. He balanced himself and then jumped to the fourth floor balcony.

"Come on," he yelled up.

Kate followed his lead.

Above them, all chaos seemed to have broken loose. They could hear the smashing of glass and it felt like the roof might cave in.

"We don't have much time," Kate said.

"Where is he?" Quinn asked. "I didn't see him up there."

Quinn looked down to the ground below, but it was too dark to see.

Quinn swung himself over again and dropped down to the third floor balcony.

"Come on down," he said.

He helped her down to the third floor.

Quinn felt blind. He could not tell what was happening above and he still had a sinking feeling some other trick was waiting for him below.

He swung himself over the balcony and dangled his legs over the edge again. But this time, when he looked down, he could see him.

The Headless Horseman stood on the ground below the hotel, waiting for him.

"Holy shit," Quinn yelled. "Kate, start climbing up."

Quinn could see the Horseman moving now, as if to start climbing the balconies himself.

Quinn tried to balance for a second, before pulling himself up to the third floor balcony. But when he looked down to see if the Horseman was pursuing, he lost his footing and fell the three stories to the ground.

Kate screamed. She watched Quinn fall in slow motion to the ground. The Horseman stood below him, waiting.

He'll kill Quinn, she thought.

But as soon as Quinn hit the ground with a large thud, everything changed. One minute the Horseman was there, striding toward where Quinn lay.

And then he wasn't. He disappeared as if he was never there at all.

Kate looked everywhere and she heard nothing from upstairs anymore either.

She scrambled down the last remaining balconies and hurried to Quinn, who lay unconscious on the ground. Kate looked all around her, but there was nothing anymore.

The Headless Horseman was gone.

Chapter 20

"For those that were chosen, there is always the time of trial,
Crowley said. A time when the chosen two's destinies are not set. It
is the most critical point for any Prince of Sanheim. Only by
understanding his cennad and himself will he be able to do what
must be done. Only by staring wide-eyed into the abyss will he
survive."
—Horace Camden, "The Prince of Sanheim"

Kate was having trouble deciding where to look. She tried to stay focused on the road, but she kept looking at the back seat where Quinn lay.

She should have called an ambulance, she knew. She should never have moved him herself. But she had panicked and did not want to take the chance that the Horseman could come back. There was no time to think about why he had disappeared.

Thank God they were in a big enough town that there was a hospital. They had noticed it on the way into town. It must serve most of the surrounding area—it wasn't huge, but it would be enough. She wanted him to be okay. She tried sensing something about him—in the hotel room, she was pretty sure she could hear what he was thinking and vice versa.

But now she got nothing. She didn't know what to tell the hospital and it was only now dawning on her that the hotel would want some type of explanation for a wrecked room and vanished customers.

She shook her head and glanced back again at Quinn.

Please let him be okay, she thought. Please let him be okay.

She was unsure what to think or do. If their problems had seemed bad 12 hours ago, everything now was much, much worse. And she still had only a limited picture of what was going on.

Only a day ago, they had been worried about one vicious killer. Bad—really bad. And now? Were there two? Was one working for the other? Who was she kidding anyway? What kind of being could literally spring out of your dreams and attack you? It was too much.

Thank God Quinn had left his cell phone in the car. She picked it up while still driving and called Janus. She had to trust somebody and he was one of the only ones left.

He answered immediately, sounding wide awake even though it must have been around four in the morning. She remembered Quinn telling her he always sounded ready for action.

"It's Kate," she said.

"What the hell is going on, Kate?" Janus asked. He sounded concerned. "I tried to call you guys again last night. The police are out looking for you and Quinn's place looks like someone ransacked it before leaving."

"You've been there?"

"I was looking for you guys," he said. "Look, you may have decided that now is a good time for a romantic romp somewhere, but there is some bad shit going on and I can't get a hold of anyone."

"I'll explain later," she said.

"Wait a second, Kate, I..."

"Quinn's hurt," she said. "He's unconscious and I don't know..."

She broke off. This was simply too much.

Janus' voice changed.

"Just tell me where to meet you," he said.

"I'm taking him to Bluemont Hospital," she said.

"Bluemont?" he said. "In West Virginia?"

"Look, I'll explain later. But I need help here."

"I'll meet you there as soon as I can."

Kate pulled into the emergency entrance and thought a minute before leaving Quinn in the car.

What if the Horseman came back? Or what if Lord Halloween somehow knew where she was? She felt trapped. And very alone. She hadn't realized how grateful she was to share everything with Quinn until he was no longer there.

She ran into the hospital.

"My friend," she told the nurse. "He's in the car. He fell three stories. He's hurt."

The nurse stared at her in total disbelief.

"You moved him?" she asked.

"Yes, but that's done," Kate said. "Please. I need help."

The nurse summoned three others and they went to the car to retrieve Quinn.

*****

Janus showed up a little more than an hour later, having driven as fast as he could push his Jeep. Kate stood outside the room where Quinn was being examined. She couldn't tell what was going on. The doctors had tried to attach Quinn to monitors earlier, but the machines had appeared on the fritz.

"What happened?" Janus asked, looking in.

"Quinn fell," she said. "We were being chased in our hotel room and he fell off the balcony."

Kate sat down.

"Chased by who?" Janus asked. "What the hell is going on?"

Kate started to explain. They had been stalked by Lord Halloween, they had fled. And then someone had followed them to the hotel room and attacked. She didn't know how to bring up the dream or the very real ghost of a horse that destroyed the hotel room door, or any of it.

"So Lord Halloween found you there and just attacked full on?" Janus asked. "I don't get it. Why didn't you call the police?"

"I don't think it was him," she said.

"Who else would it be?"

"Quinn said that you and he found something weird out by the Phillips farm?" Kate asked.

"What about it?" Janus asked. "Some nut carved a strange word into a tree."

"The same person who did that attacked us tonight," Kate said.

"I don't get this," Janus replied. "How do you know it's the same guy? How do you know it's not Lord Halloween?"

"I don't understand it all, Janus," she said. "There is some strange stuff going on. I can't explain it all."

Janus looked in the window. "Is he going to be okay?"

"I don't know," Kate said and stood up to look back at the doctor examining Quinn. The light above the bed was flickering and the doctor appeared to be calling for a nurse to help. "He fell a long way and landed on his back."

"Jesus," Janus said and sat down. "Why didn't you guys tell me what was going on?"

"It was my fault," Kate said. "I was so paranoid, I didn't want Quinn to tell anyone."

"You didn't think you could trust me," Janus said and looked at her coldly. "So what has changed now?"

Kate wasn't sure herself. But Janus was the first one she had thought of for help. It was who Quinn would have called. And her view of Janus was different too.

Before, she had seen him as slightly obnoxious, but now she knew things about him. About Christina, his long-term girlfriend who had left him abruptly two years ago. She knew he had been devastated, that Quinn had to talk him off of the roof of his apartment building. The only person who could have known this was Quinn and he had never said anything. But whatever happened in the hotel room must have connected their memories somehow. Quinn trusted Janus, so now so did she.

She shook her head. This was insane.

"Quinn trusts you," Kate said. "He told me we could count on you. And I need help now."

"Look, I'll help, but you have to understand, it was crazy yesterday," Janus said. "They found another body. I talked to one of Quinn's police sources. He said the police think the guy was killed around the same time as Fanton."

"Was there a note?" Kate asked.

"Definitely," Janus said. "But I don't know what it said. Neither did the source."

"What does Kyle think?"

"That's another thing, Kate," Janus said. "Laurence's been going nuts. It may be the weekend, but he couldn't reach any of his star reporters. Kyle didn't answer his cell or his home number. And I couldn't get either you or Quinn. I was beginning to wonder..."

"Has someone been to Kyle's house?" Kate asked.

Janus shook his head.

"Not that I know of, yet," he said. "I went over to Quinn's and that's when I found the place a mess. The police were already there. They said there had been some incident at the hotel and they needed to speak to both of you."

"We left in a hurry," she said.

"So I gathered."

"Is it odd for Kyle to go this long without checking in? It is the weekend..."

"Kate, this is the biggest story in Loudoun's history," Janus said. "He wouldn't just drop off the face of the earth. Laurence is fucking beside himself. He checked in with all the reporters after I couldn't get in touch with either Quinn or Kyle."

"The rest are okay?"

"I think so," Janus said.

The doctor came out then.

"Are you the person who brought him in?" the doctor asked Kate. She nodded.

"How is he?" Kate asked.

"I wish I could say for sure," the doctor said. "You said he fell, is that right? Did he fall on any electric power lines, or was electricity involved in some way?"

"No, why?"

"Because I can't get a machine to work within 15 feet of him," the doctor replied. "The lights above him are going crazy too. I just thought, sometimes electrocution or a lightning strike can do funny things..."

"He just fell off a balcony," Kate said. "Is he going to be okay?"

"I don't know," the doctor said. "He's in better shape than I would have thought if he really fell three floors. He must have been very, very lucky in how he landed."

"What does that mean?"

"I'm getting him in for x-rays, but he appears to have movement," the doctor said. "He also appears to be dreaming some and has been moving in his sleep. All that is a good sign."

"What's the bad sign?"

"We can't wake him up," the doctor said.

"So what happens next?" Kate asked.

"I'm not sure," the doctor said. "We are going to run a few more tests. I don't know why we are seeing all this electrical stuff going on. We will just wait and see. I suggest you sit down and get some rest."

And like that, the doctor was gone. He didn't wait for questions, he just moved on.

Kate and Janus both sat down.

"What do we do now?" Kate asked. "We're sitting ducks here. If Lord Halloween finds out... he can come right on in. Maybe get Quinn while I'm away."

"We're not in Loudoun County, remember? He doesn't know you are here," Janus said. "And this is a pretty public place. If someone shows up randomly to visit Quinn, it's going to be a tip off that he might be Lord Halloween."

"Still, there are..."

"I know, I know," Janus said. "There are lots of things that could happen. But he is in good hands for now. I won't tell Laurence where you guys are. We can limit how many people know."

"He might have followed us," she said.

"I don't know," Janus said. "It's your other attacker I'm worried about. You said he just disappeared?"

"I don't know where he is," Kate said. "But he has a penchant for dressing up. So I don't think he will be hard to spot if he shows up again."

"You said this was connected to the incident out on Phillips' farm?" Janus asked. "The word 'Sanheim' carved into a tree?"

"Yes, why?" Kate asked.

"It's funny but... Look, I didn't remember back then, but I know that word."

"It means Halloween," Kate said.

"Yeah, but it also refers to something else, I think," Janus said. "When I was young, my Mum told me about some legend. Some Celtic thing."

"What are you talking about?" Kate asked.

"The Prince of Sanheim," Janus said. "Somebody who worships the Celtic God of the Dead and gains great power on his feast day."

"Halloween," Kate said.

"Yes," he said.

"What more do you know about it?"

"Nothing, really," Janus said. "It was just some spooky story told to kids. There was a rhyme connected with it. 'Fifty men went up a hill, none of them came down. Fifty men went to see him, none of them were found.' But I don't remember any details."

Kate's mind was racing. Whatever this was, it seemed significant. If it wasn't connected to Lord Halloween—a possibility that didn't make much sense to her—it could be related to this legend somehow. She looked back at Quinn. She needed him to be all right, but she also needed to keep working.

"I'm going to watch him," Kate said. "But I need a few things. I need you to get some stuff from our hotel, I don't care how. The files, the security tapes. We need a VCR. And I need an Internet connection."

"It's the middle of the damn night," Janus said.

Kate looked at him. "And you've never done a little midnight breaking and entering before?"

Janus smiled. "All right, but if I get put in jail, you are posting bail."

*****

Quinn was standing on a hilltop, looking out over a grand vista of earth and sky. Lush, rolling green hills spilled out before him and in the distance he could see the ocean. He was standing on a cliff, yet he felt no fear. He wondered if he jumped off if he could even fly.

"I wouldn't try that just yet," a voice said.

Quinn turned to find a man standing there. He looked familiar and then he remembered. He was the man from his dream. He hadn't remembered it when he had woken up, but he remembered it now. The man had given him a hint.

"You told me to find Tim Anderson," he said.

The man nodded. "It was just a hint."

"He didn't know the killer," Quinn said.

"No, but he knew enough," the man said. "He told you what you need to know."

"Which is what?"

"I can't tell you everything Quinn," he said. "I'd like to—I really would. But that's not the way this goes."

The man looked at the sky, which was a bright blue. Quinn could hear seagulls, feel the wind racing around him.

"Beautiful, isn't it?" the man said.

"Where are we?" Quinn asked.

"Technically, you are in a hospital bed in Bluemont," the man said.

"The Horseman? He didn't kill me?"

The man chuckled at that and turned back to Quinn.

"He might yet, but not this time, no," he said.

"Did you create him? Does he work for you?"

"I'm not familiar with the story, Quinn, but I don't believe that he works for anyone but himself."

"He's fictional. He isn't real."

"You made him real," the man said. "If he works for anyone, it's you."

"But he's trying to kill me."

"Yes, that's true."

"What's going on? Who are you? Why am I here?"

"I'll tell you a story, Quinn," the man said. "I can't say for certain that it's true. It was a long time ago and it's hard to remember. Centuries ago, a small village in what you now call Ireland was under attack from a neighboring tribe. They were losing badly. After a raid which resulted in the deaths of most of the young men and the kidnapping of many women, the town elders made a deal."

"With whom?"

"Sanheim, the god of the underworld. The deal was extreme. They had only a few young men and women left, yet their survival was on the line. They agreed to sacrifice a young man and woman—kids, really—to Sanheim. They tied them to a post, bound their wrists together and left them there to die. But they didn't die, Quinn. A few days later, they returned to the village and the young man—who had seemed just like a boy—was now a powerful warrior. The woman was his priestess. The town elders were frightened by what had happened, but pleased. Their sacrifice had been accepted."

"The man and woman left for the neighboring village the next day. Some of the women that had been kidnapped returned after that, but, according to legend, no member of the rival tribe was left alive. The town elders were very pleased. Everything had gone as they wanted. Except when the man and woman returned to them, they didn't work for the town elders. They were the ones giving the orders. And those that resisted them disappeared. It wasn't long before the two ruled the tribe openly. When there was battle to be done, the man led the charge. When there were decisions to be made, the woman made them."

"So you're the man in that story?" Quinn asked.

"No," the man said, and chuckled. "Few of the chosen live long. You'll find out why soon enough. Though he did live a very long time. In the end, he got sloppy, corrupt. They all do. Start out anxious to please and end up living for themselves."

"Who are they?"

"They are called the Prince of Sanheim. The name just refers to the man, of course. Which is an advantage, really, since no one really knew what a big part the woman played. They are two that can be joined together, in body, spirit and soul. Once they pass the trials of Sanheim, they are like gods on earth. That's what the legend says, anyway."

"I still don't get what this has to do with me," Quinn said, but he was beginning to understand.

"Oh, I think you do," the man said, and stared at Quinn. It was unnerving. The man's red eyes bored into Quinn as if he could see all his thoughts and memories. "You've always known you were different, that you were special. You feel it only a few months a year, but in those months you call September and October, you felt powerful, unafraid. If you hadn't talked yourself into being afraid, you would have reveled in the dark and the night. It's where you are meant to be."

"No," Quinn said. "I don't believe you."

He wasn't sure why the words disturbed him, but he felt like he was being shown a mirror image of himself—one he was afraid to look at.

"You do and you know it," the man said. "You are a Prince of Sanheim. You had to have the right mate—not any woman would do, not by a long shot—but this was something that was born to happen to you. Your parents knew it. They could have helped you, if they had lived."

"My parents? Were they the Prince..."

"No, but your mother knew the legend and knew it well," the man said. "She knew what you were the moment you were born. In every age, a new one is chosen. They face the trial and if they win, great power is theirs. Be glad it is your destiny, Quinn. It's an honor, and if this honor wasn't yours, you would be corpses by now. Lord Halloween would have killed you in your sleep and hunted Kate until she had joined you."

"Kate's dream? That's part of this?" Quinn said.

"Sanheim is the god of the dead, Quinn," the man said. "Who warned Kate that Lord Halloween was coming?"

"Her mother," Quinn said. "It was her mother."

"Precisely," the man said. "Talking to the dead would be a miracle in the modern world, but it's nothing compared to what power you might have. Take it, Quinn. Take it and hunt Lord Halloween as he has hunted you and so many others. It's the only way to save Kate."

Quinn's mind was racing. He looked out at the vista and felt a surge of power through him. He felt alive in every fiber of his being, like nothing could stop him. For just a moment, he thought he could see Lord Halloween's face and then it was gone. He felt alone again and empty.

"I gave you a taste," the man said. "This is the deal that you and I make. Become the Prince of Sanheim."

"I don't even know how," Quinn said. "Besides, what if I can't stop? The two in your legend—they couldn't stop, could they? Whatever power this is, it isn't good."

"Good and evil are points of view," the man said. "The only thing that matters in this world is power."

"I don't believe that."

"Then you are a fool. Power is everything. But it is yours to wield as you want."

"Why?" Quinn asked. "Why do you want me to take this?"

"I need an emissary in the world," the man said. "My last one didn't quite work out. I'm offering you power, the chance to save lives."

"But I would work for you?"

"In a sense," the man said. "But I don't care about mortal concerns. I'll need you for something else that we can discuss when the time is right. This is a gift, Quinn. Take it, use it as you will. If you want to be a knight in shining armor to those who need help, you can be that. I put no restrictions on you."

"You are Sanheim," Quinn said.

The man smiled broadly but didn't say anything. Even in that moment, Quinn wondered if he was telling the truth. There was something else in play here—something Quinn could not yet understand. He had trouble believing the man was some kind of God, or the equivalent of the Devil.

"What's the catch?" Quinn asked.

"The trial," the man said. "You have to prove you are worthy first. Some of the most promising potentials have failed this test."

"Is there a math test?" Quinn asked. "Because I suck at those."

The man didn't smile.

"I can't tell you more about it," he said. "Pass the trial and the power is yours, it's as simple as that."

"That's it? Unlimited power if I win?"

"There is no such thing as unlimited power," he replied. "There are limits. If you live to see November 1, you will experience your first one."

"What happens then?"

"I can't say," the man said. "There are rules to this game. But the time has arrived for you to choose if you are ready to be what you were born to be. Seek this power out and you can save the girl and the day. Reject it, run from it, or ignore it and you're doomed. It's as simple as that."

"What does the Horseman have to do with any of this?"

"I keep telling you, Quinn. You created him. You are what you fear. He belongs to you."

"I just want him to go away," Quinn said. "Can I make him do that?"

"Yes, but when the time comes, you won't," the man said. "I see that now. Even if you would, she won't let you. Yes, you two are very promising. I'm afraid our time is almost up."

"Wait," he said. "I still don't know what is going on. I need to know more about the trial."

"No, Quinn," the man said and smiled. It was meant to be charming, but the smile instead seemed predatory. "There are some things you have to figure out yourself. I will give you one more hint about Lord Halloween."

The world began turning then, slowly at first, but then faster. Everything was a blur of shapes around Quinn. Only the man stood out clearly.

"You're over-thinking him," he said. "You think you know his motives but you don't. He's a showman, a liar. He's hiding his true motives from you because at their most basic, they are simple motives. Figure them out and you will find him before he finds you."

Quinn wanted to ask more about what he meant, but the world had tilted. Everything was giving way. The man was gone and then there was blackness.

*****

When Quinn opened his eyes, he was in a hospital bed. Above him was a TV and it was playing the strangest movie he had ever seen. There was no plot, only figures walking past a camera. The figures didn't notice the camera or acknowledge it in any way. Every so often the action would pause and then restart. Quinn was beginning to wonder who would make such a program when he realized what it was: a security feed from Kate's hotel.

He noticed Janus was next to him, watching it and taking notes. Where was Kate? He had an image then. She was downstairs in the hospital, using someone's computer.

(*Thank God you're awake*) Kate thought.

(*What's going on? Where am I?*)

(*I'll be right up*)

But Quinn found he could access her memories. She had brought him to the hospital, called Janus and waited. The doctors didn't know what was wrong, but she had known he would wake up. She had felt him getting stronger and had almost had an image of his dreams. It looked like he had been in Scotland. In the meanwhile, Janus and she had been researching. They had been watching the security feed looking for a clue while Kate also tried to look up more information about the word 'Sanheim.' What she had found had disturbed her.

Quinn stopped wondering how he knew all this. He was linked to Kate now, he knew. He could see her thoughts and memories and she could see his. It was strange but also exciting.

Janus had not yet noticed he was awake. He was intently staring at the video screen. For a moment, Quinn thought he saw something familiar on the screen as a figure walked by, but then it was gone. He felt fuzzy and lightheaded. He doubt he was in much condition to do anything other than drool.

Kate came through the door.

"Thank God," she said again.

Janus looked confused, then at Quinn. When he saw that his eyes were open, he smiled.

"Jesus fucking Christ, man," Janus said. "You gave us quite a scare."

"Language," Quinn said in what was a pale imitation of Rebecca's near daily admonishment.

Kate came over and kissed him. He had nearly forgotten what had happened before the Headless Horseman attacked, but it all came flooding back to him. This kiss wasn't like those and he knew it, could feel her emotions as they were locked. This was not lust, but relief mixed with love.

(*I love you*) he said in his mind and she kissed him harder.

(*I know*) she responded.

She didn't have to say it back to him. He knew what she felt, what she thought. He was no longer clear on where Quinn ended and Kate began. That might have been disturbing, but it didn't feel that way. It was like letting your arm go numb and suddenly regaining feeling in it. It felt natural, like they had always been this way.

"Seriously, do I need to leave the room?" Janus asked. "You two are making me blush."

Kate pulled away and Quinn got a good look at her. She was dressed in makeshift clothes again, jeans and a t-shirt she had bought at the mall before they left for Bluemont. She looked like she hadn't showered recently and her hair was frazzled. Still, Quinn thought he had never seen anything so beautiful in his life.

(*Always the charmer*) she thought.

(*Sorry*) he said. (*I can't help what I'm thinking*)

(*Don't try*) she said. (*I don't want to try either.*)

(*What have you found out about Sanheim?*) he asked.

(*Quite a bit, actually, and none of it's particularly good. Let me show you.*)

She was just starting to call up her memories to let Quinn have a look when Janus interrupted.

"What the fuck is going on?" he asked.

Quinn and Kate had forgotten he was even there. With effort, Quinn focused his attention on Janus. He found it extremely hard to do.

It was like when Kate was around, he couldn't concentrate on anything or anyone else. That would be a problem if he didn't learn to control it.

"You guys are now officially freaky and disturbing," Janus said. "You're just staring at each other, but you are making faces at each other like you're talking. What the fuck?"

"Sorry," Kate said. "It's just..."

(*Should we tell him?*) she asked.

(*It will be hard not to*) he responded.

"You are doing it again," Janus nearly shouted. Behind him the TV continued to play security feed from Leesburg Hotel. "Seriously."

(*Tell us about Sanheim. Use words*)

"Okay, Janus, just hold on," Kate said. "I'll explain what I know. I've been doing some research on the Prince of Sanheim."

"I can't imagine you found that much," Janus said. "It was just a goofy legend. I don't even know how many people heard it."

"Under that name, I found very little," she said. "But once you start looking for patterns... he's everywhere."

(*It's not a he, it's a they. It takes a man and a woman. It's like the song, 'It takes two to make a thing go right. It takes two to make it out of sight.'*)

Kate started laughing at that and Quinn smiled. Janus just looked confused.

"Okay, it's a they," she said.

Janus was looking at them both again.

"Dear fucking God," he said. "You can read each other's thoughts, can't you?"

"Yes," Quinn said. "Though I have to say you jumped to that conclusion relatively quickly."

"I don't know how you couldn't jump to it, mate," he said. "You two are smiling at the same jokes, yet you didn't say a joke. You're talking to each other without speaking."

Quinn found Janus' reaction fascinating. He seemed unnerved, nearly frightened.

(*He is frightened.*) Kate thought. (*Wouldn't you be?*)

"Don't be scared," Kate said. "We're still the same two people."

"That's how you knew," Janus said. "That's how you knew about Christina. When you mentioned it the other day, I just assumed my man Quinn here had been blabbing, which would have been very unlike him. But he didn't say a word, did he? You could read his thoughts."

"And his memories, yes," Kate said.

"How the fuck did this happen?"

"You wouldn't believe me if I told you," Quinn responded.

"Oh, at this stage, I'm willing to believe an awful lot," Janus said.

"We'll get to it," Kate said. "Back to Sanheim for a moment."

"How is that even related?" Janus asked.

"Give me a chance to talk to you and I'll tell you," Kate said. She was testy with him, the way Quinn often was after the two had been together for several hours. Not only was she absorbing Quinn's memories, she appeared to be absorbing his attitude too.

"Oh my God this is freaky," Janus said. "I'm talking to a chick that is incredibly hot and she sounds like my best friend over there, whom I've never found remotely attractive."

"Stay with me here," Kate said. "From what I can tell, the legend of Sanheim is very, very old. I've been doing some research on the Net and it seems it was the Romans who first brought up Sanheim, a God they viewed as the equivalent of Hades."

"The Devil," Janus said. "That's the equivalent."

"It's related but not quite the same thing," Kate said. "Anyway, they invaded Britain under Julius Caesar, but Caesar at some point stopped. Historians point to the political crisis back in Rome as to why he had to return, but not everyone thinks so. He had four legions go over there with him, took two back and left one to guard what he had conquered. That's a whole legion of men unaccounted for. Official history doesn't worry about it, could just be someone's error."

"But unofficially..."

"Unofficially, he ran into the 'champion of Hades.' That's why you don't find it under any reference to Sanheim at first. But it's the same thing to the Romans. I'm not sure what happened, but apparently the two met on the battlefield. After that, Caesar headed home in a hurry."

"He was scared? Does that guy get scared?" Janus asked.

"Maybe," Kate said. "Or maybe they cut some kind of deal. Maybe he told him about political events back home. In any case, the Romans don't invade any further until a couple centuries later."

"So he's a warrior?" Quinn asked.

"He's everything," Kate said. "He's the leader, he's the general, he's the priest. And he keeps showing up in Celtic history. Not during every invasion, but he's there. He's referenced during the conquering of Wales."

"Fat lot of good he must have done us," Janus said.

"That's just it," Kate said. "He's referenced as helping the English."

"Fuck him," Janus said. "What's that about?"

"It's not the same person," she said. "Through history, different leaders are chosen and they each have their own agendas. Maybe this guy just didn't like the Welsh."

"Imagine that," Quinn said.

"Well, fuck him," Janus said.

"Does anyone mention Sanheim directly?"

"Yes," Kate asked. "A guy named Robert Crowley."

"That's the guy I told you about," Janus said. "He was the 'Prince of Sanheim.'"

"Who was he?"

"Nominally, he was a bad poet of the Romantic era," Kate said. "But he went crazy, even by Lord Byron's standards. In 1873, he declared that his father was not Sir Richard Crowley, but a powerful Irish chieftain. He summoned followers to his home for what he promised would be the revelation of the 'Prince of Sanheim.'"

"Sounds like a nutter."

"Here's what interesting," she said. "He summoned women first. And just so you don't think everyone was repressed in that day and age, many came."

"He started an orgy?" Janus said.

"I think he was looking for someone," Kate said, and she looked meaningfully at Quinn. "He was looking for the right woman."

"The kind that would live out his fantasies?"

"The kind that would trigger the 'Trial of the Cennad,'" Kate said.

"I was really hoping we were going to talk in more detail about the orgies," Janus said.

"A man and a woman joining is the key, Janus," Kate said. "There's this weird Web site some group in England set up that's devoted to Crowley. It would be disturbing if it wasn't so damn helpful. But they list all of his poetry, which is really, really bad, filled with love, sex, death and more sex. But he has an entire poem on the 'joining.' It's all about sex, of course, but this one is different from the others. This is the kind of sex that links the body and the mind."

"It links the souls," Quinn said. "Two become one."

"That's one horny guy," Janus said, and then he paused. "Wait a second. They are linked in body and mind, which means they..."

"Right," Quinn said quickly.

"You two?" Janus said. "That's how come you guys are suddenly the picture of weirdness? You had sex and now you are..."

"It's not what we are," Kate said. "It's what we're becoming. Quinn and I are linked now. I have a feeling it becomes even stronger once the trial is passed."

"Was it any different than normal sex?" Janus asked. When he saw the look on Quinn's face, he continued. "Look, normally I would just wait to ask Quinn when he was alone, but since you two are one now anyway, what's the point, right?"

Quinn wasn't going to answer. He was opening his mouth to say it was private when Kate replied.

"Very. Imagine knowing exactly what your partner wants a half second before they even know they want it," she said. "No awkwardness, embarrassment. No accidentally doing the wrong thing. It's like everything is choreographed."

"That sounds pretty fucking awesome," Janus said.

"Yeah," both Kate and Quinn said at the same time, and they looked at each other. Quinn didn't want to think about sex right now. Or rather, that was all he wanted to think about, but if he did, if they lost themselves to that again, they would be dead.

"So that's the deal. The two have sex and..."

"Sex changes everything," Kate said. "That's what Madame Zora told me when she read my future. It was in the Tarot cards: The Devil, which represented lust and sex."

"What else did she tell you?" Janus asked.

"The next card was Death," Kate said.

"Oh. I'm going to go out on a limb and say that isn't so good."

"Death can also mean transformation," Kate responded.

"Really? Because usually, when you use it in a story and whatnot, it just means death," Janus said.

"Jump back for a second," Kate said. "We aren't done with Crowley. He hosts this party, right? Women come from all around."

"So he can join with as many as possible?" Janus asked.

"I don't think so," Kate said. "So he could find the right one. The Web site is vague—everything here is reading between the lines. Crowley was basically holding try-outs. I think by himself he was just a guy, but he believed if he found the right woman and they had sex..."

"He would become the Prince of Sanheim," Janus said.

"Bingo," Quinn said.

"Which means what, exactly? All you can eat at the local Irish pub?"

"I don't know," Kate said. "I know it triggers the 'Trial of the Cennad.' But I don't know what that means."

"The Headless Horseman," Quinn said. "He's part of that trial. He has to be."

Quinn could vaguely remember his dream before he woke up. He had been talking to someone—he couldn't remember who—but the man had told him something.

"You are what you fear," he said.

Kate nodded.

(*You created him.*) she thought. (*He's your cennad.*)

(*Which means what, exactly?*)

(*It's ancient Gaelic for ambassador.*)

"Stop doing that please," Janus said. "Not all of us are tuned in to Kate-and-Quinn's FM Sex Radio."

"Sorry," Quinn said. "Look, my parents read me 'The Legend of Sleepy Hollow' when I was a kid and I loved it. Loved it. I made them read it to me every night. Finally, my Dad, as a surprise, got me the Disney cartoon version of it. And it scared the hell out of me. I couldn't sleep for weeks after that, and boy, was my Mom pissed at him for showing it to me. He figured that since I had read the story, I was ready. But I wasn't."

"So the Headless Horseman is the thing you feared," Kate said. "That's why he attacked us."

"Can I just remind everyone that he's made up?" Janus said. "He doesn't exist."

"No, he didn't exist," Kate said. "But he does now."

"Because you two had sex?"

"Dee saw him before this," Quinn said. "That man near Phillips Farm heard a horseman late at night. And that was before we, uh, made love."

"Just a guess: it was after you met me," Kate said. "Before you did, he was just a dream. Once you and I started getting closer, the Horseman became more real. But he wasn't solid flesh—ready to attack us—until we had sex. That triggered the trial."

"And the trial is what? He shows up and puts Quinn on the witness stand?"

"I could be wrong, but I think it's a bit simpler than that," Kate said. "We kill him or he kills us."

"Awesome," Janus said. "That's just great, because last time I checked there was someone else that wanted to kill you two. You are very popular with the psycho set this year."

"What happens if we succeed?" Quinn asked.

"I don't know," Kate asked. "But I do know that at least at first, everything is tied to Halloween. That's the apex of the Prince's power and his lowest point is..."

"Nov. 1, All Saint's Day," Quinn said.

"So whatever power is gained is lost at the stroke of midnight," Kate said.

"What happened to Crowley?" Janus asked. "What did he do with his power?"

"I don't know if he succeeded or failed," Kate said. "But he held his party. It wasn't a huge gathering, but it was enough. Maybe fifty to hundred."

"Fifty men went up a hill," Janus said. "None of them came down."

"What happened?" Quinn asked, but he already knew.

"No one who attended that party was ever seen again," Kate responded. "They found the castle where he threw it totally abandoned."

"Fifty men went to see him," Janus continued. "None of them were found."

"But they found something else, didn't they?" Quinn asked.

"Yes," Kate said. "The Web site had a lot to say about that."

"What did they find?" Janus asked.

"They found a message written on the wall," Kate said. "It was written in blood."

"Let me guess," Janus said. "It said, 'Need more beer.'"

No one laughed.

"No," Kate said. "It said, 'The Prince of Sanheim is Risen. May God Have Mercy On Your Souls.'"

Chapter 21

Tuesday, Oct. 24

Quinn idly tapped his pen on his notepad as he waited for the press conference to start. It was already 10 minutes late and reporters were buzzing around the small room in the police station. It was late October, but the room was hot. Quinn wanted to open a window, but he was afraid to lose his chair. It was standing room only.

There were reporters here from everywhere—*The Washington Post, The Washington Times*, maybe even *The New York Times*, he wasn't sure. They had all gotten wind of what Sheriff Brown was supposed to announce. Lord Halloween is back. After a 12-year absence, Virginia's most-wanted serial killer had returned, from the dead no less, as the man police had pinned the murders on had long since died.

None of this was news to Quinn, of course. But journalism is a pack business and the pack followed the major news outlets. The *Loudoun Chronicle* could have reported a month ago that the killer had returned, but it wouldn't matter until the bigger papers got a hold of it. Once they did, only then would the story exist.

(*I wonder why the press conference hasn't started yet?*) Kate asked.

(*Not sure,*) he replied. (*Maybe Brown wants to make a grand entrance?*)

(*Could be,*) the voice came back. (*But I'm not sure it is needed here.*)

Kate was not at the press conference—she was in fact sitting across town at her computer trying to read something on the Internet. If Quinn closed his eyes and concentrated he could see it, as she could do likewise. That this now seemed natural was the weirdest part. In just two days, Quinn almost could not remember what it had been like before. Kate was just always there, in his head, and if that might seem scary to some, it was immensely comforting to them both.

It was as if you constantly had your best friend on a cell line with you. But better. He did not need to say anything out loud, but could just think it. And the speed with which they could communicate was unbelievable. Better still was that they did not need to find words to describe how they were feeling.

The other just knew. They felt it too.

In fact, the only really odd moment had come the first time one of them went to the bathroom. But they had solved that problem quickly. It turned out that they could block the other one out—have a private thought in other words—if they wanted to. But aside from bathroom time, neither had found any reason, or desire, to do that.

(*Laurence wants you to ask him about Kyle.*) Kate's voice came in his head.

(*Yeah, I heard him tell you to call me.*) Quinn replied.

(*I didn't think you were paying attention. You were thinking about sex again.*)

(*I can multitask, you know.*)

(*I know. This is just different. I think multiple thoughts in my own head all the time. But it's kind of strange when I'm hearing someone else's.*)

(*I understand completely.*)

(*I thought we agreed we aren't going to think about sex anymore.*)

(*Yes, we did. But I'm a guy. It is a hard thing to shut off.*)

(*I know, but we agreed for a reason. No sex for fear of scary guy riding horse. That clearly triggered it last time.*)

(*I'm down with the plan, honey. I'm just saying: if you are going to listen to my thoughts, you have to know that I will think about sex a lot. It's just there.*)

(*I know. The problem is then it gets me thinking about it, too. Damn. This will be a vicious cycle.*)

(*I know, I know. We will figure this out. We will figure out how to beat this. We'll beat the trial and take it from there.*)

(*What if there is no there? What if we lose?*) Kate asked.

(*We won't lose.*)

(*How can this feel so natural? Why doesn't this feel more invasive?*)

(*I guess for the Prince of Sanheim thing to work the two of us have to be able to function comfortably together.*)

(*You talk about it—okay, think about it—like it is some design. Like somebody really thought this through before creating it.*)

Quinn thought of the man standing on the hill, the one from his dream.

(*You think he designed it?*) Kate asked.

(*I'm not sure. I'm not sure he really is who he wants me to think he is.*)

(*Why is he helping us?*)

(*He wants something.*)

(*What?*)

(*I really don't know.*)

It had been a hellish few days. They had practically had to force their way out of Bluemont hospital. Doctors had insisted they wanted to keep him under observation. The local police had questions about how a horse had attacked the local hotel, but Quinn and Kate had claimed total ignorance. They had arrived back in Loudoun County to find another reception of police, who wanted to know where they had been, when they had been attacked and why they hadn't reported it any earlier. Quinn had been disturbed to find that while the rest of the reporters had checked in, Kyle had not. They feared the worst. In fact, Quinn expected it.

Sheriff Brown walked into the room. He looked pale, haggard and approximately 20 years older than when Kate and Quinn had seen him just a few days before.

(*He looks like shit.*) Kate said.

Quinn just nodded and watched the man slowly walk to the podium. He clearly didn't want to be there. Which was odd in a way, Quinn reflected. This was a guy who loved attention, who savored the moment when Loudoun was big time news. But Quinn supposed even Brown had his limits.

(*There is something more to it than that, Quinn. Look at the way he is moving. I wonder...*)

But Brown had now ascended the platform. Flashbulbs went off. Quinn could hear the distinct whir of the TV cameras recording every second of it. For a moment, Quinn felt bad for Brown, who faced what must have appeared like a pack of wolves waiting to eat him alive.

"Thank you all for coming," Brown began. "I apologize for being late. We at the Loudoun County Sheriff's department are very reluctant to communicate with suspects in the following fashion, but we have been asked, and I have reluctantly agreed, to make an exception. I wish to make the following statement: Lord Halloween has returned. Please take all precautions necessary to guard your loved ones. No one is safe."

For a second, you could hear a pin drop. Then more flashbulbs went off and there was a bustle of activity as reporters started scribbling on paper.

"That is all I have to say for now," Brown said. "I wish to make it clear that we made the preceding statement at the request of an individual who has said this is the only manner in which he will communicate with us. We do not wish to start any kind of panic. The department is doing everything it can to make this county safe for everyone. We are working around the clock. We urge everyone to be cautious and to report anything out of the ordinary to the police."

Before he could even finish, the questions started.

"Did Lord Halloween leave you a note or has he contacted you by phone?" Summer asked. Quinn had not even noticed she was there.

"All communication with this individual has been through notes," Brown replied. "I'm sorry, but I cannot take more questions..."

But the dam had been broken.

"Is it the same murderer that terrorized the county 12 years ago?" she asked.

"How many people has he killed so far, Sheriff?" another reporter said.

"How are you assuring the safety of the county, Sheriff?"

But it was Quinn who stood up and raised his hand. Brown, who clearly wanted to leave and had already started to walk out, paused when he saw Quinn's hand in the air.

(*He knows what you are going to ask him.*)

Slowly, Brown nodded.

"Sheriff, I recognize that you are normally reluctant to comment on on-going cases," Quinn began. He licked his lips before continuing, acutely aware that he did not want to know the answer to the question he was going to ask. "But on behalf of his colleagues, we wondered if you believe Kyle Thompson's disappearance is connected to this case?"

One of the other reporters gasped. Quinn knew without looking it was Summer.

Brown paused and seemed to draw a large breath.

"Quinn, it is very difficult to answer that question without commenting on other cases," Brown began. "But I've just spoken with your editor. It's the reason I was late. For those of you who don't know, Kyle Thompson was a reporter for the local paper here. He covered the crime beat and so worked with this department for more than a decade. His disappearance was reported Sunday. We here have not always agreed with his coverage, but we respected his work. He was also a police officer for two years with this department. It is with sincere sadness that I report that at 7:00 a.m. this morning we discovered a body identified as that of Kyle Thompson. Though the body has been tampered with, pending DNA tests, we have sufficient evidence to conclude it was Kyle."

Quinn felt like he had been hit in the gut. It was the answer he had been expecting, almost. But it had not seemed real then. Part of him really believed that Kyle just blew town, even when he knew that made no sense. Kyle, who set his watch forward three minutes early so he would never be late. Kyle, who insisted on talking to everyone about wrestling even when he knew no one cared. Kyle, who would not have walked away from this story in a million years.

Quinn could feel all eyes on him. It seemed like the other reporters, for one moment, wanted to give him some measure of respect. Quinn kept his voice calm, his tone steady.

"Do you believe it was the person claiming to be Lord Halloween that killed him?" Quinn asked.

"Yes, we do," Brown said. "I'm sorry, Quinn."

And with that, Brown was gone. The other reporters threw questions at Brown as he left, some even trying to get out the door with him. Quinn sat down and stared at the floor.

(*Quinn, I'm so sorry.*)

(*We didn't always get along, but... he was a damn fine reporter. I...*)

His thoughts broke away. Somehow he became aware that a video camera was focusing on him. For a second, he forgot why. And then he knew. Because they wanted the visual to go along with the story. They had the ridiculous announcement, clearly authorized by Lord Halloween himself, but that wasn't enough. The cameras had to have a picture of grief. And Quinn was the closest thing.

(*Just walk away.*) Kate advised.

(*I hate these guys.*) he thought back. (*Where are they when anything good happens in Loudoun, or when it's just the local board meeting to cover? We're down in the trenches every day and they just show up when the bodies surface.*)

(*Just walk away.*) Kate said again. And if she felt his anger, he also felt her calm. Someone who understood grief better than he did and who might have had more cause to be angry at the vultures around them.

Quinn stood up slowly, did not face the cameras and walked out. Only Summer followed him out the door.

"I just wanted to say I'm sorry, Quinn," she said.

Quinn was uncertain how to proceed. He was so used to disliking her, it was almost difficult to see her express some sincere emotion.

"Do you want to talk about it?"

(*Is she hitting on me?*) he asked.

(*No. Look at the recorder in her hand, genius.*) Kate replied.

And there it was. It felt good to know that he could still dislike her.

"You want a comment?" he asked.

Summer raised the recorder up expectantly.

"Write this down. Now that the best *Post* reporter, Summer Mandaville, is on the story, I'm sure Lord Halloween is quaking in his boots."

Summer switched the recorder off.

"You know I can't use that," she said.

"Yeah, that's a pity," Quinn replied, and walked off in the direction of the *Chronicle* office. He had other things to think about. Some part of his brain that was still dispassionate was already thinking of how to structure the story. Methodically, he started to think about what he would say, how to tell the story of his colleague's death.

*****

Friday, Oct. 27

Kate watched the leaves blow down East Market Street, which now looked less like the historic town of Leesburg and more like a ghost town out west. Signs hung on the doors of most of the shops declaring, "Closed until further notice." Many people had simply left town.

The ones who hadn't left remained paranoid. Kate had taken notes at the local middle schools where parents had shown up to take their kids home personally, not trusting a bus to drop them off. People were afraid to leave their kids, or themselves, alone for even one second.

Not that it would help. Kate knew that Lord Halloween had wanted this to happen. He thrived on the attention, the panic and the knowledge that he could still pick people off one by one. Unless everyone simply moved out of the county, they would not be 100% safe.

She was least of all, she knew. It must still be part of his plan to kill her and more than likely Quinn too. So it was with some trepidation that she had pursued her assignments alone today. But the *Chronicle* was short-staffed. Half of the staff had elected not to come to work Thursday.

For some, it was genuine grief over Kyle. For most, it was fear for themselves. After all, if a serial killer decides to kill one reporter, maybe he will just keep going. Helen, who fancied herself the star reporter of the paper, called in sick. Buzz did not use an excuse. He had e-mailed Monday to say he would be out for the foreseeable future. Bill also did not bother to pretend. He had told Josh flatly that he was "not fucking coming in until the psycho stops picking us off."

Laurence had tried to persuade a few to come in. Alexis and Josh were in the office. And Quinn and Kate figured they were safer in a public place anyway, both from Lord Halloween and the Headless Horseman. Kate laughed to herself. It felt ridiculous even to think of it that way. But it didn't change what was happening.

So they were all being sent on solo assignments, at least to try and cover everything. Quinn was nominally following a tip, but really back at Janus' apartment—which the three of them had turned into a fortress—looking again at the hotel security tapes. It was comforting to Kate to sense him there. She had a gun for her own protection, but knew that back-up was just a quick thought away. She could even see the video when she concentrated.

She could see him in her mind going slowly through the tape, pausing every few minutes. He was bored and she laughed to herself. It was so strange and wonderful to have this other person in her head this way. She might have imagined it could be terrible, but... she felt no downside. To really know a person, to know what they think and feel, was a gift. There was no doubting his fidelity, love or commitment to her. Quinn belonged to her and she to him. She wasn't even sure they were really two separate people anymore. That should frighten her, but it didn't. The two had become one.

But it was a gift that came along with the price of the Horseman. She wondered if it would be worth it. For now, it was the only bright spot. After she finished her assignment, she would go see him. Even with him in her head, she wanted to be with him again. And maybe they could go somewhere for a while... forget about all this for a bit.

(*Stop.*) Quinn thought at her.

(*Sorry.*) she said immediately. (*I thought you weren't paying attention.*)

(*You were starting to think about sex. It got my attention.*)

(*Typical.*)

(*Hey, you were the one thinking it. Some of us are trying to work.*)

(*Okay, okay.*)

She smiled to herself and let it drop. If they were still alive at the end of the month, they would go away somewhere, together. She knew that whatever their connection was would probably be at its weakest—her research had said it could drop out altogether—but they needed a chance to get away.

(*It's a deal.*) Quinn thought at her. (*But for right now, please let me work.*)

Kate continued walking down the street and taking notes along the way. It was easier to record the shops that were open rather than the ones that were closed. Occasionally, she would stop in to interview a shopkeeper or one of the few patrons she saw.

Suddenly she heard a voice behind her.

"So how's my favorite part of the Wonder Twins?" Janus said, and Kate wheeled around, her hand already reaching into her purse for the gun.

She took a breath when she saw Janus and eased her hand away.

"Easy there," Janus said, holding up his hands. "I thought you heard me walk up behind you."

"Janus, these days, you should really call first before walking up to someone," she replied.

"I know, sorry. I was on the way to my car," he said.

"Why is it parked out here? Why didn't you park out behind the paper?"

"Are you kidding?" he asked. "And dream about how that maniac will hide in the back seat of my car and at precisely the wrong moment, turn up and stab me in the neck? I don't fucking think so."

"Right, right," she said. "Of course, you could just check your car before you leave."

"It's better out here," he said.

"Where are you off to?" she asked.

"Laurence is pulling his hair out in there," Janus replied. "He keeps trying to get reporters back in the office. He told me to go see Buzz and try to persuade him to come back."

"You want company?" she asked.

"Nah," Janus said. "Buzz doesn't know you that well. He sees you coming, he could come up with some paranoid fantasy that we're an assassination squad."

She nodded.

"Besides," he continued. "I'm wondering if he's skipped town or something. Laurence said he heard from him once yesterday, but that the connection was bad. Old Buzz could have hit the road."

"Just be careful," Kate said.

"Hey, my middle name is careful," Janus replied. "But enough about that—are you guys any closer to figuring out the Horseman? For that matter, are we any closer to Lord Halloween?"

"Just theories spinning in our head," she responded.

"I noticed you said 'our head,'" Janus said. "I guess you meant that literally. So what happens if you beat the Horseman? Can you control him?"

"I don't know," Kate said.

"And do you control him or does Quinn?"

"I don't know."

"Or can you do other stuff, like read minds, or summon spirits from the underworld, or stuff like that?"

"No, but we can shoot laser beams out of our eyes."

"Really?" Janus asked.

"No, don't be stupid," Kate said. "I told you, I don't know. Nothing in the research is conclusive. There is some trial, you either pass or you fail, and that's it. There's a Prince of Sanheim or a dead person. And what happens after that, I don't know."

"Other than to know you turn back into a pumpkin at midnight on Halloween," Janus said.

"Yes," she said. "Whatever power we get, it ends after Halloween is over. At least for a while."

"How long?"

"I'm not sure," she said. "Nov. 1 is All Saint's Day, a holy day, so I'm sure we get nothing then. But maybe it returns gradually over time."

"Let's just hope you have enough time," Janus said.

"For what? We aren't really planning to face this thing down, you know," Kate said. "I don't know that we can defeat the Horseman and we're a little busy trying to avoid someone else who wants to kill us."

"Are you fucking kidding me?" Janus asked. "It's the only way, right? Lord Halloween is smarter than you."

"Hey."

"Face it, he's smarter than everybody," Janus said. "He's one step ahead of the police, he's one step ahead of us. We have all these details on him, we know his pattern, and we have nothing. It could be anybody."

"I don't think so," Kate said. "I think it is someone connected with the paper."

"Then who?" Janus asked.

"I don't know," she said.

"Exactly," he said. "But if you beat the Horseman, you have powers, right? Who is to say you don't know who the killer is then? Who's to say you don't know where he is hiding? You get the upper hand, for once. He thinks you are harmless Kate and Quinn, but no, you're the fucking Prince of Sanheim. You're a legend."

Kate thought about what he was saying. When they had initially heard about the trial, Quinn had been confident they could win it, but she hadn't been so sure. She had convinced him they had to wait. Deal with Lord Halloween, then wait until next year to face this trial. If they could even delay it. But they were no closer to figuring that out. But Janus had a good point, the one that Quinn had made himself. It was an all or nothing bet. If they couldn't beat the Horseman, they were dead anyway. But if they could...

But Kate thought of the man in Quinn's dream. That was what the man wanted. Something told her that whatever he wanted, it wasn't good. What if it really had been the Devil?

(*He's not the devil.*) Quinn thought.

(*You don't know that.*)

"I can see you are hearing voices again," Janus said. "Tell Quinn I said hi. Look, just think about what I said, okay? I've got to run."

Janus turned and walked up the street toward his car.

"Be careful," she called after him.

Janus stuck his arm in the air and flashed the V-sign.

(*I think he is flicking you off.*) Quinn said.

Kate laughed and turned to walk back toward the paper.

*****

Lord Halloween could not believe what he was hearing. He had been so close, so close to dealing with Kate. He had been watching her for over an hour go into various shops, being a reporter. He had liked watching her move. She was very good looking. And he was enjoying the hunt. There were two more bodies the police hadn't found and he was already moving on to body number three.

And then that little fucker had gotten in the way. He had been close enough to hear them—there was an abandoned shop nearby—but he hadn't understood a word. Instead of being afraid of him, Kate was talking about the Horseman. Who the fuck was the Horseman? He briefly considered that there was some rival serial killer, but if there were, it was news to him. And what was this about the Prince of Sanheim?

I must have driven her insane, he thought.

It was the only explanation and it did nothing to soothe his spirit. If she were crazy, it seemed Janus and Quinn were too. They should be worried about him. In fact, Kate and Quinn should be dead already. But Lord Halloween knew he could not have gotten through Quinn's door without waking them up. He had decided to wait.

Now it appeared something else was going on and he didn't like that one bit.

He was keenly aware every minute he stood there was a risk. What bothered him more than anything was that whatever they were talking about seemed to be connected to Halloween. And Halloween was his day—his day. Look at this place, he thought. Shops are closed, people have fled. Because of one man. Because of him. Halloween was all about fear—dressing up as the thing you are afraid of—and he ruled it.

But Kate and Quinn didn't seem afraid. He had almost been close enough to kill them both and they were worried about people on fucking horses. Kate was meant to be his great comeback story—one that would have even brought CNN to town. Not only had that failed, but she didn't even seem worried about him.

Kate and Quinn would regret their distractions, he thought as he watched Janus walk down the street. If they had forgotten about him, then he would just have to remind them.

There were just a few days to Halloween and he planned to use them well. Long enough to do what he wanted. Long enough to make Kate and Quinn pay.

Chapter 22

Friday, Oct. 27

Quinn was considering turning off the video when he saw it.
He had concluded the entire process was a waste of time. Lord
Halloween was too careful to simply walk past a security camera.
But for some reason he kept coming back to it. In the hospital
room, he had been out of it, but he had felt sure he had seen
something.

Now he was sure he saw it again. It had been quick, just out
of the corner of his eye, something like a flash of metal. It could
have been a watch, but Quinn didn't think so. He rewound the tape
and paused. It was the arm of a jacket—nothing more. He couldn't
see the man or woman it was attached to. The jacket was olive
green and Quinn thought the shade looked familiar. Like he had
seen it before. Like he knew who the jacket belonged to.

It felt like a song that he couldn't place. He knew who that
jacket belonged to, but he couldn't place it. It was just on the tip of
his tongue. Work backward, he thought. He closed his eyes and
concentrated. He was mentally flipping through the people he knew
like old photographs when it came to him.

The piece of metal he was looking at was a medal—from the
Vietnam War. He only knew one person who wore such a thing. He

pictured it sitting on the chair at the *Loudoun Chronicle*. How many days had he seen it just lying there? And yet he didn't recognize it when it was out of place.

Dear God, he thought, the jacket. It belongs to Buzz. He had been in the hotel just before Kate's room was ransacked.

"Jesus," Quinn said.

(*Where was Janus headed?*) he asked Kate.

Kate had stopped in mid-interview when he had figured out who the jacket belonged to.

(*Buzz. He was going to see Buzz.*)

(*We have to get there. Now. He's in trouble.*)

*****

Janus drove to the end of the cul-de-sac in Ashburn, parked the car on the curb and got out. He sighed. Every time Janus saw Buzz's house, it looked like a run-down mess. Buzz had inherited it from his mother, who had died only about four years ago. But he did not seem to inherit the ability to keep it up.

The grass was long, at least three of the shutters hung at slightly crooked angles. If he didn't know better, Janus might think a crazy person lived there. Only he supposed one did. Buzz was the most paranoid person he had ever met—he had been worried about Lord Halloween way before it was fashionable.

How long had Buzz worked for the paper? As long as Janus knew about, that was for sure. And all that time, Buzz talked about sinister conspiracies concerning county supervisors or the police and when Laurence had transferred him to the business beat, Buzz had relentlessly pursued some bank in Waterford, claiming there was some check kiting scheme.

Holden and Buzz had never gotten along. Rebecca tolerated Buzz's eccentricities because he produced good copy. He showed up at odd hours, but he did consistently deliver good stories for the paper.

Janus glanced at the house. For a second, he felt a twinge of anxiety, but he brushed it away. The killings, the telepathic twins back at the office and Laurence's general attitude of panic had put Janus on edge.

He walked up the front steps and rang the doorbell. It sounded deep through the house and Janus jumped a little.

Jesus, he thought, I'm way too skittish. He rang the bell again and listened to it echo through the house. But he did not hear anything else.

Maybe Buzz blew town, like he had figured. Buzz had told Laurence he was staying indoors, but that could have been a lie. It was possible Buzz was out shopping, getting supplies. But honestly, Janus thought Buzz seemed like the kind of guy that had supplies stockpiled in the basement. He would be prepared for this.

Of course, Buzz could be ignoring the door. That made sense, since Buzz might believe the killer would actually show up and ring the doorbell.

Or Janus thought Buzz could be in some kind of danger. Maybe he was hurt, or...

He didn't let himself complete the last line of thought.

I should get out of here, a voice in his head said. The neighborhood was oddly quiet and it wasn't hard to guess why. Everyone was either gone or had locked themselves in. Four days to go before Halloween and people would not come out if they could help it.

So why am I here? Buzz was either gone or dead. Either way, Janus could not help. He turned on the doorstep and prepared to walk away.

And then a crash came from inside the house.

Janus stood at the doorway for a minute.

"Buzz?" he yelled from outside the door. "Are you fucking in there, mate?"

There was silence. Janus wet his lips with his tongue. Reluctantly, he tried the front door. It was locked. Janus sighed in relief.

"Buzz? You there?" he called again.

He took a step backward. Well, there was nothing he could do, he thought. He should get in the car and get the hell out of dodge.

But he knew he should check the back of the house as well. He should be sure that Buzz was not just lying somewhere, bleeding, maybe getting his guts ripped out even now...

Janus worked to get the image out of his head.

He looked around. There was no one in sight. I have to be sure, he thought. Besides, it's a bright sunny day out. He should not be this spooked.

Moving carefully, he looked through the front windows and saw nothing. With a longing glance back at his car, Janus disappeared around the side, stopping for a second to look in the garage window. He saw only Buzz's brown BMW.

Janus continued around the house and stopped on the back patio. There were a few rust-covered chairs there, but the yard looked overgrown.

Janus' heart stopped when he saw the back door, however.

It was wide open.

Shit, he thought.

"Buzz?" he called moving cautiously to the door. "Look, are you in pain? Do you need help? It's me, Janus."

But there was no answer. Janus could see clearly into the kitchen and there was no one there. He should go, he realized. The thought of Buzz in there hurt, or tied up, kept him from running away.

Janus walked through the doorway tentatively. He tried to look around corners. But he could not see anything.

"Buzz, are you in here?" he asked again. "Listen, man, don't blow my head off 'cause you think I'm someone else. I'm just trying to make sure you are alright."

He took another step forward into the house. He saw nothing.

This, Janus decided, was rapidly becoming the dumbest move he had ever made. He reached for his cell phone and realized he had left it in the car.

Here he was, with a murderer on the loose, walking around in a deserted house. He was like one of those idiots in a horror movie. That thought stopped him from moving forward.

If Buzz was in trouble, the police could help him.

"Buzz, I'm coming in, okay?"

But Janus wasn't going to. Instead he backed slowly up, preparing to turn and run if he had to. Fuck this, he thought. He wouldn't do anybody any good if he got picked off so easily.

He walked back out the door and then turned and ran around the house to his car. He had left Buzz's back door open, but the police could deal with that.

Janus dug into his pocket for his keys and pulled them out. He kept looking behind him waiting for something to come out of the house. But nothing did.

He flipped the key on his ring and practically jumped inside the car, keeping his eyes very carefully on the house. He turned on the car, shoved it into drive and tore out of the cul-de-sac.

It was only as he looked back at the house in the rearview mirror that he saw it. There in his rearview mirror was a single yellow piece of paper—a post-it note stuck right on the glass. Still driving forward, Janus read it as a feeling of dread washed over him.

"I'm going to enjoy killing you, Janus," it said.

*****

Kate pulled up outside the building and Quinn rushed outside.

(*Gas it.*) Quinn thought as he jumped into the car.

Kate tore through the streets of Leesburg and they both hoped the police had better things to do than watch for speeders.

(*It's Buzz.*) Quinn thought, as the car turned on to Route 7 toward Ashburn, where the business editor lived.

(*He was at the hotel.*) Kate thought. (*But that doesn't mean he's Lord Halloween.*)

(*It means there is a damn good shot he is. And Janus was heading right towards him.*)

(*PLEASE SOMEONE HELP ME!*)

The voice in their heads jarred them both and nearly caused Kate to drive off the road.

(*What was that?*) Quinn thought.

(*That was Janus.*)

In her mind, she could see him. He was being moved from his car and he was in incredible pain. There was blood. She had to fight to keep her own car on the road.

(*He's dying.*)

*****

Janus turned around while driving and looked at the back seat, bracing himself for a blow. But there was nobody there.

"Fuck," he said, and faced the road again as he continued driving. His heart was pounding in his chest. He immediately reached around for his cell phone.

But it was not there.

"Fuck me," he said again.

The bastard had taken it. Janus could not remember locking his car, he had been so concerned about what was going on in the house.

He pulled the note off his mirror and slammed on the accelerator again. He would head straight for the police station. If someone was going to jump out at him from his trunk or somewhere, let it be there.

He looked in the rearview mirror and felt his heart skip a beat.

A car was behind him. And not just anyone's. It was Buzz's beat-up BMW and it was gaining on him. The sun reflected off the car's windshield, so Janus could not make out who was behind the wheel, but he had a feeling it wouldn't be someone who wanted to stop and chat.

"Fuck you, then," Janus said and sped up. He flew through a stop sign and turned right abruptly, narrowly missing a parked car on the street.

The key is to stay calm and get to the police station. There was no way whoever was behind him would think of going there. He hoped.

He rounded another corner and noticed that while the car behind him was gaining, it did not seem to be trying to overtake him. For the life of him, Janus could not figure out why.

Janus tried honking his horn—though he did not see other cars on the road. Everyone was hiding from the guy that was behind him. But maybe someone would hear the noise and call the police. No sense stopping at any of the houses on the way. There was no guarantee they would be home, and even if they were, no guarantee they would let him in or not be killed as well.

Without even attempting to brake, he swung out onto Reservoir Road and started to pray. He had gas, he thought, looking at the meter.

The key was to stay ahead of him and to stay calm.

But the BMW had gained on him and was now very close. If he braked at all, the car would ram into him. Janus floored it. If a cop pulled him over for speeding, that would be a good thing.

He had just six miles to Route 7. There were bound to be other cars on Rt. 7—someone who could help him.

With new fear, he saw the curve ahead. Since he came to this county, he had hated this curve. It was the kind where you had to slow down a lot or risk flying into the ditch. Janus had covered at least four accidents here and none of them were pretty.

But if he had to slow down, so did his pursuer, right?

He reluctantly pressed the brake.

Nothing happened.

"Fuck a duck," he said. He hit the brake again. The car didn't slow. He felt no resistance and instead saw the curve coming up at a rapid 60 miles an hour.

Behind him he noticed that the BMW had dropped back.

And then Janus knew what had happened. The killer had cut his brake lines. In his mind, he saw the image of a man underneath his car cutting his brake line as Janus stood on Buzz's back patio.

Janus pumped the peddles and watched the speedometer crawl down. It was 45 miles an hour now on a curve recommended at 15. He would just have to hope he was slow enough.

He braced himself and tried to take the turn as best he could. At first, he thought he might make it. But his Jeep leaned heavily to the right and then he could feel it tipping.

At least I'll probably die in the crash, he thought.

The Jeep ran off the road, hit the ditch and flipped on its side.

Janus came to moments afterward. He was hanging in his seatbelt, the windshield shattered and he thought he could taste blood on his tongue.

Please think I'm dead, Janus thought. He hung there attempting to look lifeless, wondering if soon it would not be an act.

He heard footsteps approaching the car, heard the car creak as someone climbed up on it and opened the door.

"You almost made it, Janus," the voice said.

Janus felt a hand reach across him and undo his seatbelt.

He was insanely tempted to look at the man, but he didn't. He had to appear to be dead. It was the only thing that could save him.

"But close doesn't quite count, does it?" he said.

Please think I'm dead, Janus thought again.

He could almost sense the man looking at him.

"Hmmm, maybe it got you worse than I thought," the voice said. "Or maybe you're just faking. Like you faked all those photos."

Janus felt a sharp pain in his leg as the man dug in a knife.

He didn't think quickly enough to stop himself from crying out.

"There, I thought so," the man said, and the knife cut deeper.

The pain was excruciating. Janus' eyes flew open and he looked at the man already pulling him out.

Janus did not believe his eyes.

"No," he said, but it came out as a whisper.

Janus felt in no condition to resist. He tried to move, but every limb seemed to be in shock.

The man hefted Janus up and then lowered his body down to the ground away from the Jeep. The pain was unbelievable.

"You can blame this one on your friends," the man said. "You weren't on my list until they started avoiding me. It hurt my feelings, Janus. And I think you are the right way to send a message about this."

Janus wanted to sit up, but the man began dragging Janus across the ditch.

Janus felt himself slipping into unconsciousness. He must have been hurt worse than he thought. A car, Janus thought. He would need a car now. Maybe someone would come by.

But there was nothing.

I'm going to die in broad daylight, Janus thought.

But the man was still talking.

"All those photos," he said. "I know you faked them. I know because nobody is that good. It's ridiculous, of course."

Janus didn't even process what he was talking about. He recognized his assailant, of course, but everything seemed different than the man he had known before. It was as if the man before and this one was not the same person. They only looked the same.

The man dragged Janus to the BMW.

"I bet you've been wishing for a car. I wouldn't. Unless it was an army, I would just kill them too, you know. Say I found you after the accident, stab them in the back as they looked at you. Easy, you know. People just naturally trust me, always have."

Janus decided then to give it all he had, before he was in that car and would never be heard from again. He lifted his head up and shouted as loud as he could, a cry into the wilderness he prayed someone would hear.

"PLEASE SOMEONE HELP ME!" he yelled.

*****

"Can you see anything else?" Quinn asked her. He could see her vision in his mind. When he tried to call something up, he got nothing.

"Someone was putting him into a car, Quinn, but I couldn't see who. He looked bad. There is blood on his face."

She picked up the cell phone.

"911," a voice answered. "What is the emergency?"

"A friend of mine called," she said. "He said someone was following him, trying to run him off the road. I lost contact with him. I think he could have been kidnapped."

"Did he give you his location?"

Kate tried to think. In her mind, she could see a curve in a road. But she didn't know the county that well. She tried to show the mental picture to Quinn.

"Tell them it's off Reservoir Road," he said. "Tell them that curve where a lot of accidents happen."

Kate relayed the directions.

"What time did he call?" the 911 operator asked.

"A few moments ago," Kate said, her voice completely calm. She knew how to impart information even while panicking on the inside.

"Did he see who his attacker was?"

Kate didn't even look at Quinn. They knew nothing about the kidnapper, that was the worst part. She had a vague idea from the image of Janus that he had known who it was, but it was blurry.

"He didn't know," Kate said. "He only called quickly."

"Was he armed?" she asked.

"I have no idea," Kate said.

But the attacker would have been armed, of course. He would have had a knife.

"Okay," the operator replied. "A unit is on its way. It should be there shortly. I need to get your name…"

Kate hung up. They could trace the cell phone, but it didn't matter. She didn't want to be on the phone. Instead, she looked at Quinn.

"Get out my gun," she said.

He nodded and grabbed her purse and started looking through it. He pulled out the gun and looked at it as if it were an alien thing. In her mind, Kate showed him how to load it, which Quinn did even as they continued to tear through town.

They ran three red lights before she turned onto Reservoir Road. That distinctive curve was miles away—an eternity, he thought.

As she continued driving, she glanced in the rearview mirror.

"Fuck," she said, and put her hand on Quinn's thigh.

Quinn didn't need to look behind him. He already saw it clearly in his mind.

They were no longer the only thing on the road. Behind them, the figure of the Headless Horseman had appeared. And he was gaining on them.

*****

"Now, Janus," the man said, and kicked Janus squarely in the stomach. "We don't like it when people talk too loudly at the table."

The man kicked him again.

"Goddamned boy," the man said again. "I'm disappointed. I thought you would put up more of a fight. The last one, well, he was too easy. And you were too. Young kids. You guys these days are so soft."

Janus said nothing. He thought his right leg was broken, it hurt so much.

And he had a feeling of time loss, so much so he wondered if there was internal bleeding. He felt himself slipping, like he might go unconscious at any moment. Maybe that was a blessing.

"And shouting like that," the man said, "Who did you think was going to hear you?"

The man picked Janus up and threw him into the back seat of the car.

He opened the front door, took another look around to see if anyone was watching and then got in the car. It was a clean operation, the man thought. He started the car and began to drive off.

*****

"What do we do?" Kate asked.

"We ignore it and hope he goes away," Quinn replied.

Kate looked in the rearview mirror and simultaneously sped up. How the hell the Horseman could be gaining on them in a car was insane. Didn't this thing have to play by the rules? It was a horse after all. Horses cannot outrun cars.

"I don't think that is a very good plan," Kate said.

"Got a better one?" Quinn asked.

Kate nodded toward the gun on Quinn's lap.

"Maybe," she said.

"You are planning to shoot a headless phantom?" Quinn asked.

"We have to at least try, right?" she asked.

"But we will need that ammo if we catch up to Janus," Quinn said. "We need something to fight off his attacker with."

"I know, I know," Kate said. "But we are going to have two problems at that point instead of one."

Quinn looked at the speedometer. The car was at 75 miles an hour now. They would be at the curve in two or three more minutes.

"We have to do something," Kate said. "He's gaining on us."

Quinn turned around in the seat and looked behind them. Even in broad daylight, the Horseman was a terrible apparition. If anything, he looked worse. You could see the decay on his cloak and the horse looked as if it was being tortured in an effort to make it move faster. The only difference from the last time Quinn had seen him was what was in his hand. It wasn't a sword.

"He has a pumpkin," Quinn said.

"Well, that's better than a sword," Kate shot back.

But this was not just a lump of orange vegetable. Instead the thing had a hideous grin carved on it—a demonic face—and it was on fire.

"It's on fire," Quinn said. "The pumpkin is on fire. I think he is trying to catch the car on fire."

How the hell could the Headless Horseman know about flammable gasoline? It was absurd.

(*He's us, remember. He has our knowledge.*) Kate thought.

Quinn looked in front of him. Just another minute or two down the road. But Quinn could see they were not going to make it.

The Horseman appeared ready to throw and he was in good distance to do it.

(*Take the wheel.*) Kate thought.

(*Are you insane?*) Quinn asked.

(*Do it now, Quinn.*)

Quinn grabbed the wheel and tried to keep the car steady. Kate rolled down the window and grabbed the gun from Quinn's lap. He saw she must have put the car on cruise control to keep it going at a steady pace. That would have to change before they hit that curve or there wouldn't be much left of their car.

(*You ever done this before?*) he asked.

(*No, but I saw it in one of the Terminator movies.*) she replied.

(*How reassuring.*)

Kate aimed the gun carefully, trying to balance it even while the wind ripped around her and threatened to yank the gun out of her hand.

She decided to aim for the horse, by far the bigger target. She fired off the first shot with her pistol, but the shot went wide.

Quinn tried to keep the car steady.

Kate waited and watched. She had to block out everything. She could see the flaming pumpkin in the Horseman's hand, a ball of fire that would be unleashed at any moment. She had to stop it. She concentrated on nothing but the horse. She blocked out the Horseman and his echoing laughter that seemed to be in her head more than anywhere else. Only the horse. Please let this shot count.

She fired again and the horse or its rider seemed to know it was coming because it leapt into the air.

But the horse was not quite fast enough. Instead of being hit in the chest, the horse was hit in the leg.

The Horseman appeared about to throw his pumpkin, but then suddenly he was gone. The horse and its rider vanished.

Kate shouted out in triumph, before feeling the car swerve beneath her.

She nearly fell out of the car, but grabbed on to the hood and brought herself back in.

"Quinn?" she asked and looked at him.

Kate had to grab the wheel and quickly slid back into the driver's seat as she looked at Quinn. He was looking at her in shock. His left thigh was covered in blood.

"Your shot.... Your bullet... It hit me," he said.

*****

Janus didn't know where the car was headed and he felt like he was coming in and out of consciousness.

"I'm going to enjoy this," the man said. "You know that right? It's good when people are strangers, but friends, true friends, are so much more satisfying."

Janus opened his eyes. He was in the back seat of the car. There was blood on the seat—his, he thought.

But on the floor there looked like more dried blood—and it definitely was not his.

The man didn't seem to regard Janus as much of a threat and he could see why. His leg was certainly broken—he felt only pain there and blood seemed to be coming from his forehead. He felt dizzy and confused.

I'm going to die here, Janus thought and grimaced. Die like a fucking ponce begging for his life.

The man kept talking.

"You know I had to wait 12 long years to do this. Do you know how hard that is? To see the vermin all around you, every day. To talk to them, smile at them, act like you are one of them. But I'm not one of them, Janus. No, no, I think I've proved that. I'm invincible. I'm unstoppable. I am a force of goddamned pure fury bent on hell and fire."

I wish you would fucking shut up, Janus thought. Dying would be preferable. He moved on his side slightly and felt on the bottom of the seat.

Nothing. Fuck, he thought. I will not die like this. I will not die afraid and in pain. He would finish this his own way, not on this asshole's timetable.

His hands continued to search the seat.

Nothing. Janus wanted to cry in despair.

Concentrating, he felt his own pockets, hoping desperately for something he could use. But there was nothing but a couple of crushed cigarettes and his silver lighter.

Maybe I could have a smoke before I die, he thought. Or maybe...

He felt a surge of hope course through him.

Janus tugged at his jeans to pull out the lighter and hoped to God it would be enough.

*****

Kate tried to keep the car steady as Quinn pulled a stack of McDonald's napkins out of the glove compartment and began pressing them to his leg.

"Oh my God," she said. "I'm so sorry."

"It hurts," Quinn said. "Jesus, who the hell knew it could hurt so much?"

The blood seemed to practically pour out of his leg.

"How the hell did that happen?" Quinn asked.

"I shot the horse. I shot him in the leg."

"Is it gone?"

Kate looked in the rearview mirror.

"Yes, but..."

"How the hell did a bullet end up in my leg?" he asked.

"I don't know," Kate said. "Evidently, when I hit it... it must of..."

"This is just great," Quinn said. "How the hell are we supposed to defeat this thing if hurting it means hurting me too?"

"The bullet must have severed the connection," Kate said, and she put her free hand on him in an attempt to stop the bleeding. "It jarred it somehow. Just like you falling and becoming unconscious did it."

"Fuck," Quinn said again and held on to his leg. It felt terrible.

"We have to get you to a hospital," Kate said.

"No time. We need to find Janus or we may never find him."

As he said it, he saw the bend up ahead.

"Up there," he pointed.

Kate slowed down and brought the car to a halt.

On the side of the road was Janus' Jeep. He dreaded finding him in there. But worse, he dreaded that he wouldn't.

"Look," Kate said, and pointed to the side passenger door of Janus' car. It still stood open.

"He must have pulled him out of there," Quinn said. "Can you check it out, but quickly?"

She looked around the car, found an extra t-shirt in the back seat and handed it to him to put against his bleeding leg. She got out and looked around the wreckage, glancing inside the front door.

"There's blood," she called out.

All the windows were shattered and glass lay everywhere. Getting down on her hands and knees, she looked through the vehicle for anything that stood out. Fluttering down at the bottom of the wreck, she saw a yellow note. She didn't pick it up, for fear her fingerprints would contaminate it. But she could guess what it said.

She crawled out of the wreck and could hear the sounds of sirens far away.

"Come on," Quinn yelled from the car.

"Where do we go next?" she asked.

"I don't know. We drive."

"What if we don't find him?" she asked.

"I don't know," he replied. "I just don't know."

*****

Janus gripped his fingers around the lighter.

God, he felt weak. He saw more fresh blood on the seat. Whatever the wreck had done to him, it clearly was serious. And maybe that was the best thing, he thought. Better to die this way than in whatever fashion this psycho had in mind.

"God, I've enjoyed this," the man was saying in the front. "It's been a load off my mind, I can tell you. Always having to think about it, seeing it in your dreams, that's the worst part. But actually acting again, letting the emotions free. Nothing beats that, Janus, old boy."

Janus held the lighter like he was holding on to an edge of a cliff. Things were blurry now and he had this kind of sickish feeling all over.

So this is what it feels like to die. Some part of him rebelled against it. He could just lie there, true, and hope to go peacefully. But he wanted something more than that. He wanted to hurt this bastard, maybe stop him for good.

He decided he would settle for just surprising him—stopping that sanctimonious laugh of his. Janus didn't have to be the victim that got away. He would settle for being the one who helped even the score—just a little.

"You were the icing on the cake, you know what I mean, good buddy?" the man said. "I've been looking for a way to win back your friends' attention. When I heard you were heading out to see old Buzz... man, it was perfect. Today is ripe with blessings, Janus old boy. Not for you, of course, but you don't matter."

Janus could feel the car moving at a more reasonable speed now. He felt it turn left at some stage and wondered where they were headed. Somewhere remote, he thought. Somewhere nobody would hear Janus screaming.

He held the lighter, moving his hands to the switch that would turn it on. He had always been proud of this little silver thing, engraved on the back with his initials. His uncle had given it to him for his 18th birthday. His parents had hardly approved, but that made it even better. It was a real smoker's lighter, the kind that you lit once and stayed burning until you capped it. For him, the acrid smell of the burning oil had been nearly as addictive as the smoking.

"They're going to talk about this for ages, you know," the man said. "I've got big plans. I'll take care of your little cronies on Halloween or before, and once I do, I've got a show-stopping number planned. Little kids in a row. I can't say much, but I can say crucifixion is involved."

"You're insane," Janus managed, not sure if he should just stay quiet or not.

"Oh, you're awake, are you?" the man said and turned to look at him. His look was one of pure disgust. For a moment, Janus worried that he would see the lighter and know what Janus had planned. But he turned back around again.

"God, I'm disappointed in you. Thought you would put up a fight. But you are such a dumb ass, you didn't even know your brakes were cut."

He laughed a dry chuckle, more to himself.

"I'm thinking I will save your buddy Quinn for last. You know his girl and I go way back, don't you? I should have gutted her after I killed her mom, but I thought it would be more fun to come back later. I stand by that decision. I really do. She's had years to think about what I will do to her."

Janus grimaced and started to feel some strength come back as cold fury rose in him. They had trusted this guy, called him one of their own, and instead he was cutting them down one by one. And in his mind he could see Quinn hanging on a cross.

With tremendous effort and nearly crying out in pain, Janus pushed himself up slowly, gripping the lighter in his hand.

"Maybe he will fight a little better than you," the man continued. "I'm a little worried I drove him crazy. Him and his little girlfriend. What was that obtaining power on Halloween? But it ends on Nov. 1? Well, that is inconvenient, isn't it?"

Silently, begging the man not to look in the rearview mirror, Janus sat up. His head felt like it weighed a million pounds. All he wanted was to lay back down and fall asleep. But he had a feeling that if he did, it would be forever.

Instead, he brought the lighter up with his right hand. For the last time in his life, he lit it, hearing the satisfying hiss as a small flame sprang to life. Janus could smell the oil burning and he breathed it in.

"Your ending won't be smooth," the man said. "I'll keep you alive long enough that you'll wish you had died in that car crash."

The man laughed again.

Janus slowly brought himself forward, holding the small flame in his right hand.

"Hey wanker, don't you ever get tired of hearing yourself talk?" Janus said and as he hoped, the man turned his head to face him.

Moving quickly, Janus stuck the flame of his lighter into the man's face, shoving it into his right eye.

The man tried to ward it off at the last minute, but was too late. The blow connected and he screamed as he felt a searing pain on his face.

The man reeled, taking his hands off the wheel. The car spun out of control, knocking Janus back.

"Happy fucking Halloween," Janus said, before everything went black.

*****

Kate and Quinn kept driving while looking for anything that might help them. When they came to a four-way stop two miles past the accident, Kate stopped.

"Where do we go?" Kate asked.

Quinn shook his head.

"I have no idea," he said.

Kate tried to reach out with her mind, but it felt like she was running into a brick wall.

"Do you have a scanner?" Quinn asked.

"I should have thought of it before," she said and reached behind her seat to pull it out.

It had been the first thing she bought in town. Somehow being attuned to police movements was comforting. It could tip you off to a story and tell you what was going on in the world.

He turned it on now, plugging it into the cigarette lighter. They both listened.

They heard reports of an accident and Quinn prayed for something else—a speeding car, somebody yelling somewhere, anything unusual that might tip them off.

Two minutes later it came.

A report of another overturned car, this one off Houseur Road—only two miles away from where they were.

Kate shoved the car back into gear, turned left and sped off.

The pain in Quinn's leg was gradually subsiding, the bloody T-shirt still wrapped around it. Still, he thought it felt better and wondered briefly what that meant.

In a few minutes, they saw it. A beat up BMW lay on the side of the road, having run straight into a tree.

Kate pulled over beside it and she jumped out with her gun in hand. Flipping the front door open, she saw nothing except some blood on the side window.

But in the back...

"Quinn," she said.

Quinn was out of the car, limping with severe pain, over to the BMW.

"Oh God," he said.

In the back was Janus. Quinn opened the door, even as Kate was on the cell phone. She kept her eyes peeled out nervously as well. She could almost sense that *he* was here, the one who had haunted her half of her lifetime. The one she desperately wanted dead.

But she saw nothing in the woods by the road. She told the police there was an injured passenger and where, knowing they must already be on their way. She wondered who had spotted the accident and called it in.

Quinn was leaning over Janus.

"Will he be alright?" Kate asked, guessing what the answer would be.

But instead Quinn pulled his head out of the car.

"No," he said quietly. "He's dead."

Kate passed him the gun and stuck her head in, but it was no use. There was blood all over his clothes and it looked like Janus had a bad wound on his head. Janus was dead and no amount of CPR was going to bring him back.

Quinn was staring at the tree line. All he felt inside was a blind hatred. All he wanted was to make that bastard pay.

"I know you're out there," Quinn screamed finally. "And I'll bet this wasn't part of your sorry little plan. I'll bet he got you good."

Kate looked again at the blood on the window. A glint of sunlight off something silver caught her eye on the front seat and she stuck her head in the car again. Janus' silver lighter lay open but extinguished on the seat. She couldn't think of how it came to be there. She picked it up.

"He must have done something," Kate said, and handed the lighter to Quinn.

"Yeah," Quinn said, looking at it briefly before putting it into his pocket. "I'll bet he did."

Quinn didn't cry and he looked again at the trees around them. There was no sense in trekking in there—the killer could have long run away, and even if he didn't, he would have some advantage.

But Quinn thought Lord Halloween could hear him.

"He died fighting," Quinn called. "Not like you will, you soulless bastard."

Kate put her arm around him. She looked into the woods, but there was nothing. No trail, no broken branches. Nothing that said where the killer had gone.

The forest on the other side of the road was more open, but again, they saw nothing.

"You hear me?" Quinn called out. "You want us, then come and get us. You coward. I'll see that you die quivering and alone."

He stood there, clenched with a bottomless fury.

Kate knew what it felt like, but didn't join in.

It wasn't until after the police came, after they made their statements, after they were home, that it all came out.

Then there was sobbing.

Chapter 23

Sunday, Oct. 29

Quinn and Kate were the last ones out of St. Gabriel's Episcopal Church, letting Rebecca and Laurence file out ahead.

Standing on Cornwall Street, Quinn saw Rebecca take another tissue from her purse and dot her eyes. It occurred to him he had never seen her cry before.

"I hope you both will join us for the reception," Rebecca said, her voice slightly shaky.

(*I can't.*) Quinn thought. (*I can't keep doing this.*)

(*You don't have to.*) Kate replied.

(*But I do. I really do.*)

"Sure," Quinn said out loud. "Your place is..."

"Just off Wirt Street," Rebecca said. "You are welcome to follow me."

"We'll be along," Quinn said. "I just need to go back to the paper and grab some stuff."

"Are you sure you want to go back there?" Laurence asked him.

How old he looked, Kate thought. He looked like a different man. He was pale with dark circles under his eyes. How many editors see three of their reporters disappear or die in three weeks? What does that do to you?

"I have to go back there at some point," Quinn said. "And I wanted to pick up a book Janus left in the darkroom. He brought it in three weeks ago for me to borrow and I kept forgetting to pick it up. I just..."

Quinn broke off. He took a slow breath and waited.

"It's okay," Rebecca said gently.

She made a move as if to hug him and stopped. Quinn barely noticed.

"Take your time," Rebecca said. "If you end up not feeling like it, that's okay. We understand."

Quinn nodded, and Laurence and Rebecca turned and walked down the street.

He and Kate watched them go.

"Laurence is right," Kate said quietly. "Are you sure you want to do this?"

Quinn nodded again, and the two walked down the street. St. Gabriel's was just over a block from the office.

The memorial service had been hard. Quinn had said a few words—said goodbye to his best friend—without breaking down. It had been a quiet affair, just the paper's (remaining) staff, Janus' family and a few others.

The truth was Quinn didn't feel sad through most of the service—he just felt angry. He felt like it was the only emotion holding him together.

"There is this thing inside of us," Quinn said finally as they walked. "I don't know if it is good or bad, and I no longer care. I just want to unleash it—to send it toward the bastard that killed Janus, Kyle and maybe Buzz. I want to make their murderer pay."

"I know," Kate replied. "You know I'm right there with you."

Quinn laughed with no humor. He watched leaves blow down the deserted street. It was twilight and the sunset reflected orange off the clouds above. It should be a beautiful day, Quinn thought.

But the day was hollow.

"How do we do it?" Quinn asked. "We're crazy, do you know that? We shouldn't even be believing this..."

(*I can feel and hear your thoughts, sweetheart.*) Kate said. (*The time for questioning is over.*)

(*I know. I just wish all my questions had been answered.*)

The least of them was how his leg had completely healed. By Friday night, there was barely a trace that anything was wrong. Quinn was healthy again.

Exactly how that had happened was unclear. From everything they read, somehow Quinn and the Headless Horseman were now tied together.

"It must draw its strength from you," Kate said out loud. Though they could talk in their heads, sometimes it felt comforting to say things out loud. "It's based on your fears. So I hurt it, but that hurt you too."

"So what kind of chance does that give me?" Quinn asked. "How can I beat him if I can't hurt him? How can I hurt him if that would only hurt me?"

"I hurt him, not you," Kate said. "Maybe this has to be about you and him. Maybe I'm just tagging along for the ride. I'm the trigger."

"No way are you just along for the ride," Quinn said.

She put her hand in his and squeezed it. Quinn felt lost. His best friend was dead and he was a marked man. His girlfriend was also a target. The odds of coming out of this alive were getting slimmer every day.

"I'm so tired of being afraid," he said.

"Believe me when I tell you, I've been there," she replied. "But I think we have only one choice. We figure out a way that you beat the Horseman and claim whatever power we supposedly get out of it. This is a fight for your soul. For my soul. If we win, we get power. If we lose, it's over anyway."

"What if we win and lose our soul anyway? What if we shouldn't want this power? I can't remember, but in one dream, I got a taste of what it felt like and..."

"What?"

"It didn't feel right, somehow. Whatever I was tapping into. There was no fear, no doubt."

"Sounds great so far."

"But I felt less human, somehow," he said. "Like something had been taken from me. Something basic. What if this power is evil, Kate?"

"Do we have a choice?" she asked. "We've been chasing Lord Halloween all over. We aren't any closer to finding him. What if this is the only way?"

They stopped walking in front of the *Chronicle* building. Quinn took a deep breath before opening the door. Kate and Quinn walked through.

The air felt heavy. None of the paper's lights were on and the setting sun cast unusual shadows.

Kate and Quinn both waited.

"He's not here," she said finally.

(*How can you be sure?*)

(*Because I just know.*)

The two walked through the paper for the first time in days. The place felt like a tomb to Quinn, and even with Kate's assurances, he still felt as if someone would jump out at them at any moment.

He glanced around him nervously.

(*God, I'm such a fool.*) Quinn said.

(*Why?*)

(*Look at me. I'm shaking and scared of my own shadow. I'm like...*)

Quinn stopped in the editorial area. He finished his thought.

(*I'm Ichabod Crane.*)

(*Don't be ridiculous.*)

He let the images wash over her—showing a frightened Ichabod jumping at shadows on his way home at night. Later, the terrified schoolteacher clutched his horse for dear life as the Headless Horseman chased him.

(*It's not ridiculous.*) Quinn replied. (*Don't you see? Since this started, I've done nothing but run away—from the Horseman, from Lord Halloween.*)

(*We had no choice.*)

(*But still, this is all playing out like the book.*)

Quinn and Kate stood in the middle of the newsroom staring at each other. To any observer, the sight would have been bizarre. Neither was saying a word.

(*How so?*) Kate thought.

(*Well, I'm Ichabod, you're Katrina van Tassel, and Lord Halloween is Bromm Bones.*)

(*Give me a break. Bromm Bones wanted Katrina for himself. Romantically.*)

(*Lord Halloween still wants you for himself. He just wants to kill you instead of marry you. But the point is that Ichabod never faced up to Bromm or the Headless Horseman. All he did was flee.*)

(*Quinn, you are just upset.*)

(*I know.*)

He sat down in Kyle's chair. Quinn felt like he was betraying his old colleague even by doing that. Hadn't he always wanted Kyle's beat? Hadn't he tried to...

(*Stop it.*) Kate said.

Quinn put his head in his hands.

(*We have no plan. We have no idea who Lord Halloween is and we don't know how to beat the Horseman to tap whatever powers we might gain. We have nothing.*)

(*That's not true.*)

(*It isn't? Lord Halloween could be anyone. He's probably Buzz. Whoever killed Janus was in that house and used Buzz's car.*)

(*Who would be stupid enough to use their own car?*)

(*It could be Josh, or Laurence, or Redacker. It could be Ethan for all we know—or Brown or Bill. Hell, it could be Rob or Steve who work over in the eastern Loudoun office. Or it could be no one we know.*)

(*We've been through this.*) Kate thought. (*This seems personal, that's why we are assuming it is someone we know. Someone wanted to get Janus because they either knew him or wanted to hurt us. Probably both.*)

(*Was that true of Fanton? Or Kilgore? Did he know them?*)

(*Lord Halloween has had a thing about this paper from the beginning, Quinn. Of all the papers that mentioned him, he only sent letters to ours. He killed several employees. Why would he be so focused on the* Chronicle*? Because he either works here or has some reason to hate us. It's the only thing that makes sense.*)

(*None of this makes sense.*)

But Quinn's mind was turning now. He saw Buzz's jacket in the security video. The crime scene at Kyle's house, the conversation with Anderson.

(*My God.*) he thought.

It wasn't there yet, but he was on to something—pieces of a puzzle he should have put together.

(*What if Lord Halloween does have a motive?*) Quinn thought. (*What if it wasn't random?*)

(*There was nothing linking all the victims.*) Kate responded.

(*Not all of them, no. But you said it yourself. It was about this paper. What if it was always about the paper? From the beginning?*)

(*You mean it's Ethan? He's the publisher. He's doing this for publicity?*)

(*No. No. The man in the dream said we were over-thinking it. Lord Halloween is just a man, he said. So who gained from the murders the first time around? Who got something he wanted?*)

(*Jesus.*) Kate said.

And they knew. They both knew. It clicked into place. All of their looking and it had been right in front of them.

(*How do we find him?*) she asked. There was fury in how she asked it. (*He's hiding.*)

Quinn's mind was racing furiously.

(*Even the girl. He killed the girl downstairs in the basement. It wasn't random. Anderson said everyone thought she was hitting on them. What if Lord Halloween thought it too? What if that was just petty revenge, not really about Anderson at all?*)

(*Never mind that now.*) Kate said. (*How do we find him?*)

(*We go to the police.*)

Kate laughed out loud and it startled them both.

(*With what? A half-baked theory? They will laugh us out of town, for obvious reasons.*)

(*What do you suggest?*)

(*We call him.*)

(*He's going to pick up his phone?*)

(*We leave a message for him to meet us.*)

(*Where?*) Quinn asked, and Kate flooded his mind with photos. Pictures of a field, a road and a covered bridge—the Old Phillips Farm.

(*Are you crazy?*) he asked. (*I can't do that. That's where my dream takes place.*)

(*That's where the Horseman will meet us.*)

(*And you want Lord Halloween there as well?*)

(*Yes.*) she said.

(*This is an awful risk.*) he thought. (*What if Lord Halloween doesn't show? Or what happens if I can't beat the Horseman? There's too much that could go wrong.*)

(*Time is almost up. Halloween is almost here. This is our one chance. Even if we're right, and it is who we think it is, who's to say he won't get away?*)

Quinn thought of all the reservations he had. Even if they won, what would they be then? What kind of power would he have? And wasn't that also a risk?

But Kate took his hand.

(*Whatever this is, it bound us closer together.*) she said. (*It can't be all bad. I want this to happen. And so do you. You said it yourself. You're tired of being afraid all the time. Do this and you will be the thing others fear.*)

Quinn slowly nodded his head.

(*I have to take the Horseman first.*) he thought.

(*We, Quinn.*)

(*No, last time we tried that, I ended up shot. The Horseman is my fear. I have to be the one to face him.*)

(*Do you know how to defeat him?*)

(*No. But I'm beginning to have an idea. Not running from him would be a start.*)

(*I'll help you if I can.*) Kate said. In the dark of the *Chronicle* building, she pulled his head towards her and kissed him. It felt good, and that overpowering sense of lust started creeping back in.

(*We have to stop.*) Quinn said. (*If we win, we will have plenty of time for that.*)

(*You have to promise me something.*) Kate thought. (*If you beat the Horseman, and Lord Halloween shows up, you wait for me.*)

(*If I'm as powerful as you said I would be, do we need to risk it?*)

Kate shook her head.

(*It's not that.*) she said. (*I want to be there when you face him. I want to watch him die.*)

Chapter 24

"Fear is your salvation, my friends. Do not shy from it. Do not run from it. If you do, it will control your path. It is only by grasping it and absorbing it that we can truly understand it, that we can revel in it and turn its power into our own. Fear is not the enemy. Fear will set you free."
—Letter from Robert Crowley, Oct. 31, 1873

Tuesday, Oct. 31
All Hallow's Eve

Quinn pulled onto the road feeling the butterflies in his stomach. He eased the car back from his not-very-fast speed of 15 miles an hour. It was tough even to go that fast without feeling like the car was shaking all around him. Easy does it, he thought. Easy does it.

Some part of him still wanted to run. No matter how angry he was, no matter that he wanted to face this thing once and for all, it was hard to put himself in a position where two bad things were liable to happen, maybe at the same time. Even if ol' Headless didn't show up, Kate and Quinn had made sure someone else would.

My God, we are desperate, he thought. There must have been another choice or some other way. But they couldn't think of any. The Horseman would be here. To defeat Lord Halloween, Quinn must destroy the Horseman. And Quinn could think of no more worse spot than here, heading into a trap of his own making.

And what did Quinn have to protect him? Nothing. Not a gun, which he had no idea how to use and would probably end up in the hands of his assailant anyway. Not a knife or a sword. Nothing.

He had come empty-handed, unless he counted Janus' lighter, which he still carried in his pocket. It was the only thing he had of Janus. And if he was going to do this, he needed all the support that he could get. He hoped it would be his good luck charm.

Not that he was entirely alone. Kate was waiting a couple of miles away. When he needed her, she would be there. He just wondered if it would be in time.

(*I'll be in time.*) she thought.

(*I know.*)

The road got bumpier and Quinn knew he was only a mile from the bridge. Not that he believed it would keep him safe, as it had in the dream. Quite the contrary, given whom he thought would be waiting for him. But it was one of the few landmarks he knew on the road.

A large popping noise came and Quinn felt the car shift violently to the left. He pressed the gas to keep it steady, but knew immediatcly one of the tires had blown.

He brought the car to a stop and got out.

Outside the car, he saw the problem immediately. The two front tires were both blown. He leaned closer to the road and saw why. Nails had been laid across the road.

Quinn shivered.

(*Well, we knew he would do something.*) Kate thought.

(*Yeah, but I thought I would at least get to the bridge.*)

(*Don't let it throw you.*) she thought.

(*Easy for you to say. Or think, rather.*)

So Quinn's car was out of it. And this meant the trap had been sprung. Lord Halloween was here.

Quinn looked up the road and then behind him nervously. The scene was too familiar. The moonlight shone brightly through the treetops, which waved slightly in the breeze. How many times have I dreamt this scene? But this time it's real. He took some comfort in the fact that this was the last time he would have to make this trip. One way or another.

He thrust his hands into his pockets and walked down the road. He was only about a mile away, he thought. He moved slowly, however. As much as he wanted to run, he was afraid of doing so. Whatever was planned for him at the other end of this little trip, he did not want to run in blindly.

And then he started to hear it. The sound was far away now, but in the distance he could hear a horse at full gallop. Quinn knew it would be here soon. He started jogging, but did not push himself too fast. It would not be good to run out of energy already.

He looked behind him, as he had hundreds of times before in his dreams, and saw nothing. Nothing but the forest on all sides.

Looking ahead, he hurried. Maybe the Horseman would find him too soon. Or finish him off. And Lord Halloween would find nothing out here.

Quinn picked up the pace and saw the field on his right. He had stood there only a week before, looking at a tree carved with the word Sanheim.

The sound of the horse was louder now. Quinn chanced a look behind him. Did he see it already? That figure at the end of the road, riding with his cape unfurled behind him?

(*You will have to face him.*) Kate thought.

(*I know.*) But he kept running instead. Now that the moment was here, he didn't want to face this thing. He wasn't ready.

Quinn reached the curve in the road, ran around it and could see the bridge ahead.

In that moment, the question of who might be waiting for him under the bridge was gone. Instead, the dream reasserted itself—he needed to get to the bridge.

Quinn hoped he would make it in time. He looked at his watch. It was almost 10 o'clock. Quinn heard the hooves louder now and then heard something else—the sound of menacing laughter.

He turned to look, actually stopping dead in his tracks. And there in the distance he came, tearing around the bend in full fury. A headless figure astride a horse, with a blade swinging at his side.

(*How could I ever think this was a good idea?*)

(*You have to face him, Quinn. You have to face him before you get to that bridge. You can't go in there. It's not safe.*)

But he could feel her fear as well as she saw the thing bearing down on him. The Headless Horseman crossed the distance between them as if it was nothing.

(*Move, Quinn, now!*) she called.

Quinn's only thought was for the bridge. But he knew he would not reach it.

Instead, he panicked and darted into the trees on the side of the road. Quinn ran through the forest, with tree limbs tearing at him. Everything seemed horribly familiar.

The Horseman did not stop. He followed at full speed, and the noise sounded as if the trees themselves were being thrown aside to make way for the headless Hessian.

(*What do I do?*) he yelled out in his mind.

But now he heard nothing, nothing but the terrible sounds behind him. Quinn suddenly felt very alone.

He ran deeper into the woods, afraid to look behind him. He went to the left, hoping the Horseman would not see the change fast enough to cut him off. But he seemed to predict Quinn's moves. The crashing sounds were near deafening.

Quinn turned to the right again, back the way he had come earlier. He had to reach the bridge. Some part of him knew he would not be safe there either. He had to find a way to face this thing before he got there. But he couldn't think clearly anymore. Around him, he heard what sounded like trees being ripped from their roots.

Quinn's hands were now scratched and bleeding. He saw ahead of him a break in the trees and knew that the bridge would not be far beyond it.

The Horseman was almost on top of him. Quinn looked behind only to see the horse's hooves about to crush him. He dropped and rolled to the right, and the Horseman shot by.

As the Horseman sliced his way through the forest and came about, Quinn threw himself to the left again and heard the sword slice near his head as the Horseman came by.

Quinn darted forward and zigzagged through the trees. He had to get out of there.

And suddenly he was out. He stumbled up the hillside. The bridge was 20 feet away.

Quinn ran and waited to hear the sounds of the Horseman behind him. But now he heard nothing.

Quinn didn't stop to look back. He did not know what had happened and he didn't care. He almost jumped to the bridge.

I'm going to make it, he thought. I'm finally going to make it.

He stole a look behind him, but nothing appeared to give chase. Instead Quinn stepped into the enfolding darkness of the bridge and could have dropped to his knees in thanks.

As he crossed the threshold, though, he saw another figure move in the shadows right toward him. It happened so fast, Quinn could not block anything, and suddenly someone grabbed him by the shoulders.

Quinn tried to break free of the grasp, but the figure held him steady. For a second, Quinn was worried it was the Horseman. That somehow he had gotten into the bridge and had been waiting for him.

"Calm down, Quinn," a voice said as he struggled. "I don't know what you have been running from. But you look like hell. Relax."

Quinn suddenly focused on the face before him. At first, a sense of relief washed over him. A friend was here, he thought. Someone who could help him face what was out there in the darkness waiting.

And then all the memories of the past few weeks flooded back to him like a punch in the stomach. Quinn had not escaped anything. He had traded one monster for another.

The figure in front of him was Kyle Thompson.

*****

"Hello, Quinn," Kyle said and smiled benevolently, still holding his arms. "So nice to see you here."

Quinn shook himself loose and practically fell over. By reflex, he looked again to the road behind him, but there was nothing there.

Quinn started, momentarily at a loss. They had known, of course. They had figured out who Lord Halloween was. But that was theory, this was reality.

"Quinn—honestly you've looked better. You look, and please don't take offense at this, like shit."

Kyle looked different than when he had last seen him. There was a large mark just below his left eye. It looked like a burn, one that wasn't healing well.

"I've been wanting to congratulate you on your new relationship with sweet Trina. I had been expecting her too, you know."

"You're a sick fuck, Kyle," Quinn said.

"You know what's sick, Quinn?" he said. "You are the second person to learn my identity and not go to the cops. Is there something in the fucking water around here that makes people act so stupidly?"

"Buzz," Quinn said. He tried to send a mental image to Kate, but there was nothing. Whatever was blocking them from communicating was still doing so.

Quinn could barely see Kyle. The moonlight crept just to the edge of the bridge, but they stood toward the middle, where the light appeared to be swallowed whole.

"Yes, Buzz," Kyle said. "Dear old paranoid Buzz. He came to warn you two, did you know that? He came to the hotel once he figured out that Kate was really Trina."

Quinn thought of the security video and nodded. He had seen Buzz's jacket, then. It was one piece of the puzzle that hadn't worked with the theory, but now it fell into place.

"So one day I find Buzz skulking around my house, even sitting in my chair," Kyle said. "For the life of me, even now, I can't think of why he didn't confide in someone. He could have told the police, or you, or Laurence, or somebody. I don't get it, I really don't. When I saw him in that chair, I thought the game was up. Seriously, he should have at least passed a note, or left something in his will, right?"

"He was paranoid," Quinn said. "Just like you said."

"Yeah, he had that whole thing with the police," Kyle said as if reminiscing good-naturedly about an old colleague. "I thought that was pretty funny, actually. I have to say—Buzz was not on my target list at all. I never liked him, but he was respectful of me. Not of Kyle Thompson, I mean, but Lord Halloween. He was always talking me up. Talking about how I would come back, about how the police would never catch me. I thought he was a pretty good PR man myself. It is a real shame he had to die."

"What happened?"

"Well, Buzz pulls out this gun and starts like he is the psychopath. I thought I could bluff my way out at first, but he didn't go for it. No, he knew he had the right guy."

"How?"

Quinn waited for Kyle to make a sudden move, maybe pull a knife, but he seemed enraptured by his own story.

"Who knows?" Kyle said. "I went to his house and there was a file on me that was unbelievable. He had detected movement patterns, sketches, a whole bunch of stuff. It was a pretty accurate record. I mean, I didn't stop killing in those 12 years, did I? And Buzz somehow could see my work all over the place. Out in West Virginia. On the Appalachian Trail. Most of the time he got it right. But I still don't know how he landed on me.

"So he sits there with a gun in his hand. Now I don't like guns myself. I think they are overly violent and not as... artistic as a serious person would like. A knife—that is a weapon I can really embrace. But good 'ol Buzz waited too long. I think he wanted to ask questions or something. He told me not to move, but I knew what was coming if I stayed still. So I jumped. He fired and missed me. I, on the other hand, did not miss. I never miss.

"He had guts, I'll give him that. Not like you—running through the forest like a man being chased by a bee.

"So I looked at Buzz and realized it was time for Kyle Thompson to sail out of the picture. It was very liberating, Quinn. I just sliced and diced, and suddenly I didn't have to worry about how Kyle looked anymore. Kyle was dead. And all I had to do was call Laurence once and talk with a really low voice. He really thought I was Buzz. That man is an idiot."

"The police identified your body. They even had DNA testing. We couldn't figure out how you pulled that off," Quinn said.

"Come on, Quinn, catch up," Kyle replied. "I mutilated Buzz's corpse and killed a police courier that was taking the DNA sample for testing. I replaced the kit with some of my DNA. No one even thought about why I would kill a police courier. That is the benefit of being random all these years. When you do it on purpose, nobody knows."

Kyle cocked his head to the side and grinned.

"Am I scaring you?"

"How many people have you killed?"

"I've lost count," Kyle said. "I really have. But now it's my turn to ask questions. You figured me out. How?"

"You just said it yourself. Not all your killings were random over the years."

"Good. Very good."

"This whole 'Lord Halloween' thing was a shtick, wasn't it? I mean, you enjoyed killing people, but you could have done that without drawing attention to yourself."

"I had become quite good at it," Kyle replied.

"But you invented Lord Halloween. Why?"

"I think you must know," he replied.

"It was so simple we didn't see it," Quinn said. "Tim Anderson said you were always hanging around, that you were obsessed with the paper. You wanted to be a reporter."

"Not just any reporter, Quinn," he said. "I wanted to cover crime. I enjoyed it. I reveled in it. Crime was the beat for me."

"But they already had a crime reporter."

"And he was good," Kyle said. "No, he was fantastic. There was no way they would give me that beat as long as he was there."

"So why not just kill him? Why invent a whole persona?"

"For one, it was a fun challenge," he said. "I'd been killing for years, but changing patterns, changing methods, ensuring not to draw attention to myself. This was different. This was a direct challenge to God and man to find me. Secondly, I wasn't even a reporter yet, Quinn. If I had killed Tim, someone else at the paper would have taken his place. Then I would have had to kill them. At what point would someone figure out what I was up to? No, I had to create a disincentive to being the crime reporter. It had to be a job no one wanted 12 years ago. And it worked like a charm. Anderson ran off and... there I was."

"The girl in the basement? She wasn't random either, was she?"

"No," Kyle said. "She wasn't. I went on three dates with her, did you know that? I thought the whole fireman-thing would really work, you know? But she just wanted to be 'friends.' And man, was I cool about it when she told me. But I knew she was into Tim. Everyone was into Tim. So I made sure she was on the list."

"Why not kill Tim?"

Kyle paused at this.

"Because he's the only one that truly stood up to me, Quinn," he said. "His last article was begging for me to kill him. So I didn't. He wanted death. I thought surviving would be harder for him. And it was."

"Why now? Why bring Lord Halloween back now?"

"Look around you, Quinn," Kyle said. "The world is dying. Journalism is dying with it. How long before Ethan sells the paper? The *Chronicle* is struggling and you know it. It's not the business it once was. Even the mighty *Post* is going to die soon. So I wanted a good story before it all went down. And Lord Halloween was the best story this county ever had."

Kyle paused and Quinn could see him smiling, even in the darkness.

"Of course, that was before someone tried to hone in on my story," he said. "Before someone tried to steal it from me."

"I never did, Kyle."

"Oh, who could blame you?" Kyle said. "Lord Halloween is a sick, sick fuck. I'll admit I'm laying it on thick. The theatricality that comes with that persona is addictive once you get started. But it's not me. Lord Halloween will have his final stand tonight, and I'll move on. Maybe I'll get a reporting job in Bluemont, what do you think? You could have joined me, if you hadn't left that message on my cell phone—a dead man's cell phone—asking to meet me here. You were a good reporter."

"I am a good reporter," Quinn said.

"Yeah, gotta say—I just don't think of you in the present tense anymore," Kyle replied.

He laughed. But far from a maniacal laugh, this one was quite casual.

"You know, I'm really enjoying this," he said. "All the others I wanted to put on a show for. You know? To live up to their expectations. But I'm just chatting with you. It's very freeing."

"So glad I could help," Quinn replied.

"It was more than just the paper, though," Kyle said. "I did this because it's what I do. To know that every October, you aren't *like* the bogeyman, you *are* the bogeyman. You are the thing that keeps people up at night, the bump in the dark, the figure they see out of the corner of their eye. You own these people. Is that enough for you?"

Kyle took a step forward. Quinn backed up.

"Hang on, hang on," Kyle said. "I wouldn't want you to go running through those woods again. I thought you were acting all crazy. But I guess you aren't exactly acting, are you?"

"I'm not the crazy one here," Quinn said.

"Oh no?" Kyle asked. "What was all that shit about the Prince of something or other? I thought I must have heard your girlfriend wrong, but you must believe some of it. Why else would you be here? Why not call the police and try to set a trap? I assumed that's what you were doing, but they didn't know a thing. I checked."

Kyle checked his watch.

"It's about 10:30 now, champ," he said. "I guess you have an hour and a half to take the 'great power' and defeat me with it. Right?"

Before Quinn had time to react, Kyle rushed toward him, flashed his knife and cut Quinn on the arm.

Quinn didn't take any time to respond. Instead, he leapt into the middle of the bridge where it was darkest.

He could still see Kyle closer to the edge of the bridge, but Quinn knew he was well hidden.

"Fuck," Kyle said. "That was fast. But I still saw blood, my boy. I still saw you bleed. So I guess you don't have supernatural abilities after all, do you? What was that bullshit, anyway? Something you cooked up for the girl? Was this just a ploy to get into Trina's pants, Quinn? Her mom would not have approved."

Kyle's voice echoed in the bridge.

"Listen, buddy, you can skulk in the shadows all you want," Kyle said. "But I have all night. Granted, I did have plans, but you know what, this 'Lord Halloween' stuff is kinda overblown anyway. I can kill them just as dead on Nov. 1. Oh, but wait. That's the day you lose your superpowers, right? When you become a real boy?"

Quinn was shocked Kyle knew about any of this. But he must have been close enough to overhear them at some point.

"You aren't invulnerable either, Kyle," Quinn said. "How did your face get so messed up? Did Janus give you a taste of your own medicine?"

Kyle stepped into the shadows and Quinn lost sight of him. Slowly, Quinn started moving backwards.

It was pitch black in there. Quinn didn't know why they built the beams so close together, but there was no light inside. He couldn't see where Kyle was and he heard nothing.

"So it's hide and seek, is it?" Kyle's voice echoed inside the bridge. "I can play that. I'm the one with the knife. What have you got?"

It was impossible to tell Kyle's position. His voice was bouncing off the walls around them. Slowly, Quinn backed up again and hoped his voice would pull off the same effect.

"Where are you going to go, Quinn?" Kyle asked. "The minute I see you in the light, I'm going to find you. And believe me, I'll catch up. You may be younger, but I have had more training, if you know what I mean."

Quinn said nothing. He worried he could give away his position.

"Where is your girlfriend, anyway?" Kyle asked. "She was supposed to be here, wasn't she? She left the message, after all, asking for us to meet here. So what's the deal, Quinn? You hoping to take me down by yourself?"

Quinn had backed now to the other side of the bridge. He was so close to the edge that he worried Kyle could see him. He couldn't stay here. Eventually Kyle would find him and Quinn had nothing to protect himself.

He had to complete the original plan. He had to get the hell out of here and face the other monster first.

"Come on, Quinn," Kyle said, and his voice sounded frustrated. "Where are you?"

Quinn knew he had to be quick. He darted out into the moonlight and immediately ran into the woods.

*****

Behind him, he heard Kyle yell something—obviously aware that Quinn had run away. But Quinn thought he had a jump on Kyle, regardless of his "training."

Quinn didn't know where to head. He wasn't sure what was in front of him, but he had very few choices.

Fortunately, the woods on this side of the bank were not as deep, and Quinn quickly came out into a clearing. Ahead of him was a barn—the old Phillips' place he guessed—and an overgrown pumpkin patch. It was the only place Quinn thought to go. He moved across the field as fast as he could, reached the barn, and collapsed against one wall.

His insides felt like they were burning. Quinn couldn't tell what was wrong, but he had been feeling it build up even while he was in the bridge. He lay his head against the side of the barn. Maybe Kyle wouldn't find him.

He wished he could hear Kate in his mind, but the connection still seemed to be blocked. From a distance he heard the sound he had been waiting for. There was precious little time left, and while the trial had evidently been delayed, it was not over.

The sound of horse hooves approached. Quinn didn't move. He was too tired to face both of them. He had thought he would have some idea of how to defeat the Horseman, but he was just exhausted.

The sound of hooves got closer. Good. At least it will be the Horseman that gets me and not Kyle. The sound was ringing in Quinn's ears. The Horseman was almost on top of him. He came pounding into view a second later and wheeled to face Quinn.

Quinn stood up, still leaning against the barn, and looked at his opponent for what felt like the first time. Nothing about the horse looked right. Its eyes glowed a deep red and there was blood on the edge of its mouth.

The figure on top of the horse was dressed in black, and now Quinn could tell it was a decayed uniform. Just like the story. A Hessian mercenary hired to make war on the colonists, his head removed during battle by a cannon ball.

The rider did not move. His horse snorted and pawed the ground, but he remained fixed there.

Quinn stepped away from the barn and walked toward him. "Let's finish this," he said.

It was as if the Horseman had been waiting for it. He swung out of the saddle and dropped to the ground. He unsheathed his sword and took a step toward Quinn.

Quinn stood his ground. He had no plans or ideas. He was not even sure he could bring himself to fight back. But he was done running. He was done being afraid.

The Horseman came forward and held out his sword while Quinn stayed motionless. The Horseman raised his arm and prepared to bring down the stroke that Quinn knew would kill him.

He heard it slice through the air, but at the last moment he jumped forward, straight into the Horseman's chest. The sword went awry, falling to the ground, and the Horseman momentarily fell back.

Quinn didn't know where the strength had come from—he had no idea he was going to make a move until it happened. He realized he would not just stand there and die meekly.

The Horseman seemed as surprised as Quinn, stopping momentarily. When he bent down to pick up his sword, Quinn jumped for it at the same time, beating him to it.

As Quinn picked up the sword, the Horseman hit him squarely in the chest, a blow that sent Quinn into the air before crashing near the barn door. But Quinn had held on to the sword.

Quinn stood up and waved the weapon uncertainly in front of him as the Horseman strode toward him. Maybe this was a way—if he could slice the Horseman with his own sword, he could finish him.

The Horseman closed the gap between them quickly and Quinn cocked back his arm to swing the sword. But he was too inexperienced and the blow was awkward. The Horseman dodged it easily and then hit Quinn again. This time the blow knocked the sword free from Quinn's grasp and tossed him against the barn door, which creaked open behind him.

The Horseman strode over to his sword on the ground and picked it up.

So much for the idea of killing him with his own sword, Quinn thought. He backed into the barn. Inside was the smell of mold, decaying hay and gasoline. Quinn thought it had not been used in years. Unlike the bridge, the barn's wood slats were far apart and moonlight streamed in everywhere.

Quinn saw a ladder to a loft in the barn and headed straight for it. He scurried up it and started looking around for something—anything—to use against his opponent.

The Horseman followed Quinn into the barn and never slowed his pace. He started to climb the ladder, sword in hand, but Quinn kicked the top of the ladder, attempting to jar it loose. The Horseman tried to slice at his foot, but missed, and Quinn heard the satisfying sound of tearing wood, as the ladder came free.

The Horseman jumped off before it crashed to the ground.

"Did you think this would be easy?" Quinn asked. He moved around in the loft, still looking for a weapon of some kind. There was nothing but an old gas can.

The Horseman stood on the floor of the barn, his body following Quinn's movement. But for now he stayed in one place.

"You got your smarts from me after all," he said. "So you can't be that stupid, right?"

Quinn was talking just to hear himself speak. He wondered how late it was.

Was it 11:00 p.m.? He could try and stay up here for an hour, couldn't he? Then the Horseman would be gone. But he would be back next year. And then Quinn would have all year to dream about his return, waiting for next October. Quinn wasn't doing this again. This had to end tonight.

Quinn faced him from the upper level.

"Do you know how long I was scared of you?" he asked. "I was five years old when I saw the Disney cartoon. And you scared the shit out of me. It took my Mom days to calm me down. Every time I walked through the woods, I half expected to see you there."

The Horseman stood impassively.

"I'm not sure why I was so scared," Quinn said. "I think I didn't like the idea of poor Ichabod, hanging on to his horse, just trying to get home. And you wouldn't let him."

The Horseman moved suddenly, throwing the sword in the air in Quinn's direction.

Quinn dropped to the ground and heard the sword slice barely above his head. The entire loft shook and Quinn could feel it about to give way.

Below, he heard the Horseman laugh. The sound bounced around the walls of the barn and seemed to come from inside Quinn's head as well.

Scrambling to his feet, Quinn saw the sword along the back wall and picked it up. He held it in front of him, but felt ridiculous. He had no idea how to use the thing.

The Horseman strode over to the right barn wall and began pounding on it. At first, Quinn was not sure what the point was, and then it became obvious. Each blow sent a shiver through the whole building, and the wood groaned beneath Quinn's feet. The loft was going to fall down, if the whole building didn't first.

Quinn would have to get out of here. He held the sword in front of him, unsure of what to do next.

Boom, another blow came, and Quinn heard his floor giving way. Not thinking, Quinn dropped the sword, grabbed the gas can, still half full, and winged it in the Horseman's direction.

Although Quinn had never been much of an athlete, his aim could not have been better. The can caught the Horseman fully in the chest, knocking him back and over. Quinn saw gasoline spill out on top of him.

He didn't wait. He picked up the sword and threw it to the floor below, then dropped down himself.

The Horseman was still on the ground. Quinn picked up the sword and headed straight for him. This could be his only chance. He was not sure where to cut so decided he would hit him right in the chest.

He never got the chance. The Horseman picked himself up and as Quinn tried to bring a blow forward, the Horseman caught his wrist. And squeezed.

Quinn felt incredible pain and immediately dropped the sword. The Horseman released him, reached down to pick up the sword, and prepared a blow for Quinn's head. Quinn punched the Horseman in the chest to knock him back. But the Horseman appeared unfazed.

Quinn stumbled back and looked around for any other kind of weapon. He ran over to where the gas can lay on the ground. So far it was the only thing that had done him much good.

The Horseman paused for a moment and seemed to watch Quinn's movement.

Quinn picked up the can and stood looking at the Headless Horseman.

The Horseman came toward Quinn, and Quinn decided to run. He needed to find a better weapon than this. Maybe at least a stick or something outside could help stop any blows. As Quinn ran out into the night again, the Horseman was right on his heels.

He turned to look behind him as the Horseman brought his sword through the air. Quinn dropped to the ground and kicked at the Horseman's knees, hoping to throw him off balance. The Horseman fell backwards.

Grabbing the gas can again, Quinn lurched away from the Horseman, scrambling to stand up. But he tripped over something and fell headlong into the pumpkin patch. The gas can came loose and fell to the ground, spilling gasoline as it went.

Quinn landed on two pumpkins. Flailing, Quinn tried to right himself. He could hear the Horseman getting up.

Quinn grabbed a pumpkin and ran forward, trying not to trip over any other pumpkins. At the far edge of the patch, he turned and cocked back his arm to throw the pumpkin, but nearly dropped it. It was too slick and smelled of...

The Horseman paused for a moment, as Quinn and he faced off across the overgrown garden.

Kate had assured him he would know what to do. And now—finally—he did.

Reaching into his pocket, Quinn pulled out Janus' lighter.

"You know what?" he asked. "For years, I've identified with Ichabod. But I think that's over."

He flicked the lighter with his left hand and lit the pumpkin on fire.

The Horseman started to move toward him, but it was too late. Quinn cocked the flaming pumpkin back, oblivious to the intense pain in his hand, and let it fly.

The pumpkin hit the Horseman full on in the chest and he immediately caught fire. The Horseman stumbled back and now Quinn laughed.

"I'm not Ichabod Crane," Quinn said. "Go back to Sleepy Hollow, you headless son of a bitch."

The Horseman was consumed in flames. The sword disappeared in a flash and the Headless Horseman appeared to burn from the outside in, collapsing in on himself. There was a mist of fire and smoke and then he was gone.

Quinn sank to his knees. His hand was in pain, but he was happy for the first time in a very long time. He had won. He felt a stirring in his blood, as if the fire were starting to spread through him. But it felt good.

Quinn had won. He had not believed he could but he had done it. He was so relieved that he barely noticed the other figure striding toward him, who moments later stood in front of him.

"You know, Quinn, a lot of screaming and burning stuff is not the best way to hide," Kyle said, and pulled a knife from behind him. "Let's finish this."

Kyle brought the knife down toward Quinn's neck.

Chapter 25

Halloween

Kate stood by the bridge, shining her flashlight into it, and holding her gun. Her connection with Quinn had been lost. She had sensed the Horseman getting closer and then she had been cut off. She came immediately, but was forced to park behind Quinn's car and walk to avoid the nails on the road.

There was nothing here and she fought down a sense of panic. Had Kyle gotten him? Or had the Horseman? And were either of those two, or both, now coming for her? Waiting for her?

But she heard nothing. She shone a light into the bridge and saw no trace that anyone had been there. She should have come along. She should never have agreed to stay back. They were in this together and they needed to face it that way.

She thought she heard far off laughter from up the hill. She started to walk up it carefully. As much as she wanted to help Quinn, it would not be a good idea to alert everyone to her presence. She was meant to be a surprise.

She moved up the hill steadily and then felt something strange. She stopped.

All at once a flood of images came to her, and she fell to the ground. The Horseman riding toward Quinn, dismounting and chasing him. A barn and...

A flaming pumpkin. She saw that clearly now, and all at once it was like someone had flipped a switch—she felt a burning sensation all through her.

It was happening. She saw Quinn again clearly now— actually felt him in her head—as he fell to the ground after the Horseman went up in flames. It was like it had been before in the hotel room as they made love, only stronger. She knew everything in Quinn's head—and more. So much more.

She could see Kyle approaching and knew his plans. She could see his thoughts, his past, even where he had been hiding since his "death." She knew it all.

Just a moment ago, she had been scared, nervous. Now that was gone. The night felt alive around her. She could feel the wind whipping the branches, the snakes on the trees, the worms in the earth. She felt everything.

There was nothing that could harm them anymore. She felt the power in her like a fire. Sadness, anxiety and doubt had been burned away. Kate started laughing and it was a joyous and awful sound at the same time. It was the laugh of someone who had seen the darkness and been consumed by it.

She saw in her mind as Kyle walked toward Quinn with the knife. She wasn't worried.

(*Send him to me.*) Kate said in her mind, and she felt the answer hundreds of feet away. She barely needed to bother. Quinn wasn't Quinn anymore, but her second half: the second part of the Prince of Sanheim.

Kate turned and walked steadily back down the hill.

*****

Kyle expected his knife to go cleanly into Quinn's neck. It was considerably quicker than he would have liked to be, but he had only 40 minutes left before Halloween was technically over. This whole process was taking more time than it should have. After Quinn had disappeared into the woods, Kyle had lost his trail momentarily before he heard Quinn shouting. He really must have driven the guy crazy. He needed to finish this, find Kate, and move on.

But Quinn moved faster than Kyle thought possible. Quinn stopped the blow and held Kyle's wrist in his hand without looking up.

When Quinn did look at him, he wished he hadn't. Kyle looked down into a face he barely recognized. Quinn's eyes glowed a deep red and there was nothing in them that indicated fear. Or anything at all.

Startled, Kyle tried to free his wrist, but found he could not.

"Am I scaring you?" Quinn said, and the voice wasn't right either. It was both lower and higher than it should have been. It sounded like the voices of several people talking out of one mouth.

Kyle let the knife drop. Quinn released him and smiled.

Kyle's mind reeled for a minute.

"What the hell is happening?" he asked.

Quinn's smile turned into a grin.

"I thought you would have figured that out," Quinn said, still in that strange voice. "You heard it so clearly with all your eavesdropping."

"No," Kyle said. "That stuff was shit. You are nuts."

But Kyle faltered. Something had come up behind Quinn—a huge black horse whose mouth looked like it was dripping blood.

"Holy fuck," he said out loud.

Quinn did not turn, even as the horse's head hung over his shoulder.

"You know, I told Kate recently that our fears do not define us," Quinn said. "I said it was what you do with your fear that matters. I was wrong. We are what we fear. Or what we fear is us."

"This isn't happening," Kyle said, but he took two steps backward. "This is a trick. You dressed up that horse."

"It's just a ghost story, Kyle," Quinn said. "Only this time it's Bromm who loses."

Kyle took another step back. He did not even pause to pick up his knife.

Quinn was changing. For him, it was as it had been in the dream—that brief moment when everything was suddenly right with the world. He was no longer afraid. He didn't need to be. All the dark places of the world were open to him now. The horse—the horse that had only moments ago terrified him—was calling to him. Quinn knew who he was; what he was.

Before Kyle's eyes, Quinn began to change form. His image seemed to shudder in the moonlight and transform. Kyle was forced to look away.

"This is a trick," he said again, but even he didn't believe it anymore.

When he looked back, Quinn no longer stood in front of him. He had been replaced by another figure, a man in a black fraying uniform. A man with no head.

"Impossible," Kyle said under his breath.

He kept backing up and nearly tripped over his own feet.

Slowly the Headless Horseman moved to the horse and swung into the saddle. He unsheathed a sword from the scabbard at his side and held it aloft, letting the moonlight reflect off it. There was a terrible ringing in Kyle's ears. The horse reared back as the rider swung his sword in the air.

The image stayed burned in Kyle's mind as he turned to run. He could already hear the sound of hooves behind him.

The Headless Horseman was riding again.

*****

"Fuck this, fuck this, fuck this," Kyle said, fleeing down the hill he had tracked Quinn up just a few minutes before. He nearly lost his footing three times, but stayed moving. He ran through the trees with all of his might, pushing branches out of his way.

He didn't know what was going on or what had happened. One minute Quinn was kneeling on the ground, just Quinn. The next? He didn't know. This couldn't be real. It just couldn't be.

He arrived at the bottom of the hill and looked back. In the moonlight at the top of the hill, he could see the Headless Horseman. Kyle heard a deep laugh that felt like it rippled across the landscape.

For the first time, it occurred to Kyle that he might die. He took off running again, hearing the crash of trees as the Horseman began to descend the hill.

Kyle ignored the bridge, running to where he had parked his car earlier in the evening. If he could make it there…

The laugh followed him and seemed to echo everywhere. But Kyle never stopped running.

He raced down the road and looked behind him. The Horseman came down the hill at a full gallop, his sword slicing through branches along the way.

Kyle saw his car ahead and frantically tried to pull his keys from his pocket. But he had trouble grabbing them and he felt terribly slow.

He could hear the Horseman gaining on him with every step. I'm not going to make it, he thought.

Kyle wrestled the keys from his pocket and signaled to unlock the car door.

As the Horseman closed the distance between them, Kyle threw open the driver's side door and jumped inside. He started the car and threw it into reverse, pushing it as fast as he could.

The Horseman was almost to the car.

"Shit," Kyle said again.

He backed up, trying simultaneously to keep an eye on the rearview mirror so he could see behind him, and look in front to where the Horseman was gaining.

He could not keep driving like this. If he did, he would crash into a ditch and be stuck on foot. Kyle slammed on the brakes and turned the wheel, trying to turn the car around as fast as possible.

The Horseman kept coming and vaulted over the car. Kyle strained his neck even as he shifted into drive to try and see where it was.

When he brought the car forward, he saw the Horseman facing him on the road.

Kyle fought to hold down his panic. The man astride the horse looked more like a decaying corpse than a person, his rotted uniform on and a tattered cloak cast out behind him. As Kyle watched, the Horseman pointed his sword in the car's direction.

Figuring it was his only chance, Kyle floored the accelerator. Cars can run over horses and besides, there was no other place to go.

The horse stood there, Kyle waiting for the inevitable collision or to see the horse move out of the way. At the last minute, the Horse jumped again, easily moving out of the car's path.

Kyle pressed the accelerator down and the car lurched forward faster. He would just have to pick up enough speed to outpace the thing.

How far was it to the highway? He cursed the dirt road he was on. He needed to get real speed, but the traction was keeping the car going only 45 miles an hour.

The Horseman appeared to be keeping up easily, gaining ground even. As Kyle watched, the Horseman disappeared from his rearview mirror to the right.

"Shit," Kyle said again. It was coming up alongside the car. "You aren't real, you fuck."

Kyle watched in his rearview mirror as the Horseman swung his sword. The blow connected, smashing the rear windshield. Kyle felt glass shards hit him in the neck and he shut his eyes momentarily.

The car jerked to the left. Kyle opened his eyes quickly and tried to keep it on the road. He moved his car to the right and the Horseman dropped back.

Kyle saw with some relief that the main road was in front of him.

He saw the Horseman fall back even further in his mirror.

"What are you playing at?" he asked himself.

He accelerated to Route 7 in front of him and did not even pause at the stop sign as he finally pulled his car onto a paved road. Kyle shouted in triumph and pressed the accelerator to the floor.

"Let's see if you can keep up with this," he said.

He looked in the rearview mirror and saw nothing.

He breathed a sigh of relief, but kept the car moving fast. Its speed edged up to 80 miles an hour.

He was uncertain what his next step should be. Quinn knew who he was—if Quinn even still existed—so staying put was out of the question. He sped past houses, through stop signs and streetlights. If the cops were out here, they would just have to pull him over. He could deal with them.

Kyle knew he had to go back to his base of operations. There was too much stuff there for someone to find. If he acted now, hopefully Quinn would seem like a lunatic. After all, the DNA test would still confirm his "death."

He kept his eye on the rearview mirror. Still nothing.

He had left the Horseman in the dust.

He sighed again and slowed down. It wouldn't do to get a ticket. He should go back to base, pick up his stuff and leave town.

Maybe someone would believe Quinn or maybe not. It wouldn't matter. Kyle Thompson would disappear.

God, but it was frustrating. He had been so close to finishing up here. And now he was just running away. He checked the clock in the car. It was 11:40 p.m.

Just 20 more minutes and he wouldn't have to worry about the Horseman anymore. That part he remembered from Kate's conversation with Janus. Given what he had seen, he had no choice but to acknowledge some of that shit must be true.

He just hoped the deadline was one part that was real.

He pulled off on Mulberry Lane, still constantly keeping one eye out for anything behind him. At an empty post where a mailbox should have been, Kyle turned left, confident that no one had followed him.

Go in, grab the stuff and go. Deadline or no deadline, it wasn't worth sticking around to find out. Winding his way down the long driveway, he pulled the car up to the house and stopped.

For once, he wished that this house had not been his choice for a base of operations. It was rundown, its steps were treacherous, and every creak of the floorboards could be heard throughout the house.

But that was what had made it perfect. It was Charles Holober's house, the poor schmo whom police had tapped as Lord Halloween the first time around.

From the beginning, Kyle had known it was a perfect spot. Nobody wanted to buy the land, even in the days where everything was being plowed down to make way for new luxury townhomes. Not here. A house built in a swamp standing on rotten stilts.

Kyle could not keep his collection items at his own house. That would have made for easy discoveries by any curious person. So Holober's it had been. Kyle had befriended him 13 years before, a lonely schizophrenic hermit with a house in the swamp. Kyle had set him up of course—he had wanted a patsy for police to find so they would stop looking for the real killer.

And Holober's place remained an excellent hiding spot. No other houses for miles, and the creaky floorboards would easily tell him if anyone else was around. It was like a built-in alarm. Kyle had kept all his trophies there. The news clippings, the stack of post-it notes, mementos.

But now he wished he hadn't. Kyle had never been afraid of the house before. After all, he was the thing that other people should fear. He was what went bump in the night.

Kyle got out of the car and checked his watch. 11:45 p.m.

But he was growing nervous. Far away, he thought he could hear a sound and it was getting louder.

"Damn," he said, and climbed the steps.

He would be safe in here. He opened the door and went through.

*****

The air in the place was stale and had a rotten odor. The house still had electricity, thanks to a generator Kyle had maintained in good order.

Kyle flipped on the light. But nothing happened.

"Damn," he said again, and the sound of his own voice made him jumpy. He must not have charged the thing, he thought.

He waited for his eyes to adjust to the dark, which they did only slightly, and moved forward. He banged his leg into the couch as he tried to make his way to his bedroom.

He crossed the living room and heard the floorboards groan beneath him. He stopped a minute and listened for any other sounds. Kyle shuddered.

Outside, the sound was unmistakable and getting closer. The pounding of horse hooves. How the hell had it followed him? But, really, was that the most surprising part of the night? He doubted it.

Kyle knew he did not have much time.

He went into the bedroom and pulled a duffel bag out of the closet. He could barely see, but he knew where most of the things he needed were. Just the newspaper clips and mementos and he would be on his way. He checked his watch again. 11:48 p.m. In 13 minutes, he would not need to worry about this anymore.

He reached onto the bed for some of his papers. He couldn't see them, but he had prepared them just this morning. They were a new identity for himself, so he could move this show to some other town and start over.

But instead his hand closed around a single small piece of paper.

In a panic, he reached all over the bed. But all that remained was a note.

He picked it up—a small yellow post-it note with writing on it. He pulled it close to his face so he could read it.

"You are not alone, Kyle," it read.

Kyle dropped the note in shock. He wheeled around and faced the living room.

"Who's here?" he yelled.

But no sound came back. Just silence.

Kyle bent down to the duffel bag and pulled out his emergency back-up plan. A gun.

"I hate using this thing, I really do," he said out loud. "But don't think that I don't know how. I was in the service for a long time, you know."

"Oh, I know," a voice in the darkness came back. It sounded like a woman's, or was it a man's voice as well?

"Quinn? Is that you?" Kyle called out, and held the gun in front of him.

"He's here, in a manner of speaking," the voice came back. "But he is also outside, getting closer. And when he gets here..."

"Fuck you," Kyle said. "Fuck you and your parlor games."

He held the gun in front of him and walked out of the bedroom door. He left the duffel bag behind. Let the cops find him. He just needed to get out of here.

"Come on, Kyle, you were always the one who liked parlor games," the voice said. "You played one with me, remember?"

"Who are you?" Kyle asked, but he knew. He had known from the moment he found the note on the bed. It made no sense. How could she have known where to come?

"See you real soon, remember?" Kate's voice came back.

Kyle tried to tell where the voice was coming from. He tried to look for her, but he couldn't see.

Outside, he could hear the sound of the horse getting louder.

"Look, Trina," Kyle said. "I'll cut you a deal. You call all this shit off and I will go away. I'll leave you guys alone—I will be out of your hair forever."

Nervously, Kyle lit the light on his watch. It was 11:52 p.m.

"I don't think so, Kyle," Kate said.

Kyle thought now he could hear where the voice was coming from. He turned to the right and fired the gun. The blast was nearly deafening in the small house. He heard the bullet slam into the wood grain.

"Nice try," Kate said.

"You see? There is still something left in me," Kyle said. "Let me go and I will just walk out of here."

"Oh, you are free to leave, Kyle," Kate said. "But I think you will find a friend waiting for you outside."

The sound of horse hooves had stopped. It meant only one thing, Kyle thought.

"He's here," Kate said.

His knees felt weak and he noticed his hands were shaking.

"He can't get me in here," Kyle said.

And then he heard a large crashing noise from below. The whole house shook.

"Think again," Kate replied. "Actually, he could walk up the steps if he wanted to. But we have a different idea."

The large crash came again and again. The whole house felt like it was breaking apart.

"Not very stable here, is it?" Kate asked.

"If this house falls in, it will hurt you too," Kyle said.

"I doubt it," she replied. "I think I'm beyond that kind of thing."

Kyle looked at his watch again. 11:54 p.m.

"I'm not going to let the clock run out here, don't worry," Kate said.

"Then come and get me," Kyle said. "I'm not moving."

A large crash happened again and Kyle felt the floor shake. It was going to fall in.

But then a figure moved across the floor. He could not believe he hadn't seen her before. She grabbed the gun out of his hand and punched Kyle in the face.

He stumbled back and heard the floorboards creak as he landed. There was another crash from below, and the house now tilted on its stilts. Furniture started sliding. Kyle felt the coffee table hit him in the leg.

Before he could move, something hit him in the stomach. Kyle went sprawling across the floor.

"Looks like the house of cards is beginning to collapse, Kyle," Kate said.

Kyle tried to get up. He got to his knees and was hit in the head from behind, falling forward again.

A voice was in his ear.

"I could kill you, you know," a female voice whispered. "I would even enjoy it, as you did. But I think I would rather see you run."

He turned over and tried to throw the figure back.

But when he looked into the face above him, it was not Kate that he saw. It was her mother.

"What's the matter, Kyle?" Sarah asked him. "Seen a ghost?"

With all his might, he tried to push her backwards and get up. She easily dodged him, but stepped back.

"This is not real," he said.

"I could have taken another form," Sarah said to him. "I could have been your worst nightmare. But this one felt the most fitting."

Kyle stumbled back and looked at her. He blinked hard again. "This isn't happening," he said again, and nearly lost his balance as another crash caused the floor to tilt even further. "What are you?"

Sarah crossed the floor and leaned into Kyle's face before he could block her.

She whispered in his ear.

"We are the Lords of Halloween, Kyle," she said, and pushed Kyle through the front door. "The *real* Lords of Halloween."

Kyle landed on the front stoop and felt intense pain in his back. His arms flailing, Kyle tried to pick himself up. He did not look back into the house. Instead, he tried to make it down the stairs, which were coming apart even as he walked down them.

He stumbled off them and tried to run to his car. Even from here, he could tell that the tires were slashed. Cut by a sword.

Kyle heard the pounding of hooves behind him. He did not dare look back. Instead, he ran forward as fast as he could and looked at his watch. 11:58 p.m.

Just two more minutes. Just two more minutes and he would be safe. I can't die like this, he thought.

He heard a blade being unsheathed behind him. He ran faster now, throwing all his energy into it. He had always come out on top. He would again.

But the Horseman was gaining on him. He looked at his watch again, willing it to go faster. 11:59 p.m. and 30 seconds.

He felt the horse breathing down his neck and dodged to the right to try and avoid him. Thirty more seconds and he would be free, Kyle thought.

He jumped now to the left and felt the Horseman slice the air near him as he went by.

Kyle stopped, dropped back, and watched as the Horseman wheeled around and then halted. Kyle looked from his watch to the Headless Horseman, who stood there impassively.

10 seconds, he noted.

The Horse reared back and Kyle backed up some more.

He glanced at his watch. 5 seconds.

But the Horseman did not move. Instead the horse held his position in the air and came to ground at exactly midnight on Kyle's watch.

Kyle looked up and shouted, waiting for the figure of the Horseman to dissolve in front of him.

"I won, you stupid fucks," he shouted, grinning, and looked back at his watch.

It was ten seconds past midnight.

But the Headless Horseman still stood there. Kyle felt the smile fade from his face.

The Horseman surged forward, his sword in the air.

Kyle looked at the specter with disbelief.

"But it's midnight," he shouted. "It's midnight. You are supposed to..."

The Headless Horseman's blade came sailing through the air and Kyle at the last moment threw up his arm to try and ward off the blow. It didn't help.

The Horseman cleanly lopped off Kyle's head. The look of surprise, terror and confusion was still on it as it sailed through the air and fell to the dust just as Kyle's body crashed down.

The Headless Horseman wheeled about and rode up to the figure that had come out of the house.

Kate, now once again looking like herself, walked over to Kyle's body. Absentmindedly, she stroked the horse's mane as it drew up beside her.

Kate leaned over the body and pulled on Kyle's watch. She held it up to her own.

"What do you know?" she said. "It's three minutes fast. Just like he always taught us."

The horse reared up and the Headless Horseman laughed. Kate just smiled.

Epilogue

A week later, it was a *Loudoun Chronicle* exclusive, a double by-line by Kate and Quinn. "Lord Halloween: The Real Story."

Police had stayed quiet after the discovery of the Holober house, which they had searched after an anonymous tip. There they collected Kyle's real body and drew their own conclusions, mostly the right ones.

However, the police were so concerned about being burned again by announcing that Lord Halloween was finished that they delayed saying anything at all. Instead, they only said that their investigation continued.

Kate had found Buzz's papers inside the Holober house and kept them. With Buzz's portfolio in hand, it was not hard to completely retrace Kyle's steps over the past few years.

It was a huge hit when the *Chronicle* announced who the killer was and that he was dead. What followed was a definitive account of the serial killer. When it had started and even what he had planned. The last bit they attributed to police sources, who had found a paper in the Holober house that was a draft of a note that Kyle had written. In it, he talked about crucifying kids.

Kate knew much more than what she could say. She had seen into Kyle's mind, after all, and there was much laid out there that couldn't come from any portfolio. But Quinn and Kate kept that mostly to themselves.

As they did their role in any of it. While paying tribute to the losses of Janus and Buzz, they removed any trace they had been involved. The police never knew who called them out to the Holober house and were never certain how Kyle had been killed. It wasn't until later that Sheriff Brown began to worry about it.

In those early days, he was still surprised by his good fortune. Once Kate and Quinn's story broke, he rushed forward to claim credit for stopping the killings.

Quinn's greatest satisfaction came the next day. The story in *The Washington Post*—written by none other than Summer Mandaville—was forced to quote the *Loudoun Chronicle*. Without access to Buzz's portfolio themselves, she had precious little else to use for her story. Kate and Quinn's story simply had too many wonderful details to ignore. And so the great *Washington Post* gave the *Loudoun Chronicle* credit. And that was not the only paper. CNN ran a whole story on it, borrowing liberally from the two reporters work, but at least giving them credit. Ethan Holden was on cloud nine for a week.

For the rest of the paper, it was more bittersweet. The killer, after all, had worked among them for years and been responsible for the deaths of two of their own. And for Quinn, the memory of Janus was ever-present.

The next staff meeting was mercifully short. Laurence said a prayer for their fallen colleagues and moved on to new business.

But Kate and Quinn did not attend. Riding on Holden's good will, they took two weeks off, the first to see Kate's father.

After that, they didn't have set plans. They just wanted to go somewhere quiet for a while, and be by themselves.

They had lost their abilities at the stroke of midnight, as promised, and no longer had the connection to each other that they had in the previous weeks.

That proved to be a problem, because each had become accustomed to knowing what the other felt like at any given time. They knew, though, that their abilities would come back, stronger than ever, eventually. In the meantime, the two were getting used to communicating the conventional way again. It was frustrating.

"So how long do you think we have to wait?" Quinn asked her on the car ride up to her dad's.

"I don't know," Kate said in the passenger seat. She was half-dreading trying to explain her actions to her dad, though she was thankful Quinn was along for the ride. "There's very little literature on it. Not forever though. Maybe February, March?"

"Shit. That's a long time."

"I know," she said, and put her hand on his knee. "And we don't even really know what it will be like. We only had a few minutes as the true Prince of Sanheim. And we were a little focused on revenge at that moment."

"I look forward to it," he said.

"Me too," she replied, and leaned back in her chair.

She thought a minute.

"What is this going to mean?" she asked. "What do we do with all this stuff when we get it back?"

"I don't know," he replied. "Band together and fight the evil plots of Lex Luthor?"

"No, really. I'm serious."

"I don't know," Quinn said. "And I'm worried."

"About?"

"The man in my dream," he said. "He wanted something and we gave it to him."

"Maybe he was trying to help?"

"For what purpose? He wants something, and part of that plan was our becoming Prince of Sanheim?"

"Well, just because we are now doesn't mean we have to do what he wants," she said.

"We don't really know that, though, do we? The power we had. It felt good, right?"

"It felt exhilarating," she said.

"But it didn't feel *good* in the other sense of the word, did it? It didn't feel right."

"I don't know what you are talking about," she said. "It was the best I've ever felt. And I saw into you, remember? It's the best you've ever felt too."

"I know," he said. "I'm just saying that this could change us."

"Good," she said. "The way I see it, whatever bargain we struck, we got the better end of the deal. We have each other, and when the time is right, we will be unstoppable. Power doesn't automatically corrupt, you know. We will know how to use our powers in the right way."

Quinn was silent after that. Maybe she was right.

"I did do one thing I didn't tell you about earlier," Kate said.

"Which was?"

"I left them a note," she said.

"Who?"

"Sheriff Brown and the rest of the police."

"What did it say?"

"Oh, nothing," she said, and she smiled.

"I hate that you can keep secrets," he replied, but he was smiling too.

"That's just it, Quinn. I can't keep them for long."

"Seriously, what did it say?"

"Ask me later," she said. "You'll find out."

They sat in silence for a few minutes.

"Well," Kate said finally. "Where do you want to go once we see my Dad?"

"I did have one idea," he said and grinned.

"Which is?" she asked.

"I put the brochure in the glove compartment," he replied.

She opened up the compartment and found a single brochure with the picture of a small town in autumn on it. Kate laughed out loud.

"You have to be kidding me," she said.

"I figured we should visit our roots."

She opened the brochure up.

"Welcome to Sleepy Hollow, New York," it said. "Where legends and magic await."

"Sounds perfect," Kate said.

PS File: Letter #1
Date: Nov. 1, 2006
Investigation Status: Open
Contents: Classified

Dear Sheriff Brown,

Some of what we tell you will be lies. This is necessary to protect us both. We were the ones who killed Lord Halloween—that part is no lie, we assure you. Where you failed, we succeeded. Let us be clear up front: we will tolerate no further incompetence from you or your staff. You have let dozens of people die at the hands of a madman. You can claim victory over Lord Halloween—we bear you no ill will if you want to hog credit—as long as you understand that you had nothing to do with it. Without us, he would still be out there. Without us, he would still be killing.

Why are we writing to you? Because you are going to hear stories, lots of them. Stories that do not make sense; stories about monsters and ghosts. Some know these stories already—just ask your own son. These stories will be true. In the absence of divine intervention from above, Loudoun County will receive assistance from down below. The monsters are out in force. Continuing the ban on Halloween will not stop us.

But let us be clear: the innocent have no reason to fear us and we will give them none. Only those that lurk in shadows to strike at others have a reason to panic. To those that murder without cause, we are their worst nightmare. To those that desire retribution, we are their greatest ally.

There are times in life when one must make a stand. We intend to do so. Our medium is the one best understood by every being on this planet, from the lowly maggot to us—fear.

We will be the thing people fear. Our name already sends a shiver down the spine of the guilty, and soon it will be synonymous with the creeping darkness.

We are night. We are October. We are flesh rendered and torn. We are the rider that was promised long ago, the harbinger of fall: We are death, riding on a black horse.

You can call us the Prince of Sanheim.

THE END

Acknowledgements

This novel, my first, has gone through multiple iterations over the years, and owes debts to several people. I first started it in 2001 in part because of a contest sponsored by the National Novel Writing Month. I will always be grateful for participating as it forced me to finally put pen to paper to write a novel. Unfortunately for me, the novel was awful and it took me two years or so to rewrite it.

My first reader was my wife, Maia. I know every writer thanks his or her spouse and says it would not have been possible without them. But this is literally true in my case. If she had disliked the book in any way, it simply would have ceased to exist. However, she genuinely enjoyed the novel and it was a treat to watch her read it. She was also the novel's first editor, making significant changes and contributions throughout the text. Every author needs a good editor, and Maia was mine. She pointed out plot holes, helped with descriptions, and generally improved the manuscript in every way.

Once the novel was finished, Maia was its biggest champion, even when I was consumed with self-doubt. When I wondered if it was any good, she reassured me. When I crazily wanted to publish it as an ebook, she helped. She was incredibly supportive as I sought to revise it and she read it multiple times with enthusiasm. I am deeply grateful for her ongoing love and support.

I have a few other debts to repay. Although he did not live to see its completion, this novel's tone and structure owes a lot to the late novelist Thomas Disch. I was fortunate enough to take a class with him at the College of William and Mary and he gave me invaluable advice about writing, much of which guided me through the writing of *A Soul to Steal*. Disch was a significant source of inspiration.

I also would like to thank the late Liz Frost, a former coworker of mine at the *Eastern Loudoun Times*. She talked openly and honestly about her attempts to write a novel, and she helped inspire me to do the same. Although she died shortly after its publication, her novel, *Queen of Denial*, is excellent and I recommend it highly.

I worked for a real community paper in Loudoun County for a few years and am very grateful for the experience. Although the setting obviously inspired me, the characters in this novel are not based on my former colleagues. The *Loudoun Times-Mirror*, which is more than two centuries old, is a well-respected paper with high ethical standards and great journalists.

I would also like to thank Holly Frederick of Curtis Brown. She read the novel and suggested several ways it could be improved, all of which I have tried to incorporate. The novel is much better as a result.

I'd like to thank Travis Pennington of Pro Book Covers for his work in designing the fantastic cover for this novel. He came up with the design and was then extremely patient with my never-ending series of tweaks to it. I also appreciate the help of Brian Gill and my wife, both of whom painstakingly looked at each different version of the cover and helped suggest improvements. I'm grateful to Kirsten Curtis for the wonderful author photograph.

Last but not least, I'd like to thank my family and friends, especially those who have helped promote the novel. If you liked it, please review it and tell your friends on Facebook, Goodreads and Twitter. For anyone interested in a sequel, you will be happy to know that this is the first novel in a trilogy about Quinn and Kate. Please like my Facebook page at www.facebook.com/asoultosteal to read updates, blog posts and other information.

Best wishes,
Rob Blackwell

Made in the USA
Lexington, KY
11 October 2013